INVITED HOSTILITY

INVITED
HOSTILITY

Innate Hostility Sequel
A Kevin and Cole Novel

BRIAN DAVID SIMMONS

Publisher's Note: This is a work of fiction. Names, characters, places, and incidents either are the product of the author's imagination, or are used fictitiously, and any resemblance to actual persons, living or dead, events, or locales is entirely coincidental.

Invited Hostility by Brian David Simmons

Published by Bright Crescent Sky. Bright Crescent Sky can be emailed at brightcrescentsky@pmt.org. Follow us on Facebook or visit our website for events, information, reviews, and new releases. Our website is brightcrescentsky.com. To contact Brian Simmons, email him at brian@brightcrescentsky.com.

Library of Congress Control Number: 2023919472

Library of Congress Cataloging-in-Publication Data is available upon request.

International Standard Book Number (ISBN):
979-8-9859323-4-8 (print)
979-8-9859323-5-5 (ebook)

Cover by Melissa Thomas, Luminare Press

Printed in United States of America

To those in law enforcement that put
right and wrong above politics and perception.

Acknowledgment

Maureen, Joni, Cindy, Rex, and Neil wrestled through the unedited *Invited Hostility* text to provide comments and corrections and help make the final version great. Thank you.

Chapter 1

Meek and Submissive

Bob Goddard, or at least that's what he had called himself for the last three months, sat on the steps with a beer missing from the six-pack at his feet. He had almost forgotten who he really was; there were periods of peace in the distant past for Hamilton Cole Davis but they had long vanished along with his real name. Of late, Cole chose rocket scientists for his aliases, Bob Goddard being just the latest. Peace and living within society's perception of right and wrong were now his goals. Live and let live, harm no one, eyes down, no conflict, no violence, politeness, meekness, and anonymity were his challenges.

The "Projects," as they were referred to, in Queens was now his hiding place. Two kids in front of the adjacent apartment building were having some kind of an altercation. An openly visible drug deal was taking place as money was exchanged between two teens. Several transients with shopping carts full of worldly possessions were milling around. A few younger kids played, as children do. A young African American girl had two doll-like pink ponies and pranced them around. She was providing the words as if the mommy pony was talking to the smaller one. Cole had seen her many times before and the game was always the same: prance, prance, prance, and then the larger pony would say something to the smaller one.

If only his childhood had been as simple as this little girl's. She was probably ten or eleven. His life was such a contrast. At ten, he was learning how to hate Blacks, Hispanics, Orientals, and just about everyone who wasn't a direct descendant of the Confederate States of America. There was never any play: no toy trucks, no swing set, no electronics, not even a television for cartoons. His youth was all training and hate-filled rhetoric of the Patriot Rebirth Society compound near Coeur d'Alene, Idaho. Cole's earliest memories included rally slogans and chants repeated many times over. *White Power, White Pride World Wide, White America for White Americans, The Fourteen Words*, and other hate-filled slogans that Cole tried to purge from memory. The cesspool of hate fed on itself and the hatred grew to levels where killing was seen not only acceptable, but as a preferable means to an end. And that's where the training came in.

At age five he was already proficient with a .22 caliber rifle at a hundred feet; at eight he knew where to thrust a knife that assured a kill; at ten he had mastered military style hand-to-hand combat with many forms and variations of martial arts intended to maim or kill one's adversary; at age twelve he had mastered the long gun and could proficiently kill a target at two hundred yards. All training was offense. Defense only had the purpose of posturing for strike-first offense.

Field drills and shooting skills were honed with only one objective: kill Blacks, Mexicans, Orientals, or anyone else who challenged their bigoted beliefs. At age twelve he could also hold his own against much older youth in the martial arts combat arena. His mother was so proud when he earned a second-place finish in the compound's Summer Fest Youth contest; he could still see her beaming face.

How different his life would have been if his childhood had been somewhere else, even this garbage dump called the Projects. Maybe he could have had a toy truck and horse trailer for the girl's pink ponies. The sun was setting and a woman emerged from the stairwell in the adjacent building. Cole couldn't help noticing that she was damn good-looking. That's a joke, Cole thought. His mother would roll over in her grave if she knew he was ogling a black woman. The woman called out, "Samantha," for the little pink pony girl and they both retreated into the stairwell.

As the sun set, Cole retrieved another beer from the now warming six-pack. The homeless began preparing for another night under cardboard. Drug deals escalated and groups of teens hung around with nothing better to do. Cole's thoughts returned to his mother and the final day of the Patriot Rebirth Society compound.

His mother and father, along with the other extremists, trained relentlessly for the day *They* would come, whoever *They* were. The end came late one night as the compound was converged upon by the ATF and

FBI with helicopters, armed personnel carriers, and hundreds of foot soldiers.

They had finally come. Cole was deafened by whirling helicopter blades, loudspeakers demanding submission, and gunfire. The Davis cabin was at the edge of the compound with the south wall protected by a mountainside of dirt. Cole emerged from his bedroom, ten-inch knife in hand. His mother and father had taken up positions at window gun slits. They had selected close-combat AK-47s from the arsenal of weapons inside the cabin. His mother scanned east and called out "Clear." His father moved from the west wall to the north wall, and back again, peering through window slits searching for the army he knew was coming. Cole's father motioned for him to move to the munitions cache and yelled "Ammo." Cole retrieved an armload of fifty-round clips from the cache and left half of them within reach of his father and the other half near his mother. He saw tears in her eyes and she reached out for him, setting aside her AK-47 and hugging him with all her might. "Live. Live son. Live to fight another day," she pleaded. "Hide in the cellar and submit. Do you hear me? Do not die here tonight."

"No," replied Cole. "We will kill the government bastards." Barrages of gunfire from across the compound rang out in what seemed like thousands of rounds and drowned out his words. He repeated them: "We will kill the government bastards."

"Four advancing two-by-two on the north," alerted Cole's father as he fired his AK to unleash a hail of 7.62 mm Kevlar piercing bullets. Body armor worn by the advancing ATF agents proved ineffective and all four dropped.

Cole's mother stared deep into his eyes and pleaded, "No, you will live tonight."

"I can take at least ten of them before they take me," Cole insisted.

Bullets from an ever-increasing assault team peppered the bulletproof steel and composite window guards. An occasional lucky bullet wisped through a firing slit and embedded itself in the interior of the cabin. The racket outside was becoming increasingly all-encompassing. Cole's father fired again, and again, adding to the deafening clamor. He changed out a fifty-round clip, which momentarily provided the opportunity to speak.

"You must live," his mother shouted at the top of her lungs. "Now get your butt in the cellar."

Cole glanced at his father, now again rapidly firing at the advancing soldiers, whose number had now become uncountable. Cole's father turned his head towards Cole and yelled, "Go."

"Live Cole—live," she commanded.

Cole retreated to the cellar door with horrid feelings of inadequacy and fear for his parents. As he opened the cellar door, he heard his mother's AK-47 fire a sustained blast and then cry out, "At least a dozen on the advance!" Gunfire continued continuously from both sides as Cole reluctantly stepped down the ladder into the cellar and closed the door. He thought he heard his father take credit for more kills, but voice sounds were barely audible.

The advancing ATF blew the cabin door off its hinges and deployed flash bangs. Even Cole, hidden underground, was stunned by the reverberations of the blasts. The army came rushing in with fully automatic fire spraying the interior of the cabin. Surrender was not an option for many of the supremacists, his mother and father included. His mother was killed and his father was severely wounded, only to later die in a jail cell.

In the aftermath, he was whisked off to Boston where his grandmother took custody of him. Life with her was the exact opposite of that of the compound; it was filled with love and caring, which left him even more confused. Cole learned to suppress and hide the hostility of the compound and gained acceptance into his grandmother's world. Cole pretended normalcy throughout high school and eventually college. He became very good at the lie, but it was always there, just beneath the surface, ready to erupt and do harm to others. Sometimes the hostility emerged, like on the high school football field where he was immensely successful as a running back. But it was all a lie, just as today was a lie. He glanced at the crushed beer can at his side. Was his soul like the crushed can: empty of any hint of remorse, trodden beyond any possible repair? Could the lies of forced normalcy ever refill the can?

The black woman he'd ogled earlier, presumably Samantha's mother, stepped out of the stairwell. Even in the dim light, Cole could see she was decked out to the nines with a short-short pink skirt, blazing red low-cut top, and high heels. He took a double pull from his warm beer. He watched every step as she seductively wiggled her way towards the street and then disappeared as she headed towards the platform for the Seven train.

He yearned for a normal relationship with a woman. Not just the one-night stand this woman could offer. But a real relationship that would survive the test of revealed secrets, a woman who was a kindred spirit and could accept him for who he was. He was saddened by the memory of Dominique, the one that could have been the love of his life. God, he missed her. But then, he had no right to ever ask God for anything.

The evening quieted, except for some distant commotion in an apartment far away. The Seven train that seemed to rumble right overhead during the day had quit running. There was no sign of Samantha's mother. She probably had a date, or maybe several dates, that would leave Samantha on her own for the night. Cole thought about heading up the stairwell to his apartment, but he hated it and the increased isolation it brought.

The only thing it really provided was anonymity. A few extra hundreds kept the building supervisor happy and Cole off the list of official tenants.

The night quiet turned into only distant sounds from far-off traffic. Cole imagined the pitter-patter of a rabbit along the building, but quickly realized it had to be a rat; after all, this was New York. He could just barely make out the small figure along the building wall, no more than twenty feet from him. Even in the dark, Cole knew that at twenty feet he could put a subsonic .22 caliber bullet right through the little varmint's eye and the sound would be so subtle that no one would awaken. His adrenaline surged but Cole suppressed it immediately. There was no place for the hunt, the thrill, or the hostility of his past life; he forced the calming by reminding himself of his goals. He would have his peace and live below the radar like millions of other New Yorkers. Someday he might regain normalcy and maybe even get a job, wear a tie, buy a house out by La Guardia, and drive into Manhattan every day. He could be a financial analyst on Wall Street, he fantasized. But then rational thought returned and crushed the fantasy; it could never be.

Cole's thoughts drifted to Kevin, his only true friend in the world. Living in the Projects was a matter of choice. He and Kevin had more money than could ever be spent in a lifetime. But money draws attention and attention had to be avoided at all costs. The FBI, CIA, and a whole host of other government agencies probably still had him on their radar. And maybe the Islamic world still held a grudge over the Quaraysh Unity. But it was the criminal elements that he feared the most. He and Kevin had relieved some forty of the nation's nastiest drug dealing, human trafficking, smuggling, larcenous enterprises of their laundered money and left them ten-to-one leveraged in the red. The reality of it all was that the whole world was a threat. Cole contemplated the essential questions he'd asked himself hundreds of times: Would they ever forget? How long would it take? Would he have to stay in hiding his entire life?

Cole popped the top on his fifth beer. A bump in adrenaline alerted Cole before any sight or sound recognition emerged from the dark. Yet, someone or something was approaching from the south; he felt it instinctively. It was time to flee and scramble up the stairs to his third-floor apartment. It could be the Project's security cops or some kind of a night patrol, which would have Cole trying to answer why he would be stupid enough to sit out here at this hour.

Cole's night vision focused on three distant figures approaching in the virtually non-existent light. As they came nearer, their features became more visible and Cole began his assessment. It was three black men: two in baggy pants and sideways ball caps and a third in common street clothes. The stupidity of Cole's life materialized in his mind. Was there nothing left in life except the adrenaline rush? "Damn," Cole cursed under his breath.

Cole took another swig of beer as the dim light reflected off some kind of bling hanging around the neck of the leftmost gang member. "Could be advantage, mine," he thought. He forced the audible self-talk, "Damn it, let it go." The Queen's Projects allowed him to stay off the grid and meld into society's poor where anonymity is the easiest.

But the innate hostility within him had its own arguments. He didn't have to be here. Cole Davis, Cody Calhoon, James West, Varner Von Braun, Bob Goddard, or whomever he chose to be could easily find another hiding place. He could just move on and find another location, another safe haven. "No," he commanded himself.

The one on the left had some kind of bag slung over his right shoulder, a kid's backpack for school, or a daypack of some kind. Whatever was in it would be of no use; they wouldn't have time to retrieve whatever was in it, even if it was the most lethal of weapons like an Uzi or folded stock AK. The punk on the right slipped his hand into his pocket and Cole knew it meant gun. Small pocket—small gun, maybe a nine-millimeter with a three-inch barrel and small grip, which also meant small mag, he conjectured. Probably a cheap Czechoslovakian semi with an overly compressed mag spring to pack in as many rounds as possible. The other two probably also had some type of pocketed weapon but they would be at least a second and a half behind. It wouldn't be a fair fight; the three punk-ass gang-bangers wouldn't have a chance.

The adrenaline rush soared like it hadn't in months and the hostility argument grew stronger. As they approached and their shapes became clearer, he contemplated each of many variables and visualized his moves and those of his potential adversaries. The one on the right with intentions of using a pistol was dead at anything less than sixteen feet and he had no clue that he was about to die. The punk's best chance was a shot at eight feet. Anything more than that and the panic of conflict, along with poor accuracy, would guarantee a missed first shot. But he would never get the shot off because even a slow man can close sixteen feet before a rookie, like this punk, could even aim. If it turned out to be a knife instead of a pistol, Cole's attack would be the same. Gun or knife, Cole would wait to see it; it would be the punk's choice. As soon as the weapon showed in the hand, Cole would terminate his life—and that of his comrades.

Colors were now becoming visible: blue and black. The gang-bangers on the left and right wore Yankees jerseys and the one in center wore a Detroit Tigers jacket with a bold Roman style "D" on the left front. Cole surmised they each had an earring in the right ear and a black rag sticking out of their right back pocket. They were Disciples, one of the most well-organized and ruthless gangs in America. Almost like terrorist cells, the Disciples had a hierarchy based on twelve with lateral and upper leadership unknown to lower levels. Their base was Chicago but they controlled and ran drugs from Brownsville, Texas to Madawaska, Maine. In his past life, Cole had interfered with their drug trade at the Brownsville crossing and learned to know them well. They were ruthless and had no inhibition when it came to torture and murder, which included all imaginable forms of rape, dismemberment, skinning, filleting, and beheading.

Their mentality would not allow them to pass Cole tonight without some form of physical abuse. They would use demands for his Mets ball cap and beer as an excuse. That is—if Cole chose eyes down, no conflict, no violence, meekness, and preservation of anonymity. But in the end, the hostility argument won out.

They neared their sixteen-foot circle of death and Cole discreetly flexed and tensed his muscles in preparation for combat. These weren't children; they were each a good two hundred-twenty-five pounds and probably spent their bored hours pumping weights. It would require tact and precision to execute a frontal assault, but it was far from the first time. He visualized each move and counter-move. They would approach to within seven or eight feet and begin with some kind of verbal assault. He would just stare. Then the one on the right would pull the weapon in an attempt to reinforce a feckless administration of torment, but Cole would be there first with a burst of energy slamming his left fist into the center of the middle punk's chest and simultaneously, with his right hand, catch the other punk's hand emerging from the pocket with the weapon. Cole's oversized hand would easily capture the punk's hand and weapon from below and begin an upward lift. Cole would then smash his left hand down at the apex of the punk's arm accelerating the punk's weapon, still held in his own hand, up under the man's chin. Cole would then either help the punk plunge the knife up through the soft tissue between the mandibula and jaw or help the punk pull the trigger of the pistol sending a bullet up through the mandibula, mouth, and out the top of his head. Either way, he would be the first to die. The punk on the far left would be the second. Cole would whirl to his right with a roundhouse kick to the man's midsection and then, with reversed momentum, spin hammer his fist just forward and above the punk's left ear, which, when delivered with enough energy, would kill him instantly. This would leave Cole in close quarters and over-rotated relative to the remaining punk. Cole would reverse his rotation and drive his right elbow full force into the punk's nose driving nasal and maxilla bone fragments into the man's brain. It would all be over in less than four seconds. Cole's adrenaline level surged. The approaching punks had no clue they were within seconds of death.

As they crossed into the circle, the center punk whispered something to the other two. Cole imagined he heard the words "not" and "business" over the shuffling of feet but captured nothing more. Their pace slowed. The conflict was only moments away. He studied each man's face intently for confirmation of the battle that was about to take place. But something was wrong. Cole wasn't the focus of their attention. The punk in the center glared at Cole but not the other two. The one on the right with his hand still in his pocket wasn't even looking in Cole's direction. Cole recognized signs of fear in his eyes: distressed, darting, and averting any one focus for more than a fraction of a second. The punk on the left also had signs of fear in his face but his eyes were focused straight ahead as if he was consumed by anticipation of some future event, something in the adjacent building. As they neared, the man in the center locked eyes with Cole as if conflict was imminent. His stare was intense as if he could read Cole's thoughts. The man's glare was unwavering as they closed the remaining few feet. Cole's adrenaline level exploded.

But then the man in the center calmly said, "Good evening, sir." Cole stared deep into the man's face and tried to penetrate his thoughts, but got nothing. "What the hell," Cole mumbled confused, and could only continue to stare.

As they plodded onward towards the adjacent building, Cole was more than just befuddled. This was not like any Disciple behavior ever witnessed, heard of, or practiced. Then, as they exited their circle of death, Cole observed elbow movements of the center Disciple. He reached across his mid-section to retrieve something under his jacket. Had they made me? Is he about to empty a nine-millimeter clip at me? How could I have missed it? Cole cried in his mind. "Over-confident fool, Damn," he scolded himself. They were beyond sixteen feet, which meant flee. He bolted to his feet, spun, grabbed the stairwell door handle, and was halfway up the first flight of stairs before turning to see what he expected was a Disciple taking aim. But it wasn't so. Something in front of him occupied both hands and all three continued walking away. Then Cole saw the cell phone come to punk's ear and Cole slumped to the stairs. He exhaled, put his face in his hands, and reflected on the thought that he was about to kill three innocent men. A man with no remorse and on the edge of hostility is fundamentally broken, yet it is a choice. Or is it? He broke down. Is this an addiction: the adrenaline, the violence, the killing? When will it end? Why can't life be normal? Is it pos-sible to be normal? Emotion and self-reprimand slowly subsided and yielded to reason. Try harder he resolved, just make the damn choice and stick to it.

Lying awake that night, in his third-floor apart-ment, he replayed the events over and over and over in his mind. Had he made the right choice tonight? It just wasn't right: "Good evening sir." Their behavior was all wrong based on everything he had learned living in the underbelly of society. It was not in their nature to pass up the weak. They should have tried to take his Mets cap and last beer. It was that simple. Something was wrong.

Eventually, the thoughts subsided. He had Mets tickets for tomorrow and Crocker, the league's last true knuckleballer, was pitching. Sleep eased in as he envisioned an un-hittable baseball floating past a Rockies batter.

Chapter 2

AMERICA'S MOST WANTED

ONE WEEK EARLIER, DEEP IN THE NSA HEADQUARters building at Fort Meade Maryland, NSA Director and USCYBERCOM Commander, Blaine Higgins, prepared to make his presentation to representatives from the highest echelons of government, including heads of the FBI, DIA, CIA, and Homeland Security. Higgins had kept full details of Operation Cool Fool limited to a key eight individuals within the NSA. But expenditures of nearly half a billion dollars meant that he now had to increase his circle of trust in order to continue, and hide, his current rate of expenditure.

"Let me begin," he started and then stared at each one to make sure he had their attention. "Note that the computer I am using is forty years old and incapable of connecting to any network of any kind and the file that I am going to present from is on a floppy disc that I will destroy immediately following this presentation. We have a security breach like none other in the history of the United States and my careful actions will become apparent to you as I go through my presentation. There can be no communication of the topics we will discuss today in any electronic form. That means no emails, Excel files, PowerPoint files, Word files, nothing. Furthermore, the contents of what we are about to discuss today cannot be verbally disclosed to anyone, in any form or forum, for any reason. That includes the President of the United States. This is of the utmost secret of discussions, as you will learn."

Higgins glanced at the director of the FBI and then continued, "This is currently just a NSA operation. However, Evert Hooster assigned six of his best agents to my task force, but they report directly to me. In total, I have sixty-four very specialized individuals working on the task force. But just to be clear, even the task force doesn't have full view of the operation details. I have limited full disclosure of all details to only eight key individuals. I will not expand that number today so expect only a high-level overview. Don't ask for more."

Higgins pointed to his first chart and began his presentation: "It all started with Julian Assange. In 1990 Julian Assange created a simple routine that broke passwords by trial and error. He hacked under the name of Mendac using a modem and broke into the US Air Force 7th Command computer system at the Pentagon. He gained access to secret Desert Storm information, which included battleground strategic plans, casualty numbers, troop numbers, and communication protocols. It was our first true cyber-terrorist attack and he alerted us to our vulnerabilities."

Higgins pointed his laser at the second chart and continued, "Brad Williams was our second experience with cyber assault. He accessed FBI files and identified agent names, addresses, and assignments. All of which were published on the emerging internet. As a result of these first two assaults on national security, along with a growing number of cyber hackers with their viruses, worms, and Trojans, the United States government was forced down a path of ever-increasing complex electronic defenses. Since 1991, we have literally spent over a trillion dollars securing our strategic and intelligence information." Higgins paused and then continued, "But it never seems to be enough. The ever-increasing multiplicity and evolution of hacker technology continues to encroach on our ever-increasing complex security measures.

"In 1997, Hugh Chon acquired a partial list of CIA operatives abroad. He actually had the gall to blackmail us and sell them back to us at a cost of one million dollars each. We paid his ransom, but eventually, we caught up with him and I think you all know his fate. Our friends the Mossad did us a favor and Mr. Chon is no more.

"In 1999, Kevin Mitinck was the world's most wanted cyber-terrorist. He hacked banking systems, CIA computer exchanges, personal and business computer systems, and just about anything else accessible. He developed codes and commandeered government and university computers, linking them through amazingly creative and efficient slave/master systems. He was feared by government officials high and low because of his capabilities. It was rumored that he could start a nuclear war by simply whistling into a phone. The thing about this guy was that he never stole any money or compromised national security. He just hacked because he could and because the son-of-a-bitch enjoyed screwing with us. In the end, we only got him on misdemeanor crimes and he only served two years. As soon as he was released, he went right back to hacking, except legally. He became a computer security expert making millions contracting out to major U.S. companies. We characterized his behaviors and used them to help profile another Kevin, which I'll get to in a minute.

"In 2005, a simple thumb drive was used to copy ballistic trajectory data for our Minuteman missile system. Lieutenant Johns simply logged on using his credentials to a Nellis Air Force Base computer and copied off the data. He subsequently sold it to the Chinese.

"In 2013, we have Edward Snowden. He absconded with generally peripheral data and policy information, which just provided formal documentation of things many Americans already suspected.

"In 2015, we had a team of hackers from Turkistan eavesdropping on House Intelligence Oversight Committee email. They captured three months' worth of emails and posted them with Wiki Leaks.

"Then we have the turmoil caused by Andre Chkonovich during the 2020 election. Trump was partially right. I'm not saying Trump would have won, but it would have been awful close. Chkonovich and his team figured out how to dupe the election software. It took us years to reconstruct how he and his team had actually assured Biden the win."

He paused and then continued, "The hackers are always right behind us, nipping at our heels, as we continue to strengthen our defenses. We hire the best and brightest computer whiz kids and geeks in droves to build and test impregnable walls to keep the attackers out. And for the most part, we are successful. All the breaches to our defenses have been kept to outer levels with—yes—sensitive information, and—yes—it has hurt our national security and worldwide credibility. But no one has gained access to our most protected top-secret information. That is, until Kevin McKuel."

Higgins advanced his slides and displayed a picture of a young man in his twenties. His face was gaunt with unremarkable facial features. He had black, greasy-appearing, long hair. The eyes were magnified by wire-framed glasses and the lips formed a devious looking half smile. Higgins thrust his arm at the screen, pointed at the picture, and raised his voice, "This cyber-geek bastard makes all those in our history look like kindergartners."

Higgins paused while they all studied the photograph before continuing: "This picture was taken twelve years ago. Since then, he has gone underground and we have no record of his whereabouts. He has no family and only a few acquaintances that we can identify. His expertise twelve years ago was in data storage on both media and cloud. In some form or another, he developed, or at least contributed to, cloud protections in use today."

Higgins paused and looked around the room. He advanced his slides. "We believe he gained access to super-cooled super-computers running in the basement of this building. They are so secret I hardly know they exist. In combination, they are a full-up quantum computer system using entanglement processing. These computers working in parallel can crunch AES 256-bit encryption and house some of this country's most guarded secrets. There is no external access to these computers; terminals are housed behind a security system so robust that access by an unauthorized person is virtually impossible. It has retina and facial recognition access controls, in addition to armed guards and video surveillance monitoring. Primary, secondary, and tertiary identification are required just to gain entrance to the terminal room. Once inside, terminal access is guarded by a series of user-unique questions and passphrases. Yet somehow Kevin McKuel logged on, used the system, and stole information. The system is classified as top-secret and, once logged on, a user has full access to other systems within the NSA, CIA, DIA, DARPA, and DHS. In summary, he has the ability to access all—I repeat all—of this nation's electronic information and only God knows what he would do with it!"

"Our AI profile predicts with a fifty-seven percent probability that he is not a mentally stable individual. Currently, he is righting wrongs as some kind of bizarre hobby. He uses social and other media to assassinate those in positions of power who have committed some kind of indiscretion. Recall Chuck Wiener's posts on Facebook and the shit-storm it caused in the media. Does anybody actually believe Weiner posted pictures of his wiener? We believe Weiner's real crime was that he used his influence as a congressman to have his nephew excluded from charges brought against four of his fellow students at Texas A&M for gang-raping some co-ed. In some kind of righteous attack, Kevin McKuel set the stage to make sure Weiner would lose his position of power through scandalous news reporting and ultimately be forced to resign."

"And there's many more: Senator Cranston's tweet about an affair with some hussy from New Orleans, Buffalo narcotics division commander caught on traffic and private surveillance cams associating with known drug dealers, and others. The son-of-a-bitch sneaks in spyware as part of a startup routine without even a single keystroke from the user. And we can't track him. He uses electronic aliases and then disappears: first, it's a 70-year-old woman's computer in Wisconsin, then it's the LAPD in California, next it's a Department of Agriculture computer in San Luis Obispo."

Higgins advanced his slides again. "Operation 'Cool Fool' is strictly off the books and off all electronic media systems because we don't know where he'll go next. We don't know what he has access to, and we don't want him to know that we're after him. He could be monitoring our internal email, searching our project files, or learning about our internal budgets. If he finds anything that suggests we are on to him, he will just go deeper, farther from our ability to reach, and that's unacceptable. Because—he is the most dangerous man in the history of U.S. intelligence. And keep in mind, it's not just the NSA that's at risk. Kevin McKuel is a threat to all our agencies."

Higgins paused. The audience was dumbfounded and he knew questions would develop. After all, it was their agencies that were threatened, which meant not only were the Nation's secrets at risk but also their personal careers and aspirations. And until this moment they had no clue the threat even existed. Higgins advanced the slides.

"We believe we know Kevin McKuel; we have used every scrap of personal information, every identifiable life event, every action and reaction to build an AI-generated character profile with an associated 3D interactive hologram. Our key operative has spent ten months, fourteen hours a day, seven days a week interacting with the AI hologram."

The director of Homeland Security interrupted, "How does all that help track this hacker?"

"The artificial intelligence generated profile takes all things into account and predicts the very essence of the individual, including cyber transgressions."

"Sounds like mumbo-jumbo physco-illusion crap to me, but okay," the Secretary of State commented.

Evert Hooster, head of the FBI, raised his hand and asked, "What computer system did you use for the AI?"

"Good question. We have four IBM ET1 super-computers isolated in a Faraday cage. They have never been connected to the internet or anything else and wouldn't know how to communicate even if they were. The only wire connected to them is from a completely independent and standalone power generator. We installed archaic DOS 2.0 as an operating system and a virgin version of AJACK, our artificial intelligence routine. Then all profile data is input by hand or self-learned by the AI."

Another question came from the small audience, "What national security data did he steal?"

"We are not exactly sure what he stole. But we do know that he created a program to run in the back-ground and crunch 256-bit encryption. We also know that he used the computer system to access data within the Financial Crimes Enforcement Network."

"So what exactly is his crime, other than being able to hack our systems?"

Higgins thought for a moment and then answered, "It's more what he could do, rather than what he has done. Whether of his own choice or coerced by a foreign power, the risk of compromise is too great. We just can't afford to have an individual with his capability on the outside. It's that simple."

"What does that mean exactly? Are you proposing deadly force?"

"I prefer not to answer that question directly. Please don't ask questions along those lines," crisply replied Higgins.

"All very interesting but you haven't given any details on how you're going to catch this Kevin McKuel."

"I won't either. Operation Cool Fool details are fully known only to eight individuals. And I intend to keep it that way. "

"Then how do you expect us to support you?"

"Gentlemen, please. I can give you a little more information. But this really has to be it. We are coming at this from multiple directions with operatives. I will tell you that we also built an interactive AI hologram of a known associate of Mister McKuel and are closing in. Our operatives' team has spent countless hours interacting with the AI reflection to learn about, and how to manipulate, him. Other than that, you are going to have to trust me. When the details come out, you will understand why. That's all the details I intend to provide today. I need two things from the intelligence community. First, I need to keep the effort fully funded, but off the books and with no oversight from any damn Congressional committee. Second, I need to draw upon your resources at a moment's notice with no questions asked. These are huge requests I make of you but the consequences of my failure will be your failure as well."

A slow rumble of conversation started in the conference room and soon escalated to all parties talking at once. Higgins stood at the front of the room and waited. He knew they needed time to sort it out in their minds and amongst themselves. The director of Homeland Security stopped talking first and sat back in his chair. The others, one by one, followed suit and the room eventually became silent. The director of Homeland Security looked at those around the table and received an unrequested indication of concurrence from each: a nod, lift of the hand, smile, or blink of the eyes.

Higgins watched the preceding and got the response he knew he would. He closed the meeting with the promise of a follow-up in two weeks and a parting comment, "In two weeks, I expect to report back to you that Kevin McKuel has been dealt with. I believe you know what that means."

Chapter 3

LIU CHEN

LIU CHEN SAT MOTIONLESS STARING AT HER CELL phone. Her current situation felt so weird. Life had been all work for as long as she could remember. Ever since being adopted by Rolf and Lana Chen in San Jose, her life had been dictated by others. Rolf was CEO of his microchip design and manufacturing company and expected his adopted daughter to someday take over the company. There were no dolls or playgrounds in her childhood years as her father pushed her to excel in Java, C++, Python, Haskel, PIC, and other computer languages. There were no boyfriends, slumber parties, or proms in her teens as she focused on advanced, lightning-speed, miniaturized processors intended to revolutionize supercomputers.

Her mother, Lana, pushed as hard as her father did. Lana had her doctorate in advanced artificial intelligence applications and expected Liu to master multivariate, parallel, programming techniques to enable instantaneous real-time AI response. When she wasn't programming for her father, she was programming for her mother. The company's supercomputer became her only physical friend. Large Language Models (LLMs) became her life. The application challenge was to create a system that could run on even the most limited computer, perhaps even just a standard laptop. Code had to be extremely efficient in its processing and draw on compact data sources for its background data.

Intensity of work left a huge void in her life. She filled that void with friends of her own creation; AI was magical. She created crude representations of girlfriends and Conrad. Conrad was her favorite AI characterization. She made him smart, witty, handsome, and very muscular. She sometimes pondered: what could have been, if he had been real?

Liu graduated from high school two years early and was accepted at Carnegie Mellon University in Pittsburgh. She excelled at general cybersecurity and quickly completed her undergraduate degree. MIT in Cambridge offered her advanced studies in AI and she was immediately accepted into their graduate program. The challenges were both hardware and software: how do you get a machine to respond faster than the human brain? Then, to further complicate programming challenges, add the complexities of behavioral characteristics and self-learning. Conrad was never far from her thoughts as he became her doctoral thesis and project. Conrad went from a crude 2D entity to a fully 3D-projected hologram. Maybe "love" was too strong a word. But Conrad filled her desperate need for acceptance and, yes, love.

Now, here she sat in this awkward situation staring at her phone. Conrad was so much easier to deal with.

Would this real man accept her for who she was? What social skills did she really have? The answer was none. How could this work? Tears moistened her eyes and were on the verge of running down her cheeks. Liu yearned for comfort from Conrad. But that was out of the question as she waited for the text she knew was coming. And Kevin could never know about Conrad.

Kevin McKuel began opening the gift he'd just received; it was an absolute thrill because he never got presents from anyone. The wrapping theme was not birthday or Christmas; it was an exotic non-descript pattern theme with bright colors. He ripped at it like a three-year-old at Christmas. But it was double-wrapped. He laughed and went after it again. As the present emerged, he smiled. It was a Probaris-Lebram smartphone providing absolutely secure communications. The note inside said: "It's just like mine and fully ready to go—Liu."

Kevin immediately texted Liu Chen: "Thx so much. UR awesome."

Liu texted back: "UR welcome. I just wanted to make sure we could CMEKT."

Kevin texted: "Did U know I can't even hack this phone."

Liu texted: "I doubt that. U can hack almost anything."

Kevin texted: "Maybe. But it would take serial quantum computers using EP to crack the AES encryp."

Liu texted: "O I know. I love it when U talk technical."

Kevin texted: "Even my Fugaku clone with 2,566 TFLOPs couldn't crack it."

Liu texted: "That's a lot of TFLOP! My Exascale doesn't even come close."

Kevin and Liu's technical exchange continued for hours. Most of the exchange was technical, but gradually breeched the line into personal. And that made Kevin nervous. She could never know his past, at least not the details. Liu was so smart that even the slightest slip would set her off on a deep-dive web search that could expose him. She had already discovered the easy to find information. She knew about the cabin in Bear Lake, Utah where he and Cole had faked their deaths. Liu was curious for more.

Liu texted: "So what are U afraid of?"

Kevin couldn't tell her the whole truth and struggled for the right partial answer. Kevin texted: "I know UL find out if I don't tell U, but it's got to be kept secret. My friend and I have enemies, lots of them. Islamic nations, drug dealers, all sorts of criminal elements, and maybe the government would send people after us if they knew we were alive. PLS don't ask for more. And PLS don't search for more on the web. U may draw unwanted attention."

Liu texted: "U make it sound so scary."

Kevin texted: "It is. PLS let it go for now."

Liu looked to her left and texted: "I guess I know why U wouldn't send me a picture of URSLF."

Kevin texted: "Y, but I love the picture U sent me. UR face is so beautiful and I love the color of your eyes."

Liu texted: "Now U R flirting. My cheeks are all puffy and Oriental eyes aren't very pretty. U R just saying that. But it's OK. I like it."

Kevin texted: "I mean it. U R very pretty."

Liu blushed, looked again to her left, and texted: "I like U too."

As the day wore on, Liu eventually texted: "I missed breakfast. We could get a table at Roberto's? Early dinner?"

Kevin texted: "I'm not that hungry. Why don't U just order in with MD?"

Liu texted: "K. Then I have some work to do."

Kevin texted: "What is it this time?"

Liu texted: "GPS trackers, two secure laptops, and four cell phones. I need to get them to UPS in the morning. Going to be a late night."

Kevin texted: "Then I'll remote the Fugaku and take care of some stuff. Talk tomorrow."

Liu texted: "K. E-kisses good night."

Chapter 4

FORTY-MILE-PER-HOUR
FASTBALL

ONE THOUSAND MILES SOUTH IN HUNTSVILLE, ALA-
bama, six-year-old Tommy Delahe woke early with
thoughts of baseball. He'd hardly slept all night
thinking about the big game: mighty Mustangs
against the fraidy-cat Cheetahs. When he ventured
downstairs, his father was studying the sports section. Tommy knew his father would miss the big
game, as he did most games, but Tommy would
provide all the highlights.

Tommy studied the newspaper with his father,
looking at pictures and getting free commentary. His
dad loved baseball almost as much as he did and baseball was everywhere. Big leaguers were already racking
up home runs in the race for new records. Las Vegas
had already made projections on the College World
Series playoffs; Stanford was favored to be the colle-
giate champion. The Huntsville Times Sports' section
featured the Houston Astros win over the Los Angeles
Dodgers on Friday. Huntsville and Salt Lake Triple-A
got recognition in minor league stories of their own.
The Local section of the paper covered the Red Stone
High School win over Tupelo. Time had escaped Reed
Delahe as he and Tommy poured over each story, but

this, like most days was a workday. Tommy's dad wished him well in the big game, gave him a hug, and left him in the care of his nanny, Miss Johnston.

Elizabeth Johnston was a real bargain for Reed. He had brought the young woman out from Utah to provide a nanny for Tommy. She was more than he could have ever wanted. Not only did she take care of Tommy, but she also took care of many household duties as well. He paid her twice their original agreed-upon sum and he still felt like he had a bargain.

The day wore on as temperature and humidity increased. Finally, the magic hour arrived and Miss Johnston drove Tommy to the Huntsville Youth Center. Parents eagerly awaited the start of the game. It was the thrill of seeing their child snag a fly ball, make an out, or just hit the ball that drew them from the comfort of their air conditioners to the miniature baseball field.

Parents of the Cheetahs cheered as the batter approached the batter's box. It was Caroline's first at-bat and she towered above all the boys on the team. Both teams referred to her as "Big Caroline" because of her intimidating size and ability to make those all-important outs at first base. The umpire stood behind the pitching machine holding the ball above his head and little Tommy Delahe stood at his side. Big Caroline nodded and the umpire fed the ball to the machine. The ball came out of the machine with a "thuwamp" and sailed in right over the plate. She swung and her hit whistled past the pitching machine and Tommy; it was a line drive that bounced behind the pitcher's mound and rolled all the way to second base. Caroline, smiling with pleasure at her accomplishment, watched the ball all the way to the second baseman's glove. She started her charge for first base as the second baseman picked up the ball and launched it in a huge arch toward first base. Caroline ran with all her heart, each foot leaving a little puff of dust behind. Caroline didn't hear the screams of excitement and encouragement from her mom and dad; her focus was on first base and Joe Bob. Joe Bob was the only one who could steal the excitement of her remarkable hit. How could he do that to her? Maybe her mamma would make her safe anyway, she thought as she pounded down the baseline. Joe Bob stood with one foot on first base and his glove arm fully extended skyward. He turned his head to look at Caroline just as the ball fell into his mitt. The umpire made a fist and motioned with his arm. She was "out" and the cheering shifted from one set of parents to another.

Caroline stopped three-quarters of the way to first. Tears gushed from her big blue eyes and she let out the first of many chirping squeaks. The squeaks increased in frequency and her head bobbed with each one as she held back from outright balling. Her hunched-over body was motionless and her arms dangled towards the ground, outwardly showing the suffering of her defeat.

The first inning ended scoreless. But the second and third innings proved to be exciting as the score advanced: Cheetahs—seven, Mustangs—eight. The game time limit expired making the fourth inning the last. The game would be over if the Mustangs could hold the Cheetahs scoreless in the top of the fourth. The coach told Tommy that their best chance of preventing runs was to put him at home as catcher.

Baxter was first up to bat for the Cheetahs. He wiggled back and forth as he twisted his feet into position and then gave the pitching machine an evil eye. His hands wrenched the bat, oozing sweat-laden dirt from between his fingers. The umpire fed the machine and its "thuwamp" startled the anxious Baxter; he swung well before the ball got there. He was luckier on the second pitch and ticked the ball back toward the pitching machine. As Baxter took off for first, Tommy flung off his catcher's mask and charged towards the mound. With catcher's gear clanging and banging, he scooped up the ball and fired it towards first. It was a remarkable play; Joe Bob caught the ball and tagged Baxter before he got to first. One down—two to go.

The second batter up struck out bringing back the top of the order, Big Caroline Shuler. She had recovered from her emotional defeat and had singled her last time at bat. Her team cheered her on, expecting her to tie the game. At the plate, she towered over Tommy and whispered, "Runt."

Caroline didn't disappoint her team; she hit a grounder past the third baseman. The ball hooked left and the left fielder scrambled to retrieve the ball. Without thinking, he threw the ball towards first as Caroline stomped on second base and accelerated towards third. Joe Bob scurried towards the ball, picking it up and then dropping it. The coach yelled, "Throw it home. Throw it home." Caroline's coach waved her on towards home as Joe Bob recovered the ball. He threw it towards home and Tommy, the team's best chance of ending the game as winners.

Tommy met the ball in front of the plate and squeezed it in his mitt. Caroline was at full speed heading for home. With only a fraction of a second to spare, Tommy jumped into position on the base-line, extending his mitt forward and reinforcing its position with his other hand. He squeezed the ball ever tighter at the moment of Caroline's full-speed impact. The mitt caught Caroline in the stomach and Tommy's locked elbows pole-vaulted her into the air launching her over home plate. She landed flat on her back as Tommy went over backward slamming onto the plate. He raised his glove hand and turned it towards the umpire to show the ball still firmly held in the mitt.

The umpire looked away, shook his head, made a fist, and then quietly said, "Game."

Caroline managed to roll onto her stomach and raise herself on her elbows. The wind was gone from her lungs and the ensuing outburst of tears and bawling refused to come.

"That was uncalled for. He should be out!" yelled a mother from the sidelines and then quietly added, "Shouldn't he?"

Encouraged by the vocal outburst, another mother yelled at the umpire, "That boy shouldn't be allowed to play. Throw him out of the game."

An Oriental man sitting downfield with two others, also in suites, began laughing and clapped.

The coach's wife yelled back, "Sore loser."

She stood and mustered her anger as a heavy-set man next to her in a fold-up captain's chair chimed in, "This is seven-year-old baseball. That was just plain unnecessary. They had another ups."

The woman, who had first mustered her anger, directed a verbal assault at Tommy, "Hey! You little craphead! What do you think that was? I'll tell you. That was a horrible thing to do and you should be punished!" Fueled by her anger, she pointed at Tommy and yelled in the direction of the parents, "Who does that little boy belong to anyway?"

The petite young Miss Johnston, Tommy's nanny, stood up and started to speak but was stopped by an outburst in her direction, "Are you going to do something about that little boy?"

Miss Johnston calmly replied, "No, it's baseball."

Calmness of the reply further infuriated the outraged woman. And when Caroline's mother ran onto the field to comfort her daughter, furor of the screaming woman reached a climax. "It's the parent's fault. Little boys don't just do that without being taught!" she screamed.

The Oriental man's laughing could be heard. At one point, it became quite boisterous and drew curiosity from several parents.

The coach's wife and two other Mustang mothers shouted back at the woman, accusing her of poor sportsmanship, teaching the kids a poor lesson, and having an outrageous hairdo.

Caroline finally got out a cry and then burst into all-out wailing. But Caroline's crying was quickly drowned out by the continued tirade of the insanely outraged woman. She screamed at the parents, "You're all the cause of this. Somebody should punish that little boy! He's a monster! You can't just sit there!"

Then she again lambasted Miss Johnston, "Your little boy is a beast. You need to do something about him!"

"I'm not sure what he did wrong," came Miss Johnston's calm response.

TOMMY HAD HEARD ENOUGH AND THE CRAZY LADY was being mean to his best friend. Miss Johnston had been his babysitter for two years and she was the only mother figure he had ever known. That crazy lady had better shut her fat mouth and leave Miss Johnston alone. Tommy worked the fingers on his right hand using the mitt on his left to get them into position and then displayed his middle finger to the crazy lady and all her friends. He had no idea what it meant, but he'd seen it before and this seemed like the right time to *flip'em-off.*

The strange-looking Oriental man, sitting away from the parents, again started clapping. Tommy looked at him. That's when he knew *flipin'em-off* was definitely the right thing to do.

"Did you see that? Did you see what he just did? I can't believe it!" Again, the out-of-control woman pointed at Tommy and exploded, "If your mother doesn't do something about you, I will! You're not going to get away with that. I'm going to—to. . ."

The stuttering and puzzled look on her face didn't stop Tommy as he methodically took the baseball from his catcher's mitt, entered a full windup, and then hurled his forty-five-mile-per-hour fastball at her head.

She screamed, "You little bastard!" just before the ball hit her square in the face and rebounded with the sound of crackling cartilage. She let out a final scream, "Oh God," as blood gushed from her nose and she bolted from the field shrieking unintelligible gibberish, leaving chair, purse, car keys, and child behind.

The strange-looking Oriental man laughed and again began clapping. The clapping continued until Miss Johnston hurried onto the field and took Tommy's hand.

Tommy glared at the speechless parents, players, and coaches as he was dragged from the field.

Even Caroline paused her crying long enough to watch Tommy being led away. Tommy's catcher's gear clanked and banged all the way to the parking lot. He looked back at all the stares coming from the ball field wondering what the big deal was. Miss Johnston opened his door and quickly fastened his seat belt as he settled into his seat. He inquired, "What about my bat?" but got no reply. Moments later, the ball field was out of sight as they sped away.

Chapter 5

THE DEVIL'S SERVANT

TIME HAD ESCAPED REED DELAHE AS HE BALANCED sales projections against the upcoming layoff. As Vice President for Operations, he was the number two man at Westcom in Huntsville, Alabama, which demanded long hours including Saturdays and Sundays. This evening's task was extremely unpleasant having arrived at the conclusion that twenty-seven percent of the workforce would lose their jobs. Military sales for radiation-hardened integrated circuits and control packages had been second-sourced and future procurements were going to be cut in half. Even the specialty sensor and circuit contracts they had locked up through "black customers" with top-secret projects were being reduced. And the commercial market for animated amusement ride electronics was a disaster; sales had just dried up.

Westcom was the only company Reed had ever worked for and he had given it his heart and soul to make it successful. He first went to work for Westcom while working on his electrical engineering degree at the University of Alabama. He spent four years working on the floor and understood the blue-collar mentality all too well. Layoff rumors were already circulating and that meant reduced productivity, quality problems, and possibly even intentional equipment sabotage.

All his education and past successes were no match for the problems that lay ahead for Westcom. After Reed got his Bachelor's degree, he spent four years in the Design Engineering section while getting his Masters in computer science and then finishing up a Ph.D. in electrical engineering. It didn't take him long to move into the management ranks after he helped land some critical commercial contracts and got special recognition from customers. He had furthered his career with his relationship with customers and truly understood the necessity of satisfying their needs. Although it sometimes made him uncomfortable, on occasion he had discretely provided products and information that bordered on disclosure of sensitive classified information. The distinction between commercial and military programs was not always that clear and Westcom not only condoned, but also rewarded, his actions and quickly promoted him through the management ranks.

The computer behind him beeped to break Reed's intense concentration on the documents spread out on his desk. He whirled around to read the notification on the computer screen: "8:00 Dinner with Ken Kuoto, MTC of Taiwan." Reed sighed and picked up the phone. He dialed home.

It was answered with a sweet feminine voice on the second ring: "Delahe residence."

"Hi, Liz. I'm afraid this is going to be another late night. I've got customers in and you know what that means. Are you and Tommy okay for tonight?"

"We're fine."

"Groceries, a movie, ah—anything you need?"

"No, we're fine. Really. Just a minute."

Reed could hear her pose a question as she moved the phone away from her mouth: "Tommy, do want to talk to your Dad?"

The simple "no" from the background brought on intense feelings of guilt. Reed had dedicated his life to the company, which drove his wife to pack up and leave for a life with "more excitement," as she put it. Now, he was neglecting his son. He instructed Liz to tell Tommy that he'd be home for dinner tomorrow. When she did, an insouciant "okay" from the background further aggravated his feelings of guilt.

Liz Johnston replied, "We'll expect you tomorrow at six sharp. I'll prepare a special Mormon stew."

"Mormon stew, huh?"

"I got the recipe at Relief Society. I'm sure you'll like it."

"They certainly teach young Mormon women home-ec stuff. I really appreciate all you do for Tommy and me."

"Thank you for the compliment. We'll see you tomorrow."

Reed organized the papers and documents on his desk, switched off his computer, and glanced at the photograph of Tommy on the wall. He hustled down the stairs to the front exit where he swiped his badge through the card reader and exited the building into a blast of hot, humid air. A glance at his watch told him it was going to be tight; the Lexus would have to bend the speed limit a little, he concluded. He slid into the driver's seat and the Lexus instantly came to life. The tires chirped when he quickly went from reverse to drive after backing out of his front-row parking space. He accelerated, racing out of the parking lot and onto the onramp for Ride Out Road. He didn't wait for the car in front of him to merge into traffic; instead, he floored the Lexus and crossed immediately over to the fast lane. The car quickly reached eighty miles per hour where he backed off on the accelerator pedal. He swung back to the right, passing a slower car in the fast lane, to exit onto University and then into the parking lot of the Regal Hotel. He found a convenient parking spot, leaped from the Lexus, and hurried towards the entrance.

A limousine sat at idle under the covered entrance; one man stood at the rear of the car and another at the front. A third man was talking to the doorman. As he approached, he garnered their attention and all three started slowly moving into position to intercept his path. Ordinarily, he would have thought mugging, especially with their intimidating size, but they were dressed in three-piece suits, clean-shaven, with short hair, and wearing spit-polished black shoes. He imagined an unusual bulge under the left arm of the man on the right. His thoughts immediately went to the CIA. Reed maintained his stride, walking straight towards them. Probably not the CIA, he guessed, more likely one of my customers from the NSA black world. This is more their style; they don't like some aspect of our company R&D and want me to change it or they want me to make some unqualified change to one of their products. You never see the black jokers unless they want something from you. Must be, he concluded as the distance between them closed.

"Good evening Mr. Delahe," said one of the men in a very quiet but firm voice. "How are you this evening?"

"I'm just fine. And how about yourself?" replied Reed, still weighing the challenge of a discussion with the CIA or NSA.

"Oh, we're exceptional. But Mr. Kuoto has found the restaurant menu unsuitable for his tastes and would like you to join him for dinner elsewhere. You can join him in the car and we'll drive you."

Reed was wrong about these jokers being from the NSA black world, even though they behaved like it. Ken Kuoto was a potential commercial customer that he'd never met, but this was way out of character for commercial customers. He offered an alternate plan, "Why don't you just tell me where we're going and I'll drive myself and, if you like, you can just follow me."

"No. Mr. Kuoto always insists on having things his way. He'd like you to join him in the car. I believe, sir, that he has some business to discuss with you and would like to utilize travel time in the car."

It went against his better judgment and gut feel. He almost said no, but he desperately needed to land whatever deal with whoever, even if it meant climbing into a limousine with three goons. He conceded, "All right, let's go."

One of the three held the limousine door for Reed and then followed him inside to close the door behind. Interior lights were dim and Reed struggled to make out the features of this mysterious Mr. Ken Kuoto. He extended his hand and offered an introduction, "My name is Reed Delahe."

"I know who you are."

Reed continued to hold his hand out in the silence. The other two goons took positions in the front of the limousine and the car began to move. Finally, Reed withdrew his hand and folded his arms. He maintained the silence, which was a negotiating technique he'd learned from the Orientals: maintain silence and your opponent will be compelled to speak. Somehow this already felt like a negotiation. The limousine turned left on University, eventually passing the strip clubs defining the fringes of Huntsville City limits. The ride was becoming increasingly uncomfortable for Reed and eventually he broke the silence, "Where are we going?" He got no reply.

"Look, Ken. I'm feeling a little uncomfortable with this and I'd like to know where we're going."

"You should feel uncomfortable," replied Ken with an Oriental accent.

"What is this? Huh?" Reed shouted.

"Just a little private business; I have something I want you to do for me."

"We can do business back in Huntsville."

"I don't think so," replied Kuoto as the limousine turned down a dirt road.

Reed peered out the window and meekly asked again, "Where are we going?"

He got no reply. Fear, frustration, and anger triggered wildly irrational thoughts. He lunged towards the door handle, only to be thrust back in his seat by the goon next to him. With the fear-driven strength of ten men, Reed repulsed the goon, sending him bouncing against the far door. Reed grabbed the door handle and pushed the door partially open when he felt a grasp tighten around his throat; the grip continued to tighten, freezing his motion and starving his lungs of air and his brain of blood. It was then that he got his first real, but momentary, look at Ken's face: Oriental showing the wrinkles of age with eyes of fire and bushy eyebrows. Reed felt faint and dropped back into his seat. The goon, having recovered from the impact, reached across and pulled the door closed.

"You are so naive," said Kuoto as he settled back into the darkness.

Reed's breathing returned to normal and, as the blood began returning to his brain, he considered his future actions. For the near term, he would have to just sit and be patient, but he would run given the first opportunity. Since giving up cigarettes and coffee, he had jogged a mile some mornings and was getting in shape. Surely he could outrun the oaf brothers and an old man. The limousine had taken them into a wooded area that might be to his advantage. Guns were his fear; he hadn't seen any yet, but it was more than probable they had them. He would have to zig left and then right until he could disappear in the darkness; it always worked for the good guys on TV. Given the four-to-one odds, it was the only chance of escape that made sense. He caught himself in mid-thought: you are a stupid fool, full of false bravado, and will just end up dead.

The limousine pulled to a stop in the middle of the dirt road. Reed's eyes and thoughts dashed back and forth, reconsidering an escape. The two men from the front of the car got out and moved to positions at the front and rear. Reed glanced to the front and rear and concluded: I can do this.

Ken broke the silence and interrupted his thoughts, "Do you think we are going to kill you? I hope so because we very well could."

Reed was paralyzed with the unknown.

Ken continued, "Do you credit yourself with past successes of your company? I suppose you also believe that your promotions to Vice President of Operations were because of your abilities. How naive. Why is it that you get premium prices for products in such a competitive marketplace? Perhaps because you are a good salesman? I don't think so. Let me offer you a piece of reality, Mr. Delahe. Your success is my doing and now I want something in return."

Reed thought it, but didn't say it: Bullshit! Instead, he chose to let the Oriental ramble on.

"You see, I represent a very large and powerful organization that can dictate your success or failure. We can ensure contract awards, manipulate your board of directors, and guarantee your future. Would you like the position of CEO with twenty percent growth of your company every year for the next ten years? How about a guaranteed annual salary of four million with an equal bonus? This is a much more pleasant picture than the one you are currently faced with: declining sales, reductions in force, your dismissal from Westcom, prosecution for disclosure of classified information, and ultimately your own financial ruin and then imprisonment. You can either become CEO or be imprisoned. The choice is entirely yours. What do say, Reed? Which will it be?"

"I never gave anybody classified information!"

"Not really, but the Westcom XL6 IC design and Grand Prix animation software can be construed as equivalent to a Next Generation Interceptor guidance and control system. The only real difference is radiation hardening of the circuitry. With a little negative press and the appropriate expert witnesses, your demise is assured."

Reed knew he was right; amusement ride animation software and hardware weren't that much different from classified missile control elements. Beads of perspiration formed on his forehead. It was the gray line that he and his company had walked many times, but this was different. Whatever Kuoto was about to propose, would surely put him on the wrong side of the line. Reed inquired, "So what is it I have to do?"

"Nothing much, just use the components I provide for SAV sensor and optic data communication. Your delivery date is rapidly approaching for your NSA customer. We wouldn't want you to be late."

"That's a top-secret program. We have extreme controls imposed on us that preclude my specifying much of anything. Most of the time I don't even know where components go."

"Indeed. This is why you will be so well rewarded when you make the appropriate physical substitutions."

Without thinking, Reed blurted out his response: "That's blatant sabotage and you can go to hell!"

"I am disappointed, Mr. Delahe." Kuoto bolted from the darkness coming face to face with Reed and again grasping his throat. "You leave me no choice but to use a different tact. Pick a number, Mr. Delahe!"

Reed grabbed Ken's arm with both hands, wrenching and pulling on it. But the more he pulled, the tighter Ken squeezed.

"Pick a number!" shouted Ken. "Pick a number between five and ten, now!"

"What?" squeaked Reed.

"Pick a number!"

"Eleven," replied Reed with defiance and confusion.

"Black or White?"

"Gray," managed Reed with more defiance.

"I'll take that as 'black.' Male or female?"

"Female."

"Very well then," said Ken calmly as he released his grip and returned to the darkness against his seat. "Wait for the newspaper, a week from tomorrow. It'll be Sunday's front-page headline complete with pictures and it will be of your choosing. You have chosen an eleven-year-old black girl to be tortured and killed. The details will be especially messy. And they will be just for you, Reed."

"You're crazy," Reed screamed and then sprung forward wielding a right hook with all his might. His fist impacted Ken's left cheekbone and then rebounded across his nose, fracturing the metacarpal of his middle finger as it crunched cartilage. The goon lunged forward with a football tackle slamming Reed against the door. Ken's nose spurted blood profusely and he let out a pain-induced whimper. With the goon pressing Reed hard against the door, he felt the uncomfortable presence of cold steel jammed against the underside of his chin.

Ken scrambled for a towel from the console of the limousine and yelled, "Kill him!" But then quickly recanted, "No, wait." Ken slipped back into the seat with his head back trying to slow the blood coming from nasal passage veins.

This is it, thought Reed. I didn't have to do that. I'm dead. At least I got in one good hit. God, please look after Tommy.

"Mr. Delahe," said Kuoto and then paused. "You continue to disappoint me, but it doesn't change anything. Now get out!"

The door behind him opened and he fell backward; his legs were thrust outward flopping him, heels overhead, to rest on his stomach. Reed lifted his head to look upward at the oaf with a pistol in the doorway. He would remember that face, along with Kuoto's, to the grave.

The figure receded from the doorway and Ken appeared. Even in the partial light, Reed could see the damage he had caused; the man's nose was ratcheted sideways. The white shirt hiding behind his tie and three-piece suit had turned bright red.

Ken spoke slow and deliberately, "The walk back to Huntsville will give you time to think. Sometimes darkness provides powerful revelations. Consider your success or failure. Consider the death of a young girl, which you have caused. Will the paper do details of her horrific death justice? I am sure you will find that we can become business associates."

The door of the limousine closed and the engine started. It crept a few feet forward and then stopped. The power window lowered and Kuoto's face appeared.

"One other thing," said Kuoto. "It was a real exciting afternoon watching your boy at today's baseball game. It's Tommy, isn't it? Too bad you weren't there to see it. I enjoyed it immensely. Perhaps his fate will be the same as an eleven-year-old black girl."

The tinted window began its upward travel as tires spit dirt in Reed's face. With thoughts of Tommy and overwhelming feelings of despair, Reed just lay at the side of the road and watched the taillights disappear into darkness.

Chapter 6

E-Kisses

Liu had completed her Ph.D. and then revolted against her parents. Life was not life without something more than microchips and AI. She had briefly worked for the CIA International Cyber Crimes Division but that just didn't work out. She had her own cubicle in a sea of cubicles, which afforded some degree of isolation. But there were so many people and the expectation was for coordinated investigations. She had to make presentations, provide regular verbal reports, and work in a team environment. Liu was terrified by the whole work environment. Personal interaction and relationships were what she thought she wanted. But the CIA was just all so overwhelming: too much and too fast. She was miserable. Maybe she was destined for a life of isolation. Maybe Conrad was as good as it was ever going to get.

Liu found the comfortable interaction she was looking for with internet sales, sometimes on the dark web. It was all text and email. She offered a variety of services, including specialty programming tasks, PCs with lightning-fast operating systems, GPS trackers, and specialty secure phones. Liu had also crossed the line into borderline illegal devices and offered her products on the dark web. For the right price, she could provide her computer "PINGS" software that could remotely capture cell phone text messages, photos, call history, web history, contact list, and more. On secretive websites, Liu also offered equipment far superior to the government's StingRay, Dirtbox, or V800/F800 cell phone listening technology. With Liu's Capture and Spy suite of software and hardware, any cell phone conversation could be captured. Additionally, the cell phone microphone and camera could be turned on without the owner's knowledge, even if the phone was powered down.

The dark web is where Liu first met Kevin. He was just shopping, just learning what was available. Kevin was different from all her other customers. He had technical questions that overwhelmed her; some of his questions were so futuristically complex that she could not, nor anyone else for that matter, answer. Some say opposites attract, which was absolutely not true with Kevin because she was mesmerized by his brilliance. Could a friendship be built on technical commonality? Liu pondered, Could Kevin ever replace Conrad?

Now Kevin had one of her specialty Probaris-Lebram cell phones. Her phone chimed. She read Kevin's text: "It's Sat night. What R U doing? Want to play a game?"

Liu texted back: "Just waiting on UR text. E-kisses to U."

Kevin texted: "K."

Liu visualized Kevin's face blushing with the text and realized just how big a step that was for Kevin. He was such a social isolationist, maybe worse than she was. How would he react to a real kiss? For that matter, how would she, herself, react to a real kiss? And then what might follow? No—never, she concluded.

Liu texted: "What game do U want to play? We could do Mortal Warrior?" Liu waited for what seemed like minutes. Why didn't he respond?

Kevin finally texted back: "It's more real than U know. It's psychotic sickness. It's hate-grown hostility. It's disgusting. It's blood, guts, tendons, fire, guns, knives, torture, beatings, and death. And it never f-ing ends!!!! It makes me sick and I don't want to be reminded. Hell no!!!!"

Kevin had a temper. She had struck some kind of a rare nerve and quickly came up with something absolutely non-threatening. Liu texted: "Sorry. How about chess?"

Kevin instantly texted back: "K."

Each with a chess board on their cell phone, the game began. Liu led with a pawn. Kevin advanced with a rook. As the game progressed, Liu struggled with each move along with Kevin's reaction to Mortal Warrior. He'd never shown any indication of a temper before. And he'd never sworn before. She went back and re-read Kevin's text several times. It just didn't make sense. But then, the temper had disappeared as quickly as it had appeared.

Liu slid her bishop to put both Kevin's queen and king in jeopardy. Kevin sacrificed his queen. Liu knew Kevin could see the end. Six more moves and she would have him.

Kevin texted: "Mate."

Liu texted back: "R U????"

Kevin texted: "Maybe. I mean, could be. If U wanted, I mean."

Liu texted back: "?"

Time passed. Liu knew she had Kevin speechless. But now what? What would he want? She'd read that men want only one thing. No. No. No, she told herself. This was all so very strange but yearnings were growing inside. It was all so confusing. Intimacy was not an option. But then again, what would it be like? Then her phone chimed.

Kevin's text read: "E-kisses"

Liu was so relieved that it wasn't something more. She quickly texted back: "E-kisses, E-kisses and more E-kisses to you."

Chapter 7

Vacation

Sunday was met with overwhelming misery and a night without sleep. Reed waited until eight to emerge from his bedroom and greet Tommy and Elizabeth in an attempt to create an illusion of normalcy. But his hand was in as much pain as his soul and the distress was obvious to both Liz and Tommy; he saw it in their faces. He forced down breakfast and got the game and obnoxious woman summary. Tommy talked. Liz talked. But his mind was elsewhere. Was he to believe Kuoto? It would be a week until he found out, but then it would be too late. What could he do? Was it just a nightmare?

First thing, he decided, was to have his hand looked at. He insisted Liz and Tommy accompany him to the hospital. X-rays confirmed a fractured metacarpal and sent him on his way with a removable brace and Tylenol.

The second action was impromptu. It was an instant vacation as he tried to explain it to Tommy and Liz. Without returning home for clothes or anything else, they headed for Memphis. Reed chose to skirt the top of Mississippi through Corinth where they stopped for complete sets of clothes, toothbrushes, luggage, and other needs. En route, Reed booked rooms, one for him and Tommy and one for Liz, at an upscale hotel. He booked three nights knowing he would only use two, but it was the kind of deceit he had learned on TV. He drove the car deep into its accelerator and kept a watchful eye on the rearview mirror. He began to feel better about himself; maybe this was all for nothing, he concluded.

That afternoon, after checking in at the hotel, they strolled up and down Beale Street listening to the Jazz tunes flowing from the small bars and looking in the windows of the many varied shops. The following morning they booked a cruise on a real Mississippi paddle wheel boat that took them downriver at a lazy pace. Reed relaxed. On the return trip, Reed contemplated abandoning this now silly vacation and returning to work. He hadn't even called to let them know he wasn't coming in. He decided to call tomorrow, just before leaving the hotel.

The third day of vacation was filled with a full day at the Mississippi River Museum. But instead of returning to their rooms, Reed, Tommy, and Liz went straight to the Lexus, climbed in, and drove off. The Lexus phone sync alerted Reed to the incoming call but he chose privacy and put the phone to his ear.

"Reed, what is going on?" inquired his secretary. "No word, no anything. Are you all right?"

"I'm fine. I just need a couple days," curtly replied Reed.

"What's wrong Reed? You have never just not shown up for work."

"Nothing is wrong. I'll be back in several days," he commanded and terminated the call.

It was the beginning of rush hour and Reed checked his mirrors for black cars and studied faces in adjacent cars. Tommy and Liz were confused and inquiring. Weren't they going to the zoo tomorrow? What about their new clothes? Where were they going? Reed failed a reasonable explanation. He announced the new destination as Nashville and pressed to five over the speed limit as traffic lightened. Reed again secured a hotel room with his phone, only this time it was a low-end, budget dump off the normal tourist track.

Outside Nashville, they found a Walmart and repeated the purchasing adventure with more sets of new clothes. When they arrived, Reed paid cash for the rooms and registered with a misspelling of his last name, "Delatee," that the clerk at the counter missed when checking his ID. Reed was rather proud of himself for the deception.

No one liked their rooms: horrid beds, marginally functional TV, and the faint smell of mold partially veiled with recently sprayed air freshener.

Morning came early for Reed. He woke Liz in the next room and then left Tommy with her to retrieve coffee for himself and breakfast sandwiches for them.

Liz and Tommy ate and glared at him outside the door as he smoked and drank coffee. Even their disparaging stares couldn't penetrate the burden that seemed to be building in his head, heart, body, and soul. Their silence coupled with stares was agonizing. He offered Dollywood and they accepted.

The mood markedly improved as they neared Dollywood. Tommy knew there were thrills and rides. He talked continuously about being able to drive his own bumper car and ram everyone. They pulled into the parking lot. Reed followed the attendants' directions and pulled into his space.

Reed got out on the driver's side and Liz got out on the passenger side. Tommy's door opened behind him and then suddenly closed with a slam. Reed turned to see Tommy in the grips of Kuoto's goon. The goon had one hand clasped around Tommy's throat restricting breathing and preventing speech. The other hand squeezed the tiny arm to control Tommy's squirming. Reed froze with uncertainty and fear. Tommy, suspended several inches off the pavement, kicked his legs back and forth, which resulted in the goon squeezing both hands tighter. Elizabeth, with the car partially obscuring her view, just froze.

The goon stared at Reed, smiled, and then spoke softly, "Kuoto wants you to know that he can have Tommy over to play anytime it's convenient." And then he released Tommy, who exploded in a flurry of kicks to the man's shins and punches aimed at the man's groin. Liz started around the car with eyes wide and puzzled. Her lips parted in astonishment at Tommy's tirade of profanities, most of which she had never heard before. One of Tommy's punches got lucky and resulted in a distressed look on the man's face; the goon backed off several steps and covered his genital area with his hand. Tommy followed, spewing profanities and swinging relentlessly.

The kicking and flailing ended as Reed stepped forward and put his hands on Tommy's shoulders. Reed replied, "That won't be necessary."

A confused Liz joined Reed and Tommy. She leaned heavily into Reed's side as the goon said, "Maybe Elizabeth would like to come over to play as well." Liz leaned harder into Reed's side and he put his arm around her. "No, that won't be necessary," Reed replied again.

"Very well then," stated the goon in a chipper tone and walked away.

Liz put her arm around Reed and clung tight as all three silently watched the goon meander off towards the ticket booth and entrance to the park.

Liz broke the silence, "What was that about?"

"We're leaving," commanded Reed, and then quickly opened the rear door for Tommy. He protested but climbed into the backseat as directed. Liz scurried around the car to her seat.

"Who was that, Mr. Delahe?" she inquired with fear in her voice.

"He was a mother puckin, corn-po, ass wipe, peanut brained, dickhead!" yelled Tommy from the backseat.

"That's enough. Where'd you learn that crap?" retorted Reed.

"Well, that's what he was," sassed Tommy.

Reed looked over at Liz. Although she was fourteen years his junior and fully a woman in her own right, she still seemed child-like. Feelings of fatherhood surged and he now felt the added burden of having Liz involved in this ugly business. He deflected her question, "I can't answer you right now but I will soon. I'm so sorry my problems have now involved you." He reached over and touched her arm realizing that, in the two years she had served as Tommy's nanny, today was the first time they had ever physically touched. They exited the park and headed towards the freeway. Reed was going to take them home, at least for appearance's sake. The following morning he would sneak them off to Atlanta to hide out with his ex-wife. She wouldn't like it, but he would leave her no choice.

As Tommy nodded off in the back seat, Reed told parts of his story to Liz: Kuoto, the ride in the limousine, how he broke his hand, the goon, and the threat against Tommy. He excluded any reference to the eleven-year-old black girl. She listened intensely and didn't speak; she didn't even ask questions. Reed explained his plan to Liz. Reed would drop her off at the airport on their way home and she would rent a car. She would then drive it to the backside of their block, park it, and then sneak between houses to the back door of the house.

She and Tommy were to sneak back to the rental car early in the morning. They could then flee to

Atlanta. For a distraction, Reed would bolt from the garage in the Lexus and drive like an escapist in the other direction. This was as good as any made-for-TV movie scenario Reed could imagine; it would work.

Reed called his ex-wife and explained the visit was a good opportunity for Tommy to spend some time with his mother. He would be no trouble because his nanny was coming with him. She objected, but Reed won out in the end. Reed watched Liz's facial expressions as the conversation dragged on over the Lexus sync system.

ELIZABETH WAS LESS THAN ENTHUSIASTIC WITH the whole discussion. Reed's ex-wife was a self-centered, selfish person. She questioned how someone as nice as Reed could have ever been married to a woman as nasty as the one on the car speaker. As the conversation progressed, she was contemplating a plan of her own. Elizabeth knew where to find real safety and security.

Chapter 8

Escape

That night, after having parked the rental car and sneaking between houses as Reed had instructed, Elizabeth organized her thoughts and put the elements of her plan in place. She made calls on her cell phone in the secrecy of her private bathroom. Plane tickets were purchased on her credit card; she was now committed.

Elizabeth set her alarm for three AM. When she awoke, she habitually reached for the light, but then remembered Reed's instructions. This was a lights-out morning. Elizabeth quickly dressed and shouldered her previously packed backpack. She crept into the hallway and was startled by Reed. She almost screamed but was calmed by his assuring whispers.

Reed waited in the hallway while she woke and dressed Tommy. Tommy was eager and thought this was some kind of adventure. Elizabeth didn't dissuade him otherwise. Fully dressed, she helped him shoulder his little clothes bag. They joined Reed in the hallway and then all three crept downstairs. Reed whispered as he reissued instructions for his plan. Elizabeth and Tommy would work their way back between the houses to the rental car. After the interior light of the rental car went on and then off again, they were to wait two minutes. Reed would be watching for the light to be sure they were ready. When he saw the light, he would run to the garage and jump in the Lexus. Before the opener even completed opening the door, Reed would race the Lexus out of the garage and head for Decatur. They wouldn't miss him; he was going to drive fast and erratic. After two minutes, Elizabeth was to start the car and make the four-hour drive to his ex-wife's house without stopping.

Tommy chimed in, "I have to pee."

Elizabeth shook her head in agreement. Reed helped Tommy find the toilet in the dark. Elizabeth stared out the window and started a countdown of her own, fourteen hours to go.

Reed and Tommy returned. Reed reached out his hand and touched Elizabeth's face, "Take care of my boy, please." He then opened the back door for Tommy and Elizabeth and whispered, "I love you both."

Elizabeth followed the plan to letter of Reed's instructions right up to the freeway exit sign for the Atlanta International Airport. She pulled into the airport and followed the signs for long-term parking, where they abandoned the car and caught the shuttle.

Tommy twisted and turned looking out each window. He was full of questions about which airplane, could they get hot dogs, and could he fly the jet. Elizabeth was consumed with nervousness and didn't answer.

Check-in was easy and they proceeded to TSA Security. Elizabeth never let Tommy get more than two steps from her and held his hand tight. Elizabeth set Tommy's book bag on the conveyor in front of hers and then lined up for the personal scanner. Tommy went through first and Elizabeth quickly followed. She knew something was wrong when the TSA agent called for a "bag inspection." They searched Tommy's bag and found a pocketknife with a four-inch blade. Tommy had taken it from his father's dresser the night before and sneaked it into his bag. When Tommy figured out they were going take it, he lambasted them with a profane and embarrassing tirade. She was going to have to work harder on correcting that behavior. TSA let Tommy and her through with a scolding, but they now owned the knife.

The "plane train" whisked them off to the B concourse and then it was just a short walk to their gate. Elizabeth studied the people in the gate area. It all looked normal but she wouldn't let go of Tommy's hand, which was as much for her comfort as his security.

She didn't relax until they had boarded and found their seats. Elizabeth breathed a sigh of relief when the plane pushed back from the gate and the engines started. She checked the security of Tommy's seat belt and he inquired again for at least the fifth time, "Where we going?" But Elizabeth was mentally exhausted and focusing elsewhere. The hard part of her plan was done. She considered her private countdown. The flight was four hours and then maybe another four. Eight hours to go and they would be safe.

Chapter 9

DETAINED

AFTER GETTING ELIZABETH AND TOMMY OFF, REED had driven to Decatur. And then drove back to Huntsville and Westcom. He passed up breakfast for another pack of cigarettes. They were almost gone and it wasn't even noon. His secretary had complained several times that he was stinking up the entire floor and violating the In Door Clean Air Act. He didn't care and finally told her to find another job if she didn't like it.

Reed picked up the phone for the sixth time, dialed the police, and then slammed it down again. *What am I going to say? Some girl, somewhere, sometime may get killed. And why? So somebody can make a point. All of which would make me sound like a babbling idiot.* He stared out the large picture window overlooking the parking lot and wondered if Kuoto was out there somewhere watching him with binoculars. Even so, he had to do something. Reed picked up the phone again and this time he let the call go through.

The officer on the other end of the phone was polite and took the information: Ken Kuoto, limousine ride, and murder of an eleven-year-old girl. But the call left little hope for action, with just a promise that a detective would get in touch with him. Reed sat at his desk staring at the phone. He instructed his secretary that he would only take a call from the police department. For all others, she was to either handle it herself or take a message. What would the Sunday newspaper say? He couldn't get the question out of his mind. He laid his head down on the desk and closed his eyes; the thoughts just wouldn't go away.

The phone next to his head buzzed and startled him. He grabbed the phone; his secretary announced that she was transferring the call he had been waiting for. Moments passed before the connection finally clicked through.

"Who's this?" Reed asked impatiently.

"Detective Hastings," came a calm response.

"Did you get my information? An eleven-year-old girl may die."

"What makes you think so?"

"Ken Kuoto, a businessman from Taiwan is going to kill a girl just to make a point."

"Based on the information you gave the desk, I did a little checking before I called. I talked to Mr. Kuoto of Right Time Computer Sales. He was staying at one of our local hotels but had to check into the hospital after being assaulted. I'm reviewing the report as we speak. Are you going to be at your office for, say, the next hour?"

Reed blurted out, "I can do much better. I'll pay you a visit. I'll be there in fifteen minutes."

"That would be excellent Mr. Delahe. I'll be expecting you. Just ask for me at the desk."

"I'll be there," concluded Reed. He felt much better; at least now some action would be taken. The only word he got from his secretary was a curt "bye" as he hurried from the building. When he grasped the steering wheel of the Lexus, he realized he had left the wrist brace in his office and the metacarpal on his right hand was a painful reminder of previous events. It didn't slow him down though; he accelerated out of the parking lot and onto Rideout Road. He jumped on the eastbound freeway, staying just a few minutes before exiting downtown, and within less than ten minutes he was at the Huntsville Police Department. Inside he was greeted by a female police officer behind a glass window who promptly notified Detective Hastings of his arrival. Detective Hastings soon emerged from behind secure doors and invited him back; the curt manner of the greeting was surprising to Reed but he brushed it off as rudeness.

Once deep inside the secure confines of the police department, Reed was shown a seat next to Hasting's cluttered and very unimpressive desk. Before any conversation, an officer stepped to the front of Hastings' desk and advised him, "It'll be a few more minutes, maybe fifteen."

Hastings just nodded and then coldly stared at Reed. Unnerving silence broke when the detective changed his demeanor and asked, "Would you like a Coke or something?"

"I don't think so," replied Reed, a little surprised.

"You realize, of course, that you have the right to remain silent and that anything you say can be used against you in a court of law. You have the right to an attorney during questioning and . . "

"What?" interrupted Reed.

The detective set a tape recorder on the desk between them, turned it on, and then continued, "I said you have the right to an attorney."

"Yeah, I heard that but I haven't done anything. I'm here to talk about a little girl."

"Okay. But I still have to ask," said Hastings in a very friendly and reassuring voice. "Do you understand your rights as I've explained them to you?"

"Yeah, I understand, but what's that got to do with anything? And what's that recorder for?"

"I just want to make sure we capture everything accurately. And should we end up in court, this will help remind everybody what was said here today. That's okay with you, isn't it?"

"Sure, I, ah, guess so."

"Good, then why don't we start with Mr. Kuoto? Tell me about him."

"He told me he was going to kill an eleven-year-old girl."

"He just told you he was going to do this?"

"Yes, damn it!"

"Is that when you hit him?"

"Yeah, I hit him as hard as I could. I hit him so hard that I did something to my hand."

"Yes, I see that. Would you mind if we got a photograph of your hand? I have a little camera right here."

"I don't know what that has to do with it. But take your picture."

Hastings snapped several pictures of Reed's hand before asking, "How many times did you say you hit Mr. Kuoto?"

"Once. But it was a solid punch and I drew blood."

"Yes, I believe you did. But I rather suspect you hit him more than once. Come on, just tell me," Hasting pleaded with a very friendly and coaxing tone.

"No I only got in the one punch before I was thrown out of the limousine and they pointed a gun at me."

"They you say. Let's put that aside for the moment. I'd like to focus on the punches you got in on Mr. Kuoto. How did it feel?" asked Hastings with a nasty little smile and then continued, "Little Chinaman bastard and all? Come on. I know it's all pent-up inside. What do you really think of the squinty-eyed little bastards? Just let it out. You'll feel better."

"No," said Reed and shook his head.

"Well, you did a number on him. So tell me why you and Mr. Kuoto were having this discussion in the hotel parking lot. It seems like a strange place for a meeting."

"It wasn't in the parking lot; it was out in the county off Highway 72. I went for a ride in his limousine."

"Mr. Kuoto has no limousine."

"That's bull!"

Just then another officer interrupted the interrogation and handed Hastings a folded piece of paper. Reed got a glimpse of it when Hastings unfolded it. At the top, it read, "Warrant for Arrest." The detective smiled ear to ear and gave Reed an evil stare. The second officer took several steps back and placed his hand on the holstered weapon. Reed's eyes sank to the floor to focus on the officer's shiny shoes; his stomach turned as he realized he'd been had in more ways than one. He looked up and made a plea that he knew Hastings and the other officer would not believe, "Officer Hastings, you have to believe me. There was no parking lot. You are making an incredible mistake. This is all part of a horrible mistake, I'm telling you."

"Mr. Delahe, please stand and put your hands behind your back," interrupted Hastings.

"You're a fool; you don't get it!"

Hastings burst from his chair, to spin Reed out of his chair, and flop him to the floor. In the same motion, Reed's arm was uncomfortably jammed high up on the middle of his back as Hastings explained, "You don't get it! Maybe I should add resisting arrest." As the pat down began, Hastings informed him, "You are being charged with assault and I have already explained your rights to you. After booking, you'll go to a holding cell and be given the opportunity to call your attorney within the timeline allowed by law."

Chapter 10

ALABAMA HELL NIGHT ONE

THE HUNTSVILLE CITY HOLDING CELL HAD A SOUR smell of vomit and feces. Although probably twenty by twenty feet, it felt incredibly cramped, especially having to share it with other guests of the city; there were six of them. By appearances alone, Reed was sure they were guilty of whatever crime they were charged with; they were not like him at all, he convinced himself. Reed stood with his back to a corner briefly glancing in the direction of each one, but avoiding any chance of eye contact, as he pondered what each might have done. A big black man sat alone in the middle of the bench seat against the wall with his eyes closed; he appeared to be peacefully sleeping, but Reed suspected otherwise. The bright penetrating lighting of the cell was surely enough to illuminate the insides of the man's eyelids. He was dressed in clean jeans and a perfectly white T-shirt, which was in stark contrast to the other occupants. The most frightening of the other occupants had wild eyes that darted back and forth as he irregularly and unpredictably paced the cell. His head shook from side to side occasionally and his arms jerked with each pace amplifying uncertainty in what he might do. He was very lean and the tattered clothes almost hung off him, leading Reed to the conclusion he was some kind of drug addict. He sized up the others as well concluding he was incarcerated with a habitual drunk driver, a construction worker charged with a bar fight, and two barely eighteen juveniles who were caught shoplifting. The puzzle was the big black man sitting alone on the bench.

It was now after five and he had not been given a chance to call his lawyer; in fact, he had been ignored following fingerprinting, photographing, and check-in processing. The most uncomfortable of processes had been the full body search, including all cavities, which had been a horribly humiliating experience. Reed decided that the next time an officer came to check he would speak up. Time passed. The pacer continued to pace and the others kept their distance from the man on the bench; they knew something he didn't. The most approachable looked to be the construction worker sitting on the floor against the wall. Reed slowly worked his way down the bars to the wall then took the few steps to the man. Reed glanced at the others in the cell; the move was made without attracting attention to himself and he slid down the wall to sit next to the construction worker.

"Not interested in company," came a curt response along with a stabbing glare.

"I was just looking for a little information on how all this works; that's all. This is my first time in jail and I'm just trying to figure it all out. I haven't been able to talk to anybody, call my lawyer, or anything. Don't I get a phone call or something?"

"Depends," reluctantly stated the man.

"On what?"

The man snorted and then responded, "You're white; you should have been out of here by now."

"What does that have to do with it?"

He snorted again, "Anybody else in here white? Anybody else in here wearing dress pants and a white shirt? You're pretty stupid."

"I don't get it?"

"You must have pissed somebody off. If you haven't made bail by now, you're staying till morning. I'd say they don't want you out tonight."

"That's nuts, why would they do that."

"Don't know. I'm here because I hit a white man dressed kind of like you down at the Silk Lace. They are going to make this as uncomfortable and difficult for me as they can. It's kind of like teaching me a lesson. First, I shouldn't have been in a strip club where there were only white dancers. And second, I should never hit a white man, pretty straightforward really. It'll be forty-eight hours before I get to make a phone call and, even then, they'll hold me as long as possible."

"That doesn't sound fair."

"Ha," the man chuckled. "Do you even live around here?"

"Yes, out towards Madison."

"Could have guessed."

"Is there any chance they just forgot I'm here?"

"None at all; see the smoke-colored ball on the ceiling," the construction worker said as he nodded upward. "They are watching your every action and probably listening to the conversation you and I are having right now. I just wonder what trouble I'm getting myself into by talking to you."

A guard appeared at the entrance to the holding cell interrupting their conversation. Reed jumped up and quickly moved towards the cell door. The guard commanded, "Back."

But Reed continued to the door grabbing the bars and pleading, "When do I get my phone call?"

"I said back," shouted the guard as Reed was jabbed through the bars with a nightstick. Reed let go of the bars and stumbled backward a few steps. He wheezed and then inhaled slowly. The guard shouted again and Reed complied, backing up to the opposite wall. The construction worker was next to him as were the other occupants of the cell. The exception was the man on the bench who ignored the commands of the guard. He was motionless on the bench with his head now turned towards Reed; his eyes were open and they were staring directly at him.

Engorged whites of his eyes stood out against the dark black background of the man's massive face; the stare didn't waiver and Reed shivered with the cold that comes with fear. Reed looked away, but watched from the corner of his eye; the man's eyes didn't even blink. Why me? Why is that man staring at me? I don't know him. I never saw him before. Could it be because I'm white; that's it, concluded Reed.

The guard barked, "Ramon Smith and Demy Shandon please step forward." The guard pointed down the hall and the pair gingerly exited the cell.

"Hey, what about me? When do I get my phone call?" Reed shouted. The guard gave him a fleeting glance and then waved his hand as if magically commanding the cell door to close. Reed shouted again, "I'm entitled to a phone call. I want my lawyer." The guard glanced at him again and even frowned a little, but didn't acknowledge the request. Reed persisted and continued to shout his pleas as the door clanked shut, but all to no avail as the guard and the two shoplifters disappeared from sight. When he turned from the bars, the big man on the bench was still staring. Reed shuttered. He met the stare momentarily before the man closed his eyes and resumed the fraudulent slumber.

Throughout the evening, the scene was repeated, letting out the drunk driver next and then the drug addict. Clarence, who turned out to be a machinist rather than a construction worker, and Reed had become somewhat friends throughout the evening. Each time the release scene was repeated, Clarence commented that this was quite unusual. Clarence had been arrested on two previous occasions.

These releases were extremely strange, especially after hours; it would have taken an act of God, or at least direction from the City's Chief Justice, to arrange bail, which was all very confusing and suspicious to Clarence. So much so that, when his turn came, he declined stating that he would rather wait until tomorrow morning. It was only under duress and threats from the guard that Clarence complied.

Reed stood at the bars again making pleas as Clarence and the guard moved down the hallway. Reed was now alone with the big black man on the bench and could feel the stare stabbing him from behind. He didn't want to turn around for fear of having to look at the man; Reed just held tight to the bars.

Lights in the cell flickered and then strangely went out. Almost instantly, Reed felt the strong grasp of a hand on the back of his neck. As his head was forcibly turned, the big black man licked Reed's cheek, starting at his chin and ending at his hairline; the saliva was disgusting and stank of putrid breath. Reed tried to scream for help but his head was promptly bashed against the bars. Reed's right side was repeatedly punched, with each successive blow seemingly harder than the previous. Each time Reed tried to scream, his head was mashed even harder into the bars. The man turned Reed's head toward him and whispered, "Just a taste of things to come."

Reed was hurled across the dark cell, rolling to the far wall. In the dark, he heard quick footsteps and saw the towering figure standing over him. Reed was jerked to his feet by a handful of hair and hurled back towards the bars. He was struck with a jab just above the belt and then took another almost immediate shot to his kidneys. As he winced over, an open hand slap struck the side of his face hard enough to return him sideways to the floor. An evil deep whisper resonated in the cell, "Does the boy wants to play?"

Reed scrambled across the floor away from the man but was grabbed by his ankle and whisked sideways crashing into the bench. He rolled under the bench and quieted his breathing hoping to avoid detection in the nearly non-existent light. The man strolled over and sat on the bench directly over Reed and said, "Hiding will do you no good. We have all night to play." And then began kicking him with both feet swinging. Reed was struck in the stomach, then the groin, and then again in the stomach, which was more than enough motivation for Reed to quickly crawl forward and then roll out from under the bench. He rolled a dozen times before coming to his feet and positioning himself in the boxer's stance he had learned in a self-defense class. The bench squeaked as the man stood; Reed didn't see the man until he was directly in front of him and then let go with a series of rapid one-two punches at the man's midsection and face. Although he never made contact, it worked; the man stepped back. But then, Reed was surprisingly knocked backward off his feet with an open hand pop to the chest that took every wisp of breath from him. The man spoke angrily, "I'm not supposed to break anything. But if you keep that up, I will." He stepped forward and added, "Try this," as he landed a kick to Reed's groin. Nausea now added to the loss of breath to incapacitate every fragment of strength. The huge hand reached down out of the darkness and grabbed a handful of hair and pulled Reed to his knees. He heard the man's zipper open as the man again spoke in an evil tone, "Have some of this you little bitch. Suck on it." Reed managed a partial breath and struggled forth with everything he had to place an uppercut swing to the man's groin. The man released his hold on Reed's hair and Reed rolled free to the bars. He heard the man moan in pain and step away to the far wall.

Reed stood and, with some imagination, he could just make out the silhouette of the man standing with one hand against the far wall. It was like a time-out, both recovering from the round. Minutes passed without movement from the far wall giving Reed a chance to regain normal breathing and the nausea to subside.

This is insane. Where are the guards? "Help, guard, help, get me out of here!" he yelled. The reaction from the far wall was instant and the man charged. Reed screamed, "Why are you doing this?" But he got no answer. At the moment of impact, Reed spun right avoiding being smashed between the charging man and the bars. The man crashed into the bars, sending reverberations throughout the structure. Reed continued down the barred wall away from the man, who now advanced at a much slower pace, but he was coming. At least Reed could outrun him, but that was of little benefit in the little cell. Oh God, he thought as he turned down the adjacent wall, the man had cut the corner and intersected his path. Reed was pressed hard against the wall by the man's forearm and held there by massive force. Reed was pounded by stout jabs to the right side of his back, each one causing him to jerk and straighten, yet not enough to cause internal damage. The man tired of the torment and thrust Reed aside back toward the bars. Reed stumbled but managed to stay on his feet. He could not turn his back to the man again, he thought, but it was too late; the man swung an arm around Reed's head and placed him in a stranglehold. With the man's arm under his chin, Reed was lifted off the ground and the man whispered in his ear, "How about I just give it to you, right here right now?" He then laughed and flung Reed across the cell.

Torment continued throughout the night. Reed was physically and mentally exhausted as a faint glimmer of light eventually appeared from a window somewhere down the corridor. Reed's hopes for an end to the torment blossomed when the lights came on. The night of terror was over and now surely he could get help. The man slowly walked over to the bench and resumed his position. He motioned with his lips, "Tonight," and then closed his eyes.

Chapter 11

METS BALL CAP AND BEER

JAMAL, WARREN, AND ISAAC MOVED GINGERLY through the shadows. Warren carried the backpack with needed supplies and Isaac carried the only fire-power. If they ran into police, Isaac would be the sacrifice and get hauled off to city lockup, leaving Jamal and Warren to complete the assignment. Supplies in the backpack could easily be explained as work supplies and the cops were sure to let them pass.

If they ran into other trouble, Isaac had the option of using his nine-millimeter. But Jamal had his own special set of skills and knew the nine would really never be necessary; Jamal had extensive martial arts training and no one was his equal.

Jamal, Warren and Isaac were all seasoned warriors of the street. Warren and Isaac proudly displayed their colors. They were part of the Disciple Nation. Isaac and Warren were Second Rank, two levels up from common Foot Soldier, and usually would have had at least a dozen brothers to handle duties like the one at hand. But this assignment was of special importance and high dollar value, and they had been specifically requested by Jamal. Jamal was First Seat. Ordinarily, they would never have known who First Seat was in the organization because of the need to protect superiors. Warren and Isaac had local knowledge, histories, and a track record for evading the cops. Neither had ever even been arrested, despite numerous killings, which thoroughly impressed Jamal.

Jamal himself had started with the Disciples at the age of fourteen in Chicago. He had quickly proven himself with the assassination of a schoolteacher who was about to testify about high school drug use and sales. The murder gained him entry as a Foot Soldier. Over the fifteen years since, he had honed a very special set of skills that made him invaluable to Disciples. Torturous interrogation and elusive assassination had become his specialties. To support his profession, Jamal had become a master at Jeet Kune Do and Krav Maga. Martial arts provided fundamentals that maximized an individual's pain and facilitated the extraction of information. It also provided for quick and efficient assassination.

Like Isaac and Warren, Jamal had no documented history, which helped keep him from suspicion for the many murders he had committed. His successes had allowed him to advance through the organization and gain recognition from those above. He knew his General well and the other First Seats, but could only speculate on the identity of General's Don.

Jamal had been sent to numerous cities throughout Mexico, the Midwest, and the East whenever his special skills were needed. Most of the Disciples Nation's money came from running drugs up from Mexico and providing distribution and sales throughout the East and Mid-West. But they also took on contract jobs and this is where Jamal excelled. He had been brought in from Chicago to plan and carry out tonight's contract.

The hour approached eleven and they advanced on the building ahead. Arrangements had been made and entry was planned for eleven. Jamal saw the figure first: a man sitting on the steps under the light. Jamal studied the figure. It was very strange because that man's white ass would end up in a dumpster on any street he had ever known. What a fool! He was in plain view under the entry light of the stairwell. Jamal began sizing him up. He looked average size, at least from the profile view, with average length hair and some kind of ball cap. Jamal couldn't find anything distinguishing or out of the ordinary, except for the man's intense stare. Did this dumb-ass anticipate what was coming or was he just stupid?

Jamal re-affirmed absence of video surveillance, both on this building and their destination. Overhead, at the stairwell entrance, there was only a single light. Absence of video was the advantage of working in neighborhoods such as this one. Anywhere else, the video challenge would have made tonight's activities much more difficult. In upscale areas of New York or Chicago, the average Joe Blow was videoed or photographed over three hundred times in a day.

Jamal continued to interrogate details about the figure as they approached. Warren and Isaac would have ordinarily assaulted the man. It would be so easy. At ten feet, the options were wide open. Isaac could plug him with the nine. Warren could have charged from ten feet and killed the fool in any number of ways: a knife to the throat, kidneys, femoral artery, or a number of other lethal options.

As they got closer, the figure took a swig from what looked like a pop or maybe a beer. He was also wearing a Mets ball cap, which had the right color. What was he doing? Is he asking for it? Jamal knew Isaac was contemplating actions too when he slid his hand in his pocket.

As they neared, Jamal learned over first to Warren and then to Isaac to whisper, "He is not our business tonight." When he repeated the instruction to Isaac, who he knew had his finger on the trigger of a nine, he emphasized the words "not" and "business." They both understood and kept by his side as they approached.

Jamal continued to assess the lone figure. He was better built than Jamal had first thought. His shoulders were wide and he potentially had strength in the arms hidden under the loose-fitting clothing. As they got closer, Jamal became even more alert with uncertainty. Revealing features of the man were somewhat hidden, but neck size was an indicator of even more strength. With continued study and assessment, Jamal speculated and surmised that the man's features were solid, yet not excessive, which left the figure potentially agile as well as strong. But then the man was short, probably less than six feet.

The man just stared in some kind of eerie trance. The closer they got, the more uneasy Jamal became. As the distance between him and the man closed to less than ten feet, Jamal's senses exploded and his entire body tingled. Something was wrong; conflict was imminent. Jamal contemplated Jeet Kune Do and Dim Mak quick kill options; he opted for commotio cordis, a lethal single blow directly above the heart. But the man would make the choice; at the first sign of movement, Jamal would lunge forward and the man would die.

Jamal didn't break eye contact until the last moment. As they passed the man, Jamal said, "Good evening sir." Now, with his back to the man, his audible sensory awareness went on maximum alert. The kill would be the same except that he could now time the commotio cordis with body rotation to fully maximize the force of impact.

Distance increased as a disconcerting revelation entered Jamal's mind and his senses scolded him. What if a nine-millimeter was now pointing in their direction? What if the man was out to avenge some past killing like a vigilante do-gooder or something? That could be the reason for his stupid behavior sitting out on the steps. What if it was all an act and they were now his targets? "Shit," mumbled Jamal.

The SOB could be a member of the BOZY, Aryan Nations, or Stoners; however, with no tattoos or colors, it was doubtful, but impossible to be certain. His senses continued to scream at him; it was all wrong. Yet he chose not to turn and forced the march onward to gain distance. Distance was working to their advantage as pistol shot accuracy diminished with each step.

Jamal relaxed a little as distance increased beyond pistol accuracy and there was only silence from behind. He regained his focus and reached into his inner jacket pocket to retrieve the smartphone he had been provided. He dialed Herme and then, as he brought the phone to his ear, Jamal heard the stairwell door behind them crash open. He jerked around to see the man dashing up the stairwell. It didn't make sense; something was still very wrong.

Chapter 12

Disciples from Hell

They were heading for an identical stairwell in a building directly across from where the man had been sitting. The glass door had been removed, presumably broken and just not worth replacing to the slumlords that profited from mostly subsidized housing. All typical of other buildings Jamal had seen in many cities across the Eastern and Mid-Western States. After the first ring, Jamal pulled the phone from his ear to verify the time; the display showed 10:59 then updated to 11:00; they were on schedule.

Herme answered on the third ring, "Yo, man."

"We're here. We set?"

"Yeh," came Herme's shaky reply.

Jamal knew the sound of fear when he heard it and Herme had it. Herme was a local Foot Soldier with limited skills who was brought in especially for tonight's action. As they talked, Jamal studied the stairwell where the man had been sitting. He was nowhere in sight. It bothered Jamal that the man could potentially identify them. Maybe he had made a bad decision tonight, Jamal reflected.

They entered the stairwell and quietly worked up to the third floor. Herme came down from the fourth floor and met them. Warren placed a piece of tape over the peephole of the apartment door opposite the door of interest. Herme had the key in hand and was about to insert it. Jamal raised his hand in a signal to wait.

Jamal looked at Warren and asked, "Confirmed eleven? No mistakes."

"Birth certificate," Warren whispered back.

"Okay then, let's do this thing. Suit up," commanded Jamal.

Warren fished in his backpack and came out with plastic Tyvek suits: one for each himself, Jamal, and Isaac. As the three slipped on the suits that covered everything from shoes to hair, Herme inquired, "Where's mine?"

"Do you want to make Rank Foot Soldier?" questioned Jamal.

"Sure."

"Then this is the way it gotta be. Initiation time, here tonight—your opportunity, Herme. Do you know what that means?" coaxed Jamal.

"I think so. But nobody eber told me what we doing here tonight."

"Just do as I say, Herme, and it'll be fine," smoothed Jamal as he interlaced his fingers to seat his plastic gloves. When the three had completed donning their plastic suits, Jamal raised his hand and listened to the silence. The apartment across the hall was quiet, as was the stairwell.

"I think I want one of those," said Herme pointing at Jamal's head-to-toe suit.

"You can have one if you want, Herme," replied Jamal. "But this is a special time for you. We have all had our special time and now it's your time. We have planned this just for you; trust me, you are going to enjoy this. And when it's all done, you will be a Rank Foot Soldier. Next time it will be you in the suit and you won't have so much fun. Now, are you sure you want one tonight?"

"It just feels strange."

"It always does, Herme," further assured Jamal. "It's the thrill of adventure, man. This is a once-in-a-lifetime thrill that we have all gone through. Sometimes I wish I could go back and do this again for the first time. I'm so excited for you Herme." Jamal smiled and placed his hand on Herme's shoulder. "Just do as I say Herme and you won't be sorry."

"Okay," agreed Herme in an uncertain voice.

Jamal's smile widened and he raised his hand to command a few moments of silence.

When he was satisfied with the silence, Herme got a gestured okay. Herme carefully inserted a key into the lock and rotated the tumblers. The door opened slightly but was restrained by a security chain. Warren was ready and inserted bolt cutters through the opening to snip the chain. All four stealthily entered and closed the door behind them.

Again Jamal signaled a pause and listened to the silence. He clicked on his tiny LED flashlight and surveyed the surroundings. It was a tiny apartment with a joined living room and kitchen and it was obvious that the couch was being used as a bed. The kitchen was clean and neat with a single glass and plate recently washed in the drying rack. Clothes had been neatly arranged on bookshelves that supported a small TV. The clothes belonged to a woman; Jamal could clearly identify two extremes in style: casual as might be worn by a bank teller and risqué as might be worn by a hooker. The latter he expected, which was additional confirmation that things would go as planned.

Jamal signaled towards the short hallway and pointed at Herme. "Lead the way," Jamal whispered.

Herme focused in the dark down the hallway where a glimmer of light emitted from within a room to the left. Herme led the way. Jamal, Warren, and Isaac followed. They entered the room lit by a small nightlight to the smell of baby powder topped by a slight lemony aroma. A small figure lay motionless and almost silent, except for subtle sounds of breathing, in the bed before them. There were dolls and pink pony figurines on the nightstand next to the bed. An oversized stuffed rabbit sat on the bed next to the tiny figure. The figure sighed and the lips smacked, bringing all four to a stop.

Breathing resumed and Jamal pointed and motioned the commands: Warren on the legs, Isaac on the hands and arms, and he would prevent the screams. He held up his right hand with three fingers extended and then dropped them, one-two-three.

They each reached in and captured the child whose eyes exploded open with terror. Jamal forced a pair of rolled-up socks in her mouth and then strapped them securely in place with a large zip-tie extending around from the back of her little head. Her hands were zipped-tied as well. Tears boiled from her eyes in confusion and terror.

Jamal flipped on the light switch in the tiny bedroom, turned to Warren, and asked, "Time?"

"Eleven fifteen," stated Warren. By now, mother finished her trick and is whacked out on skag. We've got at least three hours."

Jamal commented to Herme, "Look at that. Isn't that the prettiest little thing yo eber saw? Okay, Herme, you're up."

"What?" inquired Herme.

"Right now, Herme. I told you this was your special night," said Jamal. "Now jump up there on the bed."

Herme was still confused with all that was happening but complied with Jamal's instruction. Jamal continued to give instruction and encouragement.

"How that? Awesome job Herme," complimented Jamal when Herme completed.

Jamal then instructed carving of the words "Tommy Boy," The figure on the bed was held tight as Herme carved. But when Herme completed the task, it read, "TOMY BOY." Close enough concluded Jamal. They had made the right choice with Herme, as he struggled to accomplish even this simple of tasks.

Throughout the early morning hours, Jamal continued to instruct Herme. At some point, the child's eyes glazed over and just stared off into space. Jamal had seen the look before, most recently two days earlier in Atlanta. He, along with a local 14-year-old wanna-be, had paid a visit to some uptown bitch. She was supposed to provide them with the whereabouts of this Tommy Boy; she failed and died. Although, truth or lie, she would have died either way. The rape, torment, and ultimate death were dispensed differently, but the end-result was the same as it would be tonight.

When Herme completed his directed deeds, Jamal and the others stepped back. The real purpose of tonight's actions was for pictures. Jamal clicked the cell phone camera repeatedly to capture every detail of Herme's special night out.

Jamal, Isaac, Warren, and Herme stepped out of the small living space into the stairwell and quietly closed the door. Warren checked his piece of tape on the peephole of the opposing apartment door; it was still in place. Herme started to speak but Jamal scowled at him and put a finger to his lips. It was tight quarters in the stairwell and they bumped and elbowed each other as they stripped themselves of their plastic suits. Warren collected the three suits and compacted them into a black trash bag. Jamal, Isaac, and Warren all kept their hands gloved throughout the process. Herme just watched with an impatient look on his face.

Jamal thumbed the smartphone and posted all the pictures from the night's business to the pre-established Facebook page and then copied and pasted prewritten captions and text.

Herme asked, "What are you doing? What's all that for, anyway?"

"Be patient. We don't want the moment to escape. Do we?" replied Jamal as he continued to work the phone with his thumbs. When the Facebook posting was complete, he also posted the photos to Instagram and X.

Jamal handed the smartphone to Herme with his still gloved hand. Warren followed, carefully handing Herme the backpack.

"I suggest you dispose of this stuff," Jamal said to Herme in an almost remorseful tone. They exited the stairwell in silence. The evening's business was complete.

Chapter 13

Alabama Hell Night Two

Breakfast was served on paper plates, but no sooner had the guards departed when the big man came across the room to tower over Reed sitting on the floor.

He demanded, "That's my breakfast. Give it to me."

Reed had only taken two bites and the man's untouched plate was across the room on the bench. Reed grabbed a handful and shoved it in his mouth before throwing the plate at the man in a show of bravado. "There," he managed as he tried to swallow. This was now survival and he was hungry.

The man's eyes swelled and focused pupils at the center of huge whites pierced Reed's soul. "Wait until tonight," the man whispered wickedly and slowly. "You're going to lick it up off the floor and then we're going to have some more foreplay—tonight."

Reed swallowed. He tried to hold eye contact but couldn't and had to turn away; tears began to form in the edges of his eyes and his emotions swelled. He let out a whimper and then another as a tear slid down his cheek.

The man laughed and repeated, "Yes, tonight," and then returned to the bench.

Reed shivered and let out another whimper as his thoughts took over. How could this be happening to me? Don't I have rights? The police have to be in on this. How am I going to survive another night? He'll make me do horrible things. Oh God, what am I going to do? I wish I were dead. Stop it. Get a grip on it. You damn crybaby. With great restraint, Reed withdrew feelings of destitution and forlornness and wiped his face. Survive, that's what you do. Even if it means the worst—survive, he concluded.

Mid-morning they brought in an old man that looked like a street bum; his clothes were tattered and dirty. Reed could almost smell him from afar and didn't give him the courtesy of a single word. Two other young men were brought in before noon that Reed guessed had been busted in some kind of drug-selling sting. Neither appeared stoned or incapacitated, but they looked the part. Reed didn't speak to them either. Shortly after lunch, the street bum was summoned to the barred door and let out. Clarence must have been right; even a white street bum spent less time in holding than a black man. Mid-afternoon they brought in a man with no shirt; he looked drunk and just ornery enough to have hit his wife. The cell filled quickly after that with an additional six residents; Reed categorized and analyzed the probable crime of each: a gang banger, a car thief, two more shoplifters, a home burglar, and another drunk driver, only this time white. All the while, the big black man sat motionless, eyes closed, on the bench. All the occupants of the cell knew to stay away from him.

Just like the day before, each was individually summoned to the cell door and led down the hallway. Five o'clock came and went; the cell was empty except for Reed and the big black man. Reed glanced at the man; his eyes were open and he was staring directly at Reed. The man's lips motioned, "Tonight."

Dinner was served late, a turkey bacon club, and a bottle of water. Reed forced down repeated large bites before the guards left and then took a swig of water. The man was standing next to him at the bars and the demand came as soon as the guards left, "Give it to me."

Reed did. In a single motion, he dropped the water bottle and came across with a stiff jab to the man's nose with his left; it was a solid hit and blood rushed from the man's nose.

"That was uncalled for," he said and smiled, ignoring the blood. "You didn't even wait for the lights to go out. I am going to mess you up tonight."

Reed spun and ran to the far wall taking another bite of his sandwich. Blood running across the man's mouth and off his chin was sprinkling the front of his T-shirt, making him look more terrifying than before; he looked like a vampire that had just taken a bite. Reed forced down the final bite of his sandwich and smiled inwardly; the man had lost this round. The man took two steps towards Reed and Reed quickly began anticipating his options, but then the man turned and strolled to the bench and resumed his position. Before closing his eyes, he again mouthed, "Tonight."

Reed returned to the opposite wall and slid down to sit with his knees in front of him. He enjoyed the moments of peace and savored his victory over the sandwich. A feeling of bravado emerged. Tonight he would stay on the offense.

But it wasn't so. The lights flickered and went out, leaving total blackness for unadjusted eyes. The torment continued like it had the night before.

As morning neared, the man commanded, "Ready my sweet. I think we have had enough foreplay."

"It isn't foreplay," cried Reed. The tears now gushed forward and he let the sobs become vocal; he tried to hold back but it was all too overwhelming.

"I think you're ready. Come on over here and we'll be friends."

Reed let his body slump while holding the bars and just sobbed. Rapid breaths accompanied fragmentary bawling and Reed didn't hear the man approaching from behind. Reed had been abandoned by the world and he was alone with this man; this was his destiny and there was no escape.

The man put his hand on Reed's shoulder and insincerely consoled, "There, there."

The touch was repulsive, bringing the sobbing to an end and replacing feelings of doom with raw hatred. Reed screamed, "I'm going to kill you." The cell reverberated as Reed was smashed between the massive man and the bars. The man grasped Reed's wrist and jerked it across between them spinning Reed, as the man's other arm slid around Reed's throat to close in a headlock.

Reed whimpered "screw you" with fleeting bravado as the headlock tightened.

"I'm tired of this!" said the man angrily for the first time in two days. "I could snap your neck right now. Don't you understand that I own you? I decide when you eat and what you eat. I decide when you'll be my delight and you will comply. Make no mistake about it."

Reed gasped for the air and the man mistook it for another "screw you."

"God damn it," the man screamed and squeezed harder. "What is it with this 'screw you'? You have no idea what you're in for." The man jerked Reed left, then right, swinging him back and forth as the headlock was tightened.

Blood had quit flowing to Reed's head challenging consciousness and he almost welcomed the snap of his neck, but it didn't come. At the moment of losing realization, the man tossed him to the center of the cell and then followed with a kick to roll him to his stomach. Reed gasped for air as the man stepped around behind and let loose a brutal kick between Reed's legs.

"Spread 'em bitch," he yelled. "I'm going to show you 'screw you.'"

Reed tried to rise to his hands and knees but the man's foot shoved Reed from behind forcing him back to the floor. "Let this be a lesson to you," the man said and increased the weight on Reed's butt. "When you get to the Alabama State Correctional Facility, they are going to tattoo tits on your back and pass you around. You won't be somebody's bitch; you'll be everybody's bitch. How's that for 'screw you?'" He snorted and then reached down with both hands and ripped the back of Reed's pants through the waistband and down the center seam. "Oh Christ, you crapped your pants; God damn stinking mess." The man stepped back and then kicked Reed between his splayed legs.

Reed jolted with pain but there was no resolve left; he would let the man do anything and do anything for him. Reed just laid there, in the middle of the cell, bawling.

Chapter 14

Saturday's Fool

Within an hour of the Facebook posting, Herme's page had been identified by the FBI in Quantico and Facebook instructed, agreeably so, to remove the page. Herme's page had six underage girls as friends, all with past cordial communication; however, his posts within the past week were seeking a sexual experience like none other. The crafted verbiage in the posts cloaked Herme's desires, yet was quite transparent to an interrogative reader. But it was the 3:00 A.M. post of pictures from a "night out," as Herme described it, which alerted the FBI Cyber-Crimes Division.

The final picture showed a small black girl with arms dangling, head titled, arched back, carved message on her tiny chest, and impaled on what looked to be a broom. Her delicate little legs had been amputated at the knees and placed on the floor beneath her in a pool of blood. The posting included boastful verbiage of finally doing it and really getting off. It was despicable, heinous, and sickening to even the most hardened law enforcement officer who saw it. The FBI was furious at the crime and offered any and all assistance to the NYPD to track down the perp and ensure justice was properly administered. But that wasn't necessary because the idiot perp, Herme Menders, had listed his hometown as Queens and left a roadway of personal information; the NYPD was only hours from finding Herme Menders. Three uniforms and two suits nearly got into a fistfight in the squad room at the Queens Precinct over who was going to make the arrest. Whoever got the opportunity, it was doubtful Herme Menders would live. Shouted arguments were specific about how it should be done and continued until the ranking officer on duty took command.

Detective First Class Clifford Jerkins barked assignments at three uniforms and a suit; they would be the arrest team and the arrest would be made before shift change at eight. He barked orders and commanded that Herme Menders would not be killed by the NYPD. That could easily occur in prison when his fellow inmates discovered what he had done. The job of the NYPD was to pick this little piece of shit up, read him his rights, and collect evidence. Nothing more, he forcefully emphasized to his small team. He further reminded them that they don't have a body; all they have is photographs.

Jerkins went on with instructions and interrogation strategy. He concluded with a final reminder to the team, "Remember, no one lets the perp know we don't have the body, at least until after I offer him enough lies and deceit that he gives up the location. And I want the prick before dayshift at eight!"

The three uniforms and suit drove straight to Herme Menders' mother's apartment building. Jerkins stayed in constant contact with them and coached them through gaining access to Herme's apartment. They woke Martha Menders from her sleep, lied about faults with the fire alarm system to gain entrance to the apartment, and arrested Herme, who was deeply asleep on the couch. They were en route back to the station house by seven. Jerkins was pleased.

Clifford dispatched another suit and an army of uniforms to begin a physical search around Herme's apartment building, which would be even further expanded when the dayshift arrived. But maybe they would get lucky. Clifford Jerkins worked on preparing his questions and interview strategy while waiting for his first glimpse of Mr. Herme Menders.

Before most New Yorkers had even had their first cup of coffee, Herme Menders was in custody in interrogation room number one. Jerkins approved the overtime and sent eighteen more uniforms to help with the search around Herme's apartment. Jerkins studied Herme on the video feed. Herme paced nervously in the room. His clothes looked clean and his hands washed. Jerkins strained to interrogate the details of the video feed. Could he be so lucky? It was almost indistinguishable from his skin, but it was there: dried blood on the backside of his left arm.

Jerkins chose to wait until the Saturday dayshift captain arrived. This was too important a case to blow and everything had to go just right. He wanted to plan the actions going forward and run through his interrogation strategy with someone equal in experience. He needed Menders to give up the body. And just as important, he needed the dayshift captain to start working on investigation actions: search warrant for Herme's mother's apartment, DA briefing, expanded search and resource assignment, and a court order for physical inspection of, and the taking of samples from, Herme's body. Although it was Saturday, Jerkins knew that anyone seeing the photographs would eagerly rise to the occasion and help nail this despicable bastard.

Chapter 15

Saturday—Escape from Hell

After two nights in the Huntsville holding cell with the giant on the bench, Reed didn't respond when breakfast was served. He just lay there in his torn and tattered clothing facedown with the weight of his head pressing his cheek hard against the floor. His life was over. Take me now he pleaded in his mind.

The two guards were prompted by his inactivity to enter the cell and verify he was breathing. They left and the big man consumed his breakfast, as well as Reed's, and then resumed his apparent slumber.

Reed slowly went about pulling himself back together. Best he could, he tore strips from the legs of his tattered dress pants and fastened the rip in their seat back together. The big man never moved. Reed redressed and resumed his position against the cell wall.

Shortly after nine, the guards returned. "Visitor for Reed Delahe," they announced. The guards escorted him down the corridor to an interrogation room of some kind without speaking a word. He wasn't handcuffed; he was just left alone to think. For the first time in two days, Reed felt some glimmer of hope. Would they let him out? And then his thoughts went to Tommy and Liz. Were they safe? Had their escape to Atlanta worked? Had his ex-wife taken them in as agreed? He loved that little boy and no harm could ever come to him, however this thing worked out. He would do whatever they wanted, including the treason they demanded. They had won.

Tumbles on the door lock rotated and the door opened. His lawyer, Pete Matheson, entered. It was strange, in that he had never had the opportunity to make the call. Reed stood and greeted him warily, "Pete," and then extended his hand.

Pete Matheson grabbed his hand with both of his and commented, "You look like shit."

"Really. I'm lucky to be alive after two days in this hellhole with a monster kicking the shit out of me. Can you get me out?"

"I'm not sure?"

"What do you mean?"

"I got a call at home this morning from Detective Hastings. He explained a mix-up in the system and told me they were holding you. He said you had confessed to beating some Mr. Kuoto and didn't request an attorney so they hadn't made any efforts to provide you an opportunity for calls. That's where the mix-up came in and he apologized several times for not being a little more proactive."

"Interesting—do you know why I'm here? Do you know why Hastings didn't want me to make any calls?" replied Reed as he studied Pete's face for a sign of collusion.

"Hastings explained the charges to me. It doesn't sound good. You beat the crap out this Mr. Kuoto and then fled to Memphis."

"What?" interrupted Reed.

"Just what he told me, Reed. We'll have plenty of time to sort it out."

"Okay, Okay. What else did he tell you?"

"You hid out for a few days in Memphis and then returned to work on Thursday. You called him and made some kind of confession. I'll get a copy and see what he claims is a confession. Then Reed," Pete stuttered before continuing. "Hastings told me that he—a—that he has your assault of a fellow inmate on video."

Reed burst from his chair and exclaimed, "I assaulted him?"

"It's alright. It doesn't matter at this point, Reed. We'll get a chance to see all their evidence and challenge it accordingly," calmed Pete as he raised an open hand and encouraged Reed back into his seat.

"This a frame job, you know that! Hastings is in on it. In fact, they're all in on it."

"Perhaps, but at this point, they are charging you with the assault on Mr. Kuoto, plus an assault on Mr. Henson, but downplaying the trip to Memphis because it could be construed as interstate evasion, which is a Federal offense. They assured me they would like to keep this a local matter."

"I'll bet," replied Reed curtly. "How about getting me out of here?"

"That could be a problem. It's Saturday and I need a bail hearing. I'll work on it, but don't count on it."

"What does that mean?"

"Monday, maybe," replied Pete meekly.

"You gotta do better than that, Pete. I'm still in the cell with this big black prick that wants me for sexual favors. I'll die if I spend another night alone with him."

"I must have missed something. Is this the Mr. Henson that Hastings alleges you assaulted?"

"If that's his name! I've been locked up with him for two days and yes I hit him. In fact, I'd like to kill him."

"You keep that to yourself and don't ever repeat it to me or anyone else. I'll pretend I didn't hear it for now. But you can never say those words again to anyone. Do you understand me?"

"Okay, Pete."

"But you say he's still in the same cell with you, even after the alleged assault?"

"I can work with that. We can get that changed immediately and potentially use it to our advantage in getting the charge dropped."

"That'll save my life, Pete."

"Okay then. I'll go to work on getting you moved out of the cell and then we'll talk some more this afternoon," concluded Pete as he stood. He started towards the door and then stopped and turned. "Couple other things—I'm good at divorce and such, but I'm going to have to bring in some help on the Mr. Kuoto thing. Are you all right with that?"

"Sure Pete. Whatever it takes. Thanks a million."

"Yes, well that may be what it costs you before this thing is done. The other thing is Tommy. The detective called in Family Services when they executed the arrest warrant. I'm assuming Tommy's with that nanny you hired, but they'll want to verify his well-being."

"He's safe, Pete. And yes, he's with Liz."

"Family Services will have to verify. Where are they?"

"Safe, Pete. Safe. But I'll keep their whereabouts to myself."

"Um, okay. We'll see how that plays. I suspect poorly."

"That's the way it's gotta be."

"Okay. Last thing—don't say any more to the cops. Nothing you have to say will help your situation," Pete advised and pressed the buzzer next to the door. The door opened and Pete exited.

Reed was not returned to the holding cell with the monster. Instead, the cops held him in the interrogation room. Reed created his own hell during the first three hours. He paced back and forth repeatedly until he was physically exhausted. He wanted a cigarette. He wanted Kuoto dead. He wanted the monster dead. He wanted his son. He wanted this all to end.

His concern for Tommy tormented him to the brink of tears. Had he done the right thing by sending Tommy to his mother? Would Tommy's mother accept Liz? Maybe Liz wouldn't tolerate the bitch, then what?

But that was only if they had gotten there. What if his plan hadn't worked? Could they have been followed? What if Kuoto found Tommy? What would Kuoto do?

Something changed around noon. Reed was escorted out of the interrogation room for a shower and given the opportunity to clean up. He was allowed to use restroom facilities in private, which was in stark contrast to the public toilet of the cell. He was provided a clean change of clothes, not exactly his size, but acceptable. Lunch was served and he was given repeated opportunities to be escorted to the restroom.

Pete Matheson was let into the room mid-afternoon. Reed knew he'd been responsible for the improvement in treatment and thanked him. But Reed sensed something was wrong before they sat down at the table. He saw it in Pete's face. Reed was afraid the Family Services people would be as big a problem as Kuoto. Reed needed to keep Tommy safe and hidden at all costs.

Pete started with the troubling issue Reed knew was looming, "You've got problems. But there are other things you need to be aware of."

"Tommy, I know. I told you he was safe," interjected Reed.

"No Reed, that's not it."

"What then?"

Pete hesitated and then spoke, "Just information, and I'm sorry to be the one to tell you this, but there's been a murder."

Reed's heart stopped and his eyes instantly swelled with tears. Tommy had consumed his thoughts throughout the day and his mind instantly concluded the worst of all possibilities. He looked at Pete across the table, folded his arms on the table, and then dropped his head to cry. At first, it was just sobs and then it turned to all-out wailing. Tommy was all that really mattered and his son's death was his fault.

Pete reached across the table, put his hand on Reed's shoulder, and comforted, "I didn't realize you cared that much for her."

Reed jerked his head up, "What? Not Tommy. Is it Liz?"

"No Reed. It's your ex-wife. I'm sorry."

Reed's sorrow turned to jubilation as he rejoiced and thanked God that Tommy was alive. The tears dried up instantly and he smiled at Pete before realizing what this meant; Kuoto had Tommy and Liz.

When Reed's jubilation subsided, Pete continued, "They found her yesterday in her apartment. She failed to show up for a lunch date with her boyfriend. He found her when he went to check her apartment. She was killed sometime Thursday night after she went to bed. It wasn't very pretty. She was raped and then stabbed multiple times. Money, jewelry, and personal items were taken from the apartment by the perp. He wasn't very smart though; he pawned her jewelry and an engraved silver plate you must have gotten as a wedding gift.

The engraving had both your names on it along with the date of your wedding."

"I don't remember it, Pete."

"Anyway," Pete continued. "The perp left all his personal information on the pawn ticket and they picked him up yesterday. The Atlanta cop I spoke to this afternoon told me they have a rock-solid case. They have DNA, fingerprints, murder weapon, video of him entering the building, and more. From my point of view, the unfortunate thing is that the perp is only fourteen and could end up in the juvenile system. He could be out in four years. But then maybe they'll try the little prick as an adult. We'll have to wait and see."

Reed's heart sank. "Where was Tommy?" he asked a puzzled Pete.

"Tommy wasn't there. There was nobody else there."

"Yes, there was. Tommy and Liz were there," Reed insisted.

"I don't think so. But I'll check with the Atlanta detective."

Reed chose not to tell Pete about the Kuoto threat to the eleven-year-old girl. Instead, the focus of the afternoon discussion was on getting Reed out on bail. Pete had gotten the Huntsville PD to embarrassingly admit they had made a mistake by leaving Reed in the holding cell with Mr. Henson after the assault. They agreed to talk with Mr. Henson and convince him not to make an issue of it, which would allow them to then drop the charges. The assault charge for beating

Mr. Kuoto in the parking lot was more difficult. Pete had been trying to get a bail hearing but was having very little success. Pete had contracted for help from a law firm specializing in criminal defense; he was confident they would have the necessary contacts and knowledge to expedite Reed's release. The good thing was that even if he had to stay here another night, it wouldn't be with Mr. Henson.

They parted with Reed's final request for Pete, "Find Tommy." But Reed knew he could not fulfill that request. Reed needed to get free of this jail and let Kuoto know that he would do as requested.

Shortly after Pete departed, two deputies escorted Reed to a small cell that had been antiseptically cleaned. It had a single cot, sink, toilet, single chair, and small table. When the deputies closed the barred cell door, one of them asked, "Is there anything we can get you Mr. Delahe?"

"No this will be fine," he replied and was then left to his thoughts. He was sorry his ex-wife had been killed. She deserved a lot of things but not that. Although she'd aged since their marriage, she was still beautiful. He remembered the fun times and replayed some of the parties and travel they experienced together. She was always the highlight of any party and so much fun, but that changed when she got pregnant with Tommy. She became dissatisfied with life and displayed it in vicious tirades blaming Reed for taking her life away from her. Shortly after Tommy's birth, she filed for divorce. Their divorce had been brutal and a financial disaster for Reed. She ended up returning to her life as the party girl and Reed funded it.

The afternoon wore on and dinner was served. It was almost edible. He wondered what Kuoto was feeding Tommy. Was he in a cell similar to this one? Kuoto surely wouldn't kill a six-year-old boy. Or would he? What about the black girl? He wouldn't really kill her either. It was all just a way for Kuoto to get his damn radiation-hardened chips and circuitry into U.S. satellites, concluded Reed.

What would the circuitry do, he pondered? Was all this worth sabotaging U.S. satellites? If they wanted to sabotage a satellite, there were easier ways than circuit board substitution. And certainly, a faulty circuit would be discovered during system checkout and testing. Reed's radiation-hardened chips and control circuitry were just a small part of the overall complexities of a satellite. Satellites relied on an immense bank of sensors to provide diverse spatial, temporal, and spectral resolutions. All of which was transmitted to the ground for data re-assembly, interpretation, and post-processing. How could Reed's chips and circuit board make any difference in the larger picture? It just didn't make sense.

Reed's thoughts shifted back to Tommy. God, he loved that little boy. Reed eventually drifted off to sleep with the promise to himself that he would never miss another baseball game.

Chapter 16

SATURDAY'S KINDRED SPIRITS

LIU CHEN HAD WORKED MOST OF THE NIGHT ON HER specialty orders and got them ready for UPS pickup in time for a one-day special delivery. She was too tired to start up a conversation with Kevin, besides he was busy with his remote to the Fugaku clone. Sometimes he would get so engrossed with his computer that he was oblivious to anything around him. He wouldn't respond to texts or anything else when he climbed into his own computer world. It was weird.

Liu undressed, slid into bed, and pulled the covers over her head. Having missed a night's sleep, Liu thought sleep would come easy. But it wouldn't. Traffic noise from the street out front seemed to roar by. A plane heading for La Guardia or JFK sounded like it flew right over the house. And then was followed by another. She heard noises from inside the house. First, it sounded like the floor creaking. Or maybe it was just the structure responding to increasing warmth of the sun. Then she thought she heard something from the attic bedroom above, but dismissed it as well.

Her thoughts were of Kevin. Kevin was so different from Conrad. Physically, Kevin didn't come close. And he had a different kind of wit. Maybe it was because she had created Conrad as an opposite and Kevin was more like her. Conrad offered controllable interaction, fantasy, and the comfort of knowing he wasn't real. With Kevin, there was always the fear that things could become more personal. Intimacy was frightening. She wasn't about to share secrets with anybody. And then intimacy might lead to something more. That just absolutely was not going to happen. No way, she told herself.

So why did she like this Kevin so much? It had to be because he was so much like her, she concluded.

Bob Goddard, AKA Hamilton Cole Davis, stared at the floor of the second car back of the Seven train as it rattled and wiggled its way toward Citizen's Field. The train was so full there was barely enough room to breathe and he could feel a small Oriental woman's shoulder low in his back. The only good thing was that, even in a post-Covid world, most people on the train continued to wear masks, which helped obscure his appearance for the ever-present surveillance cameras. The Oriental woman, dwarfed by the crowd, had to dislike the ride more than he did. She was no threat, as were most of the passengers squeezed in against one another. To his left were two teens sporting Mets ball caps, presumably also heading to Citizen's Field. Behind them was a well-dressed, slightly tall man about Bob's height wearing a long overcoat, which was unusual for a Saturday afternoon. This would have ordinarily raised concern, except for the man's timid and submissive mannerisms.

Bob pulled his Mets ball cap down, adjusted his mask, and studied a petite woman three people to his right. He watched her through shifting and swaying bodies and identified the inconsistency: her movements were minimal compared to those around her as the train rocked down the tracks. It wasn't because of a handhold or something to lean against that made her different; it was actually a well-toned body, balanced and alert with reaction. She was an anomaly and her eyes were on the discrete prowl, similar to his. She allowed her long brown hair to drape forward from her partially titled head to conceal the sides of her face and obscure movements of her eyes. She was good, but not good enough. Her error was that she allowed too much eye movement instead of allowing the brain to interpret its images from peripheral vision. Had she spotted him? Probably not, but who and what was she? Should he fear her? Or was this just part of the paranoia that came with living a life burrowed underground in the plain sight of humanity?

In another life, he could have followed and tracked her every movement to learn first of her home and then ascertain every detail of her life and heritage, all without her having any knowledge of his presence. It wouldn't matter if she were Metro Police, FBI, or a Mafia assassin. Bob's resource, Kevin, was capable of penetrating the deepest of databases and he was momentarily distracted by the thought of his only real friend, Kevin. What was he doing? The last time he heard from Kevin, he had taken up fishing, which was hugely out of character for him.

His instincts transitioned from the mild and timid Bob back to his past and he felt more like the Hamilton Cole Davis he had once been. Cole turned slightly to his left pressing back against the small woman behind him. His broad shoulder now towered over her, increasing what had to be a state of claustrophobia, but it allowed him to see past the man in front of him and catch a faint reflection of the woman's face off the dirty window. She was pretty, about thirty, small figure, hair that fell just below shoulder length, and bangs trimmed at an angle below the level of her eyes, further allowing her eyes to roam. Eye color and other distinguishing features were not discernible, but Cole captured enough definition that he would recognize her if he ever saw her again, even with a mask on. The Seven Express passed through a station reducing the backlight on the window and Cole got a clearer reflection. She was not just pretty; she was gorgeous. So much so, he almost missed the small billowed hump in her white button-up top, just above her right hip.

She was a right-handed shooter and she was carrying! It was holstered inside the belt to obscure its shape and maximize concealment. It had to be a subcompact, nine-millimeter at best, single stack in the mag. Maybe ten rounds at most: a very small pistol. Cole raised his right hand to his Covid mask and blew through his fist as he thought and then spoke imperceptibly to himself,

"Sig Sauer 238." Then reconsidered, "no"—the small Sig was too big to conceal on her figure, even with a loose-fitting top. It had to be a .22, maybe a 32ACP, with a six-round mag, maybe a little Beretta Tomcat, or something similar. Cole's oversized hands could hardly shoot such a tiny and ineffectual weapon. With a size of less than 2.5 by 3.5 inches, Cole could nearly conceal it in a closed hand. The gun was only effective at extremely close range, less than ten feet—more like five, and even then only when one emptied the mag at the target. It was not a cop's weapon, which made her something else.

The Seven Express slowed as it neared the next station. Cole allowed his body to shift with the motions; she did not. As the doors opened, she worked her way through the steadfast horde of Mets fans and exited the train. Bob waited, decided on impulse, and then slipped off the train at the last moment, giving breathing space to the small Oriental woman. He had anticipated a day in the sun watching knuckleball pitching, drinking beer, and providing boisterous instructions to the ump, but she was more interesting at the moment; plus the Mets played again tomorrow and he had a ticket. Cole moved into the crowd waiting for the next train as she moved towards the platform exit. Just as she disappeared from sight, he made his way to the exit. He watched her move off in a northerly direction from the elevated vantage point of the train platform. When she disappeared around a building corner half a block away, Cole ditched his Mets ball cap and bolted from the platform, hustling at the limits of drawing attention to himself. He hit the bottom of the stairs and ran across the street dodging an irate horn honking New Yorker. His quick gate and long stride allowed him to close on the corner of the building in a matter of seconds, just in time to see her enter the second stairwell. Four floors with two doors per floor meant Cole had her down to one in eight in a city with a population of ten million; he smiled. He realized this was nothing more than silly stalking, something for idol worshipers and paparazzi, but his adrenaline was now pumping and the feeling brought remembrance and a smile to his face.

Cole meekly stepped forward into visible space. He slowed his pace and allowed his shoulders to hunch forward and narrow, which left only his oversized hands as an identifiable oddity. He allowed his fingers to overlap and cup slightly minimizing their overall apparent size, but the hands would potentially still be the one item someone would remember. As he moved towards the adjacent building, he surveyed the surroundings in search of a discrete vantage point.

The parking lot was full, each space marked and allocated to an apartment. As he moved along the edge of the lot, he saw them: two men in a Chevrolet parked in a visitor's space. They were clean-shaven, both white, and wore nice shirts. The car was running with the windows up, obviously running the air conditioner. As Cole walked past, shoulders hunched and looking straight ahead, he noticed the exempt license plate. The nondescript white car was a no-frills city or state vehicle of some kind. Cole would have made the occupants as low-level undercover cops except the car had no indications of being a functional police car. It had no lights hidden behind the grill, no shotgun rack between the occupants, and no markings of any kind. And the two men, if they were truly doing surveillance, were way too obvious. Certainly, she had made them as well.

Cole strolled past the parking lot to a small park where he found enough vegetation to observe without detection. It also had a canopy of tall trees that shielded him from the view of any upper-floor window in the building. It was farther away than he preferred but it was as close as he could get and still remain clandestine.

It turned out to be a stalemate known only to him: them watching her, him watching them, and her probably also watching them—everybody watching. The hours dragged on. By now Crocker was probably pitching his sixth and final inning but leaving the Mets leading by three, Cole surmised. He pictured her with binoculars standing two feet back from a third-floor window studying the idling car. She was waiting and watching, but waiting for what? Maybe the shift for the two in the car would end and they would be replaced by another pair in another city vehicle.

Maybe she was waiting for a chance to sneak back out, which is what Cole really hoped.

A well-dressed man emerged from her stairwell and strolled out to a Tesla. Most of the cars in the lot were of the mid-price range establishing the income level of the residents. However, simply owning a car in New York was an indication of a healthy salary. The man wore a suit with a white shirt and red tie underneath; a power dresser headed for a Saturday afternoon in the office, concluded Cole.

A woman, with what appeared to be a small sack of groceries, came around the corner, walked to the adjacent stairwell, and entered. This whole thing was silly, Cole considered. First the adrenaline rush last night and now this silly stalking game he was playing today. Consider it a downpour in the bottom of the eighth and just call it.

Cole considered his options. He couldn't go to her but maybe she could come to him. He speculated, based on her appearance and behaviors, that she was intensely aware of her surroundings. And she was obviously capable of taking action. Maybe she was even skilled at martial arts, he speculated. Although with the 32ACP on her hip, the use of physical force wouldn't be necessary. But he liked the thought anyway.

For him, any action would mean loss of anonymity and Bob Goddard might have to disappear forever. But his life had become just mere existence in the anonymity he had created. Still, he was managing what Kevin called "innate hostility" and he hadn't resorted to any behaviors of his past. Cole weighed the options. The smart move was anonymity, but intrigue won out.

Cole stepped from the bushes and strolled out into the parking lot. He set his sights on the idling Chevrolet as he crossed behind a Focus, Nissan, and a dozen other non-descript cars. He didn't look up but sensed she was watching from an upstairs window. He again envisioned her holding the binoculars, only this time studying his every move. When he reached the back of the Chevrolet, he stopped in plain view of the rearview mirror and turned to stare with an artificial look of bewilderment. Cole then pulled the phone from his pocket and stepped back a few paces to expand the field of view for the cell phone camera. He snapped two pictures and then moved to get an angled side view of the car. He had their attention. The driver moved his head to follow Cole in the side mirror. The passenger wasn't so discreet; he just turned his head and stared. Cole gave the car a wide berth as he made his way between adjacent cars and around to the front of the Chevrolet. He kept his distance and again raised the cell phone to snap more pictures. The concern was evident on their faces and Cole knew he was about to get a reaction. He also speculated she was asking herself, "What the hell is he doing?" He could almost hear her saying it. Cole moved closer, nearly to the bumper of the car, and aimed the phone directly at the driver to snap his picture. As Cole shifted to the passenger, both doors flew open.

They were big men. But this was to be a show. Cole feinted a look of fear and surprise as he quickly snapped another photo of each. The combination of a scared pathetic victim look and the unwanted photography bolstered their charge; Cole just froze. The driver struck the first blow with both hands open pushing Cole backward and commanded, "Give me the damn phone!" The passenger moved around to Cole's rear and yelled, "Now, ass-hole!"

Cole meekly responded, "No," and then looked down.

"You're going to give me that phone one way or the other," stated the driver. The passenger, now directly behind Cole, grabbed both his arms and pulled him tight.

Cole taunted, "Is that the way you give it to your mother?"

From behind, the man let go a solid right to Cole's kidney. Cole wheezed and hacked. The driver reached in and grabbed Cole's hand in an attempt to remove the cell phone. He pried at the fingers to no avail. Cole's grasp was secure and beyond the man's ability to open, which just further infuriated him. The driver held Cole's hand in his left and repeatedly smacked down on it with his right fist. It probably hurt the driver's fist more than it hurt his hand. As the driver hammered away, Cole wondered how long he would keep up this game of patty-cake. Was she watching?

"Give it to me," the infuriated driver demanded and then landed a forceful punch to Cole's mid-section; Cole keeled over with pain, but also for show.

The passenger had him from behind pinning his arms against his sides. The driver jabbed again at Cole's mid-section again and demanded, "Give it to me!"

"No thanks, ask your partner," suggested Cole.

"What?" exclaimed the driver and then pounded again and again at Cole's stomach, left—right in succession and then over again. "You are the dumbest asshole I have ever met. Now, give it to me!"

"No thanks, but your partner has been rubbing against my ass and should be up for it."

The passenger let loose his grip and spun Cole around to land a weak back-handed slap and then went for what would have been a solid jab to Cole's solar plexus had Cole not deflected it with his right. This guy needed to be watched closely.

The driver then took a cheap shot to Cole's jaw. Cole went with the punch and flopped to the pavement. The driver kicked him in the stomach and the passenger kicked him in the back. He had just about had enough. Then, he saw her.

She stepped from between two cars and demanded, "What the hell?"

Cole lay on the ground staring up at her, consumed by her presence. Beautiful was an understatement; she was absolutely gorgeous. Her voice was feminine, yet commanding, and Cole's mind replayed the words she had just spoken, "What the hell?"

She stood with feet squarely planted and shoulders square, postured for the confrontation. Her blue jeans were tight-fitting and she wore the same loose-fitting, button-up, white top he'd seen earlier. Her hair was so brown it was almost black. It fell along the sides of her face to just below her shoulders but her bangs were cut at an angle to half cover her left eye and give her a look of mystique. Her skin was tanned similar to his, but smooth as a baby's behind. Her face presented itself with a perfect balance of remarkably perfect eyes, nose, lips, and chin. Her eyes were dark and difficult to simply assign a color to, perhaps a very dark blue. It was all accented with just a touch of makeup here and there to bring it all together as perfect. She was astonishing.

"He has something of ours," replied the driver.

"I don't think so," she replied. "Just get back in your car and go somewhere."

"We're not going without that camera," demanded the passenger and glanced down at Cole.

"I know who you guys are and you should just go," she commanded.

Cole continued to study her. The features of her figure were small but in perfect proportion to her over-all petite frame. He noted that the slight pillowing on her hip was now much larger; he envisioned that she had traded up for something more lethal. A 1911 would have been his choice for lethal, but that's a big heavy gun. She would have chosen something lighter, yet something still with a punch. Maybe a forty in a Glock or XDM, he speculated. The weapon would be held in hands that were perfectly proportioned in every way. She would slip her delicate fingers around the grip and extend her forefinger to rest on the trigger, he thought. He noticed a small oddity for such a beautiful woman: her nails were neatly trimmed yet unpainted.

She slowly moved in an arc around the men as a staring contest developed. Cole watched her every move from his prone position on the ground. Each step was easy, silent, and graceful. She glided around until she was within only a few steps of Cole's feet and stopped to concentrate on the staring match.

"If you know who we are, then you know we're not going to leave without his phone," replied the driver. "And we do know what we are doing. It's you that's in trouble."

"You'll be the ones in trouble if you don't just leave," she commanded.

"I don't think so. We're only here to send the message that you're being watched. And we can watch you in more ways than you can imagine—anytime, anyplace. There is nowhere to hide—nowhere to run. That's the trouble you're in—bitch!"

There was momentary silence and she looked at Cole and asked, "How about it? This ordeal ends now if you give them your phone."

Cole looked up at her and meekly asked, "It's my only cell phone and I want to keep it; what do you think I should do?"

She didn't hesitate, "Give it to them."

Cole extended his arm and held the prepaid smart-phone out to the driver. "Okay," he said from his position on the ground.

Cole wasn't concerned about the phone. It was completely untraceable back to him. Bob Goddard had purchased the phone with no contract and prepaid minutes. During the conversation, Cole had discreetly wiped the phone clean of prints. If they had resources and gained access to the phone contents, they wouldn't find anything useful. The address book of the phone was empty. The only calls in history were untraceable back to anyone in particular. The phone or its features were never used in any manner that left evidence of his existence. It was the way he had come to live. They might find the photos interesting; but after each picture had been snapped, Cole had instantly saved it to the cloud. He had also discreetly captured a picture of this amazing woman. When they figured out he had sent off copies of the pictures, along with the unusual absence of information on the phone, their suspicions would rise. Unfortunately, it also meant they would be back for him. Cole sighed, so much for anonymity.

The driver inspected the phone and then inquired of Cole, "Why in the hell were you taking pictures anyway?"

She intervened and instructed them to leave but Cole answered anyway, "Waste of taxpayer dollars. You guys are sitting there in a city vehicle, with its engine running, playing phone games on city time. I was going to turn you in."

The passenger pointed at Cole and said, "You know what turning us in will get you, right? More pain for you. We have your phone. So keep your mouth shut!"

As the passenger lectured him, Cole watched the actions of the woman from the corner of his eye. She put her left hand on her hip and her right hand on her Glock such that the outline of the gun was apparent to both the driver and passenger. This was her show of lethal force, which meant that if they came back after her, they too would bring lethal force. Mistake—hers, concluded Cole.

She turned to Cole and commanded, "Tell them you won't say anything. Tell them it was a mistake and you'll forget all about it."

She was naive in her request but he complied, "I won't say anything."

"There, now go!" she commanded to the driver and passenger.

Both the driver and passenger stared at Cole. Cole avoided eye contact, nervously looking down and away and then back again, producing the Bob Goddard appearance of weakness. They accepted this answer more than his verbal response.

She commanded again, "Go!"

Cole didn't get up, just watched along with the woman, as the two retreated to their car and climbed in. The car backed out and then drove off with a squeal of tires, leaving her standing over him.

She looked down at Cole and asked, "Sorry about all that—and sorry about your phone. Are you hurt?"

"Some," he replied.

"Do you need a doctor?"

"No."

"How can I help? Call a cab? Help you to the Seven?" she asked. "I'll pay for your phone? How much?"

Cole raised his hand, shook his head, and said, "Enough." He stood and then continued, "No more false pretenses. Do you know what a kindred spirit is?" he stated as he stared into her eyes.

"What is this?" she suspiciously replied.

"No lies. I saw you on the Seven this morning doing the same thing I was doing. You live your life with everything and everyone around you a threat. Every face you encounter is interrogated, subjected to a mental threat assessment, and then racked, stacked, and placed in memory because someday you might see that face again. And for your face, every other set of eyes, every video surveillance camera, and every person with a cell phone camera is a threat. I know you."

She stepped back and put her hand on the concealed pistol revealing its threatening shape. "I think you need to leave."

"I will after you hear me out—if you still want me to. Just for clarity, the Glock on your hip is only a limited threat."

"It's not a Glock," she retorted.

"Then it's a XDM, forty cal., compact."

"How do you know?"

"Because I capture, analyze, and judge every detail that might be a threat." Cole paused and then continued, "And by the way, the 32ACP strapped to your ankle is absolutely no threat. You were carrying it on your hip this morning on the train."

She stepped back again and Cole saw a change in her eyes from wary to fear, fear someone was breaking into her world. She didn't speak, just stared as her mind recounted events. Then, he saw the subtle twitch in her eyes at the moment of recognition and she confessed, "You were there. Mets ball cap." Her eyebrows twitched again as it instantly came together. "You followed me. You baited me into coming to your rescue. You took a beating just for this meeting. Why?"

"Kindred spirit," Cole answered.

"What?"

"I told you no lies." Cole explained further, "My life is one of isolation. I have no real interaction or honest sharing with anyone. I saw you as a kindred spirit. I saw you as a woman of mystery, a woman of intrigue. I saw you as a woman I could be friends with."

She slowly shook her head, but with noticeably weakened conviction said, "No. I think you better go."

Cole was staring into her eyes but also now noticed movement in the small park he had observed earlier. Cole raised his hand to partially obscure part of his face and turned slightly.

She recognized the behavior and inquired, "What is it?"

"Just threats, threats that are everywhere and they never leave: a figure behind a darkened window, movement of a curtain, change in a person's pace, shifting eyes on the train, turned face in a car, glint of unexplained light, or the rustle of a bush fifty yards behind you. We're being photographed."

"Let's walk," she stated without turning to look and stepped in his direction. "What's your name?" she demanded as she stepped alongside him. He turned and walked next to her as they moved directly away from the park. He could sense the high-power zoom lens of a real camera on the back of his neck and imagined the shutter clicks in his ears.

"Real or most recent," he asked.

"Real," she replied as a command and gate for any further communication. "You said 'no lies.'"

In almost a whisper and directed toward her ear with a cupped hand Cole answered, "Hamilton Cole Davis." He dropped his hand and added, "Please don't ever repeat it. You can call me Bob for now. And yours?"

"Julia Addison, I go by Julie." She stared at him, paused, and then added, "Bob doesn't fit."

He looked into her eyes and then conceded, "Okay, just Cole then, no last name—ever, please."

They proceeded to her stairwell and he followed her to the third floor, where she excluded him from entrance to her apartment and instructed him to wait. Upper floors in an unknown stairwell violated Cole's senses. You never enter a place where you haven't established preplanned escape routes. The stairwell had none, unless he could gain access to the fourth-floor apartments, but that was problematic in that he didn't know what was on the other side of the door. Or once in the apartment, was it a trap? He knew better than to just wait, but the acquaintance with Julie was worth it.

Julie closed the door behind her and leaned against it. She closed her eyes. This was just too bizarre. Who would get the crap beat out of them just to say, "Hi, how's it going, want to be my friend?" Was he for real? But she knew he was. And now she had him right outside her door. It would be better for him if he just left, especially with what she knew. He should run like hell. She considered the options: cops—no way, leave him out there until he got bored—not probable, shoot him in the arm and send him running for the hospital—doubtful. For all she knew, he might shoot back. No, he wouldn't, she already knew.

There was also something about him that she was refusing to admit. He was different from any person she had ever known. Secretly she knew him very well. He knew nothing about her but assimilated bits of observation to establish her persona: her paranoia, her gun, and her heroine reactions. His powers of perception were scary accurate, which meant she would have to be extremely cautious not to let him get too close. He was honest; holy crap was he honest.

Coffee, that was it, she decided. Julie traded out the XDM, which was actually illegal in the state of New York because of its high-capacity magazine. As for her 32ACP, it was legal and she was authorized to carry it. She changed her top to a light blue one of a similar design and ran a brush through her hair. She opened the door and stepped out. He was still there.

"Coffee," she said. "Buy me a cup of coffee."

He said, "Okay, lead the way."

She didn't like having him behind her but she trotted down the stairs in the lead. When she exited the stairwell, she turned to watch his reaction to the video surveillance camera at the entrance. Sure enough, he looked down and ensured there was no captured image of his face. She also noticed his build. Lying on the ground in the parking lot, he had appeared somewhat diminutive. But now his size and strength were apparent.

His strides matched hers as they walked side by side. She tested and accelerated just a little. His stride increased to match; this man with the true name of Cole was instinctive. She kept her part of any conversation to a minimum with the expectation that he would feel compelled to provide more information. But the walk was, for the most part, silent.

She took him to a small mall with an open food court that included a Starbucks. Before they got to the Starbucks, he insisted on stopping at the Phone-Mobile store. Cole knew exactly what he wanted and ordered it like fast food: three prepaid Black RC smartphones each with an unlimited three-month plan, and three cheap flip phones with a prepaid three-month plan. He paid cash, which got her attention. The total bill was a little over ninety-eight hundred bucks. He slipped one of the smartphones in his breast pocket and dropped the others in a bag. Julie had never heard of a RC Black phone; what the heck was that?

She ordered a pumpkin latte and a piece of banana bread. Cole ordered a large black coffee with no cream and no sugar. Nasty she thought. She chose a table near the wall and sat with her back to the wall. Instead of sitting opposite her, he chose the chair to her right with his back to the surveillance camera in the opaque globe. For a few moments, they just stared at each other. The feeling that she liked him asserted itself, but that had to be out of the real equation.

He pulled the smartphone out of his pocket and commented, "These things are amazing." He thumbed the screen and she tried to see what he was doing but he angled the screen to keep it from her view.

"What kind of phone is that?" she asked.

"It's a Rubik's Cube black phone. Several manufacturers make black phones. It's just a little faster than a typical I or Android. And it still has limited security features. But the phone keeps Google, the phone company, or anyone else from using triangulation or GPS to track its location. Except it still uses cell towers, which gives away its location when in use. It also keeps phone conversations from being directly intercepted by almost everyone. Everyone, that is except the United States government."

"Are you afraid of the government?"

"Yes."

Cole continued to tap the screen and study its display. Silence between them grew deafening as minutes passed by. Finally, her curiosity got the best of her and she asked, "What are you doing?"

He replied, "Reading about you."

She scooted her chair back an inch and snapped, "What?"

Calmly and politely he replied, "You heard me."

"Show me," she demanded.

"Almost finished," he said, paused, and then continued. "Born in Buffalo, twenty-nine years old, father Edward, mother Jeanette, B.S. in Criminal Justice, never married, work for the New York State Department of Taxation."

He had just violated her sanctity and she lambasted him, "You butt, where'd you get that! That's my information!"

She saw a partial apology in his face before he answered, "Impressed?"

"Not at all!" she replied with feigned ire.

"Bad start for a first date, huh?"

"I guarantee you this is not a first date. I don't know what it is!"

"How's the pumpkin latte? Any seeds?" he said, which caught her completely off guard.

She couldn't help but yield to a small smile. "No. There's no seeds." she said and submissively shook her head.

"How's this," he said. "Born in Idaho, thirty-three years old, father Cole, mother Rachael, M.S. Aerospace Engineering, never married, entrepreneur. That makes us even."

"I suppose," she said. She had assured herself earlier that she wouldn't allow it to happen, but it was happening anyway. She did like this man, which would only complicate things.

They talked about the parking lot incident as the afternoon disappeared. It was too soon to let him in on her problems and provide the reason for the parking lot watchers. All that would come later. She was becoming quite convinced that he would help. He promised her names and a full complement of details on the men in the parking lot by tomorrow. She inquired how, but he declined to offer any information about his sources. He said providing his personal information had put him at extreme risk and she needed to respect that; his discomfort was obvious.

Cole gave her one of the activated flip phones from the bag and they exchanged numbers. All was memorized, nothing was input into the phone memories. He told her it was only good for one call to him and then she was to destroy it. He instructed her to smash it then and force it down the garbage disposal. He frightened her when he explained it and made her promise. She was to avoid any electronic trail that could link her to him. It was all very discomforting and his problems were obviously worse than hers. Maybe they were kindred spirits.

They agreed on a rendezvous time and location for tomorrow. They would meet at Citizens Field for a baseball game. She had never been there so this would be a true date, at least as he categorized it. Cole promised tickets right behind home plate and an afternoon of excitement, beer, and bratwurst. It was an easy ride out to the end of the Seven from her apartment. Maybe she would even see him again on the train, which made her smile.

Cole devised a plan to work their way back to her apartment. He would take a circuitous route and come in through the park. If she never saw him as she came in from the street, then all was clear. He touched her hand and said, "See you tomorrow," as he got up and walked towards a different exit than they had come in. She watched as he exited and then made her own way out. As she walked down the street towards her apartment, she conceded that maybe she would like someone to be there watching. That way she would get to spend some more time with this kindred spirit.

She entered the parking lot just at dark. All was quiet in the parking lot and there was no Cole. She would have to wait until tomorrow.

Chapter 17

Rush Order

Cole watched her as she came around the corner. Even from afar, she was beautiful. She stepped into the building entrance and disappeared. He stayed put in his clandestine location to watch and be sure she was safe and the watchers didn't return. He would have liked to join her but felt like he might be advancing too fast. Besides, he still needed to have her background more thoroughly investigated before this developing relationship went any further. All he had were the basics, but Kevin would complete a thorough investigation. He needed to call Kevin.

She was quite sensitive about her personal information, thought Cole, even though what he had given her was readily available online. Certainly, she knew it was all easily accessed. This was just the beginning too, he thought. By the time Kevin got through looking into her background, he would know every aspect of this woman's life.

Cole had had his smartphone set to instantly store his photos in the cloud. Earlier in the day when he snapped photos of the driver, passenger, and Julie, all had been posted to a cloud server that only he and Kevin had access to. Kevin, being the curious sort, would have already transferred the photos to a two-hundred-sixty-four-bit encrypted location and gone to work on all three. Kevin had almost instantly sent Cole the preliminary data, just based on her name. But it would go much deeper than that.

Kevin could confirm who Julie was without even knowing her name. He'd probably start with any number of databases to match a name with her photo using facial recognition software. It could have been the New York driver's license division or any place else he could access a database with names and photos. Cole envisioned Kevin rattling away at his keyboard going two hundred words a minute developing some kind of code that would hack into the New York driver's license database. Once he verified her name, Kevin would delve into every aspect of her life. If Cole's pictures were good enough, Cole hoped Kevin could do the same for the Chevrolet driver and passenger, especially the passenger. Cole had a bad feeling about him.

Cole hadn't talked to Kevin in months, but now it was time. At best, Kevin would be pleased that Cole had learned to manage his "innate hostility," as Kevin called it. Cole could report months of peace and harmony living amongst the New Yorkers.

Cole waited thirty minutes and then crept off in the darkness, eventually making his way back to the tram station. In-route, he called Kevin. The conversation was one-sided, direct, and specific. Cole made his requests known and disconnected before Kevin could start on one of his usual tirades.

Kevin was concentrating on the photos Cole had posted. Julia Addison was who she said she was, at least from a quick look. Like Julia, the two men were from some taxation branch of New York State. While he continued to study the remote connection to the Fugaku, Kevin texted Liu: "Can U do a rush order?"

Liu texted: "I'm pretty tired. But for U. Sure. What do you need?"

Kevin texted: "An encrypted satellite phone and two cell phone signal transmitters that can be kept mobile and recharged on subway trains."

Liu texted: "Satellite phone is no issue. Transmitters I'll have to think about. It's Saturday. Thought we were going to spend some time together tonight?"

Kevin texted: "So did I. But this for my friend."

Liu texted: "K. Maybe someday UL tell me more about him."

Kevin texted: "U don't want to know. Trust me."

Chapter 18

SATURDAY AFTERNOON HORROR

MARCY OGALSBY REACHED THE THIRD-FLOOR LANDing after a horrible night. She waited tables and flirted for tips during the week at the Austrian Beer Chalet, but made her real money Friday and Saturday nights working the downtown area. Stockbrokers and well-to-do businessmen were much better tippers when they got the real item, and she was the real item. She reported some of the Chalet tips but never reported any of her Friday or Saturday escort income, as she liked to call it. This kept her on the low-income list and qualified for subsidized housing, while still having an ample income to spend and enjoy. She worked every angle to make her, and her daughter's, life as comfortable as possible.

Friday night had been a rough one. She worked two Johns and made nearly a grand before the third John sought her out. She provided him full service, which made her an easy six hundred. The John was extremely satisfied and they both got high afterward. Ordinarily, she would only accept crack. But last night, she was convinced to do a little H with the guy. And that was all she could remember until waking up alongside an alley dumpster.

As she stood on the landing searching for her key, her head pounded to the point of blurring her vision and her body trembled with distress. The key was somewhere in her little bag. Her money was surprisingly all still there. She was briefly distracted by the money and shuffled over the edge of the bills to get another reassuring count. While counting the bills, she stumbled forward and dropped the bag. Eventually, Marcy found her key and poked it at the door handle. It was amazing she had even found her way home, she thought. Leaning against the wall and forcing her focus, she found the key slot. The key found its way into the slot and the tumbler rotated.

Marcy entered the silent apartment and considered the day of the week in her foggy mind—Saturday. Samantha would ordinarily have been watching TV, she always watched TV. She would sit on the couch for hours, with her little pony things lined up on the armrest, watching cartoons and other for-girls-only shows. Marcy was glad the TV was off; she didn't know if her headache could handle it.

Marcy looked at the couch, which is where she usually slept unless Samantha was watching TV, of course. In which case, she would just nap in Samantha's bed. She considered just crashing but thought a hot shower on her neck might provide some desperately needed relief. She stumbled towards the hallway, stopping briefly at the kitchen cabinet to retrieve and quickly swallow four or five aspirin. The world was spinning;

maybe she wouldn't make the shower. Marcy entered the short hallway, with the bathroom on the right and Samantha's room on the left, and stumbled the first couple of steps. Bathroom light was off. Samantha's light was on, which helped Marcy decide to pass on the shower. She stumbled the remaining steps to Samantha's doorway and then raised her eyes from the floor.

She stood motionless, her breathing stopped, her heart rate accelerated, and her eyes ballooned. When Marcy's breathing returned, it was with screams that penetrated every room, in every apartment, in her entire stairwell, and beyond. She screamed and screamed and screamed. She screamed until the NYPD, summoned by a neighbor's 911 call, broke down the door and entered the apartment. She stopped screaming only momentarily when they gently grabbed her and escorted her away from the sight and into the living room. She resumed her tormented release and continued screaming even as they helped her downstairs to a waiting ambulance.

Chapter 19

THE HEREAFTER

COLE ALMOST MISSED HIS STOP THINKING ABOUT JULIE, but jumped off at the last second, just ahead of the closing door. He continued thinking about her and fantasized about their upcoming date. As he approached his building, he was suddenly aware of police activity, police activity everywhere. A patrol car passed him on the street. Rotating lights from a hidden source between the buildings flashed outward and splashed onto the roadway; the light had to be from at least two patrol cars, speculated Cole. Another cop car passed in the opposite direction. If he didn't act in the next few seconds, he feared an encounter. And that would not play out well. Another cop car slowed behind him and followed him as he walked. Keep inconspicuously moving, Cole decided, and then went around the corner of his building to find a crowd of on-lookers. He joined them and worked his way to their center where he was protected from view by the police but also able to see ahead.

Cole peered over and between the heads in front of him. There was a police line guarded by yellow tape stretched between two patrol cars. Paramedics were escorting a screaming woman out of the stairwell to a gurney. They laid her down and tried to start an IV. She bucked and fought as they tried to work. One of the paramedics reached for her and she landed a backhanded blow to the side of his head. He stumbled but didn't go down. The woman continued to scream and flail. With the assistance of three police officers, the remaining paramedic was able to restrain her to the gurney. The other paramedic shook off the blow and returned to get the IV in place.

Interesting Cole thought, but felt the need to flee to the security of his apartment. He glanced over his shoulder. The path was clear. A woman to Cole's left asked if he knew what happened. Cole replied "No" and the woman in front of him turned to explain. "That hooker what go out eber night leabin her daughter at home all by herself. Somebody came and kilt that child in a real bad way. Post to be pictures on the internet."

Cole slowly backed out allowing people to fill in as he worked his way to the edge of the crowd. The crowd extended nearly back to Cole's stairwell and he easily slipped away. Cole entered his third-floor apartment and left the lights off. Out his kitchen window, he could see into an identical apartment in the adjacent building. There were four uniformed and two plain-clothes cops in the living room having a conversation. It was apparent they weren't very concerned about pro-tecting a crime scene, at least not in that room. Cops and investigators seemed to be taking turns entering and exiting the hallway leading to the bedroom.

Cole watched late into the evening with binoculars. They managed to get a small gurney up the stairs and into the front room. There was some kind of discussion with pointing and direction; most of the cops exited the front room and went to the stairwell. The gurney was positioned in the front room. Two men in white waited with the gurney; a third entered the hallway and returned a few minutes later with the child in his arms. "My God," Cole gasped.

They laid her on the gurney and took a couple of pictures. They'd probably already taken a hundred others. Then, with some discussion, they propped her up on the edge of the gurney while the photographer positioned himself. This was horror beyond anything Cole had ever seen. "My God," he again mumbled. The child's legs had been amputated and she was impaled on something. Through the binoculars, a carving on her delicate little chest was discernable, "TOMY BOY."

Cole focused on her face and saw the unimaginable. Her eyes were wide open. They locked onto his and drew him across the expanse to bring him face-to-face. She penetrated the very core of Cole's soul. His entire existence was flooded with indescribable sensations he'd never known before. It was more than horror; it was pure unadulterated, malignant terror. His entire being cried out. His body shook. His knees went weak. His heart raced to cardiac levels. His stomach came to his throat. His eyes engorged. Rational thought vanished. And, as the unreasoning and overmastering panic within him climaxed, Samantha Ogalsby screamed, "Why?".

Chapter 20

SUNDAY—REALIZATION

COLE LAY AWAKE FOR WHAT SEEMED LIKE AN ETER-
nity. Poor little thing. Images of her and her little pink
ponies played over and over in his mind. It made no
sense. She couldn't have been but ten. It wasn't just
that she had been murdered. It was that someone had
tortured and mutilated the child. Who would do such
a thing? What kind of message were they trying to
send? And to whom? And who was Tomy Boy? Was
it just pure evil like he'd seen in Mexico? Even so, at
worst it would have been a beheading with the head
sent to her father as a message, warning, or threat of
things to come. This was far worse. It was cruel, horrid,
and malicious.

He thought of Kevin. Cole had meant to call him
again but somehow now it didn't seem that important.
Neither did Julia. Mental fatigue yielded to a semicon-
scious state of sleep but the terror of it all continued
to churn and grind.

Four A.M. came with a jolt of realization and he
instantly came to a sitting position. "Good evening,
sir," he screamed. He'd seen them. It was the prick
in the Detroit Tigers jacket. It had to be. Cole closed
his eyes and blew through his fist as he reconstructed
every detail of the encounter. Three of them appeared

out of the darkness, one with nervous darting eyes, one with a nervous hand in his pocket, and one in the center with steady collected behavior. The one on the left also had a backpack and wore some kind of shiny necklace. Cole remembered its glint in the light from the stairwell. The one in the center had to be their leader. He showed no fear and glared with steadfast intensity. They were seasoned Disciples, somewhere between twenty-five and thirty, each of reasonable stature. Cole blew through his clinched left fist and forced maximum recall to envision their faces.

He recalled the overheard words from the encounter and judged the timing between, "…not…business…" He then reconstructed the muffled words with multiple combinations of implanted words from his imagination. He played it back and forth until he arrived at the possible whispered phrase: "Boy's not our business forget it." There were variations on the phrase, such as "Ass-hole's not the business tonight," but the meanings were all the same and they all revealed intent. They knew where they were going. And they knew what they were going to do.

The disingenuous "Good evening, sir" was just confirmation. Cole blew through his fist again and tried to recall the sound of the man's voice. He played it over and over again: deep, calm, and cool stated words with maybe a touch of accent, but not New York, Bronx, or Queens. Where, he puzzled without conclusion. Would he recognize the man's voice if he heard it again? Maybe was the best Cole could commit to himself.

What they had done sickened his stomach and even more so knowing that they were only seconds from death by his hands. Had things been ever so minutely different, had they accosted him, had the one on the right pulled the pistol, the little girl would be alive.

Cole returned to his front window. There was a single cop car sitting in front of the stairwell. The lights were on in the apartment but he saw no activity. He stood in the darkness and watched until the first rays of morning peaked over the building. He knew what he was going to do. Kevin would help him do it.

Cole retrieved the second of the prepaid flip phones and called Kevin. It was answered on the fifth ring and Cole simply said, "Game time."

"Not only no. But hell no. Asshole," came an expected response. "You can't just leave it alone, can you? I'm not going to help you with your psycho insanity. So don't ask."

"Yes, I love you too."

"You better. I'm your only friend in the whole world. I'm the only fool willing to put up with your shit. Killed anybody lately? Beat up anybody lately? You sick bastard. I told you no more games."

"The answer to your questions is no I haven't killed anybody."

"I'm impressed. Going through withdrawals? Beating up the pillow every night, I'll bet. Or have you resorted to killing small animals?" responded the impertinent Kevin and then added a screeching cat cry.

"You're a pain to talk to, Kevin. Shut it down."

"You deserve every bit of it and more. Hey, you got something going with the Julia hottie? Maybe you have turned over a new leaf and its whips, chains, and kinkosex."

"No Kevin, she's not why I called. We can talk about her later. I've got some other work I need you to do for me."

"I don't work for you and you better remember it. I work for myself and I do what I want when I want."

"You're right, Kevin."

"I'm right…so it is kinkosex. I knew it," said Kevin in a twisted reply. "I'm going to soon know everything about her."

"All right Kevin, you do that. Just research her in your spare time and include the two bozos as well. But I need you to focus on another problem first. Look up," continued Cole but Kevin cut him off by interjecting, "Did you tell her you're a psychopath?"

"Damn it Kevin, this is serious. This is no shit for real, no time for jacking around. And Kevin, we are going to play this game," retorted Cole with his patience wearing thin. "Look up the New York killing and mutilation of a little black girl. I saw the gang bangers that did it. Read up on it. Find out what you can. And then call me back so we can have a private conversation about the game we are going to play. Got it!"

"I told you—no game! Get that through your psychotic head. But I will look up the girl. One hour," conceded Kevin and disconnected.

He needed time to think and Kevin time to work. Cole showered and laid out his clothes options for the first half of the day. Cole would wear an "I love New York" T-shirt, Yankees ball cap, knee-length pair of shorts, and common tennis shoes, but only for the first half of the day.

In the afternoon, Bob Goddard would wear a button-up Dickey Mets jersey, Mets ball cap, full-length khaki pants, and the same common tennis shoes. He tried on Bob's glasses. He hated them, but they helped deceive facial recognition software by changing the projected distance between his eyes by one-point-two-five millimeters, which was beyond the tolerance limit for the multifaceted software algorithms. He quickly removed them and placed them in a little fanny pack that Bob could wear in front. Of course, the fanny pack and Covid mask also complimented the overall Bob Goddard image.

This morning he was going exploring where cameras were less of a concern. The flip phone rang. It was Kevin and it was within the hour promised.

Kevin didn't wait for a hello; he just started talking. "The prick that killed that girl is nothing but a vile -.

Kevin stumbled and then continued, "I don't even know what to call him. I saw the internet pictures. Google, Yahoo, Facebook, Instagram, and everybody else are trying to keep them from being circulated because they are the worst thing I've ever seen. At first, I thought they were a horror movie clip of some kind. But they're real. I'm sick. Thank God they caught the bastard."

"They didn't catch him, Kevin."

"Oh yes, they did. Some little twerp has been fantasizing about what he'd like to do with little girls and then he finally did it. He posted the pictures and a glorifying self-tribute to his Facebook page. I read it. They got him solid with all kinds of physical evidence. They have his DNA in her, her blood physically on him, his prints on her, his prints on the saw, his prints on the knife, his bloody footprints throughout the apartment, and his bloody handprints on a backpack. He's as guilty as it gets."

"Backpack was black with black straps. Did you get that?"

"No. Where'd you learn that?"

"I told you I saw them. It wasn't just your little twerp."

The phone was silent for several moments before Kevin inquired, "Fall guy?"

"Yep."

"But evidence is overwhelming."

"Too much so, don't you think?"

"I can explain it," slowly responded Kevin.

"Explain what?"

"The pictures," continued Kevin very slowly. "I need to do some work." Kevin paused again and asked, "But why?"

"Don't know," Cole answered.

"Game on. I'm in," came an instant response from Kevin.

"I thought you would be," complimented Cole.

"Now, how about the conversation pieces I asked for? They are going to be more important now more than ever."

"I'm still working on getting them. Time's up. Open phone line and you know better. I'll call when I have something," finished Kevin and disconnected.

Cole stood at his front window and watched a shift change of officers guarding the stairwell entrance. A short cordial hello was exchanged with the driver's windows down and then the car that had been there most of the morning hours drove off. It was still too early to venture out. Cole just stared across to the third-floor apartment. The day would start with reconnaissance, and then he would spend the afternoon thinking at the baseball game. He'd almost forgotten about Julie. She would be a distraction; maybe it was time to move on.

Liu Chen texted Kevin: "Those pics are horrible. I can't even look at them. How could someone do that?"

Kevin texted: "That's what we're going to find out."

Liu texted: "I'm sick. That child. She's just a baby. It is horrible."

Kevin texted: "And paybacks are a bitch."

Liu texted: "U and UR friend???"

Kevin texted: "Yep. Game on. Whoever did that is about to meet their worst nightmare."

Liu texted: "I don't like those kind of words."

Kevin texted: "Sorry. But this needs fixing."

Liu texted: "Is this what U and UR friend do? Fix things????"

Kevin texted: "It's the only thing we have in common. We fix shit."

Liu struggled with strange new thoughts and then texted: "Can I help???"

Kevin texted: "UL be sorry. It's always ugly. And U could get hurt—or worse."

Liu hesitated as she looked to her left. This was horrible. But she made her decision and then texted: "What can I do?"

Kevin texted: "How's the rush order?"

Liu could have verbally responded but texted anyway: "Just finished. Is that part of this?"

Kevin texted: "It is now."

Liu texted: "What else can I do?"

Kevin texted: "Start by dissecting the photos. Every pixel, every shadow, every detail."

Liu texted: "K." And then went to work on her Exascale.

Chapter 21

Sunday—Testimonial

Sunday morning Jack Johnston stood in front of Manti's First Ward congregation and stared at his fellow neighbors. He started his testimonial, "I testify that the Church of Jesus Christ of Latter Saints is the one true religion. I know it in my heart and I know it in my soul. There is no other religion. I forsake all the ills of alcohol, drugs, and tobacco. I do so without regret."

He paused and scanned the crowd of a hundred. "I give thanks to the Lord that my Elizabeth has safely returned to us and brought with her a fine young man as a new charge. She escaped those in the world that wished to do her and her charge harm." He shouted, "She escaped unimaginable threats!" And then paused and continued more calmly, "She joins us here in this place of family, community, and kinship. Here, she and her charge must be kept safe."

Jack Johnston stopped and allowed a tear to form. "The Lord sayeth thou shalt not kill. But what does that mean? Does that mean Porter Rockwell was a killer?" He paused and then shouted, "I say not!" He paused again. "If those that would do my Elizabeth harm come here, then let their fate be in our hands. I don't suggest we ward off tourists with their four-wheelers, mountain bikes, and hiking boots. But I do suggest we take action against those that would do my Elizabeth harm, just as Porter Rockwell would."

After another pause, he continued, "Utah is a gun state and we have the God-given right to use them against transgressors. So my friends and neighbors, be watchful and be prepared. Do not hesitate in your action. Remember, we are the greatest army on earth. And the army will support you in your actions. So my friends and neighbors, act swift and act with unmistakable consequence." Jack then looked directly at each man in the congregation, including the County Sheriff, and got a subtle nod.

ELIZABETH WAS SO PROUD OF HER FATHER. SHE squeezed Tommy's hand to share her fulfillment. Tommy just looked at her strangely. It was against the rules but nonetheless, she pulled out her cell phone and texted Reed: "We are safe. Do not worry."

Chapter 22

Sunday—Paper

Reed slept well. Sleep hadn't been a possibility over the past few days. The Huntsville correction facility duty officer decided to let Reed sleep in and then provided him with a special late breakfast. Reed felt rested and better fed than he had in days. After breakfast, two officers escorted Reed to the interrogation room. They were cordial and even tried some small talk along the way. His attorney, Pete Matheson, was already in the room waiting for him when they opened the door and let Reed enter. Pete was reviewing legal paperwork spread out in front of him. He turned to greet Reed with a broad smile.

"Good morning," he offered and then stood to shake hands. Pete didn't bother with small talk and got right to the matter at hand. Reed could sense that Pete was pleased with himself.

Before Reed made it to his chair, Pete proudly said, "You'll be out by noon."

"Excellent. How did you do it?"

"Well, first I got your assault charge for Mr. Henson dropped. They should have never left you in the cell knowing that you had allegedly assaulted Mr. Henson, especially since they had it on video with documented time and date. I told them it was Mr. Henson who assaulted you and challenged them to let me see the video for the two nights you were in there with him. They said it showed nothing because it was after lights out. All the video shows is Mr. Henson sitting on the bench almost the entire time. I was assured that the only interaction between you and Mr. Henson was the one incident captured on the video. But it didn't matter, Mr. Henson agreed that it was only a minor disagreement and he didn't want to make an issue out of it. The Huntsville PD then agreed to drop the charge."

Reed was relieved, but at this point, Tommy was his concern. "What about Kuoto? And I've got some things to tell you about him, Pete. He isn't who they think he is. He isn't some damn TV salesman. He kidnapped me against my will, threatened me, and probably has Tommy," Reed blurted out.

"Slow down. How does Mr. Kuoto have Tommy? You told me Tommy was safe. In fact, you refused to tell me where he was?"

"He was with my ex-wife and Kuoto killed her. Now Kuoto has him."

"No, no, no. Stop it, Reed," interjected Pete with confusion. "Your ex-wife was killed by a fourteen-year-old punk and they got him. The medical examiner got the punk's semen as evidence. They found the knife in a dumpster and it had the punk's fingerprints and her blood on it. He pawned her jewels and personal stuff and they got it on video and with the pawn ticket. And they have more."

"I don't care," shouted Reed. "Kuoto did it. I know he did."

"No, Reed. We are going to be very careful and only stay with the facts. And I remind you—don't say a word to the Huntsville PD, the DA, or anybody else, especially about what you think Mr. Kuoto may or may not have done."

"You're not listening Pete! I don't know how he did it, but he did. And now he has Tommy."

"I can only deal with facts. What facts have you got?

"The fact is," he paused. "I sent Liz and Tommy to Atlanta to hide them from Kuoto. Now my ex-wife is dead and they're gone. Kuoto has to have them. He's even going to kill an eleven-year-old black girl to prove he's serious."

"Are you hearing what you are saying? You sound like a rambling lunatic. Get yourself back on track here Reed. Mr. Kuoto has returned to Los Angeles. Your wife's killer is in jail. And I'm trying to get you out on bail, on a Sunday, in Southern Baptist country. I don't want to hear any more of it. Do you understand me?"

"Okay Pete," conceded Reed.

"Now, your bail hearing is in one hour. They'll come get you and take you next door to the courthouse in about forty-five minutes. It is all just a formality at this point and should take less than sixty seconds. It'll be one hundred grand, which is a bargain, so don't even consider complaining. I'm posting ten grand with the bail bondsman for you. It'll be on your bill with interest. At the hearing, you just say 'yes your honor' when spoken to and nothing more. If you say one word about your Kuoto suppositions, they'll march you right back here to jail. Do it right and you walk out in an hour; keep this rambling up and you won't. It's that simple. Do you understand?"

"Sure, Pete. I'll behave."

"I'm going to meet with your bail bondsman and I'll see you at the hearing." Pete pulled his papers together in an organized folder, stood, and then handed an envelope to Reed. "This came urgent for you. The guard at the front desk opened and inspected it. I guess it's okay for me to leave it with you."

Pete walked to the door, pressed the buzzer, and was gone. Reed stared at the door as it closed and then looked down at the opened envelope. He slid the newspaper out and his heart froze. He mumbled, "Please God no," as he stared at the front page. He slid down in his chair. It was five minutes, maybe ten, Reed didn't know until the shock wore off and he began to read. It was sanitized but he could read between the lines. Kuoto was good to his word. He finished the front page and flipped to find the continuation, but the page had been oddly folded. Reed used his fingernail to catch the edge of the paper and pull it from what had appeared to be just a fold. As he unfolded the page, a photo dropped face down on the table. Reed's hand shook, but he had to know. He picked up the photo. As Reed slowly turned it over, he screamed and broke down into all-out tears. The picture was horrifying by itself but the words, "TOMY BOY," hurt the most.

Two correction officers escorted Reed from the interrogation room, down the hall, and out a side exit that provided direct access to the courthouse. Reed carried the photo discreetly concealed by the newspaper. The courthouse was empty except for voices coming from the open door to courtroom number one. He was led to the defendant's table and seated next to Pete. One of the officers removed Reed's handcuffs.

Pete turned to him, handed him another envelope, and said, "I took the liberty of signing for your personal effects: keys, wallet, cell phone."

"Thanks," replied Reed and handed Pete the photo in exchange.

At that moment the judge came in and the bailiff started to say "All rise," but the judge snapped, "Skip it."

"We have before us a motion to post bail at one hundred thousand dollars in the case of the State of Alabama versus Reed Delahe," boomed the Judge. "Any objections from the prosecution? With a shake of the head and "no your honor" from the prosecutor, the judge said, "So granted," and charged out of the courtroom.

Pete studied the photo momentarily and then quickly turned it over. He stared at Reed with a bewildered look as Reed put his keys and wallet in his pocket, put on his wristwatch, and then looked at his phone. The battery was nearly dead, but it came to life, just momentarily to reveal a text. The message read, "We are safe. Do not worry."

Chapter 23

Sunday Morning—Recon

Cole left his apartment, cautiously working his way down the stairwell and, after momentarily pausing to gain comfort with the police car out front, slipped out the door and around the corner. He headed down 75th Street, going nowhere in particular but looking for just the right scene.

The condition of buildings got worse the farther he went. He stopped to study a possibility. Graffiti markings were exactly what he was looking for: "BOS," "BGD," pitchfork symbols, six-point stars, "BLOOD," and a variety of indecipherable scribblings. All of which advertised Disciple's territory. It was a deteriorated, white, three-story building with maybe five apartments per floor, each with two front windows. There was a floor below ground, but it probably only had three apartments. A fire escape located at the center of the building provided egress from the top two floors. Directly under it was the only visible entrance to the building. Two of the apartments on the first floor had plywood for windows and windows in the other first-floor apartments had been blacked out. The floor below ground also had plywood windows. Window-mount AC units protruded out from a few of the upstairs windows and were running, but those were the only sounds coming from the building. It was lifeless and quiet, as was the street behind him; it was still too early for the activity Cole hypothesized. Cole paused in front of the building imagining the interior layout: center stairwell, hallway on each floor providing access to the front apartments, and matching set on the backside of the building.

He envisioned entry and quickly moving to the second floor where, in any given apartment, he might find a Disciple still asleep. Perhaps he would find a flock of hookers clinging to each other in a large bed. Their door would be locked from the outside to keep them from wandering off in the middle of the night, resulting in lost income for their masters. If the Disciples were running drugs out of the building, they would have them hidden and under guard. At this early hour, it would probably be a single century outside a locked door with at least one more inside sleeping; both would be heavily armed. The situation was manageable but would require extreme silence. But just how many? Too many unknowns, he concluded. Entry was just wrong. One misstep or incorrect assumption and he could find himself cornered like a white supremacist facing an army of Disciples with AKs.

Cole put his hands in his pockets and walked on. Temperature was moderate but the humidity had to be pushing a hundred, which would probably keep people with AC units inside today. He needed to find a neighborhood that didn't have AC units. He walked farther down 75th and then down a one-way side street, not much wider than an alley. The neighborhood deteriorated quickly as he approached Starrett City and he soon found what he was looking for. What was once some kind of business with frontage on 69th Street, had access from the side street that was now used for a different type of business. At one time, it may have been a bakery or some kind of small business with large metal doors hinged to a scarred and worn red brick wall. Much to his delight, Cole could see a home security video camera above the first door. Its blue light was apparent, meaning it was active. The camera angled downward at whoever was standing directly in front of the door.

The building wall was tall, maybe as much as two or two and a half stories but there were no windows or anything suggesting access to an upper floor. In its day, the business used the metal doors to bring in supplies and ship out products. It probably had a jumble of scrap baking or light manufacturing equipment inside extending upward a story and a half. From a distance, Cole could see jagged cut slots at waist height in both doors. Cole maintained his pace and approached the first door. It was of heavy iron construction with no evidence of hinges or pinned flanges, which meant it opened inward. With no door handle or exterior lock, the door had to be secured from inside. The metal door had a twelve-by-four-inch slot in the center. At the top of the door, almost perfectly centered, a pitchfork had been scrolled in textbook Disciple graffiti. As Cole passed the door, he looked down trying to get a peek through the slot; it was dark and quiet inside. The second door was similar to the first, including a slot, except it had no surveillance camera.

Cole envisioned the process. A car would pull up at the first door and a runner would take the order and cash. The runner would feed the cash through the slot in the door and place the order. Then, as the car crept forward, the runner, or perhaps a second runner, would retrieve the order from the second door and make the delivery. It could be meth, coke, H, reds, or any number of drugs. The car would pull away, make an easy right on 69th, and quickly disappear into traffic. The occupants could then return to some upscale neighborhood with their goods, never having to leave the security of their car. The runners outside were sacrificial, probably juveniles, while those behind the doors were the seasoned dealers. In the event of a bust, the runners would be easily run down and the focus of the cops. By the time the cops breached the heavy steel doors, whoever was inside would have escaped by a pre-established route. And that's what Cole needed to figure out.

Starrett City is New York's worst of the worst housing projects with an inexhaustible supply of distraught people seeking relief from life's trials through a temporary high. This location satisfied that market. And

Brian David Simmons

with easy access to 69th, it also served more affluent New Yorkers with a vehicle. It was perfect from the Disciple's point of view, concluded Cole.

Cole emerged on 69th Street and looked up at the narrow front of the building. Faded lettering suggested it was once some kind of restaurant supply company. It was boarded up solid, providing no opportunity for entry. However, between the supply building and the next one, there was a narrow four-foot walkway full of trash and cardboard boxes. Cole looked both ways down 69th. Traffic was light and no one was paying attention to him; he entered the walkway. As Cole stepped around the first cardboard box, he realized it had an occupant. Cole froze. He could hear a person breathing and watched an exposed hand for signs of movement. Cole crept past, placing each foot carefully to avoid disturbing the clutter. He approached a second person sitting along the wall with his arms folded and head down. This person was male and had graying unkempt hair. The figure was gaunt and Cole estimated his stature at five-ten, one hundred thirty pounds. Neither one of these people was of interest, but then they could be alert sentries of some sort. He placed one foot between the man's splayed legs and then quietly stepped past. The walkway continued to the back of the restaurant supply building, which had a wooden door at the back corner. The door opened inward, similar to the metal doors, but this one had a door handle and an external padlock. A similar wooden door, providing access to the adjacent building, was directly across the walkway. Cole assessed the Disciples' egress options: out the wooden door and into the adjacent building or a four-foot leap across building tops. Cole looked up and concluded that was how he would do it.

Cole slipped through the ajar door in the adjacent building and quickly interrogated its darkened interior. He surmised it was once a furniture store with a showroom and warehousing on the first floor and the owner's residence or offices on the second. He found a roof access and stood a dilapidated desk on end so he could reach the access door. Working at arm's length, Cole pried off an aging lock with his knife. He verified the access door's function and then, in one quick motion, ratcheted the squeaking door all the way open. The opening was small and Cole wasn't sure his shoulders would fit through, even diagonally. He would have to go through the opening one arm at a time, which even with his strength would be a challenge. Height of the upended desk just wasn't enough; Cole could just barely reach the edge of the opening with his fingertips. He needed another foot or two, but there was nothing else sturdy enough to support his weight.

With limited options, Cole decided to move on and further survey the rest of the building. Interesting that it only had one rear entrance and, like the restaurant supply building, the front was nailed up tight.

This building was a trap with no egress option. The Disciples were seasoned criminals and Cole surmised that this building with its rear door just barely ajar was just a ploy to divert the cops. Assuming the Disciples would make their escape across the top, there had to be more to the escape route.

Cole crept back out the door and passed the two sleeping walkway residents. Back on 69th, he continued past the abandoned furniture store to the next corner; the building was continuous but the roofline dropped several feet leaving at least a twelve-foot ceiling for the Huy Nu Chang Noodle Company cafe on the corner. Cole followed the building around the corner and peered in the windows of the cafe. It was a tiny Chinese restaurant with only two tables, a small bar area, and a kitchen-serving window. It could have roof access in the kitchen, which was out of sight from the windows. The dealers could have some pre-arranged agreement that allowed them to drop into the kitchen and then just walk out the front door. An auto repair shop occupied the rear of the building and advertised twelve to twelve hours, hence its name: Midnight Auto. It had a single rollup door for cars and a small office entrance door. Cole peered through the office door window. The office was small with a single desk, chair, and sofa. There was no computer, television, or anything of visible value, although the door did have an alarm system as indicated by the keypad on an interior wall. The sidewalk out front was grease-laden. Cole concluded it was a functional shop and the alarm system was to protect mechanics' tools in the shop behind the rollup door. But this mechanic's shop was it, Cole sensed. They probably parked their vehicle inside, or maybe just at the curb, every afternoon and then walked around the corner, down the walkway, and into their place of business. If they had NYPD visitors, the dealers would escape across the roof, drop into the shop through a roof access, and then drive off in their car, all before the NYPD even breached one of the metal doors on the restaurant supply building.

Excluding the sacrificial runners, Cole put their minimum number at two, with a maximum number of five. It would take two inside to man the doors and then two or three more for supervision and shift relief. Two would not be a problem, five would. He would have to change the odds up front. Cole blew through his fist as he formulated a plan. He strolled down the street back towards 75th and the building from his earlier reconnaissance. He got a glimpse of the back of the three-story building and reaffirmed his initial conclusion: this was not a building to be entered.

Cole didn't return immediately to his apartment. Instead, he walked straight to a small hardware store and purchased a dozen paintbrushes, two quarts of turpentine, a package of fifty extra-long electrical zip-ties, a razor knife, white and black spray paint, five plastic tarps, bleach, and a tool bag. Cole saw a question form in the clerk's mind about why so many paintbrushes, but then she let it go. Shopping items bagged, he rode the Seven for only one stop and got off. New Yorkers are inattentive to their surroundings as they travel their familiar routes and none of them took notice of him. He continued a careful vigil, wearing his mask and watching for those who might be watching him as he made his way back to his apartment.

Cole sat against his living room wall, stared at his tool bag, and played through the events that would follow. Just like Mexico, he would become the target. How good were Bling-man, Pocket-boy, and Tiger-fan, he wondered? Could he take all three? They were big men who carried themselves well and no doubt seasoned for battle. His thoughts wandered to Julie and the promised baseball game. This afternoon's distraction would be the last.

Chapter 24

Sunday—Baseball

Cole stared at the tram window as the Seven rocked its way toward Willet's Point and Citizen's Field. He remembered the reflection of her face in the window: the shifting of her eyes, the unseen little smile, and the slight curl of her lips beneath the mask. The subtle twitch of her cheek was interesting. Was it a 'tell,' he considered? Then dismissed the thought and replaced it with the lure of her beauty.

Cole checked his perimeter for anyone who looked even slightly threatening, but this was a happy train full of Mets fans. Yesterday the Mets beat the Rockies five to two and the crowd was looking forward to another win today. The train slowed and pulled into the elevated platform. The doors opened and Cole moved with the crowd. The mass of people charged down the stairs and out into the open expanse leading to Citizen's Field. Cole made his way towards the entrance and spotted her from a distance. She was wearing a Colorado Rockies jersey; how could she, he thought?

She was as beautiful as ever with the near black hair mystically hiding her eyes and her perfect shape was obvious even with the baggy jersey. Cole neared and thought he saw a hint of a smile, but then she turned and looked back toward the stadium. When she turned back, Cole was within twenty feet and she recognized him instantly with a huge smile. She called out to him and waved, "Hey Bob."

The Rockies jersey was unbuttoned revealing a tight-fitting white top showing just enough to let Cole's imagination compose the remainder of her hidden features. She wore blue denim jeans stretched tight over her small shape revealing powerful leg muscles.

"Great to see you again," he replied and then reached for her hand as he neared. She let him take it in a kind of odd handshake, but then she stepped near and gave Cole a pleasant little hug. His passions soared with her touch and he felt a tingle flush through to his toes. He hadn't known anything as exhilarating since Dominique. Julie stepped back and began to speak without realizing what she had just done to him.

"I've been watching the crowd," she said. "I never realized how big a crowd baseball drew. I think there have been at least ten thousand people walk right past me."

"Anybody walked past that didn't just keep going?" asked Cole as he put his senses back on alert.

"No," she said. "Some folks smoking a cigarette before going through the gate is all; pretty harmless, except for their health and pocketbook."

"Interesting Jersey," commented Cole, and then asked, "Are you a Rockies fan?"

"Not really. It was on sale by a street vendor selling bottled water, caps, and jerseys. It looked like everyone else was wearing some kind of fan-wear. I thought I might as well join the crowd. But I think I picked the wrong team."

"You did. And you couldn't stick out more."

"Should I get rid of it?"

"It wouldn't help. You would still stick out." She smiled at his compliment and Cole smiled back.

"Okay, but I may still abandon it if it gets much hotter."

"Excellent. Shall we?" said Cole as he gestured towards the gate. They entered through the main gate with home plate tickets and were directed to a doorman up a very short set of stairs. The doorman re-checked their tickets and then opened the door admitting them to a private bar area. As they passed through the bar area, Cole breathed a sigh of relief. The Mets provided four levels of security between the general public and the sanctuary of the Gold Zone. Their tickets were checked a third time and then a fourth when they were met by an usher who showed them to their seats: three rows up and directly behind home plate. Julie plopped into a leather seat that was designed to accommodate a person three times her size. A waiter appeared and took their order. It was beer and bratwursts, just as Cole had promised.

The first pitch was thrown and Cole promptly corrected the umpire. Julie was entertained. They laughed and by the third inning, Julie was helping Cole correct the umpire. Cole had a second beer and Julie had a margarita before the seventh inning. The Mets were up by four and Cole was confident the Mets would end the afternoon victorious. Julie shed her Rockies jersey in the afternoon heat and he was now certain to be the envy of every man around him. Cole excused himself to make a pit stop and left Julie to continue with umpire corrections.

THE METS BATTER TOOK A CALLED THIRD STRIKE and the ump made a fist. Julie yelled, "What kind of call was that! That was at least a foot outside. Get real ump!" Her smartphone rang.

As the roar of the crowd faded, she answered, "Hello." But there was silence on the other end. She inquired, "Hello is there somebody there?" She looked at the incoming number, but it strangely displayed her own number, "Hello," she inquired again and was about to terminate the call when she thought she heard a response, "Hi."

A pickoff move to first had just resulted in a second Mets out and the background noise from the crowd became deafening. "What?" she challenged.

"Hi."

"Who is this?" she shouted into the phone.

"I have a message for Cole."

"Who is this?"

"I have a message for Cole. Actually, I wanted to know if your voice was as beautiful as your picture."

"I'm going to hang up. Who is this?"

"No, No. Just tell Cole he has a pickup."

"Okay, tell me who you are and I'll tell Cole."

"It's a little more complicated than that. The average storage capacity for short-term memory is seven items. How good is your memory?"

"That's it. I'm hanging up."

"No, No. This is life and death. Trust me."

"I don't even know who you are. How am I supposed to trust you?"

"Are you ready? This is important. You have to relay this message to Cole exactly as I give it to you."

"Who is this?" she demanded.

"Code, are you ready?"

"No code and no message unless you tell me who you are. You got that."

"It's life and death. Don't you care?"

"Then tell me who I am talking to."

There was a pause and a slow quiet response, "Kevin. Just tell Cole." And then he followed more commandingly, "This is code. You need to have a good memory."

"What is this; some kind of game or something?"

"That's exactly what it is. Now, how good is your memory?

"Excellent."

"Okay then. Here it comes. Repeat it back to Cole exactly as I give it to you. Ready?"

"Sure."

"Remember it in months: June, January, September, April, July, April. Picture it in front of the bar: one, three, two, four, one, seven, five and ends in twenty. Picture it burning, turn around. First word—first and last letters are the first two. What do you put in your ear?" Kevin paused and then asked, "You got that?"

"No."

"Why not?"

"I didn't understand a thing you said?"

"You disappoint me. I'll repeat it for you one more time. But this is it. Remember it!" Kevin went through it again and then added, "Repeat it to Cole, exactly." And then Kevin disconnected.

Julie closed her eyes and played it back in her mind. June, January, September, April, July, and April were obviously month equivalents for numerals. But the rest was just gibberish. She concentrated and hoped she could string it all together for Cole. She played it again and struggled. Was it burning in front of the bar—no it was picture it and picture it burning. One thirty-two, four seventeen, and five, she recounted and hoped she would get it right. Where the heck was Cole?

Cole wasn't long and sat back next to her only a few moments after the call ended but it seemed like an hour as she fought to retain the confused message.

"I got a call from Kevin," she announced.

Cole looked at her with a puzzled look on his face. "What did he say?"

"He gave me some kind of strange code."

"Okay. What was it?"

"I hope I get it right," she said timidly. "Months, no—remember it in months: June, January, September, April, July, April."

Cole held up his hand and she paused. He took a pen from his fanny pack and scribbled numbers on a napkin. "Go ahead," he encouraged. Julie relayed the message as best she could recall and Cole continued to write.

When she finished, he looked at her for a moment and then commented, "You have just been tested. Kevin likes to do that kind of shit."

"What is the code?"

"It's just an address."

"Really?" she replied as he gave her a millisecond glimpse of the napkin.

"How did you get that from my ramblings of burning and a bar?"

Cole avoided a direct answer and subtly questioned her, "He gave you his name? That is strange. Kevin is normally absolutely secretive."

She watched Cole warily fold the napkin and put it in his fanny pack. "He said he wanted to know if my voice was as pretty as my picture. Did you send him something?"

"I did."

"Okay, so what about this code business?" she pressed.

"It's an interpersonal code that only Kevin and I share. For example, you and I have a code that only we share. Consider: first date—home team's first two letters, the word AND, and visitor team's first letter plus three. Did you get it?"

"Let's see. Me, from Mets? The word "and." And U from the Rockies R plus three. That's 'Me and U,'" she concluded and clapped her hands.

"Simple, huh?"

"Yes, it is. So the only question is; did I get Kevin's message right?"

"I'll see. This game is pretty much over with the Mets up by four," said Cole and stood.

She thought about pressing for more about Kevin but that would be pushing her luck. This was a secretive relationship between the two of them and she had already learned more than expected. Julie followed him to the exit. She remembered Prospect and Bronx from the napkin but couldn't recall the number from her brief look at the napkin.

Liu Chen texted Kevin: "You have an interesting friendship."

Kevin texted back but Liu was off in thought. Internal yearnings were again developing deep within her. Kevin had a parallel life: one that resided in the world of cyber technology and then another with an absolute, unyielding bond to this peculiar friend. The cyberworld was her commonality with Kevin. But Kevin's second life was strangely rousing and stirred feelings she had never felt before. There was much more to

Kevin than she had ever expected. And the revelation was super-fueling a desire for something more.

But no—never, that wasn't going to happen. She drew on the reality of her physical characteristics and mental psyche to counteract the absolutely unacceptable thought. Liu wished she had done more about her weight; her body was far from a supermodel hourglass shape. Not only was it unshapely, but it also had other imperfections: a birthmark that never fully faded away, some other unattractive skin spots, and a few moles, one that was in a particularly embarrassing location. And her skin had never seen rays from the sun. A bikini was not even a remote possibility and a man seeing even that much was absolutely out of the question. And no man ever had, not even in college. Her body would forever stay hidden behind the colorful clothing that made her feel acceptable.

On top of that, a real relationship meant intimacy. It meant uninhibited sharing and unification. The thought absolutely terrified her. Isolation had been her security in life and it was embodied in her very essence. How could she just all of a sudden change? No, it just couldn't happen.

The internal battle continued to tear her apart. On the verge of tears, Liu covered her face with both hands. Was she just being overly self-conscious? Was she just giving in to irrational fear? She liked Kevin. But no, it just couldn't be.

Chapter 25

SUNDAY—JULIE'S PROBLEM

COLE EXITED THE BALLPARK WITH JULIE ON HIS ARM.
As he covertly surveyed the crowd, he noticed heads
turning to watch her. Being with her, he had almost
forgotten that his future was an unknown and this
was going to be goodbye, at least for the foreseeable
future. His thoughts transitioned to this evening's
reconnaissance challenge and a calling card, of sorts,
he would present to the Disciples.

They strolled across the parking lot towards the
tram station and she interrupted his thoughts. "I have
to tell you something," she started and then paused.
"Do you know what I do for a living?"

"No. Not anything more than you work for the New
York State Tax Authority."

"I am a special investigator assigned to tobacco
products."

"A cop of sorts?"

"Yes. But after last night with my two watchers in
the parking lot, I decided to do something I've been
thinking about for months. They know what I've been
working on and, if I had waited any longer, I don't
know what would happen. So this morning I remoted
my work computer and sent out a summary report
to the Governor's office. It means my life will change

tomorrow morning. I will get fired for bypassing the hierarchy, which is the least that will happen. But I think they are all involved. Hopefully, the Governor's office will act."

"Okay. What are they involved in?"

"The state of New York collects over three billion a year in cigarette tax at a rate of $9.85 per pack. Each pack gets a tax stamp authorizing it for sale in New York." She stopped halfway across the parking lot before continuing, "I shouldn't be telling you this. I don't know why I feel I can trust you."

Cole studied her eyes. Her bangs laid across her eyes with just the right eye fully visible. It was slightly moist and he sensed her distress. He reached out and touched the side of her face and she instantly collapsed into his chest. Her arms stretched around him and held him tight. He responded by holding her ever tighter. The embrace lasted for minutes and Cole again felt the tingling that this woman brought.

She quietly spoke, "I have no one to talk to; no one to trust. I think they are all in on it."

"So talk to me," Cole softly consoled.

She gently separated from the embrace and moved back a half step. She looked at him and confided, "I have evidence that members of the State Tax Authority are importing cigarettes from Mississippi at less than three dollars a pack and providing them wholesale at a discount, complete with an official appearing tax stamp. This fiscal year they have cheated New York out of over nine million dollars. They know I know and have been watching me. It's some kind of intimidation tactic they thought would shut me up."

"So now the Governor's office can take action. Did you name names?"

"Only two, but that's just the beginning. I have circumstantial information on six others, including my boss."

"All right, let's go. I'll make sure you get home safe."

She smiled at him with a girlish grin and timidly asked, "You might stay for another beer?"

"I might but I have some things to do tonight."

"Like what?" she abruptly inquired.

"Business—personal business. So don't ask. I won't tell you. It has to be done tonight," Cole said sternly.

Julie seemed content with the answer and went back to taxes. New York had the highest tax rate in the nation on tobacco products, collecting from authorized wholesalers who issued the tax stamps. You had to be a licensed tobacco distributor or wholesaler if you sold tobacco products within the State. Retail dealers got their products from wholesalers who had to register each outlet location.

Multiple levels within her department were involved in hiding untaxed cigarettes authorized for sale by duplicating tax stamp authorizations. A single, traceable stamp authorization for a lot of cigarettes would be issued by the State Tax Authority to two different wholesalers: one legit, the other not. The second authorization provided stamps for untraceable cigarettes purchased in Mississippi. The wholesaler receiving the Mississippi cigarettes didn't realize he was getting illegal products, even though they were sometimes given special discounts. The result was that each $9.85 per pack could be split between eight people in her organization. And the $9.85 per pack added up fast. She had evidence against an IT person and a field inspector with circumstantial ties to the other six.

None of her story surprised Cole; he rather expected it of officials at all levels and admired Julie for taking a stand. But filing a report, even with the Governor's office, wouldn't be effective and accomplish nothing compared to what other methods had to offer.

She continued to talk until they reached the stairs to the el and then he saw her senses engage. She had been oblivious to her surroundings the entire walk from the stadium but now she was surveying the crowd. He too had been somewhat disconnected from their surroundings while he listened to her talk; he loved the sound of her voice. The station was full of people seeking an early escape from the masses that would follow when the game ended. He judged each one as they stood waiting for the next train; Cole identified no threats and relaxed.

The train arrived and they squeezed inside the claustrophobic environment. He didn't appreciate being confined with so many people but he enjoyed having her press hard against his side and he put his arm around her. He was a full head taller than she was, which meant she must have felt confined. The train rattled onward to the first stop and the crowd thinned; she didn't back away into the available space but instead slipped her arm across his back and firmly pulled him closer. He smiled.

At her stop, they exited the train and both interrogated the people in the station. She looked at him and smiled before descending the stairs. Cole had already devised a plan to get her safely to her apartment. "You go first. I'll follow at a distance and watch your rear."

"I bet you will," she seductively whispered and started off.

He started at twenty-five paces behind her and slowed to let the distance increase slightly. And he did watch her suggestive walk, which led to thoughts of what might have been. Could she be the one? They could flee to a farm he owned in Hungary and spend long hours under an oversized comforter. They could go to the Caribbean and frolic in the sun on the beach. She has to look really good in a bikini, he envisioned. She might even accept his past, except for her righteous attitude towards simple bureaucratic crooks. Would she accept his past actions as righteous or heinous, he pondered? But she was a distraction. Maybe someday in the distant future, their paths would again cross, that is, if he survived the next few days. But only then; he had to re-focus.

Cole slowed and turned his head sideways, just far enough to capture traffic coming up to his rear in his peripheral vision: minivans, taxis, a black Chrysler, a faded red Toyota, and several other unidentifiable cars. No one was nearby on the sidewalk. It all seemed clear. He increased his pace a little as she neared her building. When she reached the corner, he was only ten paces behind her. She disappeared from his sight for only seconds before he came around the corner.

He watched her as she made her walk into the apartment building and up the stairs. All was good.

Chapter 26

PRIVATE COMMUNICATIONS

COLE RETURNED TO THE SEVEN PLATFORM AND boarded the next tram. Fading remnants of daylight radiated in the twilight over the building roofs. Cole transferred to the Five at the 28th Street station. He studied people in the train: Black, White, Oriental, representing all economic levels of life. A man in a three-piece suit stood next to a small man dressed in shabby street clothes. Here on this train, the only difference between them was just the clothes they wore. He discreetly continued his interrogation. Conversation was always a minimum on the trams, with each person in their own private little world; perhaps they were thinking about the day's events, the post-Covid world, what was for dinner, or Sunday's baseball game.

Colt turned to the man next to him and asked, "Hey, did you see today's game?"

The man looked at him with surprise but then smiled, "I didn't, but I understand the Mets won."

"You wouldn't know the score, would you?"

"Yeah, seven to six. The ninth was intense. Score tied in the bottom, two outs, and two strikes on Rodgers with Tolman on second. Rodgers drove a single up the right-field line and they waved Tolman on to home. It was a close play at home; the throw from right was dead on but Tolman slid wide and raked his left hand across the plate."

"Wow, wish I'd been there to see that!"

The tram lurched to a stop at Pelham Parkway. Cole introduced himself as Bob. They bumped fists and Cole got off of the tram. The clock was ticking and Cole had a lot of ground to cover tonight. He took off in a near run, but not so much that he would attract attention. He checked traffic to his rear, both pedestrian and automotive. He intensely interrogated every window, person, and car as he covertly made the circuitous route to the address on Prospect Street. The neighborhood was clean and nice. The narrow street was clean and the sidewalks looked swept. Small two-story homes, some with common walls, lined both sides of the street.

Cole approached the address and studied the building. It was a small 1970s-style, all brick, build-ing. It had a single narrow door on the right and a wider front window on the left, both protected by security bars. Upstairs, two windows matched the width of the door and window below. Each of the openings had an awning providing shade and rain protection. The edge of two satellite dishes showed above the decorative roof outline. The house had an alley on the left with a small subgrade window sug-gesting a basement of some kind. An unattractive white-sided home of approximately the same size shared a common wall on the right. The front of the small brick house was guarded by a freshly painted black wrought iron fence. The enclosure contained trash and recycle garbage containers. Cole considered options for egress and imagined what the backside of the building might look like. Unknowns and potential lack of egress options meant he wasn't going to enter.

Cole crossed the street and stepped up to the gate of the wrought iron fence. As he pushed a small white buzzer button, he noticed the small video surveillance camera discreetly hidden in the light fixture next to the door. The electromagnetic release on the gate buzzed almost instantly and bumped open an inch or two; Cole entered.

He was greeted at the front door by a slightly heavyset Oriental woman, probably in her thirties and dressed in wild colors. Her radical dress included swirls of pink, purple, and green, and revealed a rather large cleavage. The dress hung down below her knees and she was wearing pink and purple high-top tennis shoes. Her shoulder-length blonde hair was bluntly trimmed to just frame her face. Her slightly plump face sported a pair of glasses with a flared and diamond-embedded frame. She wore just a hint of eyeliner and a very light pink lipstick. In a peculiar sort of way, she was quite attractive. Strangely, she also somehow reminded him of Kevin.

The woman smiled at him but kept him at the front door. "Bob?" she timidly asked.

Cole kept his head slightly turned from the surveillance camera in the light fixture and replied, "Yes,
I am. I think you have something for me."

With obvious trepidation, the woman very quietly
said, "I am supposed to ask what this is before I give
it to you."

Damn Kevin he thought, everything has to be
code, and everything has to be a test. Cole thought
about it for a moment and then replied, "Private communications. Let's try that."

"Just making sure," she said as she handed him a
satellite phone. "It is all programmed and ready to go.
Kevin said you would know the number and to call
us as soon as you picked it up."

Cole's senses immediately went on high alert as
he picked up on "call us." Something wasn't right.
He subtly glanced down the street in both directions
and then tried to capture detail beyond the partially
open door.

But then she handed him a small suitcase and
added, "These are the other items Kevin said you
wanted."

It was too late to back out now and Cole had no
option but to play along, "Thank you. How much do
I owe you?"

"Oh, no. Kevin already took care of that," the
woman said.

"I guess I should have figured that," conceded Cole
as he slowly and cautiously backed away from the front

door. With his senses on maximum alert, he exited through the wrought iron gate to begin his circuitous trek back to the station.

Cole glanced over his shoulder and began punching numbers into the encrypted satellite phone as he walked. No threats were apparent but the phone call would have to be very careful and alert Kevin to the "call us" slip of the tongue by the woman.

Liu Chen returned to her computer room and sat back down on the couch. Adding to a long string of text messages, Liu texted: "Why didn't U want me to tell him about us?"

Kevin texted back: "It's too soon to tell him U are helping. Better he doesn't know for a while."

Liu texted: "K. When????"

Kevin texted: "Time will come."

Kevin was ready for the satellite phone buzz. He quickly answered and blurted out, "You were right!"

Cole tried to interrupt but Kevin just continued. "We have at least three people in the room when the pictures of that little girl were taken. The pictures have some almost imperceptible reflections and shadows, almost beyond recognition unless you take the photo apart digitally. Then you have to use algorithms to supplement between pixels and sharpen image boundaries, which makes clear images unnatural. But it enhances those that are more subtle. Basically, outlines are artificially darkened. I uploaded them.

Take a look. Work still needs to be done to take into account shadows, improve resolution, and reassemble a digital two-D representation. With that, it should be clear exactly how many of them there were and what they look like."

"Slow down Kevin," requested Cole.

"No, listen. The best image we got came from the reflection off a glass-covered four-by-six picture on the dresser. You are not going to believe this. I can make out a full image of a guy in some kind of a contamination suit and he's next to a half image of some guy without one. The contamination suit is some kind of full body covering with only the eyes showing. Look at it on your phone; it's scary, eerie shit right out of hell."

"Kevin, you need to know. There may be an 'us' on this call."

"Maybe."

"You got it covered then?"

"Sure."

"Okay, so you got my gang boys in Samantha's bedroom. They went there with purpose and they came prepared. They were sending some kind of message: the broom meant something, her legs meant something, and the carving meant something. The message had to be for 'Tomy Boy.' You need to focus on finding 'Tomy Boy' and it might go beyond New York. They advertised far and wide sending it to the national media, so this 'Tomy Boy' could be anywhere. See what you can do. I'll focus on the Tigers fan I saw that night."

"How are you going to do that?"

"I'm going to leave a calling card and invite them over for tea, crumpets, and broken legs."

"Understand. You know I get sick when you do that."

"No other way Kevin and you know it. Now in your spare time, I also need you to investigate Julia Addison's boss and coworkers at the New York State Tax Commission. See what you can find out and we'll compare notes based on what Julia told me. Also, check the cloud folder. I posted the plate number of a black Chrysler that I think was following us."

"You like her, don't you?"

"That's none of your business. I'm just concerned about the Chrysler. Call her about the taxes if you want; get the details. Don't tell her anything about our game."

Liu was listening to both sides of the conversation. As soon as Kevin disconnected, Liu texted: "UR so awesome. I've never known anyone like U."

Kevin traded his satellite phone for his Probaris-Lebram and read the text. Kevin didn't know how to respond. The text was quickly followed by another one.

Liu texted: "IWYRN"

Kevin glanced to his right at Liu and texted: "????"

Liu texted: "I WANT YOU RIGHT NOW."

Texting provided comfort and ease of conversation, especially when Liu was near. This text went right past verbal communication directly to intimacy. Is that what she's asking? Kevin cringed and his internal communication barriers squealed, "No." But when Liu touched his hand, Kevin's face turned bright red and he shivered; the touch was electrifying and ignited overwhelming desires. His heart violently accelerated when Liu gently kissed him on the cheek. His inner flame exploded when Liu snuggled closer on the couch and her body was in full contact with his. All breathing stopped when Liu gently placed her hand on his leg. Barriers evaporated and newfound passion violently raced throughout his entire body.

Kevin texted back: "K."

Chapter 27

SURPRISES OF THE HEART

EYEGLASSES WERE THE FIRST TO GO AND FLEW OFF IN haphazard directions. Kevin's heart exploded to increase blood flow to every part of his body as Liu kissed him on the lips. Kevin reacted, fully embracing Liu and pressing his lips hard against hers. His tongue met hers and all thoughts of the world disappeared; it was her and only her. They kissed again and then again. As if by natural instinct, his hand found her breast. He gently slipped his other hand behind her and undid first the clasp and then the zipper on her dress. They continued in passionate kissing and the dress fell from her shoulders.

Passion accelerated and Liu ripped open Kevin's shirt, sending buttons flying. Liu stroked his chest and then slid her hand around to his back. Kevin fought with Liu's bra hooks. They just wouldn't come free. He tugged and pulled until Liu finally had to help. Liu went for Kevin's pants next as he slid her bra from her shoulders.

The coffee table flipped over as it was kicked out of the way. Shoes and remaining clothing went somewhere as they frantically helped each other undress, all the while embracing, touching, and kissing. They fell to the couch in immaculate embrace with Kevin on top. After round one, Liu rolled Kevin to the floor and assumed the top position. "Oh-oh-oh-oh-oh," she cried. Kevin was in utopia with this magical goddess. The magic lasted for an eternity until physical exhaustion overwhelmed them both.

Kevin and Liu just lay on the floor, gently touching each other and enjoying the new found closeness. Kevin was so content, so at peace, and so in love.

COLE RETURNED TO THE TRAM PLATFORM, CHECKED his watch to establish timing, and boarded the train. It took several transfers to get back to the Seven. On each train, he discretely removed a battery-powered cell phone relay from the small suitcase the Oriental woman had given him. He surveyed the riders. When it appeared no one was paying any particular attention, he peeled off the plastic protecting an adhesive layer and attached it to the front wall at eye level. The relay was encased in a bright yellow housing with red "One Year Imprisonment" and "Tamper Prohibited" warnings. In bold red letters, it also read: "CAUTION— MAGNETIC SENSITIVITY—DO NOT REMOVE."

Cole returned to his apartment to find a single police car still parked in front of the opposing building. He changed his clothes and left his suitcase in the apartment before departing to repeat the tracks of his earlier surveillance and establish a timeline.

He had been right about both the drive-up drug distribution center, as well as the Disciples main house.

Both were a buzz of activity. After surveilling the main house, Cole made a test call to Armando to arrange for transportation the following night. The cell phone activated a relay on the Seven train and then transferred to Armando's phone. All was ready for a very special invite to the tea and crumpets party.

Cole returned to his apartment. Sleep was a challenge and he had to force the boiling adrenaline into submission. He desperately needed peace, rest, and sleep. For tomorrow, there would be no rest, much less sleep.

Monday morning came with an incoming phone call. It was Julie. He tried to put her off. But she was emotionally insistent. Cole knew the brief relationship had to end, at least for thirty days. Her timing just couldn't be worse. Julie's persistence won out and, in the end, he agreed to a late lunch.

Cole rolled over to capture desperately needed sleep. But he barely got his eyes closed before another interrupting call came in. It was Kevin.

"Good morning Kevin. Don't you ever sleep?"

"Sure. But we are, I mean, I am still working on the photos," stumbled Kevin. After a short pause, Kevin continued, "I guess I should tell you. I'm getting help with the photos. She . . ."

"What?" Cole interrupted.

"Well, her name is Liu Chen."

"Kevin," Cole paused and blew through his fist as the possibilities flashed through his mind. "How's Tobago? How are Joe and Sylvia doing?"

"Oh, they're fine, at least when I saw them last."

"Kevin, where are you?"

"I'm here—with Liu Chen. That's all you need to know."

Cole blew through his fist as the realization gained clarity, "I think I know more than that, Kevin. I already met Miss Chen. Didn't I?"

"Maybe."

"It's alright, Kevin. I trust you did your homework on her."

"Sure."

"Is Miss Chen business or something more?"

"Maybe."

"Well good for you. Just be careful. Maybe we'll all get together in Tobago when this is over."

"Oh, I called to tell you we got a clean bill of health on Julie Addison. But Liu has some minor things she wants to check."

"Just FYI. We really can't afford the Julie distraction and need to focus on Samantha Ogalsby. We'll screw up if we try to solve too many problems at once. I keep trying to put her off but she's pretty persistent."

"Could we wait on Samantha?" asked Kevin.

"Not a chance! That game is going to play, starting tonight."

"With Liu helping, you'll get plenty of support."

"It's against better judgment, but okay. Get anything on Julie's boss?"

"We're working on it."

"Call me when you do," said Cole and disconnected.

Cole laid out his clothes for this evening's adventure and then dressed for his lunch date with Julie. Everything else went into large garbage bags: sheets, linens, dishes, pots and pans, clothes, toiletries, all of it. The exceptions were a few table knives, a few medical supplies, sandwich bags, his hardware store purchases, and the clothes he'd laid out. Cole made several trips to dispose of it all in the dumpster between his building and Samantha's. On each trip, he was reminded of Samantha and her silly play with little pink ponies and he smiled. But every time he smiled, the terror struck like lightning, and the pleasant thought was banished.

Cole caught the Seven and several stops later got off in the upscale side of Queens, at least it was upscale compared to his apartment complex. He was early and leisurely strolled towards her apartment but his mind was elsewhere.

The plan required a certain amount of intelligence on the part of the Disciples and he wasn't sure they had it. But then again, there was something more to the Detroit fan. He was different from the rest and probably smarter than all the Disciples put together. The preferable option was for the Disciples to come to him because that was easier than tracking down the Detroit fan. Nonetheless, Cole began considering options for plan B if the initial invite didn't work. Thoughts consumed Cole and he forewent the usual interrogation of everyone and everything.

He turned the corner of Julie's apartment building. Julie was laid back in a man's arms; it was the driver from the other afternoon. Julie's mouth was open and her eyes were fighting for cognizance. A small trickle of blood was forming at the edge of her mouth. The driver was in front of her with his back to Cole. The son-of-bitch had just hit her. And he'd hit her hard, hard enough to drive consciousness from her mind. A third man was standing at the back of a black Chrysler with a key fob pointed at the trunk.

Three-on-one: driver and the dangerous passenger from yesterday, along with a new man with a key fob. Their intentions were obvious; Julie was about to go for a ride in the trunk. It wasn't going to happen and Cole didn't hesitate. The passenger's mouth opened to sound the alert as Cole exploded to put himself within arm's length of the driver and Julie. The passenger's body and head started a quick turn to the left as he started to yell: "fu . ." But snapped back to the left as Cole's right fist contacted his jaw with the force of a sledgehammer. The force of impact feedback to Cole's fist told him the passenger would be dead before he hit the ground. Cole's forward momentum along with the rebound from the punch left him out of position to react to the key fob man's reach for what Cole knew was a gun. And the driver was now spinning to throw Julie in his direction.

Cole caught her, whirled 180 degrees with her in his arms, and let her slide to the sidewalk in a slow fall. Cole continued around in a full spin, extended his right arm, and with all his momentum and arm length took a blind backhanded swing at the driver. But he was out of position and the back of his fist just grazed the side of the driver's face. The swing was little more than a distraction for the driver. And now the key-fob man's pistol was now fully visible; it could fire within a half second. Cole was off balance and way out of position; a shot was coming. Cole twisted, planted his right foot, and launched, in flight, at the driver. Cole's shoulder drove into him at waist level with all the mass Cole's body could muster. Like a cue ball grazing the eight ball and dropping it into the pocket, the driver was impacted sideways into the key-fob man, who was just leveling his pistol; it fired. Cole rolled and came up ready. The expression on the key-fob man's face said shock; how could he have shot his buddy? Cole didn't give him time to figure it out; he charged and landed his second real punch of the afternoon, square at his nose; the key-fob man would be lucky to live.

Cole reached down, grabbed the key fob, and then quickly scooped up Julie in his arms. He gently set her in the passenger seat. She was confused and combative when he buckled her seat belt. She swore something unintelligible at him. And then she turned towards him and vomited out the car door. Cole gently held her head as he listened to an approaching siren in the not-too-far-off distance. She retched several times until there was nothing more. He laid her back in the seat, slowly closed her door, and then ran to the other side and jumped in. The shift lever hit drive the instant the engine started and Cole quickly maneuvered the car into position for a left onto the street. He could see flashing lights in the distance and hoped they weren't watching as he pulled out. He stayed at traffic speed and watched the cop car in his rearview mirror pull into the driveway. Cole then floored the car, jerked into the on-coming traffic lane, passed the car in front of him, and then the next, and then the next. He darted out, around, and back in repeatedly until he had put three blocks between them and Julie's apartment building.

Cole turned left on a side street and slowed to a normal pace. He made several lefts and rights to check his mirrors for familiar cars following, but always kept moving in the general direction of Manhattan.

Julie was now becoming slightly coherent and questioned, "What happened?"

"You have a concussion."

"No. I'm fine," and then tugged on her seat belt and went to unbuckle it.

"You are not fine. And you are going to do exactly as I say. Now leave your seat belt on," shouted Cole.

"I'm fine and I'm leaving. You aren't stopping me. I have to find Kevin."

"Julie," Cole shouted. "Relax, give it five minutes. Do you remember what happened?"

"It's all about the show. We have to put on a good show. Don't we?" Julie rambled as drool leaked from the left side of her mouth. "I have to find Kevin."

"You did fine, Julie. Now just relax."

"Oh good," she slurred. "Did we find Kevin?"

Julie had all the signs of a concussion. Cole had experienced one or two himself. Slurred speech, confusion, and combative desire for self-control were all classic signs. She was a mess with vomit in her hair and on her hands. She'd lost bladder control sometime during the concussion. She was human after all, Cole thought.

"It'll be alright Julie," he said and reached over to stroke her cheek with the back of his hand.

She pushed him away and blurted out, "No. I have to find-" and then paused with clarity returning to her eyes, "Where are we?"

"Heading downtown."

"Where?"

She wiped the spit from her face and studied the buildings as they drove past. All of sudden she became embarrassingly aware of her condition and flopped down the visor to look in the mirror. She was a mess and Cole watched her try to pick the vomit out of her hair; had the circumstances been different, he might have laughed. Her expression was so tragic and the task so hopeless, yet she persisted.

Cole picked up the 495 and headed toward Manhattan. By the time they reached the Queens Midtown Tunnel, Julie had pretty much recovered, but remained silent.

Halfway through the tunnel, she finally spoke, "I can't remember," and then paused before continuing, "I look like crap. I'm embarrassed."

"You may never remember exactly what happened and you don't look like crap. You are lucky it was just a mild concussion because the guy who hit you made the decision; he chose knockout over death with his punch. He and his friends just wanted you peaceably in their trunk."

"Who was it?"

"The passenger and driver from the other day, along with a third guy. The driver and the third guy won't be bothering you again and the passenger will never hit another wo…"

"What?" she interrupted.

"It was just one of those things. The passenger was too dangerous. Then, in the confusion of it all, the third man, the new guy, shot the driver so he got his nose broken."

"It can't be. Are they dead?"

"Maybe, I don't know; I didn't ask them."

"This is hardly funny!" she scolded.

"Sorry."

Then confused, she asked, "You did it?"

"Did what?"

"There were three of them? Why would they shoot each other? I don't understand. And who broke the other guy's nose? You? Why do they have guns?"

"Yes, there were three. Bad aim. No, you don't understand and you may never. Yes, I broke his nose. And I don't know if they all had guns."

"You couldn't do that. I mean," she stumbled with her words. "Not that you couldn't, but I mean how? You don't have the training."

Cole replied. "I just survive."

"I still don't understand. How many other things don't I know about you?"

"Probably a few. Everybody has their secrets."

"I suppose," she pondered. "What are we going to do?"

"I'm going to hide you someplace safe for tonight and then tomorrow I'll find out what your boss has to say. Then we'll figure out how to straighten this whole thing out."

"Right," Julie sarcastically replied.

"Right," Cole assertively repeated and looked over at her with conviction.

"You're not going to hurt him, are you?" she questioned but didn't get an answer. "Oh God, they can't be dead. Can they?" she added.

They emerged from the tunnel and Cole took the first exit. She watched the East River as he drove down the FDR towards Stuyvesant Town. He watched the side streets, exited the FDR at 10th, and then backtracked to the J. Brown Park. Parking space was always at a premium and Cole circled. He passed up a parking space at the park and headed west. He passed up two more parking spots and circled the block several times before he found just the right spot. Cole parallel-parked the Chrysler between a utility truck and a Toyota. He got out and hurried around to Julie's door, opening her door and helping her step out.

"Are you all right?"

"I'm fine, but I'm a mess."

"I've got you. Just follow my lead. Can you walk?"

"Yes, but people are staring at me. I must really look bad."

"You look fine. Let's go," said Cole and took her arm. They walked slowly at first and then gradually increased their pace. They walked for nearly three blocks, then over one, and back two. Cole wrapped his arm around her and up under her arm, lifting her nearly off her feet and easing her journey. He could see pain in her eyes as she struggled to physically make the motions. Her feet didn't naturally follow one another in step, which seemed like a concentration problem as well as a physical one. She inquired several times about where he was taking her and why all the lefts and rights. Cole explained to her that it was his last resort for safe hiding in New York. If they were followed and had to flee, the next safest place was Wyoming. She inquired about Kevin. He didn't respond.

They reached an entrance to a fifteen-story build-ing with a combination of apartments and condos. "We're here," he announced. Kevin and Cole owned a condo on the tenth floor that he seldom used but kept as a safe house of sorts. Dominique was the only person, other than Kevin, that had ever been here.

"I hope Kevin has aspirin. My head hurts so bad I can hardly see."

Cole punched the keypad and then held the door for Julie as she stepped inside the air-conditioned lobby. Cole said, "Duck your head and look to the right," as they passed a security camera on the way to the elevator. Cole input a numerical code and the elevator door opened; they stepped inside. Cole inserted his key card and the elevator raced upward. The door opened on the tenth floor and they stepped out. Cole helped her to the condo and let her enter in front of him.

"Wow," she exclaimed.

The door closed behind them and Cole directed, "Aspirin is in the cabinet." He sat her down on the couch before walking into the kitchen area. She took three aspirin and might have taken more if he'd offered; she guzzled a glass of water and asked for another. Cole opened a package of stale saltine crackers and handed her several. She ate them and then a handful more from the package. A good sign, thought Cole.

He touched the side of her face, which now showed signs of bruising, and asked, "Hurt?"

"A little."

"Want ice or something for it?"

"No, but a shower would be great. I am not going to put these clothes back on. And, unless you have some small size, I don't have anything to wear. I don't have a credit card or anything. I feel awkward asking. But, can I ask you to buy me some clothes?"

"Sure. What, what size, and what color? I am pretty sure I can manage."

She provided all the requirements and Cole was off. She had requested white pants a white button-up top, ankle socks, panties, and a sports bra. He selected two of everything Julie had requested, one set meeting her exact specifications and another set meeting his liking, including lingerie. He picked up two sandwiches on his way and was back at the condo within the hour.

Julie was sleeping in the large king-size bed. She had folded the blankets back and was under a single sheet. Cole could see the outline of her naked shape under the sheet and he warmed to the thought of her company. She lay on her side in a partial fetal position with her hip gently rising upward to reveal its smooth contour. He imagined the pleasure they might share and the thought of caressing her smooth shape. Her arms were pulled in tight along with the sheet and her right thumb rested at the edge of her mouth. Cole moved to the side of the bed, delicately swept her hair aside, and checked her breathing; it was slow, steady, and warm. He moved to the other side of the bed and gently placed pillows against her back to keep her on her side, just in case she wasn't quite over the nausea. He then laid out the clothes he had bought at the bottom of the bed, each set of articles laid out together such that she could choose at each stage of dressing.

Cole moved to the dresser, glanced back to verify her eyes were still closed, and then quietly removed the second drawer. He retrieved a sheathed knife with a twelve-inch blade. He looked at Julie again and reconsidered the actions he was about to take tonight, but then the terror and vision of Samantha returned; so did his resolve. Cole replaced the drawer, gathered a change of clothes, and left the bedroom. Cole dressed in the living room, slipping his knife inside his right pull-on boot and hiding the handle under his boot-cut denims. An all-black, long-sleeved, warrior-wear shirt stretched over his shoulders and arms and a black ball cap hid his hair.

He wrote a note instructing Julie to be ever cautious, not to go back to her apartment, and, if she left, make sure she wasn't followed. The note encouraged her to watch TV, surf the internet on her phone but not to access her email. He laid out a thousand dollars on the counter, which was a loan as he called it in his note, for incidentals and a movie if she insisted on going out. It was the least he could do, considering he might never return.

He put her sandwich in the refrigerator and then reached around toward its back edge to release a hidden latch that allowed it to swing outward on air bearings and expose a small door and sliding panel. Trim hid the edges of the door and the sliding access panel cover was nearly flush making it all look very innocuous. The four-foot door was guarded by a keypad combination hidden behind the sliding panel cover. Cole quickly typed in the code and the door swung open to reveal a small dark enclave, not much larger than a closet. Cole was refreshed by a blast of cooled air from the tiny room's AC unit. A multitude of tiny LED lights and a faint hum defined the electronic equipment on the back wall. Cole listened back toward the bedroom for any signs of movement from Julie; all was quiet. He stooped and entered.

Cole switched on the overhead light, studied the small blinking LED lights, and then switched on the left monitor. He selected camera two and monitor one as he waited for the screen to come to life. Cole sat in the office chair and placed his hand on the system drive handle. As the screen brightened, he could see the black Chrysler in the top left corner. He centered the car in the middle of the screen, zoomed in slightly, and clicked the right button four times in rapid succession to send the digital recording speeding backward. Traffic zoomed by in reverse and people hurriedly marched with backward strides. There was nothing unusual. Cole reset the recording and turned off the monitor. The door clicked firmly in place and the refrigerator swung effortlessly into place as he returned the kitchen to its customary appearance.

Cole checked on Julie once again; she hadn't stirred. With sandwich in hand, he exited the condo.

Chapter 28

Invitation to Tea
and Crumpets

It seemed to take longer than usual to get to Junction Boulevard but eventually the Seven train pulled into the elevated platform. Cole waited and was the last one to exit. Afternoon light would be fading soon. He crept down the stairs, across the street, and down the block to his apartment building. He cautiously peered around the corner. There was no longer a police car stationed outside Samantha's stairwell. The neighborhood had returned to normal; a few teens were milling around and a drug deal was taking place, but there were no threats. Cole quickly moved to his stairwell and up to his third-floor apartment.

He rolled up a blue hoody and brown plastic raincoat along with four pairs of surgical gloves, tying them tight and neat with multiple wraps of computer wire.

He checked his purchases from the hardware store: razor knife, paintbrushes, tarps, spray paint, bleach, zip-ties, and turpentine. He put the razor knife, zip-ties, spray paint, surgical gloves, raincoat, and all but three paintbrushes in the tool bag. He had a special plan for the last three paintbrushes.

Cole made his way to 75th Street and approached the Disciple house. It was Monday afternoon, yet business looked to be booming. A car pulled up with the passenger window down, money was exchanged and a young woman got in the car. Another man approached on foot, conversed with someone at the door, and then was admitted, presumably to visit some young woman upstairs. Cole crept past on the opposite side of the street. The Disciple house was a fortress with at least ten soldiers, he concluded: three out front, another barely visible in an upstairs window, and maybe a half dozen inside. One of the three out front warily watched Cole as he passed.

Cole dialed his phone as he walked. Armando instantly answered. He and his yellow cab were off duty. Cole arranged for a five AM pickup at the Junction Street Metro station. Armando would be there at four and wait until seven. Fee was not discussed; Armando was always extremely well compensated when Cole requested his services and Cole knew he would be there as agreed.

When he finished arrangements with Armando, Cole accelerated his pace; the day's light was fading and the clock was ticking. Cole hurriedly raced down the alley leading across several streets and eventually onto 69th. As he approached the dispensary drive-thru, he donned his raincoat and surgical gloves. He turned his ball cap backward, hunched his shoulders forward, and, for appearance's sake, stumbled down the alley as if he were stoned or drunk. At 70th Street, he paused and watched. The day's light was almost gone. A car turned into the alley heading toward 69th and brightened the alley with its headlights. Two foot-traffic customers were nearing the first window and a single was near the street entrance. Excellent thought Cole. As the car approached the Disciple's dispensary, its brake lights came on. Then a few moments later, flashed off as the car pulled forward but then brightened again before reaching 69th Street. A second car pulled in and the process was repeated. Cole was right about the payment at the first window with pick up at the second, just like McDonald's. He crossed 70th and entered the alley. Shoulders hunched and gripping the tool bag against his chest like it was a baby, Cole staggered down the alley.

Headlights shined behind him illuminating the alley and then a car passed. It was two runners working the windows; Cole watched as the first runner retrieved cash and handed it through the first window, which was then followed by the second runner retrieving product and delivering it to the advancing car. The whole process took less than thirty seconds.

The lone figure he had observed earlier now stumbled forward. He watched the figure in front of him pay at the first window and then stumble forward to the second where he received his product. Drive-through and walk-up service, excellent thought Cole. The surveillance camera he'd observed earlier was functioning. It emitted a small amount of light directly over the first window. So far—so good, he thought, everything to plan. He just hoped they would get a good image.

The alley brightened again with headlights from behind as Cole reached the first window.

Cole mumbled, "G- Glo."

"What?" came a reply from the slot in the door.

Cole pictured a man sitting in a chair behind the door with a cash box next to him. He probably had an AK leaning against the wall next to the door and a 1911 holstered somewhere on his body. Cole repeated the order. "G- Glo," he said in a firmer voice.

"Eighty, man."

Cole maintained a feeble voice and begged, "Come on, it's fifty."

"Seventy or get your ass out a here."

Cole dug in his pocket and came out with two twenties, two tens, and eight ones. "This is all I've got," he said as he held the money in front of the slot.

"All right," came the voice from behind the door. "But don't ever come back unless you have the full bill!"

The man's hand came through the slot and Cole placed the cash in the open hand, except he dropped a twenty.

"Pick it up fool," the voice demanded.

Cole kneeled, picked up the twenty with his left hand, and at the same time slid his pant leg up with his right. He squeezed his fingers around the handle of his boot knife. Cole rose with the knife concealed from the overhead surveillance camera and reached to place the twenty-dollar bill in the man's hand, which was now rapidly opening and closing in a demand for payment.

Instead of making payment with the twenty in his left hand, Cole grabbed the man's hand and pulled it farther through the opening. At the same time, he flipped the knife in his right hand from a forward thrusting position to a downward stabbing position and then raised it above his head for maximum thrust and momentum.

The man yelled, "You f . ." but was interrupted when Cole drove the knife between the radius and ulna of the wrist. Cole leveraged against the radius to rotate it farther down through cartilage, tendons, and socket holding the ulna to the wrist. Cartilage popped with a snap. The man screamed in pain, which escalated to horror when Cole began violently hacking at the remaining cartilage and tendons.

The car that had brightened the alley with its headlights sat idling with a runner at its passenger window. Cole glanced at the faces now all staring his way in disbelief. He completed the final hack and the hand came free from its arm. With released tensile energy of Cole's exerted hold, the man on the other side of the door fell backward and Cole recoiled backward to fling the hand at the idling car—and its open window. The hand hit the inside of the windshield and rebounded to the driver's lap, which got an immediate full-throttle response.

Cole raised his knife and glared at the runner who paused, considered the bloody blade, and then took off in a dead run. The second runner didn't hesitate and followed. Cole twisted his ball cap back forward and then stared intently at the surveillance camera. He focused on the camera's little blue light as he counted to five.

Cole charged to the second door. Standing with his back to the bricks of the building, he used the butt of his knife to pound on the door and shouted, "Police, open up. NYPD, open up." There was a burst of semi-automatic fire through the opening in the door, which ricocheted and boomed with an echo off the building wall on the other side of the alley. Cole pounded and again shouted. Another burst of fire came through the opening. And then sounds of scrambling emanated from within the building. The man missing a hand was still screaming and Cole sensed a change in location from the cries within. Cole pounded on the door a third time but got no response of fire through the opening.

Cole jumped past the opening and ran for the building corner. Traffic was light and there was no pedestrian traffic in sight. He bolted from the alley and darted past the bakery and furniture storefronts. His knife, still clutched in his hand, was hidden inside the sleeve of the raincoat and the tool bag was clutched in his other. He stopped at the corner of the noodle company and peered around the corner. The noodle cafe was closed and the mechanic's shop was open. The street was clear and the roll-up door to the mechanic shop was up. Cole darted past the noodle cafe to the office entrance of the shop; he peered through the window and confirmed it was unoccupied before entering through the rollup door. It was a small shop with racks of starters, alternators, and other used and new parts on all three walls. Two cars and one utility van were in some state of repair. The car in the center stall was a vintage Chevrolet Caprice with fancy wheels and low-profile tires. Cole knew this had to be their car. A man worked behind the open hood at the front of an Accord next to it. Cole hit the grease-laden down button to lower the door and charged towards the Accord. The man's head appeared around the hood and saw Cole's charging advance. Caught by surprise, the man froze momentarily giving Cole time to brutally tackle him. The man tried to speak on the way down but the thrust of Cole's tackle knocked air out of his lungs and no words emerged. With the man on the ground and Cole's weight on top of him, Cole showed the man his knife and calmly said, "Not a word. You speak, you die. Understand?"

Cole could see fear in his eyes as the man nodded in compliance. Cole grabbed a handful of zip-ties from his bag and used one to bind the man's hands and another to bind his feet. He used two ties together to secure a grease rag in the man's mouth. The man gagged at the taste of grease and the uncomfortable-ness of the rag, but accepted it. Cole assured him, "Just be calm. Don't move. You will be fine."

Footsteps scuffed at the tarred roof above and Cole surveyed the ceiling. It was dirty white unfinished sheet rock with multiple fluorescent tube lights hanging beneath. Cole surmised there was an attic space between the flat top roof and the sheetrock. Cole saw what he was looking for, a two-foot by two-foot opening directly over the roof of the utility van. Entrance to the attic space from the roof could be anywhere, even over the noodle cafe. He could hear them working their way across rafters directly overhead. A flashlight beam flickered across the darkened opening. Cole darted for the driver's door of the Caprice. The window was down and the key was in the ignition, he removed it and put it in his pocket. From his bag, he removed the box cutter and slid the blade open. Cole moved around the front of the utility van and positioned himself in the shadows of the van and automotive shelves.

A pair of legs appeared through the opening and the first of them dropped through to the roof of the utility van. Cole stood perfectly still. The man stooped slightly and moved back to make room for the second man to drop through a large duffle bag and then a smaller bag. He slid the bags to the rear of the van and moments later the second man dropped through the opening. Cole listened to the shifting and positioning at the opening in the ceiling and also heard moaning and clumsy advance across the rafters from a straggler. Cole guessed five total: two on the van roof, two over the ceiling opening, and a straggler, probably missing a hand. A third man dropped through the opening and immediately slid off the van roof to the hood, only a few feet from Cole's face. Cole revised his plan, pocketed the box cutter, and then without sound, slowly slid his knife onto the shelf next to him.

Simply shooting them would have been the easy answer. But the sound of gunfire had to be avoided at all costs. It didn't matter; gunfire, theirs or his, would draw attention and that just wasn't part of the plan.

As a fourth man dropped through the ceiling opening, the man on the hood turned around, squatted, placed his hands on the hood, and slid off backward. Cole stepped forward behind him and then snapped his neck with rapid left-right over rotation, fracturing vertebrae with the sound of dried tree branches. It was over in less than a second. Cole stepped back into the shadows as the man crumbled to the floor.

When he hit the floor, one of the men on the van roof shouted, "Raymond." Had any of the three looked closely, they would have seen Cole but their attention was on the crumpled man. One of them slid off the van roof to the hood. Cole heard the bags flop to the floor at the rear of the van. The man slid off the hood and his place on the hood was immediately taken by another with an AK slung over his shoulder. He also slid off the hood to the floor. Another quickly followed, who also had an AK. Cole could see familiar bulges at the right rear of each man's waist concealing pistols. It needed to be close quarters and fast, because the AK count was two to none. Cole ever so slowly recovered his knife from the shelf and then took a slow deep breath as he tensed his legs and clinched the knife handle ever harder. All three stared down in confusion at their partner Raymond; surprise and now, Cole knew.

Cole took a half step forward and unleashed a side-thrust kick. Just before his knee locked into place and the full forward motion of his leg, hips, and body peaked, Cole planted the heel of his right boot directly in the center of one of the men's lower back. At a kick speed of forty feet per second and a leg weight of forty pounds, nearly a thousand foot-pounds of kinetic energy were focused on two small lumbar vertebrae; facet joints popped, cervical discs failed and vertebrae crumbled with the impact. The man flew forward with arms splayed and head tilted backward, a scream came from deep within his lungs and reverberated off the ceiling. The man's forward momentum and now uncontrollable legs tripped over Raymond to send him flying to the floor.

Cole uncoiled from the sidekick to face the two assailants in front of him. He heard a thump on the van roof and knew it was the recent amputee. The man on the right grabbed the butt of the shouldered AK and started to swing it forward under his arm. The man on the left was reaching for a holstered pistol at his side. With the knife handle firmly held in his right fist, Cole drove a blow into the AK man's jaw with the intent of a kill, but it wasn't even a knockout; the man just stumbled back. With continued motion of the knife, Cole slashed at the other man's pistol hand that was just coming level. He heard the amputee drop onto the hood of the van behind him. The knife cut across the top of the man's hand and the pistol dropped free.

In a soccer-style kick from the hood of the van, the amputee connected with the back of Cole's head. Cole's head snapped forward and he stumbled over Raymond into the fist of the man facing him. The punch caught him square in the solar plexus; Cole gasped for air. The AK knockout candidate grabbed Cole's knifed hand with both of his. Cole was dazed from the kick to the back of his head and didn't react to the second, third, fourth, and fifth blows to his midsection. In his stunned state, the knife tumbled free. The AK knockout candidate turned and, from behind, slipped his right arm around Cole's neck and cinched down in a rear naked chokehold. Cole gasped for air and pulled on the man's elbow with both hands. He turned his chin to the crook of the man's elbow, all in an attempt to ease the pressure on the airway. The other man continued hammering again and again at Cole's midsection.

The amputee on the hood shouted, "Kill him. Stick em wit his own knife. Make it hurt."

The man landing the punches stopped and looked down at Cole's knife on the floor. It was there at his feet and he reached down to pick it up.

Cole was losing to the chokehold. Blood flow to Cole's brain was restricted and color vision had shut down to black and white. The other man, now holding Cole's knife, slashed at him. Cole leaned and pushed backward, but not soon enough. The knife sliced across Cole's shoulder. The man recoiled his body and arm to maximize forward thrust and then put the knife on a trajectory directly at Cole's midsection.

Ethereal terror from two nights earlier flooded every muscle tissue, ligament, and bone in Cole's entire being and screamed: This is it! Now or die! With terrorized energy, Cole exploded, deflecting the incoming knife thrust with his left hand; simultaneously, wrapping his right leg around behind the choke holder's leg; leveraging and whipping one-hundred-eighty degrees to his right, breaking the chokehold to hurl the man in diagonal motion. Cole accelerated the forces of gravity as he focused every bit of strength into a full-force punch to the man's temple. The man and his head hit the concrete floor with a terminal bounce.

Cole's knife again came at him. He lunged sideways and followed the knife, catching the man's wrist with his left hand. He whisked the man's hand upward while rapidly firing his right knuckles at the man's kidneys. Cole stepped forward placing his right foot behind the man's leg and drew the hand holding the knife downward. Twisting the man's hand while driving the man backward, they headed towards the floor. As Cole went to the floor on top of him, the knife drove through the man's heart and only stopped when it hit concrete.

The amputee on the hood of the van looked on with disbelief. He turned and started to scramble back up to the roof of the van, but Cole caught his baggy pant leg and pulled him to the floor. Cole retrieved his knife and put his boot squarely under the amputee's chin, grabbed his remaining hand, and pulled. He then hacked, hacked again, hacked again, carved, pried, and hacked some more until the man's remaining hand separated from his arm. The amputee tried to scream but the pressure of Cole's boot against his windpipe choked out sounds. Blood spurted from the newly hatched surgery. Cole retrieved zip-ties and a paintbrush from his bag as the amputee bawled and flailed his profusely bleeding arms. Cole forced a paintbrush into the amputee's mouth; he gagged and fought it, but Cole held it in place and secured it with two zip-ties. More zip-ties were used at the elbows and feet to provide restraint. The amputee was the first to receive the "TOMY BOY" carving on his chest. The amputee's stumps and bound legs flailed to no avail as the words were carved. Cole dragged him to the Caprice and placed him in the passenger seat.

Three of the remaining four lying on the floor were dead, or soon would be. Cole relieved them of their pistols and then repeated the process: carved the words, zipped tied hands and feet, and zipped tied paintbrushes in their mouths. And then placed them, one-two-three, in the back seat of the car. The remaining man, with a broken back, was partially conscious. Cole repeated the process with him and placed him in the center of the front seat.

Cole opened the trunk and found another duffel bag; it was compartmentalized and had a multitude of drugs broken down into smaller packages. The large duffel bag the men had brought with them from the bakery had similar contents. Cole threw it in the trunk along with the other one. The smaller bag they had brought from the bakery had what looked to be about twenty thousand in small bills. Cole put the small bag into his tool bag and pulled out a can of spray paint. On both sides of the car, he wrote "TOMY BOY" in large white letters. On the hood, Cole painted "YOU ARE NEXT." On the roof, he put a large "D."

Cole got out his phone, one of the ones he had bought with Julie, and took pictures of the five men in the Caprice. The Disciples in the back seat were posed with their heads titled backward to provide the appearance of a long handle extending up through their torso. Individual close-up photos, as well as group shots, were taken before closing the doors and photographing the car. The images were horrifying. Cole paused, admired his paint job, but then reminded himself of the critical time element.

His shoulder ached and he was concerned about leaving a DNA signature. He also discovered that the knife had sliced his leg sometime during the encounter. The sleeve of his black warrior-wear Kevlar shirt was becoming soaked in blood underneath the raincoat. In the bathroom, Cole found alcohol, gauze, and medical tape. He removed his shirt and did his best to stem the bleeding with the limited medical supplies; the shoulder would ultimately need stitches. Cole used a grease-stained towel and duct tape to finish off the temporary treatment. He completed a similar duct tape repair on his leg.

Time was slipping by. He quickly put his shirt back on; the Kevlar, although thin, would slow a high-energy round and possibly even stop a lesser caliber, which could mean the difference between life and death. In a locker, Cole found blue striped coveralls with the words "Midnight Auto" on the back and a nametag of "Ted" above the left pocket. He donned it as well and then slipped the raincoat back on.

When he finished dressing, Cole hurriedly collected the two AKs and handguns. The AKs he tossed into the backseat with the triplets. He slipped two of the pistols inside the rear of his belt. The third pistol he laid in the lap of the man with the broken back. Cole took one last look around the shop and then hit the button to raise the door. He got into the Caprice next to the man with the broken back, started the car, and backed out. It was only seven blocks to his destination but he needed to get there without attracting attention.

Cole approached 75th Street from a small side street. He stopped the car, put it in the park, slipped out, and set his tool bag in a doorway. From his tool bag, he retrieved the two pints of turpentine. Before returning to the car, he checked the traffic on 75th Street and stared down the street toward the Disciple's house. One of the two men he had seen earlier was out front talking to a potential customer. The street light two blocks up was red and held up maybe a dozen or so cars. Back to the left, traffic was sparse and intermittent.

Cole returned to the car, opened the trunk, and soaked the two duffel bags with turpentine. He pulled a lighter from his pocket, maximized the flame size, and flicked the striker to verify it would meet his needs. He left the trunk unlatched and got back into the car. Cole closed his eyes and blew through his fist while momentarily visualizing the events that were about to happen. He caught a faint odor of the turpentine, which was actually welcomed. The car was beginning to smell of expelled body fluids and death.

Pictures of his companions in the car had been uploaded to the cloud. Cole typed instructions for Kevin to post the pictures far and wide on social media and to send them to every news agency in the country. The pictures were to be accompanied by the caption: "Vigilantes avenge Samantha Ogalsby's torture and death."

Traffic that had been held by the light began to pass. Cole took a deep breath and then pulled out onto 75th Street. As he approached the Disciple's house, he veered into the oncoming traffic lane, which had now cleared, and then cut the wheel hard right to point the car directly at the Disciple's house. He slammed the transmission into Park and jumped out. Customers were nowhere to be seen. The man Cole had seen earlier was still there but had retreated to the shadows alongside the building. Another man on the sidewalk turned his head in confusion and just stared. The man from the shadows stepped forward to the sidewalk. Both men, dumbfounded by the oddity of events, froze and watched as Cole pulled the two duffel bags from the trunk and set them afire.

Both men began to advance at the same time. As Cole returned to the open driver's door, their expression turned to one of recognition. Perhaps they recognized the car or the dying men in the front seat. Perhaps they recognized the duffel bags. Or perhaps they recognized the events about to occur. Both men drew pistols as Cole dropped the shift lever of the car into drive and grabbed the pistol from his passenger's lap. The man on the sidewalk nearest Cole had now leveled his sights on Cole and was only moments from pulling the trigger. The man continued to advance; Cole estimated a fifty percent chance of a miss at this range. As the car started forward, Cole rotated into a Weaver shooting stance, firmly steadied his body, and maximized his grip on the weapon. The man on the sidewalk fired; Cole returned fire with instinctive rapid-fire accuracy: front-sight-bang, front-sight-bang, front-sight-bang. Two of the three shots hit their target and the man went down.

Cole spun out of his position and ducked behind the moving Caprice. A flurry of pistol fire erupted from the front of the car as Cole moved. Cole dropped to the ground and then rolled into the open with his elbows gently resting on the asphalt and the pistol pointed in the direction of the firing man. The Caprice bounced up the curb just as Cole fired. All three bullets struck their mark and the man crumpled. But the firing didn't stop, bullets began striking the asphalt left and right, and Cole felt a twinge of pain in his lower back right side. He rolled and then bolted from his position as AK fire continued from the left upper-most building window. Cole found refuge behind the car, which was now taking the brunt of the fire. The window above was dark but muzzle flashes made the shooter's location obvious. Cole pulled one of the pistols from his belt and popped out from behind the car to return fire at the window, all with instinctive rapid fire, front-sight-bang accuracy: aiming first at the bottom right, then center, bottom left, center, top right, center, top left and then repeated to empty the fifteen round mag.

Cole dropped the empty gun and charged down the sidewalk; there was only silence behind him. As

Cole ran down the sidewalk he slipped his right hand around to his side to investigate the damage. The bullet hadn't entered; instead, the bullet's trajectory had glanced off Cole's Kevlar warrior wear shirt backed by the mass of scar tissue on his side. Although the bullet didn't penetrate, the sensitized nerves in the soft tissue of the scar made it immensely painful to the touch and pounded with every step. Cole expected to hear sirens as he charged past the first side street, but there were none. He glanced over his shoulder; vehicle traffic coming from both directions was now stopped at the Disciple's house. Occupants of the cars were, no doubt, frantically dialing 911 and sirens would be nearing soon. Several drivers and passengers of passing cars glanced at Cole. He wondered if they would be able to provide an adequate description to the police or if it would just stand as "White male." Either way, he was sure to be stopped and questioned by any cop who saw him.

Cole entered the side street where he had parked and scooped up his tool bag from the doorway without breaking stride. He put all his speed into charging down the dark alley to add as much distance as possible between him and the soon-to-be cop-filled crime scene. Cole emerged onto a fully lit street and had to break pace. The most he could do was a fast walk if he was to avoid drawing attention to himself. He crossed the street and then, at his first opportunity, darted down a darkened street to further distance himself with another fast-paced block. He continued to work his way back towards the elevated Seven line, charging through the darkness and pacing himself in the light. At one intersection, he caught sight of a cop car two blocks away and managed to conceal himself in a darkened alley. Cole removed his surgical gloves and raincoat. He rolled the coat into a tight ball and worked it, along with the surgical gloves, deep into a dumpster.

The Seven line was still running, which was a time-table relief. Cole was further relieved to finally cross underneath the elevated train platform. The train would have been faster than working his way through the streets. But every occupant of the train could potentially help police close in on his final destination. Cole continued his trek and eventually emerged just beyond his apartment building. He waited until the street was clear and then walked hastily to his building and into the stairwell.

Chapter 29

PARTY PREPARATIONS

ONCE INSIDE HIS APARTMENT, COLE DIDN'T RELAX. He stripped off his coveralls with the Ted nametag, removed his warrior-wear shirt, and went about the task of redressing the knife wound in his shoulder. Bandages alone would not stop the bleeding. This wasn't the first time; Cole retrieved his surgical needle and thread and then further sterilized them in alcohol. He mentally commanded his body to purge the sensations of nausea, light-headedness, and blurred vision that come with increased levels of pain, as he stitched and tied thirty-seven stitches across the slash in his shoulder. With the stitching complete, Cole bandaged and bound his wound as professionally as could be accomplished in any emergency room. His leg received similar treatment, but it only required twelve stitches.

Cole then finished cleaning up. Final traces that he'd ever been in the apartment had to be erased. Clothes, bloodied rags and bandages, and the like were sealed in a trash bag. The exception was one complete clean change of clothes. He re-wiped and cleaned any area where he might have touched and liberally used bleach where he thought there might be some chance of a DNA sample.

Cole then spread the tarps he'd purchased at the hardware store on the living room and kitchen floor in anticipation of the events that would follow. Perhaps soon, he contemplated. The tarps were laid out with a foot of space between the edge of the tarp and the wall on each side. Cole adjusted them several times until he was satisfied with the pathway around the edges. He opened the sliding door off the main room and verified his egress route. Either he could go up or down by scaling the half balconies on each floor, and each floor gave him the option of ascending, descending, or entering adjacent apartments.

Cole laid out his supplies on the kitchen counter: two additional tarps, large leaf-size garbage bags, rope, surgical gloves, and zip-ties. He paused and thought about what else he might need for the coming events. Cole retrieved an aluminum baseball bat from his closet and set it against the kitchen wall.

Cole glanced around the kitchen and small living room. It was as good as it was going to get. But, was he good enough? For Samantha's sake, he hoped so. The uneasiness grew in his stomach. The anticipated confrontation came with too much risk. The encounter would have to be silent and also had the requirement of no killing.

He still had one of the triplets' pistols and ejected the clip. It was a nice gun: a Springfield Armory 1911 firing a .45 caliber round. Cole thumbed a round out of the magazine and inspected it. The hollow point maximum defense round would do irreparable harm to whomever it hit. He slid the round back into the magazine, verified the functionality of the pistol, and then re-chambered the round. Cole placed the pistol in the oven and hoped he would not have to use it.

Cole sat in the single kitchen chair and dialed the twenty-seven numbers to reach Kevin on the secure satellite phone. Kevin answered on the first ring and simply said, "Here."

"Did you upload the pictures? I need them delivered far and wide to every news outlet, every face . . ."

Kevin interrupted, "What the hell did you do?"

"I got their attention. That's what I did."

"Don't you think you went too far? You really pissed them off, didn't you? Just like Mexico? You ass hole."

"They deserve whatever they get!" replied Cole then continued more calmly. "When you send out the pictures, make up a story of some kind for the media. Then, send the NYPD your latest on picture dissection from Samantha's room. The cops need to see the pitchfork Disciple in his suit."

"Liu has been working with pixel intensity and has some pretty clear images. She's amazing. There's three of them all goofy suited up. She's not going to like these new pictures."

"She'll get over it."

"This game makes me sick."

"What about Julie's problem? I'm thinking simple."

"I'm still researching it and don't have any specifics."

"We don't have time for research. Let's just do this simple and quick. I'll convince them to buy from us instead of their current supplier and then we stiff them on the buy. We'll sell them a shipping container, on dock, that we advertise has been backed out of customs before shipment and is off the books. I did the mental calculation and estimated a container can hold about eleven million packs of cigarettes, which at two-fifty a pack should hurt them pretty bad, dollar-wise. You figure out how to get the container, fill it with newspaper, and load a hundred thousand packs at the doorway."

"That's a stupid plan. What makes you think they will agree to buy from us to begin with? And then, who would spend twenty-seven and a half million dollars without inspecting the whole load?"

"I have a lot on my mind and that's the plan I came up with. You get the container, get it loaded, and get it arranged, and I'll take care of the rest."

"It's a stupid plan."

"Then come up with a better one because I want the container on Thursday."

"Cole, this is wrong. It just doesn't feel right. We should give this some more time. Let me do some research. There has to be a better way."

"No, it's got to be fast. Just do it my way. Get me that container by Thursday."

"There's no way. Three days is impossible."

"Just do it."

"I'll work on it. But you remember I said your idea was stupid."

"Get me an address for Julie's boss, some guy by the name of Greg Grimes. Do it now. I'll need the address in a couple of hours. Also, find out the license plate number of his car. Do it now. Bye," concluded Cole and disconnected.

Cole shut off the main power to the apartment and then squatted next to the wall in the darkness to think. He pulled his knife from his boot and gently let its tip rest on the deteriorating linoleum. While holding it upright with his index finger, he sent it spinning. Minute glimmers of reflected light flashed off its blade as it rotated in the dark. If he had time, there were options. He could steal liquid nitrogen from the hospital and use it to displace the oxygen in his apartment. One liter of liquid makes about seven hundred liters of gas. He did the math in his head and concluded he would need about five gallons to drop the oxygen level down to ten percent. That would be enough to cause unconsciousness without killing them and without them having any idea what brought them down. He had chlorine, ammonia, and isopropyl alcohol, which would make a nasty form of chlorine gas and bring them down as well. But preparation time was against him. Unfortunately, it was going to have to be physical.

He brought his left hand to his mouth and blew through his fist as he envisioned their actions—and his. Would they be wearing their goofy suits from hell? He hoped so. Would they come tonight? Or would it be tomorrow tonight? What if they were too stupid to get the invite? Then he'd have to work on plan B.

Then there was the cigarette scam that just complicated things. It was all just too much; mistakes and not enough time were huge concerns. If he survived the night, a pair of ears would help him make a point. Cole crafted a brief note, folded it, and put it in an envelope. Would the cigarette man take the bait?

Chapter 30

Realization

Liu Chen stared over Kevin's shoulder as he prepared Cole's photos for distribution. She shrieked as Kevin advanced the photos.

"That man doesn't have any hands. That's horrible beyond belief. How could he do that to another human being?" Liu cried. "What's that in their mouths?"

"I told you Cole has hostility issues."

"But that's horrible."

"It's payback for Samantha Ogalsby. And it's not over. See what he painted on the hood of that car." Kevin zoomed in on the hood. "'YOU ARE NEXT.' It's a baited invite to tea, crumpets, and broken legs. Remember the phone call you listened in on?"

"I had no idea this is where it would lead. Oh my God. I never imagined," pleaded Liu as she covered her cheeks with her hands.

Kevin rattled the keyboard and swirled the mouse. The pictures went out to every news agency in the country and were posted under Samantha Ogalsby's name on Facebook, X, Instagram, YouTube, TikTok, and Snapchat.

"If I'd known, I would have never agreed to help. Kevin this is the worst thing I could ever imagine," Liu cried.

Kevin eased out of his chair and put his arms around her. She buried her face in the nape of his neck and just cried. Kevin gently stroked her hair as he pulled her close.

Kevin consoled, "I felt the same way when Cole and I first became friends. It'll get easier with time."

"I can never look at him again."

"Time will heal your shock."

"Aren't you afraid of him?"

Kevin stumbled for words, "No. He's…He's my brother in this game of life." Kevin moved his hands to Liu's hips, looked directly into her eyes, and then kissed her on the lips before continuing, "And you have captured my heart in this game of life."

Chapter 31

TERMINAL PARTY

JAMAL HAD TREATED HIMSELF TO ONE OF WARREN'S youngest girls earlier in the afternoon. He had wanted to partake in some of Warren's special high grade H, but needed to stay clearheaded for his flight tomorrow. He had instead settled for just one line of crack. He chose to keep it an early evening. If he had stayed, it would have been a party and tomorrow would have been a challenge. Jamal had gotten a cab ride back to his hotel in Manhattan and finished off the evening with a couple of shots of whiskey in the bar. He had turned in before nine and now slept peaceably in his king-size bed with the gentle hum and cooling from the AC. The cell phone lying on the nightstand rang and then rang again.

"What!" he reproached the caller.

"We got issue," said the caller.

"Warren?" asked Jamal still groggy.

"We got issue, man. Have you seen CNN?"

"No."

"Check your phone. I sent you pics."

"What are they?"

"We got seven dead and two so screwed up they might as well be. Five of em got Tommy boy carved in their chest."

"What!"

"Tommy boy. Spelled just like Herme spelled it."

Jamal visualized the spelling on the little girl's chest and the fog of sleep cleared. "No way," he admonished.

"Oh yeah. He took out my drive-up and five of my boys. Hurt em real bad. Cut off their hands and shit. He loaded them up in Raymond's Caprice and delivered it to my house. He painted 'YOU ARE NEXT' on the hood. Now the cops are all over my house. I can't even go back. We screwed man. He knows."

"Who is 'he'?" Jamal confusedly asked.

"You ain't going to believe this. I checked the video feed from the drive-up and got a clear video of him. Remember the white boy sitting on the steps, drinking beer, from Friday night? It's him, man."

"So take care of it."

"You isn't listening. He took out my guys, some of them best I eber had. Cracker son-of-a-bitch got us ID'd and now he's coming for us."

"Sounds like you got a problem."

"Did you hear me? It ain't me, man. It's we and he knows who we are!"

"No, it's you! Take a damn army if you need to and end it!" said Jamal and hung up.

Jamal rolled back over and pulled the covers over his shoulder to warm him against the chill of the AC. He dozed and then remembered the steadfast glare of the man's eyes; it was him. The phone rang again and Jamal threw the covers off with irritation.

He picked up the phone and shouted, "What!"

"What, indeed my friend? Your handiwork is all over the news," said Kuoto in a devilish tone.

Jamal hesitated for a fraction of a second and considered his response carefully. Jamal spoke confidently, "Yeah. We're on it. It was some white guy that saw us go in the little bitch's building. We got him on a video feed from one of our dispensaries."

"What are you going to do about it?"

"I'm meeting with my boys in an hour and we are going to do this asshole."

"Excellent. I would expect nothing less. And your other commitment?"

"I got until my nine-ten flight in the morning, which is plenty of time to finish this business."

"Excellent. I knew I didn't need to make this call, did I?"

"Nope, I got it covered."

"Excellent."

Kuoto hung up and Jamal hit Recents to redial Warren. It was answered immediately. Jamal laid out the plan for the early morning hours. Warren and Isaac were to meet him at the apartment complex. They discussed bringing more boys but decided against it; more might draw attention and certainly Jamal could handle this white piece of shit. Warren was to bring the standard supplies, including the saw, plus the silenced twenty-two that Warren kept for him. This was a hurried job and lacked Jamal's usual planning, which Jamal knew greatly increased the chances for error. Jamal instructed Warren to find the building super and figure out what apartment the piece of shit lived in. He was also told to get a key. Jamal would meet Warren and Isaac at the back corner of the building within the hour. This vigilante mofo was going to pay and he was going to pay painfully, they agreed.

Jamal called downstairs to the concierge and requested a cab. He quickly dressed and slipped out of his hotel room to the elevator. A cab was waiting for him at the front door of the hotel when he got there. He gave the cabbie directions that would put him within a half block of the apartment complex. The cabbie sped away from the hotel and began working through the light traffic.

Buildings flashed by as he stared out the cab window and struggled with his decision. Jamal's skin radiated with a dull numbing sensation and his stomach felt queasy; this just wasn't right. Under ordinary circumstances, he would never take on a job so quickly and with so little planning. Kuoto had paid him and the Disciples millions over the past several years and Jamal anticipated more. He paid more for a job than any other customer did. It was for that reason alone that Jamal knew he had to take on this hasty assignment.

They crossed over the East River and entered Brooklyn. He had never faced a situation like this before. Could he be underestimating this vigilante? Jamal flipped through the pictures on his phone in disbelief. He studied one of three men in the back seat of the Caprice. He had tortured and killed many people and seen many horrid things, but this was eerie. Why the paintbrushes? Perhaps he had made a mistake only bringing Warren and Isaac. Maybe he should have sent in some foot soldiers first and then followed. But he was already committed. Maybe this should just be quick and clean without the tortured punishment this mofo deserved.

The cab entered Queens and Jamal thought about how it would go down. They would suit up, enter quietly, and then give the vigilante mofo a double tap with the twenty-two while he slept in his bed. In and out quickly, Jamal assured himself. The cab pulled up to the curb; Jamal paid the fare and tipped the cabbie well. Jamal stood on the sidewalk and waited for the cab to disappear from sight before walking towards the apartment complex. The early morning hours were quiet. Parked cars lined both sides of the street, but there was no traffic. He saw Warren and Isaac in the shadows before they saw him approaching. Warren had a backpack over his shoulder and Isaac had his hand in his pocket. They were whispering to one another and not focusing on their surroundings. They should have seen him approaching; maybe they weren't as good as he thought.

Jamal raised his hand to silence the whispering and avoid any greeting when they finally saw him. Jamal raised one finger and then pointed at Isaac indicating that he needed to go first. Isaac went around the corner of the building and into the light emanating from stairwells. Jamal and Warren paused at the corner of the building and waited until Isaac reached the vigilante's stairwell. As Isaac entered the stairwell, Jamal and Warren briskly walked through the open area and then entered the stairwell.

Jamal quizzed Warren in a whisper at the bottom of the stairs, "What about the super?"

"Thousand bucks for the key. Not a word to the cops or he faces the wrath of the Disciples. Super says the asshole pays cash and has no name. He ain't eber hardly seen em."

"After we finish upstairs you take care of it. No witnesses! You understand?"

"Yeah, I gets it." Warren complied and followed with a question he didn't want answered, "What about the super's bitch and kid?"

"Them too, no witnesses," whispered Jamal. "You can cap them with my little twenty-two."

They advanced to the third floor where they paused and listened. Faint voices could be heard in the apartment opposite that of the vigilante. Jamal put his ear to the door and listened carefully; it was a television left to run all night. The feeling of uneasiness swelled more so now than it had before. Jamal froze in the subdued light of the stairwell for what seemed like an unreasonable length of time for Isaac. Isaac pulled his hand from his pocket and, with both hands palms up, shrugged his shoulders to gesture a question. Jamal nodded and Warren opened his backpack. He put a small piece of tape over the peephole in the door of the opposing apartment and then quietly removed three DuPont Tychem suits. All three donned their suits, including hoods and gloves. Jamal thought suits and gloves might be unnecessary if it was a quick in and out, as he hoped, but it had always served him well in the past as a precaution against leaving a hair, fingerprint, drop of sweat, footprint, or any other indication of ever having been there.

Warren took the key and gently slid it into the door lock. Jamal touched him on the shoulder and held up his hand signaling a pause. Jamal listened intensely trying to anticipate what was behind the door. It was quiet except for the barely audible television from the other apartment. Jamal removed his hand from Warren's shoulder and Warren turned the key.

The door inched open and Warren shined his penlight inside. Safety chain wasn't latched and Jamal's nervousness increased. Warren pushed the door a little farther open; Jamal saw nothing. He flashed his light towards the kitchen, and then back across the living room. A small kitchen table and a single chair were in the kitchen but the remainder of the visible area was empty. There was something on the floor. Jamal studied it; he concluded it was a tarp of some kind. Perhaps they were getting ready to repaint the apartment. He gave Warren a gentle shove and Warren entered. When he stepped on the tarp, it crackled with what seemed like earth-shattering noise. Warren froze and turned his head to look back at Jamal. Uncertainty and uneasiness transformed into indecisiveness and Jamal gave Warren no sign. Warren continued to enter, with each step crackling and echoing throughout the apartment. Jamal stepped slightly aside and waved for Isaac to follow Warren. As Isaac entered, Jamal watched as Warren used the penlight to survey the inside of the visible rooms and down the small hallway towards the bedroom. Jamal touched the handle of the silenced twenty-two slipped under the elastic band of his pants and then entered. He stepped onto the tarp and closed the door behind him.

Jamal reached forward and put his hand on Isaac's shoulder, holding him momentarily in place, as he passed in front of Isaac to take his place behind Warren. The penlight beam penetrated the darkness. The bathroom door to the right was open and the bedroom door was slightly ajar. Warren entered the hallway and Jamal followed. Isaac crunched on the tarp behind him. Jamal thought he heard the squeak of a door hinge. Then, a slight breeze on the back of his neck brought awareness and he realized that he had made a mistake.

The windowed door off the living room opened to a small half balcony and they hadn't checked it. "Shit," Jamal said aloud just before something moving with incredible speed whistled through the air to strike

Isaac. The object swung up between Isaac's legs and echoed with a thud and ping as it crushed his manhood. Jamal recognized the sound of the object striking up between Isaac's legs. Jamal had used a bat before and its sound-crushing soft tissue was unmistakable. He pulled the pistol as he began to turn, but Isaac was upon him being driven with incredible might. He went with the momentum and was rammed into Warren; all three crashed onward down the hall. Warren stumbled and went down. Jamal and Isaac were driven right over the top of him. They crashed into the closet door at the end of the hall. It splintered into pieces and the shelves collapsed as they were both rammed into the closet. Isaac crumpled towards the floor as Jamal brought his pistol around. He heard the whistle of the bat barrel through the air again as he fired a blind shot. The bat struck Warren lying on the floor with a thud and ping, and the offender retreated. Warren moaned on the floor, crumpled in a fetal position. Warren fully blocked the hallway and Jamal hesitated. He fired another shot into the darkness and listened for its effect. He heard crumpling of the tarp to the right of the hall exit over the crying and whimpering of both Warren and Isaac, but there was no indication his bullet had struck.

Jamal focused his eyes and ears forward into the darkness, but there was nothing. The mofo had gone right and was waiting for him just inside the living room, surmised Jamal. He slid his foot forward into the back of Warren's head. Warren whined with the small addition to his pain. Jamal searched for a place to land his foot without stepping on Warren and eventually found a spot. He placed one foot after the other and worked his way past Warren. Warren's whining and whimpering were irritating; Jamal needed to take in every sound from the living room ahead. He held the pistol in his left hand and carefully worked his right hand down the wall until he found the corner and the exit to the hallway.

Jamal slipped the pistol around the corner and squeezed off a quick shot, then retreated a half step. He listened for an indication that his bullet had done some good, but there was none. He crept forward again, found the corner, and this time fired at a slight angle from the wall. The sound was different this time and he knew the bullet had gone through the glass in the door leading to the balcony. Where would he be? Down, concluded Jamal. He crept back to the edge of the living room and slipped the pistol around the corner pointing down at a slight angle. He fired the pistol and the baseball bat came crashing down on his hand to send the pistol flying; the mofo had crept around the edge of the tarp to come up on the left side.

At least now he knew where the mofo was. Jamal charged forward, planted his right foot as he exited the hallway, and unleashed a Yoko-geri-kekomi with his left foot. He felt the impact; it was a solid blow and had, in no uncertain terms, done damage. He heard the "umph" of air being forced from the man's lungs and the sound of the baseball bat rebounding off the kitchen cabinets. He visualized the mofo's position and unleashed a Hiraken-uchi, but his fist only passed through air. The baseball bat bounced to the floor and began to roll. Anticipating the target's moves, which were now slightly to the right, Jamal launched a Mawashi-geri and again struck his target, but it was too early in the travel of the roundhouse kick to have much of an effect.

Momentum of the blow out of the darkness caught Jamal by surprise. It was slightly off Jamal's center of mass and sent him spinning and bouncing into the wall, and then out into the living room where the crumple of the tarp gave away his exact location. Jamal froze, slowed his breathing, and listened for the advance of the mofo that he knew was coming.

Jamal now understood the reason for the tarp. This was a trap from the very beginning and he should have known better. The mofo knew they were coming and arranged for this confrontation on his turf. The tarp was part of his advantage, or so he thought. The mofo thought he could just work his way around the edges of the tarp, waiting to pinpoint his prey with noises from the crumpling tarp. And then launch an ambush from the darkness. Jamal would turn this mofo's plan to his own advantage.

Jamal had earned his Black Belt and Yellow Sash at an early age and continued his education, expanding into many methods and arts. Jamal had trained in Shito Ryu, Keuwa Mibuni, Krav Maga, and Shotokan. Having mastered the Kata, he had then delved into the forbidden art of Dim Mack, which included lifesaving and pain relieving methods of contact, as well as the dark side of pressure points that kill. He was the master here and this shagwa was going to die.

Jamal adjusted to the Sanchin-dachi stance and waited, listening for a creek in the floor, scuff of a foot, or breathing from around the edge of the tarp. He heard the slip of cloth against cloth slightly to his right; the man's arm had shifted against his body, scraping cloth against cloth. Jamal did not hesitate and first executed a Yoko-geri-kekomi that found only air, which he partially anticipated, and then quickly followed with a full body, head level, Nagashi-zuki that struck mass. His fist hit the mofo in the face and he heard an audible sound from the man's vocal cords. The mofo bounced off the wall and onto the tarp, now fully giving away his location. Jamal struck with a Mae-geri-kekomi that connected with full force and then rapidly followed with a Hiraken-uchi that was surprisingly blocked; the momentum of his punch had simply been swept away. Jamal followed in rapid succession with first a left, then right, left, right Hiraken-uchi but, with perfect timing, each punch was swept away by the man in the darkness.

As his last unsuccessful Hiraken-uchi was swept away, Jamal felt the man's breath in his face followed by the blow of a cupped hand to the side of Jamal's head. Jamal flowed with the punch minimizing its impact, rolling to the floor, and then quickly rebounding to his fighting stance. The blow had ruptured Jamal's eardrum and he felt blood begin to trickle down his neck. His vision, had he had any in the darkness, and equilibrium were askew and he swayed with dizziness. The tarp crumpled slightly to his left. He attacked again with rapid succession Hiraken-uchi clearing the void in front of him until he instinctively knew that his target was the optimal distance for a Yoko-tobi-geri snap kick. He accelerated all of his forward momentum and delivered the snap kick at precisely the right moment. If the full force of a flying front kick struck a target's face or chest, it would most assuredly cause death. He felt the heel of his foot strike hard mass but backpressure was light, meaning he was three inches too far to the left, yet he had still landed a solid blow. The man grimaced in pain with an unintelligible "Gaahwol," as both he and the man rebounded from the impact, crashing to the floor.

Jamal rolled and quickly sprang to his feet, resuming a Sanchin-dachi stance, and just listened. He visualized the mofo on the tarp struggling to get to his hands and knees; the man moaned, "Awe." Jamal charged with controlled paces to time a Mae-geri-keagi kick to the man's midsection. It was a solid kick and the man flopped over sideways. Jamal visualized the man's position on the floor; he uncoiled a Fumi komi stomp intended to crush the man's rib cage as he shouted "wang jin shagwa!" The stomping kick impacted with full force, except Jamal suspected the man's arms had absorbed some of the energy. He coiled to strike again and this time commanded in English, "Die now mofo," as he unloaded another stomping kick.

His foot passed through air and struck the floor. The voice from the floor coolly said, "Not yet." The calf of Jamal's kicking leg was spear-punched with two fingers in a Dim Mack point strike. Jamal heard the tarp rumble as momentum was being generated; Jamal was struck in the stomach with a kick accelerated from the floor. It was low velocity and ineffectual as far as damage was concerned, yet it was enough to cause Jamal to stumble backward, limping on a now injured leg. He couldn't let it bother him and used the mental powers of the Kata to suppress the pain. He resumed his Sanchin-dachi stance and again listened to the darkness.

Silence persisted. First, it was just seconds, and then it seemed like minutes. Jamal imagined that he could hear the man breathing and contemplated an advance. He was the master here and no one was his equal, especially not this shagwa. Jamal taunted, "I am the master here."

The man charged. Jamal anticipated the man's moves, sweeping aside the first punch. And then with rhythmic timing thwarted the second, third, and fourth punches, before retaliating with an Ippon Ken zuki aimed into the darkness at the man's solar plexus. It struck at the same time a sweeping kick took his feet out from underneath him and they both went down. Jamal rolled, sprang to his feet, and was again met by the man's assault. He shifted his blocking tactic to Gedan uke and Haishu uke to repel and flow with the incoming punches. He retaliated with a Mae geri keage kick aimed at the man's groin. His kick was defensively blocked as Jamal took another blow to the chest. He stumbled backward and commanded his body to attack even with no air in his lungs. Each rapid succession punch and kick were miraculously countered in the darkness. Jamal reverted to defense as the man countered Jamal's offense with one of his own. Instinctive rhythmic timing allowed Jamal to fend off the onslaught of incoming punches as he created his next opportunity.

Drawing the mofo in close, Jamal kept elbows tight and unleashed rapid-fire Kimzami-zuki boxer's jabs aimed in the darkness at the man's face. The first jab connected, the second glanced left, and the third and fourth found only air. A kick from the darkness struck the mid-section of his torso. He allowed his body to flow with the kick and retaliated with a Hitsui-geri kick targeted at what he visualized were now the man's unprotected genitals. The kick was perfectly executed but struck the inside of the man's still extended leg, instead of the visualized target. Both men retreated momentarily from the exhausting interchange. Jamal knew he had broken ribs to go along with his damaged leg and ruptured eardrum, all minor injuries easily overcome with concentration. His adversary had to have worse; Jamal had landed several lethal blows that, having not killed, surely would have caused severe damage.

The man charged at Jamal with a new level of energy, but Jamal was ready. He adjusted his Kata tactics and moved with increased speed to block the man's onslaught of kicks and punches and also to get an inside advantage. Jamal landed several well-placed Zuki Waza and Geri-Wasa punches causing the man to retreat allowing Jamal to further increase the intensity of attack. But then a flurry of balanced responses came from the dark and Jamal was struck again and again in his broken ribs; pain exploded and Jamal had to draw even more intensely on the mental powers of the Kata. He tried to adjust his tactics to fend off the man's advance, all to no avail. The mofo just kept coming and Jamal was less and less effective in blocking the kicks and punches coming out of the dark. Move even faster he concluded and, emerging from left-right blocking movements, dashed outside an incoming punch and slightly past the man to plant an elbow in his side. Momentum from the blow started his rotation into a Mawashi geri kick that impacted the man's midsection. The man tumbled and fell across the tarp, bouncing into the wall.

He heard the man stumbling, trying to get to his feet; Jamal knew the shagwa was done. Now it was time to finish him, once and forever. Noise from the mofo's futile attempts to get up came slightly from his right; Jamal adjusted and targeted the distance. He advanced directly at the noise, attacking with Choku-Zuki. Jamal was the master here and shouted with each advancing half-step and punch: "Ichi!" "Ni!" "Saih!" "Shi!" "Go!" "Roku!" "Schichi!" Hachi!" "Ku!"

"Ten!" came a shout from the darkness and Jamal was struck with unimaginable energy to his mid-section. His feet went out from underneath him as his forward momentum was reversed and he flew backward to the floor. Air completely evacuated from his lungs and his heart paused. His last moments of consciousness were filled with streaks of bright light from inside his eyelids and an overwhelming sense of suffocation.

Chapter 32

EXPOSING THE DEVIL

COLE HAD TAKEN MULTIPLE BLOWS TO HIS KIDNEYS, stomach, face, solar plexus, and back. He had at least two broken ribs, if not more, and his shoulder was now bleeding more than ever. Every inch of his body was in pain, even breathing was a painful challenge. He was done; there was nothing left.

Cole stared into the darkness of the hallway. Moans from the hallway reminded him that the job was not finished. If he didn't act soon, Pocket Boy and Bling Man would recover enough to finish him. But, all strength was exhausted and even the simple act of rolling to his side was beyond his capacity. The will and strength just weren't there.

Then it happened. Somewhere deep within his soul, a window opened and he got a blinding reminder of terror from the great beyond. A voice from the great beyond commanded, "Get up!"

Feeling, more than rational sense, gently grasped his hand and encouraged him upward. His mind flashed through images of Samantha Ogalsby at play and then, inexplicably, imagined her strength gently pulling on his hand. Cole rolled to his side and then slowly struggled to his feet. Pocket Boy and Bling Man were beginning to stir and becoming more of a threat by the minute.

Cole stumbled to the body in front of him and verified that the man was either dead or unconscious. Cole retrieved zip-ties from the kitchen counter, stumbled into the hallway, and secured the first of the intruders. With strength gradually returning to Cole's battered body, he managed to drag the intruder into the living room. The second man, whimpering in the doorway of the broken closet door, took a swing at Cole in the dark. Cole mustered a punch and hit him hard in the abdomen to get compliance. Cole zip-tied his hands and his feet before also dragging him to the living room. Cole also zipped-tied the hands and feet of the unconscious Kung Fu Man.

With all three secure, Cole returned to the circuit breaker box and turned the main power back on. The refrigerator hummed with life and LEDs on the stove and microwave brightened. The overhead light switch next to the front door revealed three Disciples in their suits from hell.

Two of the three were moaning; Cole cut the suit from the first one's face, forced a paintbrush into his mouth, and then secured it with a double zip-tie around the back of the man's head. As he pulled the zip-tie tight, Cole saw fear in the man's eyes; no doubt the Disciple knew his fate. The second Disciple squirmed and bucked as Cole attempted to cut away the suit. Cole held him in place with a knee on the man's chest while forcing the paintbrush into the man's mouth and completing the zip-tie operation. His eyes also flared with fear.

Kung Fu Man had a pulse and was breathing, but out cold. He also got a paintbrush. Cole sat him in the kitchen chair and added zip-ties to secure him. Cole retrieved a small vile of smelling salts from his first aid kit and waved it under Kung Fu's nose; the man stirred and tried to cough. His eyelids rose and then fell. Cole saw the whites of his eyes with the pupils rolled up in his head as he blinked. The man tried to cough again and then mumbled something unintelligible. Cole waved the smelling salts under his nose again and the man jerked with reaction. The man's eyelids intentionally clamped down hard, he slowly turned his head to the right, and then his eyes opened to stare directly into Cole's.

Cole was taken aback by the suddenness of consciousness but stared back with intensity. He maintained the stare for a moment and then explained. "You are going to die here this morning. We will start with a little lettering," said Cole as he pulled his knife from his boot.

The point of the knife easily slipped through the fabric of the plastic suit and the shirt beneath. Cole ripped open the suit and shirt to reveal the man's chest and then, without saying a word, sliced a deep "T" across the man's right nipple. The Disciple in the chair didn't squirm or even move with the carving. He just stared with hatred and defiance. Cole continued his carving until he completed the words "TOMY BOY."

Cole tired, as he realized how much more was left to do this morning. He didn't have the wherewithal. And now there was not enough time. He considered just killing them. But terror from deep inside his soul returned. He shivered. Cole made his commitment; Samantha was going to get an answer to her haunting question from the great beyond. And Kung Fu Man was going to provide it.

Torture was a language they understood. Cole stared into the man's eyes and explained, "You are going to die by my hand, but how much pain you endure is up to you. So any time you want to tell me your name, why you killed the little girl, and anything else I want to know, you just shake your head up and down and I will stop the pain. Do you understand?"

The Disciple just glared at Cole with hatred. Cole understood and answered, "All right then. Let me see what your friends have to say and you can watch because your turn is coming."

Cole turned to the man lying on the floor nearest him and quickly sliced up the front of his devil suit and shirt, but miscalculated when the man squirmed. Cole cut clear to the rib bone with the slice. Fear raged in the man's eyes. Cole ripped open his shirt; the man tried to roll over. Cole rolled him back over, dropped a knee to his lower abdomen, planted his left hand firmly up under the man's chin, and pushed. The man squirmed and cried out in his mind as Cole carved. The man's squirming made carving difficult, it wasn't Cole's best work but it would do. Cole started to move toward the third man; but the one he had just finished with tried to roll away. Cole stamped down hard between the man's legs and simply said, "Don't."

The third man had rolled to the wall. Cole dragged him back onto the tarp and jabbed him once in the stomach before starting to slice up through his suit from hell and his shirt. The man's eyes showed fear but also a reckoning of his fate. Cole's knife caught on something as he tried to pull it through the final inches of fabric. He withdrew it and sliced again exposing the man's chest and his necklace.

"This makes you Bling Man, your friend over there Pocket Boy, and the ass-hole in the chair Tiger fan. Why would you do that to a child? Anybody care to answer," asked Cole. He glared at each one for a few seconds before resuming his kneeling position and started carving the words "TOMY BOY" with renewed vehemence. Cole looked into his eyes and didn't see the fear necessary for confession.

Pocket Boy's eyes showed the most fear and Cole returned to him. He kneeled with one knee in the man's abdomen and glared down at him. The man's eyes cried out for help. Without saying a word, nor the man realize what was happening, Cole sliced his knife first across the left side of the man's head and then the right, dropping both ears to the tarp and starting the flow of blood. Cole stabbed one of the ears on the floor, brought it up on the knife tip, and held it in front of the man's eyes. "Do you want to eat this or do you want to talk to me?"

The man shook his head left and right and then up and down in confusion. Horror raged in the man's enlarged eyes.

"Okay. I'm going to remove your paintbrush and I want you to speak very quietly. No yelling, no shouting, just nice quiet conversation. If you can't do that," Cole thrust the knife down into the floor stabbing the second ear and adding it to the knife tip. He brought them both up in front of the man's eyes and then continued, "I will stuff both of these down your throat. Understand?"

The man nodded in compliance. Cole wiped the knife blade across the man's forehead leaving both ears; one slipped down onto the man's eye and he shook his head to eject it. Cole grabbed the handle of the paintbrush to stop the shaking and sliced the zip-ties holding it in place.

"Quiet now," he said as he slowly withdrew the paintbrush. The man's mouth was stretched out of shape and Cole gave him a moment to recover. "Name?" he asked.

"Isaac. Are you going to kill me?"

"Yes," Cole replied without emotion.

"Are you going to hurt me?" he whimpered.

"Yes. Your nose is next unless I get answers to my questions. Now, why did you kill the little girl?"

"It was Herme, man. I didn't do it."

"Not good enough," said Cole as he brought his knife to the man's nose.

"We were there," the man quickly said and then continued rapidly blurting out facts with almost no breath in between. "It was Jamal's contract job. Warren brought all the stuff for Herme. We supposed to make it look horrible ugly bad. The girl had to be Black and had to be eleven. Warren made sure her mother would be gone. He got a key to the apartment. Herme was the fool that did all the things to the girl, but Jamal told him to do everything. It was a message to somebody named Tommy and supposed to be a message not to run. That why Herme cut her legs off."

"Very good," said Cole and withdrew the knife from the edge of Isaacs's nose. "Tell me about the contract."

"It was Jamal's contract to do the girl. He got all the big bucks. Warren and I got twenty Gs to help make sure it went down, but that's all."

Cole did the math: twenty for Isaac, twenty for Warren, expenses, and at least an equal sum for Jamal. That made the contract worth at least a hundred thousand dollars. Who would pay so much to have a kid forgotten in America's poverty class killed? It didn't make any sense. "Who issued the contract?" he asked Isaac.

"I don't know."

Cole wisped his knife back into place next to the man's nose and demanded, "Who!"

"I don't know. Jamal does. He talked to somebody named Cuojo on his phone. That's all I know." Tears ran down the sides of his face and mixed with the blood from his missing ears. Cole stared into his eyes searching for more information and truth; there was nothing more Isaac had to offer.

"Okay," Cole said and gently re-inserted the paint-brush into Isaac's mouth. He then, with surprise and certainty, hammered the knife butt into Isaac's temple. Isaac's head snapped right, he gasped and his eyes closed.

"Next," announced Cole looking at the Tiger fan who now had a name.

Jamal turned his head slightly to the side and glared with eyes of contempt and hatred.

"I'm going to do more than remove your ears. Let me give you a preview," said Cole and walked over to Warren. "Hi, asshole," he said looking down at the man. "Unfortunately for you, Jamal over there isn't going to give me what I want and because of that you are not going to die as easily as Isaac."

Cole stepped to the kitchen and retrieved the baseball bat from the floor, rope from the counter, and four table knives from one of the drawers. He cut four short pieces of rope and tied a loop in each. He laid the rope and knives on the tarp in front of Jamal where he could ponder their purpose. Warren saw Cole coming with the bat and tried to roll away, but Cole got in front of his retreat and took a low outside swing to Warren's midsection. Then he took another, and then again, again, and again, until he feared Warren was going to lose consciousness. Cole walked over to Jamal sitting in the chair and dished out an equal series of blows, just enough to finish breaking ribs but not enough to cause fatal internal injury. Jamal timed each incoming blow and allowed his body to flow with the impact, minimizing its blow and absorbing energy. Cole swung just a little harder to compensate and continued until Jamal too showed signs of fading awareness. Cole didn't like torture and would rather have just killed them, but someone had ordered Samantha Ogalsby's torture and murder. And Cole was going to have that person's name, whatever it took.

"Look, Jamal. I can beat on you, cut on you, and you can continue to resist, maybe even for days. I don't know. Consider it this way. Cuojo, or whatever his name is, ain't going help you. And what do you owe him anyway? You're going to suffer pain like you've never experienced. And for what? You talk to me and it ends. I'll even use your twenty-two over there. A quick double tap and it's all over. All it takes is a nod. What'd ya say, Jamal? How about it?"

Cole stared into Jamal's eyes looking for an answer. The hatred had softened and the contempt had diminished, but the eyes still glared no.

"Your choice Jamal," said Cole and then returned to Warren. "It was you that brought the backpack to the torture, wasn't it? Did you bring the saw? Was that your idea or was it Jamal's? I'll bet you thought the saw up all on your own. Now, I don't have a saw. What am I to do?"

Cole slashed the fabric above both of Warren's knees and then flipped him over to finish cutting the fabric at knee level. Warren rolled back to his back as Cole retrieved two of the table knives and two of the looped sections of rope. Placing a knee in Warren's abdomen to hold him in place, Cole tied one of the pieces of rope above Warren's right knee, inserted a kitchen knife, and began to twist. He finished tightening the tourniquet and slipped the handle of the knife into the loop of the rope to hold it tight. Cole repeated the process on Warren's left leg. Warren squirmed and twisted, but with hands and feet bound, and Cole's two hundred ten pounds resting on his abdomen, it was all to no avail. Tourniquets in place, Cole stood and looked at Jamal. He saw confusion and, for the first time, a subtle indication of fear. Cole grabbed Warren's feet, flipped him over to his abdomen, and then with a single swipe of his twelve-inch blade, sliced deep into all four collateral ligaments on the backsides of Warren's knees. Warren tried to stiffen his legs with the pain and then tried to retract them as Cole sawed deeper at the ligaments. One by one they popped and retracted when their tension was relieved. Cole glanced at Jamal and saw the barrier crumpling. Cole flipped Warren to his back and then, with one hand holding the back of Warren's foot, dropped a full-force blow to the front of Warren's knee. The knee popped and the leg folded forward. Cole changed hands and repeated the knee-snapping blow to Warren's other leg. Cole lifted the zip-tie binding Warren's feet together to display the unnatural leg position to Jamal. He glanced at Jamal and finally saw signs of fear. Cole pulled Warren's bound feet forward and forced them, stretching remaining tissue, above Warren's head. Cole pulled Warren's head up between his legs and then let the zip-tie holding his feet together slip down behind his head. Jamal's eyes revealed growing fear. He let Warren flop to his side. Warren's eyes, ballooned with horror, were now clearly visible to Jamal. But Cole wanted him to know there was more and used his knife to slice through the fabrics covering Warren's buttocks.

Cole turned to Jamal and asked, "I don't think I have a broom. I wonder how far a baseball bat would go?" Cole stood, walked over to Jamal, picked up a piece of rope, and started to tie a knot. Jamal's head began bobbing up and down, first slowly and then with repeated vigor. Cole appeared to ignore his signal of compliance. The paintbrush handle reached frantic velocity before Cole put his hand on Jamal's shoulder and said, "Okay."

The paintbrush waving subsided to a small dither and Cole saw relief in Jamal's eyes.

"Can you be quiet?"

Jamal's paintbrush handle dipped up and down several times in agreement.

Cole sliced the zip-ties holding the paintbrush and pulled it from Jamal's mouth. He struggled to pull his jaw in place and swallowed several times. Cole saw peace and calmness in his eyes. The man knew his fate was in his hands, he either could die like Isaac or be tormented like Warren; he chose Isaac and would reveal all. Cole started to ask a question, but Jamal spoke first.

"Who are you?"

"Unimportant," Cole paused, "but you probably deserve some kind of answer." Cole paused again, formulating an answer as much for himself as Jamal. He answered, "I'm a displaced combatant from Hell trying to live a peaceful life. Then you came along, offended my sensitivities, and invited me to violate my personal armistice."

Jamal looked puzzled for a moment and then accepted the answer before asking, "I get the twenty-two, right?"

"If you give it to me, all of it: names, places, dates, phone numbers, and whys."

"Names: Ken Kuoto, Reed Delahe, Bonnie Delahe, Tommy Delahe, and Samantha Ogalsby," Jamal listed matter-of-factly before explaining. "I do jobs for Ken Kuoto wherever and whenever he wants them done. Mostly he just wants them to go away with no possibility of it ever getting traced back to him. This Samantha Ogalsby job was because she had to be eleven and had to be Black. I don't know why but those were the instructions. The words on her chest were supposed to be Tommy boy, but the dumb shit Herme misspelled Tommy. I don't know why we were supposed to cut her legs off; I swear those were just the instructions. I keep my kills clean when it's my choice." He paused and breathed a partial sigh of regret.

Cole calmly assured him with a partial smile, "Go on."

"Kuoto paid me to go to Atlanta, retrieve Tommy Delahe, and deliver him to Kuoto in Huntsville, Alabama. His old man, Reed Delahe, tried to hide him in Atlanta with the kid's mother. He wasn't there and his mother hadn't seen him. I verified that—and—a— she became a casualty. But I know where the kid is now. I was supposed to take a nine-ten flight to Salt Lake, pick the kid up in some town called Manti, and then drive him out of the state to Las Vegas. Kuoto is sending a private plane to pick the kid up from the private terminal at Harry Reid. I have to be there at midnight. I got the ticket and car reservation in my pocket. Check it out."

"I believe you. You gave me the what, but not the why," urged Cole.

"I don't know. Kuoto pays better than drugs or prostitution and I don't ask questions."

"How much?"

"Hundred per, with bonuses when it all works out."

"That's a lot of money," said Cole buried in thought. "How does he pay you?"

"Wire transfer from the Minh bank in China to my account in the Bahamas."

"Account numbers," demanded Cole.

"They are in my phone under notes. The phone password is two-three-one-four. Check it out. The phone is in my pants pocket."

Cole slipped his hand into Jamal's front pocket and retrieved the phone. The password gave him access and he verified the information along with a quick scroll through the list of contacts. Kuoto was there.

"Will Kuoto be at Harry Reid?" Cole asked.

"I don't know. Probably not, I think he has business in Huntsville."

"Why do you think he has business in Huntsville?"

"It has something to do with Reed Delahe. This whole thing has something to do with him, blackmail or something."

Cole felt like he had gotten most of what Jamal had to offer and stood. At the kitchen counter, Cole quickly dialed the twenty-seven numbers on the satellite phone.

As soon as Kevin answered, Cole placed his demand, "I've got a smartphone in my hand that we need to get all of the information off: notes, address book, call history, all of it. How do I get it to you?"

"Pair it with the satellite phone and I'll take care of the rest."

"How do I do that?"

"I thought you had a Master's degree. Didn't you learn anything?"

"Knock it off, Kevin! I don't have the time. Just tell me how to do it."

Kevin went through the keystrokes to allow Jamal's smartphone to pair with the satellite phone. Cole followed each step quickly and precisely until he had transferred the information. Cole returned the smartphone to Jamal's pocket. Jamal just stared at Cole with a puzzled look.

Cole checked the time. This wasn't going to work. He would find himself caught in broad daylight. "Shit," he said to himself.

Cole scrambled about quickly cleaning up the apartment. He sloshed some more bleach on the linoleum and whisked it around with the broom to obscure bloody footprints, retrieved his trash bag from the bedroom, and set it next to the front door. Jamal waited patiently for his fate and watched Cole scurry about. Warren's eyes had become comatose.

Cole picked up Jamal's twenty-two from the floor; Jamal watched him and then closed his eyes. Cole walked over to Jamal and slid the slide back far enough to see a chambered round.

Jamal opened his eyes and pleaded, "Double tap, right?"

Cole stared at Jamal, closed his eyes for a moment, and visualized Samantha Ogalsby. "Double tap it is," he said quietly and then violently grabbed a handful of Jamal's hair, jerked his head backward, and rammed the silencer of the twenty-two into Jamal's mouth, past his tongue and into the rearmost passage of his throat, bypassing his trachea and driving it deep into the esophagus. Pop, pop fired the twenty-two, almost imperceptibly. The two bullets passed through Jamal's stomach and lodged somewhere between the large and small intestines. Cole looked down into Jamal's now terrified eyes and said, "You shouldn't extend the violence and horror to children. That is unacceptable."

Cole left the pistol in place and picked up the two tiny shell casings; he spread out a tarp for Jamal and tossed the casings onto it. He cut the zip-ties holding Jamal to the chair, flopped him onto the tarp, and rolled him up. Jamal squirmed as Cole secured the tarp around him with rope. Cole then flopped Warren's legs back into a somewhat normal position and rolled him up in the tarp he was lying on, being careful not to let any of the body fluids drain from the tarp. Cole secured the tarp with another piece of rope.

Before repeating the process for Isaac, Cole retrieved the sandwich bag from the kitchen and returned to carefully pick up Isaac's ears. They had been cleanly severed from Isaac's head and still had perfect form; they were so perfect he feared they might not look real enough. Someone might assume they were a Halloween gag of some kind. Cole carefully slipped the ears into the baggie and slid its zipper seal closed. The baggie was then folded and delicately slid into his pocket.

Cole opened the door to the little half balcony and winced at the now fleeting darkness, but at least it was still quiet below. The first-floor apartment below had a small fenced area guarding bicycles and a barbecue; Cole hoped he could clear it. Cole hefted Jamal, who was the biggest of the three, over his shoulder. It was almost more than he could manage and the tarp made it just that much more difficult. His ribs now hurt more than ever. Cole took a run at the half balcony and launched Jamal with all his strength. Jamal cleared the small fence and made a blaring thump when he hit the ground three stories below. Cole instinctively squatted down with the noise and watched for light from the apartment below; there was none. Cole struggled to get Warren up over his shoulder and sensed Warren's movement, as well as fluids moving to the bottom of the bagged-up tarp. Cole took a run and sent Warren flying towards the ground to join Jamal. Warren bounced off Jamal and came to rest just beyond him. Isaac was easier, he was the lightest of the three, and when Cole launched him he easily cleared the other two and hit the ground with a thump. Cole looked below for lights or any indication he had disturbed the tenants below. He waited for a few moments and then returned to the living room, closing the door.

Cole took one last look around the living room and concluded it would have to do. He grabbed the garbage bag containing any remaining signs he had ever been there, his change of clothes, and his tool bag.

Cole turned off the light, stepped out of his apartment, closed the door, and slipped off his boots. The soles of his boots could contain residual blood that would leave a blue glow when sprayed with luminol, which could lead the cops directly to his apartment; but his socked feet would leave no trail. He knew he had forgotten something; it was just too much, too fast, and some clue, someplace would be found; but it was too late now. With garbage bag, tool bag, change of clothes, and boots in hand, Cole made his way down the three flights of stairs and out the front of the building. Cole slipped a folded garbage bag into his back pocket before leaving his possessions in the shadows at the back corner of the building. He made his way to where Isaac, Warren, and Jamal lay. The back of the building was silent and dark. Late-night TV watchers would be asleep before two and early risers getting ready for work would be up no earlier than five. It was now after five. Time was up.

Cole grabbed hold of the tarp containing Isaac and dragged it with ease across the grass that now had a light deposit of dew. The city, in the misguided spirit of beautification, had installed a park bench adjacent to a sidewalk not more than fifty yards away. The bench was in the shadows and Cole hastily covered the ground to dump Isaac next to it. Cole ran back to where Jamal and Warren lay. Jamal was next, he also glided across the dewed grass, but Cole had to grip the tarp with both hands and rapidly trudge backward to cross the fifty yards. Cole was exhausted when he dropped Jamal next to Isaac but willed himself with increased vigor. Warren was easier to drag but halfway to the bench a light came on in a ground-level apartment. Cole dragged the rolled-up tarp containing Warren even faster and made the bench just as a figure walked by the backlighted window. It was a woman who had no interest in peering out the window, as she undoubtedly was getting ready for work. Yet the threat was real; she or any tenant could sound the alert as he worked in plain sight.

Cole quickly untied the tarps and placed all three men on the bench. He untied Warren's tourniquets and blood began to spurt out; Warren was still alive but not for long. He checked Jamal's pulse; he was unconscious but also surprisingly still alive. Jamal was one tough son-of-a-bitch, but not for long. Cole gripped the pistol, still forced down Jamal's esophagus, and repeatedly pulled the trigger to empty the magazine; eleven more bullets dispensed their energy deep in Jamal's body. Shell casings pinked and tinkled as they bounced off the sidewalk making more noise than the twenty-two itself. Cole stepped back, pulled out his smartphone, and, with a flash, snapped a single picture. "Benched Disciples," he thought was an appropriate caption.

Chapter 33

Cigarette Man

Cole quickly rolled up the tarps and placed them in another garbage bag, tying a quick knot in its top to secure the contents. Another light came on in the apartment building, the second floor this time. It was well after five.

Cole took off at a dead run back to his possessions at the corner of the building. Hastily, Cole stripped off his shirt and pants. He carefully removed the baggie with Isaac's ears from his soiled pants; they were coming with him. He shoved his clothes in one of the garbage bags, and then dressed in the change of clothes he had brought from the apartment. He pulled his boots on over his now wet socks. A light in the window directly above him came on and stole his darkness. He slipped the baggie with Isaac's ears in the pocket of his clean pants, gripped his items, and headed for the Metro station, running whenever possible and walking whenever he might draw attention; he knew Armando would be there.

Traffic was increasing as he made his way down the street. Streetlights blazed and illuminated the street. He would undoubtedly attract the attention of passing cars and just hoped he would be dismissed as a street person in a hoodie. He had two large garbage bags and a tool bag, all of which helped create the image. Maybe a shopping cart would have helped, he thought. When no traffic or traffic cam was in sight, he ran until he sensed a car coming up from behind or saw one coming his way. Department of Transportation cameras at every intersection were hopefully capturing his facade rather than his identity. Some of the glass-protected electronics would only capture a digital still image but others were video and all would be recorded on a computer for inspection, if anyone chose to look. And he knew the police would. A street person would be their initial assumption and he hoped that would be as far as it would go.

Armando was there and popped the rear hatch on the minivan when he saw Cole approaching. Armando had cleverly parked outside the vision of the cameras and Cole was pleased. Cole tossed his bags into the back of the van and jumped in the back seat as Armando slammed the hatch closed and climbed in behind the wheel.

"You not look so good, boss. Okay?" inquired Armando.

"No. But it is what it is. Let's go."

"Phone GPS on maybe? I have microwave," said Armando.

Cole handed Armando two flip phones and one smartphone; he kept the satellite phone. Armando opened a small microwave oven on the seat next to him and placed the phones inside next to the taxicab's

GPS tracker. He closed the microwave door and then, quite pleased with himself, said, "All good now. Very good. No tell where we go now."

Cole instructed him to make a U-turn and go back down the street; Cole surmised that the cops trying to follow his tracks away from the Disciples would not suspect a taxi heading back in their direction. Once clear of the building, Cole gave Armando the first address. It was in Queens but timing was going to be close. Garbage pickup was already marching towards his destination. Cole urged Armando to accelerate their pace. Armando worked the main streets and side streets, turning right at red lights and timing those about to turn green.

Armando swerved into the opposing lane to pass a garbage truck creeping along to make its pickups. Cole instructed Armando to turn into the parking lot of a high-rise, pentagon-shaped apartment complex. They pulled up to a gated enclosure with four large garbage dumpsters. Overhead parking lot lights blinked off; daylight was here. Cole jumped out of the van and popped the rear hatch. As he hefted the bags, Cole instructed Armando to back the van off to the parking lot entrance. The bags seemed heavier now as he ran towards the enclosure. He heard garbage truck brakes squeal as the truck stopped just down the street. Cole hurled the garbage bags over the gate and then followed them. Inside, he buried his bags amongst the trash, one in each dumpster.

The garbage truck turned into the parking lot just as Cole exited the enclosure. He wasn't sure if the driver of the truck had seen him or not but began a casual stroll towards the apartment complex. The truck approached off his left shoulder, the brakes squealed, and the truck came to a stop at the enclosure gate. When the driver got out of the truck to open the gate and his back was turned, Cole changed directions and increased his pace towards the taxi. Cole climbed into the taxi as the hydraulic tines of the truck slipped into slots of the first dumpster. Cole and Armando accelerated into the now increasing traffic and headed east.

Cole pulled out his satellite phone and was about to call Kevin when he saw the text. Cole read the address on Menechant Street and gave Armando instructions. They were headed for the Bronx; Cole was glad it was on this side of the river, otherwise, they would never make it in time. Armando squealed to a stop at the red light only to floor the van and then change lanes in front of the car alongside. He cut left across traffic to take a side street and avoid the red light ahead. When the street intersected a main thoroughfare, Armando wheeled the van to the right and accelerated. He swerved the van back and forth into every available space between cars traveling towards the next light. His timing was impeccable and he shot the taxi through on a yellow. The sky to the east now showed a rising sun. Armando continued his frantic attack on the streets of Brooklyn.

Cole pulled the envelope with the note from his pocket. He glanced at Armando in the rearview mirror and then discreetly pulled the baggie from his pants pocket. The ears looked more Halloween-like now than before. Light red blood, still wet, coated the inside of the baggie with the ears, almost spongy-like, slipping and sliding inside the baggie with every touch. He looked again at Armando and then slipped the baggie and its contents into the envelope. He didn't seal it, just folded the envelope carefully and placed it in his shirt pocket.

Armando swerved again and then made a rapid right turn. He announced, "Two blocks. Thirty seconds." And then asked, "You want me wait?"

They passed the address as Cole responded, "No, just circle the block once or twice until you see me on the corner. I should be no more than fifteen minutes. Give me the smartphone"

"GPS on. They know where you go."

"You're right. It's all turned off, but you never know. It's just a risk."

"Roger that," cheerfully replied Armando and pulled Cole's smartphone from the small microwave oven sitting on the front seat. "I circle for at least hour. Not worry."

The van screeched to a halt at the red light and Cole jumped out. Armando made a right and disappeared from sight. Cole headed back the way they had come, towards 88 Menechant Street. Menechant Street was one-way and Cole now faced oncoming traffic. The street was a mixed assortment of 1940s construction homes and small two or three-story apartment buildings. Cars along the street filled every possible parking space. To his back, sunlight now brightened the horizon. It was already warm, yet the warmth on Cole's back felt good. He stopped at the corner of an apartment building shading five small houses, each house not much wider than the width of the parking space in front. The five houses were each unique and set back from the street leaving room for a small yard and car. Each had an iron fence with a car-width gate. A car was parked behind four of the five locked gates. Each gate and small fenced area had been personalized for each house making them all unique. The first house had the widest fenced area and no car in front of it. The building's basic brick structure was accented with colorful awnings sheltering the entrance and windows. The remaining four homes had narrower lots and also had colorful awnings. The third house over, number eighty-eight, had red awnings with white trim. An aging white Audi station wagon was parked in front; it had been backed in leaving its nose only a foot from the gate. The gate and enclosure had been extended up beyond the original five feet by an additional three, further deterring anyone from scaling the fence or gate. He searched the soffit, doorbell button, and underside of the awnings for surveillance cameras and wasn't sure; there could be a small camera tucked up under the roof eave. His eyes strained and imagined the captured image. It might not cover the sidewalk, at least based on the elevated location and an imagined downward view angle if it was really a camera.

The sun now fully blazed from the horizon. Cole looked at his shadow stretching down the sidewalk; he had to decide; time was up. He stared down the street and then blew through his fist as he contemplated options. He hurried back to a nineties Ford pickup with a whip antenna. Traffic was picking up, people were somewhere behind their windows, a woman jogged towards him two blocks off in the distance, and he knew that his act of vandalism would not go unnoticed. He pulled a hundred-dollar bill from his pocket and slipped it inside the truck through its loose-fitting side window before snapping off the whip antenna. Cole hurried back to the gate guarding the Audi and took the envelope containing the note and ears out of his pocket. He punctured the envelope at its edge and inserted the tip of the antenna inside the envelope up to its fold. He then used the antenna to float the envelope over the Audi's hood to the edge of the wiper blade. With a gentle shove, the envelope slipped under the edge of the wiper blade. Cole withdrew the antenna.

As the antenna cleared the fence, Cole saw the front door of the house begin to open. Cole, at almost a run, hurried back down the street. He dropped the antenna into the bed of the truck and then ducked in front of it. Traffic was building. Cole calculated his timing and darted across both lanes of one-way traffic without being the recipient of a blaring horn. He emerged on the sidewalk and sat down on the third step leading up to an apartment building.

The view was perfect, and also discrete. Diagonally through the front side window and back rear window of a car at the curb, Cole watched as the man stood at the front door of the Audi and pressed the button on his key fob. The man opened the car's front door and started to climb in before noticing the envelope stuck under the edge of the windshield wiper. He stood at the open door and, with a puzzled look on his face, questioned the envelope; he looked from envelope to gate, then left and right down the street, and then back to the envelope. The man let the door swing back closed and then, carefully using only forefinger and thumbnail, pulled the envelope free of the windshield wiper. The man unfolded the envelope using a pen from his pocket and read its message. Cole could almost see his lips move: "You will listen when I call or the next pair will be yours."

The man then surprised Cole. He didn't react at all as Cole had expected. He instead displayed very cautious and interrogating mannerisms reminiscent of someone with criminal investigation training. With the envelope on the hood, the man used the pen to open the flap and peer inside the envelope. Then, using only the back of his forefinger fingernail and the pen, carefully slid the baggie with the ears partway out of the envelope. He moved his head first to the left and then to the right to get an angled view of the ears. There was no sign of shock, disbelief, or fear, only the careful interrogation of a crime scene professional. Cole wondered if he had gotten the wrong address, but then he knew better. Kevin didn't make mistakes.

The man very carefully slid the baggie with the ears back into the envelope and then, with his pen, carried the envelope with him and climbed into the car. Cole watched as the man made some kind of adjustment inside the car, probably doing something to protect the envelope from loss of forensic clues and keep it free of contamination. Had he ever touched the envelope or baggie with bare hands, Cole wondered. He hadn't touched it this morning; he was wearing surgical gloves then, just as he was now. But in the past, had he ever touched the envelope? When he opened the box of envelopes, could he have accidentally left a thumbprint? What about the sandwich baggies? How long had they been in his kitchen? Three months he concluded but he couldn't be sure he hadn't touched the baggie as well.

The man reached to his visor and pressed a remote button. The car-width gate slowly swung outward and the Audi pulled forward. As the Audi pulled into traffic, the gate closed. Cole was ready when the car passed and snapped a picture with his smartphone. It wasn't a very good picture, but maybe Kevin could do something with it. Maybe he could verify this was Greg Grimes, Julie's boss the cigarette man.

Cole saw Armando approaching and stepped between parked cars. Although unnecessary, Cole waived as if flagging down a taxi. Armando momentarily double-parked while Cole climbed into the back seat.

Armando inquired, "Where to boss?"

"Metro."

"You want me take cell phone. No one to know where go."

"No. I'm good. GPS doesn't work on my phone. But thanks for looking out for me."

"Boss, you want me take to hospital?"

"Nope."

"Okay, boss. I have cleaner for blood. No worry then."

"Sorry Armando," said Cole as he looked at his right sleeve.

"Okay. We go now."

Cole dialed Kevin on his encrypted satellite phone.

Kevin answered on the first ring. "You ass. I knew you'd torture them. You are a psychotic lunatic. You know that. Only a sick bastard could do those things."

"I get it, Kevin," interrupted Cole putting an end to the tirade. "Now focus. Do you know who is investigating the Samantha Ogalsby murder?"

"Yep, I got a detective's name."

"Good, send him the photo of the last three in their suits from hell. Don't send it to the media or social media. The Disciples killed that little girl just to make a point in some blackmail scheme. A kid by the name of Tommy Delahe is next if word gets out."

"Okay."

"Let the detective know that it is over, at least as far as the Disciples go."

"I should hope so. I think you have done enough."

"After you've taken care of that, go to work on a Reed Delahe and a Ken Kuoto in Huntsville, Alabama. Tommy Delahe is in hiding in Utah with his nanny. No first name on the nanny, just Johnston for a last. This Ken Kuoto contracted for this whole thing. I'll fill you in all the details later but see what you can learn." Cole paused and then added, "And get my cigarettes."

"It isn't that easy. I mean a cargo container and a million dollars worth of cigarettes. Come on, Cole."

"No, you come on, Kevin. Hard never stopped you before, just do it."

"I don't like you."

"I know. But I love you nonetheless."

"You Ass."

"Get me a first-class ticket to Huntsville Alabama for this afternoon under the name of Helmut Hoelzer. Book him from Atlanta to Huntsville under that name."

"What do think I am? Your travel agent!" barked Kevin.

"Just do it. Get Julie Addison and Bob Goddard first-class tickets going to—say Miami. Route us through Atlanta on the same New York flight. Make sure we have a good layover so that Helmut can make the Huntsville flight. Get Julie a second ticket under another name from Atlanta to Salt Lake City Utah. Can you do that?"

"Sure, I can do that. I can do a lot of things. But you're a fool if you think she'll help you. Even if she does, do you want to involve her? Have you told her about your little psychotic mass execution problem? Does she know what you did last night?"

"I'm not sure I want to involve her but I may have no choice. We'll see. Last thing, this is Bob Goddard's last trip. This afternoon it becomes Helmut Hoelzer. Get me a car and hotel room in Huntsville."

"I am not your damn travel agent."

"But you do it so well. Bye," concluded Cole and disconnected.

Armando swerved in and out of traffic while keeping an ever-watchful eye out for police. Traffic cameras were a threat and Armando always approached with the appearance of perfect compliance with traffic laws. However, once clear of a camera, Armando pushed the van with every ounce of speed. As Cole finished his conversation, Armando pulled onto a side street out of view from watchful camera eyes. "Ready, here boss. Half block from Metro," Armando said as the van came to a stop.

"New plan. Just take me to the Wisco building in Stuyvesant."

"Ready that, boss."

It was a risk, but he trusted Armando. Given his current appearance, riding the tram would have made him a standout worth remembering. This was definitely a safer option.

The cab rocked back and forth as Armando worked through the ever-increasing traffic. His thoughts were now of Julie. He hadn't thought of her all night and now he just smiled. She was probably just waking, her scent fresh on his bed sheets. He had just met the woman and yet he wondered. Could she be the one? Could she ever understand and accept him? Could he love her like he'd loved Dominique? They could go to Hungary and live out their lives at his farmhouse. Or they could join Kevin and his girlfriend in Tobago and spend their lives on the beach. Could he reform and live a peaceful life with her at his side? Perhaps, but not until Kuoto had been dealt with.

Cole's thoughts faded and he dozed off. He didn't wake until Armando made the arrival notification: "Okay boss. Two blocks out. Sixty seconds."

Cole's senses re-engaged. What had he missed? Cole watched buildings fly passed until Armando pulled up directly in front of the Wisco building. If anybody were watching, it would be a risk for him as well as Armando. Maybe it was a bad decision, he considered.

Cole handed Armando a tightly wrapped sack with half the cash from the drive-up drugstore.

"There's extra for you this time," Cole said and smiled at Armando in the rearview mirror. "Take the rest of the day off and, as usual, you never saw me."

"Saw who," replied Armando as he handed Cole his flip phones from the microwave oven. "Very good now, boss."

Cole slipped out of the van. He pondered what Armando would think when the bag was opened; he would find probably more than a month's pay. Perhaps it was too much. But then Cole always shared the spoils of entrepreneurship with those that helped. And, in the grand scheme of things, it was just pocket change. Maybe he should buy Armando his own fleet of taxis. The thought pleased him.

Armando drove away. Cole waited a few minutes. No one was following. Of course, with the way Armando drove, no one could. Cole made the short walk to the corner of the building and waited for another ten minutes to observe, study, and analyze everything. All was in order. He entered the building, ducking his head to avoid the overhead camera, and walked to the elevator. The elevator closed creating a feeling of claustrophobia, and the not knowing of what would be outside the door when it opened. The elevator took him up and the imagined fears were unrealized. Cole momentarily paused at his front door, key card in hand wondering if Julie would still be there. He entered quietly and heard the fluffing of pillows from his bedroom. "Julie," he softly inquired.

She emerged from the bedroom and stared at him. She was as beautiful as ever, even with the coloring from the bruise on the side of her face.

"Oh," she said in surprise.

He didn't understand the surprise; after all, it was his condo. "How are you feeling?" he asked.

"Pretty good. Are you okay?" she asked as she approached.

Cole meekly replied, "Sure. Just in desperate need of a shower and a little sleep."

"Oh my God. What's dripping off your sleeve? It's not blood, is it?"

"It'll be all right."

"I don't think so! Is that a bruise on your neck? What happened to your face? My God. Is that from the parking lot?" Julie then abruptly took a half step back and commanded, "You need a doctor."

"No. Please excuse me to shower and get a little sleep. Then we can talk and maybe plan a trip."

Cole noticed an ever so slight twitch of Julie's upper cheek, which he took as a sign of agreement. She didn't inquire where or why; she just accepted the state of things as Cole stepped past her. He retrieved a medical bag from over the kitchen sink and started towards the bathroom. Julie looked at him with an inquisitive stare but didn't ask.

In the bathroom, Cole assessed his wounds: bruises everywhere, maybe three broken ribs, half the stitches in his shoulder ripped out, stab wound to his leg was also bleeding. The bullet that grazed the scar on his side had done little damage but hurt like hell to the touch. He found another grazing bullet wound across his abdomen that he was unaware of; it had to have come from Jamal's .22. Cole showered and scrubbed at the bleeding wounds. He then spent the next hour sterilizing, re-stitching, and bandaging wounds.

Clothes and used bandaging went in a plastic trash-can for later dosing with bleach before disposal. He emerged naked from the bathroom to find underwear and a T-shirt. As he extracted the items from his dresser drawer, Julie entered the bedroom and screeched, "Oh my God." Cole ignored her and pulled his underwear up.

She put her hands on her hips and commanded, "You need a doctor. We are going right now."

"No."

Cole turned around to find a T-shirt in the dresser drawer. He pulled a Mets T-shirt out.

"Your back, my God," said Julie referring to old wounds and new bruises.

"What happened to you? You have to see a doctor."

"Absolutely not," asserted Cole. On the verge of passing out from sleep deprivation and adrenaline exhaustion, Cole curtly added, "Enough! Now please, I just need a couple hours sleep."

Cole put the Mets T-shirt on, slipped into bed, and closed his eyes.

Chapter 34

Transformation

Julie let CNN run on the TV while she evaluated many disturbing and conflicting thoughts. This Hamilton Cole Davis wasn't the man she expected. His old wounds told a different story; something had been missed altogether. There was no record of the surgeries he had to have had: the grotesque scar on his side and the hundred smaller ones on his back. Where could they have come from? His actions and secretiveness, past and present, were not at all predicted. This was all wrong. How could this be?

There was something else that she refused to admit and it kept resurfacing. What's worse, it was becoming stronger. It had to be suppressed; that's all there was to it. She had first recognized it months ago, but that was her secret and he could never know.

News stories were afire with sensationalized breaking stories about self-proclaimed vigilantes that had killed or maimed a dozen Black men in the New York area. There was a brief mention of a young girl who was killed earlier in the week. But most of the reporting was on how the BLM community was in an uproar, how slow police officials had responded, how protests were expected, and how commentary experts had hypothesized origins of the perpetrators. A popular theme among the experts was that the perpetrators were part of a new sect of the Nationalist Boys that obviously had racist motives. Media experts had conclusive insight that the TOMY BOY carving left on the chest of the victims was clearly a signature of the Nationalist Boys. The TOMY part of the carving was uncertain, but the BOY part of the carving was a clear signature of the Nationalist Boys.

One CNN expert had, however, deciphered the message. TOMY was a slang acronym: Total Opposition to Mayata Yams. The acronym offensively included Hispanic and Italian variations of the "N" word. And it was signed by the Nationalist BOYs.

CNN played a portion of New York Mayor Como's news conference and then supplemented it with their own interpretation. Como was appalled at the racially motivated acts of violence perpetrated on the residents of New York. This was the worst racially motivated mass killing in the history of New York and he was calling on the Federal government to step in. The New York City Attorney General was going to file charges against the Nationalist Boys for causing racial unrest, and then eventually when sufficient evidence was developed, charges for the murders would be filed against members of the organization.

Julie switched the channel to CBS, as Cole emerged fully dressed from the bedroom. Nora Donald was just coming on the Channel: "Breaking news just in from CBS investigative reporters. They have discovered that the murders committed in New York are linked to an eleven-year-old girl. We'll take you now live to Melisa Contrail. Melisa, what can you tell us about this latest development?"

"Nora, this building behind me in one of New York's poorest neighborhoods was the scene of another grisly racially motivated murder where an eleven-year-old girl was killed and mutilated four nights ago. I'm here with the child's mother. It brings the total death count to…"

"Please turn that shit off," requested Cole.

Julie complied and responded, "The whole world has gone nuts."

Julie saw a moment of evasion in Cole's eyes as he hesitated for a response and then turned his head. As if searching for an answer, he searched the room with his eyes: first surveying the room, and then just staring at the ceiling. Internally she cringed. Did he know?

Things weren't right. The living room gave off vibrations of change. Cole studied each detail of the room: a small scuff mark on the floor from a shifting of the couch, multiple footsteps were almost visible in the imperceptible layer of dust on the floor, table light on the end table was perfectly centered, window drapes were opened just ever so slightly wider, and framed paintings on the walls looked okay but somehow their appearance was different. Had he missed these details earlier this morning when he came in?

Or had he just been too tired to notice? Very subtle and unexplainable, but taken in total, added up to the apartment having been searched, probably by more than one individual. Could they have found Kevin's secret computer room? Cole studied light fixtures and resurveyed the room. Could there be more, video surveillance perhaps? He just stared at the ceiling. If it was surveillance, that's where it would be, perhaps even a team in the apartment above. How could this apartment have been compromised? What about Kevin's security cameras? Was he followed earlier this morning and the apartment searched while he slept? If they'd wanted him, they could have taken him while he slept. Makes no sense. Searched before he came in this morning? With Julie here sleeping? How? Maybe she went out? When? Again, if they'd wanted him, they could have taken him while he slept. Was this to be added to a growing awareness about Julie? The stray thought that this was all just part of his normal paranoia was quickly rejected. Escape and evade returned to the forefront of his thoughts. "What?" he shouted within himself.

Cole blew into his fist and contemplated options before calmly addressing Julie, "Julie, perhaps I can give you some answers, but not right now. Put your shoes on. We're leaving."

"What?" Julie questioned.

"We're going for breakfast."

"What the hell, Cole?"

Cole saw the distress on Julie's face and it matched her tone, "Last night I laid some groundwork to deal with untaxed cigarettes." Cole observed the subtle little twitch of Julie's cheek that he'd now seen many times.

She conceded, "I need to freshen up but I want to know exactly what groundwork you did?"

"I worked on solving your cigarette problem," stated Cole. "I'll tell you more later. For now, just put your shoes on so we can go to breakfast."

"I don't understand, but I do know a good place for breakfast near here. It's called Hornito's. I'll take you there if you promise to tell me what's going on. I'd like to know where all the blood and bruises came from."

"I'll just say that whatever happened last night was invited and it's not at all what it appears. And it ended with a critical message related to untaxed cigarettes. Now please get your shoes on."

"I don't like this at all," said Julie as she went in search of her shoes.

With Julie out of sight, Cole sent Kevin a text, "SIAR." It was code for we are screwed. Kevin would react accordingly.

When Julie returned from the bedroom, she had done something to partially conceal the bruise on her face, probably makeup or something. Cole knew her bruises, as well as his, would continue to become more apparent throughout the day and that could be an issue.

Julie repeated her breakfast request, "Hornitos, right?"

Cole crisply replied, "Yes," as he glanced up at the ceiling again and then opened the door to the apartment. They exited without further conversation and made their way to the elevator. When they exited the building, Cole didn't bother avoiding the surveillance camera. His instincts, observations, and suspicions were now fully in sync. They, whoever they were, were watching. He knew it.

On the street, Julie said, "Hornitos is this way."

"Yes and that's why we're going this way," said Cole as he took her arm and they headed in the opposite direction. Cole flagged down a cab and Julie reluctantly climbed in. Cole instructed the driver, "JFK."

Julie demanded, "What the hell?"

"Please, trust me. I'm going to ask Kevin to work with you on some arrangements that will rectify your cigarette problem. It's the kind of thing Kevin and I do best." At each mention of the word Kevin, Cole observed that peculiar, almost imperceptible, little twitch of Julie's cheek.

"All right," Julie said submissively. "Maybe this mysterious Kevin will give me some straight answers." Julie smiled and her beauty blossomed. "When do I get to meet this mysterious Kevin?"

Cole didn't answer. His thoughts went to Kuoto.

The cab arrived at departures for JFK. Kevin had been a fine travel agent; Bob Goddard and Julie Addison retrieved first-class tickets terminating in Miami with a layover in Atlanta from the kiosk. Julie studied her tickets and Cole saw more questions forming but she said nothing. Cole adjusted his glasses and they put their masks on as they proceeded to security. Little was said as TSA passed them through security with the rest of the cattle. They had no luggage, which was a TSA red flag. But they were allowed to pass without incident. In the food court, they grabbed a breakfast sandwich, at which, Julie's only words were, "This wasn't what I had in mind."

The flight to Atlanta was equally uneventful and almost no words were spoken between them. Julie had a Chardonnay. Cole just drank water, lots of it; he was in recovery mode and his body craved hydration. Cole's mind was at work and he relished the silence and peace of the flight. It seemed as if Julie was equally content and doing some thinking of her own. At touchdown, Cole sent a discrete text to Kevin on things to follow.

As they exited the plane in Atlanta, Cole's senses went to high alert. Not because of the watchers, but because he had to find someone he had never seen before. He, or she, would be a geeky-looking type carrying a small briefcase, probably looking very nervous, probably social distancing off in the most unpopulated part of the terminal, yet close enough to the gate to see all the passengers coming off the plane. He, or she, wouldn't know who they looking for, only that they were to be at the gate and that they would be found. The finding was Cole's challenge. Everything was a game to Kevin and this was just another game Kevin had arranged: can't go to Boardwalk, if you can't get to Park Place first or some distorted BS like that.

There, Cole said to himself but then identified a second candidate. Two possibilities: one in view of the surveillance cameras—the other not. Cole stopped in the middle of the terminal and faced Julie: "This is where we part. I need you to make a call to Kevin. Use my burner phone. You'll be in his hands for a while. Can you remember a phone number?"

"Cole," pleaded Julie. "What's going on?"

"Just trust me. Kevin is an ass. But just follow his instructions." Julie's subtle little cheek twitch registered again and he continued. "The number you need to call is 555-555-0134. It'll go through some strange periods of silence and beeps, but just hang on; it will go through."

"I'm not sure I like this."

"Find someplace isolated and make the call: 555-555-0134." Cole moved forward to give her a gentle kiss on her cheek, but she shied away. Julie shook her head and Cole could see tears swelling up in her eyes.

"I'm so confused," she said and turned to walk away.

You're confused, Cole said to himself; that's an understatement. He yearned for her acceptance, but it was squelched by a growing and very uncomfortable awareness.

As she disappeared down the concourse, Cole approached the first of his possible contacts. He was just out of view of the ever-present surveillance cameras. He was a rather small man, probably still in his twenties, with glasses, tight dress pants that were too short, a wrinkled blue dress shirt, and very nervous behaviors, "Dogs fly kites," Cole said when he reached the man.

"That's not the passphrase," the small man said in an almost feminine voice.

"Um, okay. How about 'dogs fly cat kites'?"

"I don't know. It's supposed to be 'dogs fly kitty kites,' but I guess it's close enough. Here's your stuff," he said and handed Cole a small briefcase. "Mississippi driver's license, credit cards, passport, and the ticket to Huntsville. You're already checked in Mr. Helmut Hoelzer."

Nothing more was said and Cole proceeded to the departure gate for the Miami flight. He studied the people forming in line; first class at the front, then preferred seating, and finally cattle class in the rear. He spotted a man near the end of the line wearing a leather vest with a multitude of patches: Two Tours Iraq, Enduring Freedom, 435th Infantry, Afghanistan, American Flag, and many others. Cole approached. "Veteran?" Cole inquired.

"Yep. Three tours in the Middle East."

"Damn. I don't think you guys get enough recognition for what you did for this country. We Americans need to do more to let you know just how much we appreciate your service."

"Well, thanks."

"Tell you what, and it's just a small thing. Probably not supposed to do it, but I'm going to anyway. What seat do you have?

The man glanced at his ticket and replied, "42B. Center seat I suppose."

"I've got 2A. Here," said Cole as he offered his first-class Bob Goddard ticket to the man. "Trade me."

"I can't do that."

"Yes, you can. And it'll make me feel better. It's just my way of letting you know how much we appreciate your service to this Country."

"That's awful gracious of you. What's your name?"

"Bob Goddard. What's yours?

"Jimmy Fontain," said the man and took Cole's ticket.

"Great," said Cole and smiled. "I'll take your place in line and you can move to the front. They should be calling first-class any minute."

"Mister you just made my day," said Jimmy as he picked up his small backpack and headed off towards the front of the line.

Cole watched as Jimmy took his place with the rest of the first-class passengers. They soon called first-class and the boarding process began. When Jimmy entered the jetway, Cole wadded up Jimmy's cattle class ticket and put it in his pocket. He waited a few moments, stepped out of line, and surreptitiously melded into the crowd moving down the concourse. Cole was now Helmut Hoelzer and Bob Goddard was on his way to Miami, at least as far as any passenger manifest would indicate. The watchers, whoever they were, would no doubt be waiting in Miami. When they discovered Bob Goddard never actually arrived, it would take hours of video review to find the exchange in line and even then it would lead nowhere. Cole took the train to the A Concourse and headed for the Brewmaster Pub. Surveillance cameras would have him entering but not leaving, which would make the transition to Helmut Hoelzer complete.

Julie walked away from Cole and any hint of a smile turned into a frown. What she was doing, in so many respects, now just felt wrong. She studied the concourse and found a gate where the next scheduled flight was still hours away and there were few waiting passengers. She dialed the number Cole had given her. Unbeknownst to her, a device on the Seven train back in New York began processing the call. The device was in plain sight, attached to the forwardmost wall of one of the cars. In bold red letters on a yellow background, the circular sign said: CAUTION—MAGNETIC SEN-SITIVITY—DO NOT REMOVE. In the center of the sign was a small receiver-transmitter. As the train rattled down the tracks, the call was re-routed to a similar receiver-transmitter on yet another train and then re-routed again to a third receiver-transmitter in Guadalajara Mexico where the call then went through to Kevin. Julie listened and waited through a series of beeps and silence until she finally got a ringtone. The ringtone continued until she was almost ready to hang up.

"Hi," came a distant response.

"Kevin?" she inquired.

"Maybe."

"Cole told me to call this number."

"I'll bet he did. How are you, Jules?"

"My name's Julie."

"Maybe."

"What the hell?"

"Was your grandmother really from Stockholm?"

"Ah, no. I think she was from Gothenburg."

"Do you?"

"What is this?"

"Maybe it's a test. Maybe it's a game. But I will find out."

"It's bullshit," Julie abruptly replied. "Cole said you would give me instructions and you would take care of me. Now where can we meet?"

"Ooh, fiery."

"Are you trying to piss me off?"

"Maybe."

"Cole's right; he said you were an ass."

"That's because he loves me. And I bet you've got him fooled."

"That's it! I'm about done with this call."

"What grade school did you go to, then, before you hang up?"

"Clarkston Elementary. Now can we get on with this? What instructions do you have for me?"

"You were an ugly third grader. What play were you in that made the yearbook?"

"I don't know. Jesus Christ! Ass doesn't even come close!" Julie retorted nearing her frustration limit.

"Well I'll let it go for now but you should think about it. So I want you to exit the airport and get a cab to the closest Walmart. Buy a large roll of tin foil. Buy four prepaid burner cell phones with at least a hundred hours on each. Don't forget the tin foil. Cole gave you some cash. Use it to buy the phones and tin foil. Then get another cab to take you to the Best Western on Hawthorn. You have a reservation under your own name and they have an envelope for you at the check-in counter. Reservation was made using your VISA card. Get all four phones fully charged. Wait at the hotel until I call you," matter-of-factly directed Kevin and then disconnected.

COLE TOOK THE ESCALATOR UP TO THE BREWMAS-ter Pub. He quickly identified and evaluated the coverage of surveillance cameras and found a table near the window offering limited coverage and backlighting to further challenge the camera's ability to capture his features and actions. He ordered a German lager and studied the bar patrons. No one was paying any attention. He removed his green outer shirt and placed it on the back of his chair. As Cole sipped his beer, he verified the contents of the briefcase he had been given. Credit cards, driver's license, passport, and ticket for Huntsville, all in the name of Helmut Hoelzer, along with a bundle of hundred dollar bills and four bundles of twenties.

Two well-built men in suites arrived at the top of the escalator and Cole's mind began the interrogation. They exited right and never glanced in his direction, which didn't mean they weren't a threat. Just that if they were, they were really good. Waiting until the camera view was blocked by transitioning bar patrons, Cole nonchalantly inverted his reversible green shirt and slipped it on, blue side out. He then put on his mask and slipped his glasses on as he rose to leave. He hated the glasses and the mask, but the glasses hopefully deceived facial recognition software by changing the projected distance between his eyes. His posture drooped to make himself look as diminutive and non-threatening as possible. Hiding with the bar patrons, he made his way to the elevator primarily reserved for the handicapped, but accessible to all, and was soon melding in with the crowd in the concourse.

Cole made his way to the escalator down to the plane train. He boarded and remained ever-vigilant in his observations. Fake little airplane propellers attached to the tunnel wall spun as the train sped past, no doubt to provide some level of amusement for hundreds of thousands of travelers. The ride was short and he quickly arrived at the C Concourse. The gate for Huntsville Alabama was just beginning its boarding process. Cole discretely monitored the gate and assessed every boarding passenger. As the line dwindled, Cole approached the gate and handed his ticket to the gate attendant. She passed it over the reader and without any words being spoken, Helmut Hoelzer entered the jetway. He took his seat, put his briefcase under the seat in front, fastened his seat belt, and closed his eyes. The transformation was complete. At least, he'd lost anyone trailing him. At most, Helmut Hoelzer was just another passenger amongst thousands and anyone in the hunt would be in Miami searching for Bob Goddard.

JULIE DID EXACTLY AS DIRECTED BY KEVIN. SHE checked in at the Best Western under her own name and proceeded to her room with Walmart bag and the mysterious envelope given to her at the check-in counter. The envelope contained a passport, two credit cards, a Mississippi driver's license, a bundle of hundred dollar bills, and four bundles of twenties. Julie studied the passport. It had a somewhat recent picture, an official stamp, and in every way looked official. It was the name that jumped out at her, Ellie Mae Clampet. "Shit," she mumbled and pictured the ditsy blond from an ancient 1960s television show. It had to be Kevin intentionally trying to piss her off.

The call did come as promised. She let her cell phone ring several times just to make him wait. She could play insult games too.

"Hello, Kevin McKermit," she answered.

"Well, I see you're trying to be insulting."

"Why, Kermit is a very handsome frog. At least as appealing as a ditsy blond from the 1960's. And Kermit fits you so well."

"It won't work Jules. Insults are my specialty. And I just happen to like Kermit the Frog. Oh, it was McKermit. Wasn't it?"

"But now I have a visual image to put with your voice," Julie chided and smiled.

"I'll accept that. Now let's get to work. We have to make your burners functional. I want you to do exactly as I say and we'll get two of the phones set up. Take one of the phones and access 'settings,' 'access,' then 'voice.' Use the second phone to call the first."

"Okay, wait a minute," interrupted Julie as she accessed the phone's control functions.

"It's real simple, Jules. Come on. Now you're going to set it up so that the first phone will activate when it hears a ringtone from the second phone, and will then subsequently answer the second phone. Now, with an incoming call open on the second phone, the first phone will be set to accept voice commands from you. Simple."

It wasn't simple. And Julie felt like it was just more opportunity for Kevin to berate and insult her as he walked her through the process. Eventually, she got the two phones set up, both plugged into chargers, and the phones themselves positioned closely together so they could talk to each other. Then Kevin had her wrap her phone and the other two burners in multiple layers of tin foil, which seemed very strange but she complied.

"Now, the next steps are going to be up to you," continued Kevin with instructions. "Take the two phones you just set up along with their chargers, get out, hang the 'Do Not Disturb' sign on the door, and make your way out of the hotel without being seen or captured on surveillance cameras. There aren't many cameras at the Best Western so it shouldn't be a challenge."

"Okay, I can do that. Then what?" compliantly replied Julie.

"Make your way on foot four blocks east without being observed or followed to the Squire Inn and check in as Ellie Mae. Set up the phones just like before where one can call the other. Use one of the phones to call the number I gave you before when everything is ready. Then I'll tell you what's next," curtly concluded Kevin and hung up.

Julie left the hotel through a side entrance and avoided the surveillance camera by working her way down the wall. Once on the street, she made no eye contact with anyone and avoided traffic cams as best she could. The Squire Inn was AAA certified, at least that's what the sign said, but it was a dump. She had a reservation and checked in. The small Indian woman at the check-in desk hardly spoke English and took no special notice of the name Ellie Mae Clampet. Inside her room, Julie did as instructed with the two phones and called the number Kevin had provided. It strangely delayed, beeped, and then went through to Kevin.

Kevin looked over at Liu as the phone rang. Liu shook her head as confirmation and said, "Uploaded." Liu's Capture and Spy software was now loaded onto one of the two phones. All cell phone conversations would be captured. But more importantly, the cell phone microphone and camera were secretly active even when the phone was powered down.

Kevin answered the call, "All good Jules?"

"Just like you told me, Kevin. After I hang up, I'll put this phone in position with the other. But why are we doing this?"

"Just part of the game Jules. You'll find out soon enough. Now, after you return the phone to its position, simply exit the hotel room, hang out the 'Do Not Disturb' sign, and return to the Best Western. From now on, whenever we communicate it will be through the two phones there at the Squire Inn. At some point we may even use the Squire Inn as a rendezvous location," finished Kevin and disconnected.

Chapter 35

REASSESSMENT

NSA DIRECTOR AND USCYBERCOM COMMANDER, Blaine Higgins began his second briefing to the head of the FBI, DIA, CIA, and Homeland Security, along with the Secretary of State, Secretary of Defense, NSA Section Q (Security and Counterintelligence) Director, two select NSA Section Q IT specialists, and a NSA Section Q special ops liaison. Higgins put up the slide of Kevin McKuel and began: "Operation Cool Fool has demonstrated a unique new tool in our arsenal of weapons. Our characteristic algorithms allow us to anticipate every move of a known criminal suspect and then use that data to rapidly infiltrate with undercover agents." He paused and waited for the statement to sink in and then re-enforced it, "Given any situation, given any set of circumstances, given any environment, we can predict what an individual will do. We start with an intense study of the individual's psychological characteristics and then code them for assessment by parasympathetic, somatic, and autonomic AI algorithms. We call it PSIAA for short. Then numerous scenarios are input and response predictions are output. For Operation Cool Fool, it has proven more than 95% accurate. And that's why at this time, I am able to announce that we have undercover personnel on the inside and very near Kevin McKuel."

Higgins moved to the next slide. "Here in the very near future, I'm going to ask the president to allow me to offer NSA PSIAA services to all agencies. I think we could make it a standard practice across all intelligence and regulatory agencies."

Evert Hooster, the FBI director, interrupted, "Higgins I'm sitting here biting my tongue. You have no idea how pissed I am! I have two dead agents and all you want to do is give me a sales pitch. What the Hell? Now, when are you going tell us you have McKuel dealt with?"

Higgins responded, "I am just trying to explain the value of the new NSA-developed algorithm. I hope you see the value in our development capabilities."

"God dammit, Higgins!" shouted Evert. "You're not listening. I've had enough. Now, when are we going to have this McKuel character? Because I'm not going to wait. I'm going to pull the plug on FBI support."

Higgins squirmed internally, his mouth went dry, and his Adam's apple choked his breathing. He managed a response, "I think I'll go to the President when we have some concrete results."

"I'm not waiting for concrete results!" lambasted Evert. "This meeting is over as far as I'm concerned." Evert Hooster abruptly got up from his chair and promptly marched to the door. He turned, pointed his finger at Higgins, and said, "I'll give you two days and then the FBI is done!"

The director of the Secretary of Defense followed suit, "I think that's a good idea," and then, got up, and also exited the meeting.

Soon the others also left the meeting: some without saying a word, some echoing expectations for a follow-up, full-disclosure meeting in two days. Higgins was abashed. His career was on the line. Now he had only one avenue left. He exited the secure confines of the Fort Meade NSA headquarters building and made the call. He requested a meeting with the President at his earliest possible convenience.

Chapter 36

CIGARETTE MAN COMPLIANCE

JULIE SAT ON THE EDGE OF THE BED AT THE BEST Western wondering what was next. Julie took one of the tin foil-wrapped burners out of her bag and unwrapped it. She dialed the number Kevin had given her.

The call went through the two phones at the Squire Inn, to the receiver transmitter on New York's Seven train, then on to another train, on to El Paso, and then finally to Kevin. "Hello," answered Kevin on the first ring. "I've been waiting. You didn't walk very fast."

"I walked fast enough. I don't like any of this."

"Then you better just leave now. Don't even say goodbye, because we'll be done."

"You ass."

"Yes, but the game is serious. And now somebody's circus is coming to town."

"What? What does a circus have to do with anything?"

"You know exactly what I'm talking about. But don't worry. Just do exactly as I say." Uncharacteristically rapid-fire, Kevin continued, "You have calls to make and then you're going to make payments. You're going to have to be tough and efficient to pull this off. Are you ready? Get a pencil and paper to write this down."

Julie interrupted, "No memory test?"

"No time. Now are you ready?"

In a rapid-fire sequence, Kevin gave Julie instructions. She scribbled notes on the motel pad as he talked. When he was done with the instructions, he simply hung up.

First on her list was to make a call to her boss, Greg Grimes, with Cole tied in. She first called Cole, who had just gotten off the plane in Huntsville. The call was routed through Miami and then on to Huntsville. With little pleasantries, just "Are you there," then she called the second of the phones at the Squire Inn. The phone was opened at the sound of the ring tone and via recorded voice command answered the second phone. Within a few seconds, Julie was able to command, "Call 555-555-0135," which was promptly answered by Greg Grimes.

"Hello,"

Julie was fearful Cole might somehow learn things very uncomfortable for her and this call had to be very careful.

Cole spoke first: "You will listen when I call or the next pair will be yours. Do you understand? "

"The message came with ears. I'm listening."

Julie listened intently as the silent partner in the conference call. Julie pondered, ears? What the hell?

Cole continued. "You are to buy all future untaxed cigarettes from us. You will buy them by the cargo container load. You will make a lot of money. We will make a lot of money. My price is twenty-five million per cargo container. You can do the math. It's approximately $2.50 a pack."

"Pretty pricey," Grimes complained.

"I don't think so. You're currently paying $2.85 coming out of Mississippi. And you need to understand my resolve. Have you asked yourself where the ears came from? Your fate, good or bad, is within my control."

"Well, maybe that's an okay price but I don't have twenty-five million."

"Then I suggest you get it because the shipping container is already on its way. You'll get delivery tomorrow for your inspection. The twenty-five million will be wire transferred to the following routing and account number: routing number 834456920148, account number 210000986. Container 4126794 will arrive at Warehouse 4B, Gambit Inc. tomorrow morning. And you won't need pen and paper because I know you're recording this call."

"I'll have to talk to some people before I can commit to a whole shipping container."

"Whether you know it or not, you are already committed. So you better get busy, because the clock is ticking. And do a little thought exercise on where the ears could have come from. I know you still have them. I saw how methodically you collected them from the windshield of your car. And as a final note, you don't ever want me to come visit. I guarantee you that you'll lose more than just your ears. So it better just happen. Now hang up the phone and round up my twenty-five million."

Julie heard Grimes phone disconnect and said, "Cole, what the hell?"

"Now you know the plan. At least part of it. Grimes is not going to get his money's worth. He's going to be more than just a little short-changed."

"What about getting him arrested? What about my report to the Governor?"

"Grimes will have to borrow money from sources that are very demanding about repayment. With nothing to sell, he won't be able to repay and the sharks will move in. It's better that society's underbelly deals with him and his partners. It's much simpler and faster that way."

"What about the ears?"

"Later, Julie. For now, you have some more calls to make and cover our end for shipping arrangements and procurement expenses. Get our container in the warehouse. Kevin gave you bank wire expense, transfer, and fund instructions. We need you to follow through on them," concluded Cole and disconnected.

Cole was all so businesslike. Julie had more questions than answers and wasn't sure of anything. She let her facade fade for a few moments and her feelings came rushing forward. There were too many unknowns and nothing seemed right. It was just plain wrong: her job, her being here, Cole, Kevin, the cigarette scam, and the men who died. Just all of it, she thought, and tears came rushing forward.

When she regained control, she concluded it was too late. She would simply follow through on the instructions.

COLE DIALED KEVIN ON HIS SATELLITE PHONE AS he stepped out of the airport terminal and it was immediately answered.

"Hey," Kevin answered.

"What do you know?"

"Cole I'm not being an ass, but I've been telling you all along that this cigarette thing was all wrong. It's just too simple. And now if the circus is in town, it means that something else is going on. How big is the FBI, ATF, or whoever circus?"

"I was hoping you learned something. The condo on Stuyvesant was compromised. I believe searched and bugged. Not sure, but one of your paintings may have had a minicam embedded in the frame. I suspect they were very near when Julie and I left, maybe in the apartment directly above. They were really good. But a lot of it is just speculation. I haven't seen anyone."

"I'll check the feed from my cameras. Do you think they found the computer room?"

"I don't know Kevin. The computer is set to wipe the servers if the room is breached. Isn't it? You checked it lately?"

"Doing it now," Kevin paused. "Yep, no sync-bit updates in the cloud. It's dead."

"Anything on Julie?"

"Squeaky clean. In fact, she's too clean, like the Hermes thing. She is what she says she is. Everything from birth certificate to college graduation checks out. Employment checks out, everything. Her life is pretty much just all work for the state of New York. Her expenses, credit cards, finances—all clean. No extravagance or anomalies in any of it. Goes to the gym regularly. Spends her vacation time going to see her mother. Pretty normal and boring. Only two anomalies we've come up with. There is no way she would know my last name, yet she called me McKermit. You know, like Kermit the frog. She was trying to insult me. Why would she have added the Mc? Could be nothing. And then Liu is chasing something interesting, facial recognition similarities from high school yearbooks. She found one that is a dead ringer for Julie and the woman just vanished after high school, without any record or trail. Her name was Chrissy Filer from Edmond Oklahoma."

"I hope Liu is wrong," Cole paused. Thought a moment and then continued, "On the cigarette game, at least. But we've got Julie sucked in now so let's just play it. I know better than to ask, but do you have eyes on the Squire Inn?"

"Yep. I got it covered. Hotel and traffic cams are both on recorded feed. And we'll see what we capture with Liu's Capture and Spy software from the Squire Inn cell phones. Could be interesting."

"Okay, game two plays on. Game one is for me to get to Kuoto."

"How do you want to play it?

"Don't know yet, Kevin. But it'll start with this Reed Delahe character. I'm not going to waste any time. I'm going to just knock on his door and ask him."

"Be careful. The circus could be FBI, ATF, CIA, or who knows; stay away from them. And no bullshit. I really do love you."

Cole clicked off the phone and headed for the car rental counter. A mid-size had been reserved for Helmut Hoelzer. His first stop would be a sporting goods store to pick up a hunting knife. It needed at least an eight-inch blade and had to have enough mass to make it effective. Then he would find a path to this Kuoto character through Delahe. Kuoto's life was about to change, and end, Cole committed.

Chapter 37

SATELLITE

REED DELAHE TRIED REPEATEDLY TO CONTACT LIZ. Her text said she and Tommy were safe, but where? It had to be his fiftieth attempt but he dialed Liz's number again. The phone rang for an eternity before going to voice mail. The TV playing in the background again had breaking news: "Black Lives Matter activists have filled downtown Los Angeles in a show of solidarity for racial change…" Reed watched as the screen showed hundreds of people assembled in Los Angeles, many of them wearing 'TOMY BOY JUSTICE' T-shirts. How could it be, questioned Reed? "… racially motivated murders in predominately Black New York neighborhoods are the latest in a series of social injustices plaguing the country. It's clear evidence that social change is necessary."

Reed's thoughts turned to the envelope lying on the kitchen table. It had been delivered to his door by a small, non-threatening Oriental woman dressed as a house cleaner, but he knew better. The envelope contained four identical computer cards and instructions. The cards were replicas in appearance of those his company had manufactured for his "black" customer. In the secretive world, suppliers are given limited information and manufacture just their little part of a top-secret project without ever knowing the overall picture. Suppliers never know who the other suppliers are and never have visibility into the integration or use of their part. But Reed had speculated that his company's cards were ultimately going into a spy satellite of some type. His cards would be providing the data capture and relay function.

How could the cards Kuoto provided look identical to those his company had manufactured, pondered Reed? How could they have gotten the design? Did they steal it from the NSA? Did they steal it from his company? What was different about Kuoto's cards? Maybe he wasn't the only one threatened, abused, and leveraged. And then, why would data capture and relay be worth all the effort they put into this? It didn't matter. He was going to do exactly as the instructions in the envelope directed. He was resolute in doing nothing that would jeopardize Tommy.

His instructions were to swap out the original cards with the Kuoto cards. When accomplished, he was to text the word 'done' to the number provided and then drop the original cards in the dumpster behind the strip club on 72. Swapping out the cards would be a challenge. As required by contract, original cards were kept in a walk-in safe requiring two forms of physical identification, along with a memorized keypad code. Access to the safe was limited to him and eight other employees at the company. The safe was also under 24-hour video surveillance and access was monitored by an armed guard.

The door buzzer woke him from his thoughts. He wasn't up for company, but the buzzing was persistent. So much so it became irritating and he finally got up and pushed the intercom button. "What," Reed abruptly said.

"I want to talk to you about Kuoto, Tommy, Elizabeth, Bonnie, and much more. I probably have answers to things you know nothing about."

Reed took a step back. "Shit," he said to himself. He studied the image on the door cam, but couldn't see the man's face. But it was no doubt one of Kuoto's goons. What else could Kuoto want? He'd only had the envelope a few hours. Kuoto couldn't expect him to have already made the exchange. Could he? It didn't matter; Reed's ever-present thoughts of his son guided his actions. He pushed the button and released the door lock on the entry door.

A man stepped through and said, "My name is Helmut and we don't have much time so I'll get right to it. I want Kuoto. I want to know where he is. I want to know why he would commission the torture and death of Samantha Ogalsby."

Reed did a double take. Had he heard right? Not one of Kuoto's goons? Someone who knew about the eleven-year-old girl? Someone who would finally believe him? Someone who could tell him where Tommy was? "So you don't work for Kuoto?" asked Reed.

"No. Far from it. I'm his worst nightmare," calmly replied the man.

"I'm sorry. What was your name again?" inquired Reed.

"Helmut Hoelzer."

"Do you know where Tommy is?"

"Yes. He is safe for the moment with Elizabeth Johnston in Manti, Utah. But not for long if I don't deal with Kuoto."

Reed had a terrible thought. What if this is a trick? What if Kuoto is testing me? This guy can't be for real. "No. I'm going to do exactly as instructed by Ken Kuoto," Reed firmly stated. "Who are you anyway?"

The man stared into Reed's eyes with laser intensity and replied, "Look, we don't have much time. Samantha Ogalsby was the essence of innocence. She used to play with her little pink ponies outside her apartment, run around with the other children, play kid games, jump, and laugh. All the things an eleven-year-old should do. Then Kuoto had her tortured and murdered. I want the son-of-a-bitch. He will die a death like none other. And he needs to die before he can do harm to your son."

Images of the photographs he'd seen raced through Reed's mind. And now he was confused with mixed thoughts of trust. How could he trust a complete stranger? But this man's intensity and sincerity were so overwhelming; his resistance was dwindling. "What happened to your face?" Reed asked.

"I ran into an obstacle. But I'm here for Kuoto. I hope you're not an obstacle."

"Okay."

"Okay, What?'

"Okay, I'll tell you what you want to know. At least what I know." Reed started at the beginning and went through it all non-stop: limousine ride with the instruction to watch the newspaper, road trip with Liz and Tommy in an attempt to run, jail time with the monster, trumped-up charges, and the envelope with computer cards. It was like a burst of freedom to just say it all. When he finished, Reed closed his eyes and took a moment to relish the release.

Cole listened intently capturing every detail, especially about the data cards and instructions. All this was just so Kuoto, or whoever he worked for, could implement some kind of change to a satellite. If it was top secret, how did Kuoto even know of its existence? Maybe there were more Reed Delahes throughout industry and government suffering the same type of blackmail? Even so, what could be the end game? Maybe Kuoto was just a soldier because this is larger than anything ever envisioned.

Cole blew through his fist as elements of a new plan formulated. "First thing is to keep your son safe," stated Cole. "And a deal with Kuoto might be the ticket. How steady are your nerves? Do you think you could negotiate with Kuoto, face to face, without losing your nerve?"

"I have the nerve. I'd like to just smash his face."

"No. this is bigger than that. We need to keep him from going after Tommy and I need time to put some other things in motion. We'll play this in a way he'll understand. Instead of texting 'done' to the number Kuoto gave you, I want you to text: 'I will make the swap, but I have two conditions. First, you will leave Tommy alone. And second, you will compensate me for the risk. Call me.' But before you send the text, let me see your cell phone."

Reed handed Cole his cell phone. It was a Samsung readily open to eavesdropping. Cole memorized his phone number, tapped the screen as Kevin had taught him, and placed the phone next to his smartphone. With pairing complete, Cole handed the phone back to Reed. Cole input the number on one of his burner phones and texted it to Kevin.

"You are going to have to explain my presence here. Tell them I was from the FBI investigating what happened to you in jail. Tell them you told me nothing. Tell them I scared you and you're afraid of going to jail for treason. Then start a financial negotiation. Ask for 50 million dollars so you and Tommy can leave the country and go into hiding. Tell them you know it's a satellite. Try and get Kuoto to talk as much as possible. Tell them a top-secret satellite is worth 750 million and the launch is worth at least 200 million. Certainly, they can afford 50 million. Settle for no less than 10 million. You've got to be tough and they've got to know you mean it. Can you do that?"

"I'll try."

"No. You will." Then Cole pulled another burner phone from his pocket and handed it to Reed. "Wait an hour after I'm gone to negotiate and then call me on this. Use the last number dialed in 'Recents.'"

"Now this is bigger than both of us so I'm going to take one of Kuoto's data cards with me and get it analyzed. We're not going to make the exchange so don't worry about it. But you have to provide for delay and stall until I get the card into the right hands."

Cole had refused a job offer that developed out of the Quaraysh Unity imminent hostility ordeal. It was now time to accept the offer. Cole looked up the number on his Rubic's Cube Black phone and pressed Call.

The called number went to voice mail, "Once upon a time you offered Kevin and I a job. We're going to take you up on the offer. Want to learn something about top-secret satellite communications? Check your email within the hour."

Cole left through the front entrance with the circuit card hidden under his shirt. He wondered where they would be watching from. It didn't matter, though, because Helmut Hoelzer was headed straight for his hotel room. They would probably have already traced his rental car license plate and knew where he was going anyway. It would take them at least a week to figure out he was not FBI and by then it would be too late. As soon as Cole got in the car, he dialed Kevin on his satellite phone. Kevin was waiting and Cole relayed all he had learned. The data card was the challenge and the key, but analysis by itself would probably yield little. They needed the bigger picture. Cole pressured Kevin to use his Presidential access to the Nation's most secret computerized information and see what he could learn.

Kevin was more than resistant: "I can't Cole. No way. The government IT masterminds are just waiting for me to try. I've snooped around the edges and they have set traps and tracers. It's too risky."

"Then we're going to have to get the satellite info some other way. Can you still get past the CIA email security scan with a Trojan horse of some kind?"

"Yes."

"Can it reside in a forwarded email?"

"Sure. I can embed a backdoor control to capture whatever is generated or accessed on a host device. If the email is forwarded, the backdoor control goes with it."

"Can you get that CIA deputy director's email address?"

"Already got it. But Jeff Monson retired."

"It doesn't matter. I'll send you a picture of the data card. You send it to him. Send it with a message enticing enough for him to forward it to the right people. When they figure out it's a top-secret program, their curiosity will do the rest. They'll figure out where it goes and what it does. If your Trojan works, you'll have access to whatever they learn."

"Then what?"

"We monitor the negotiation between Reed Delahe and Ken Kuoto with the goal being to capture bank routing and account numbers. I've got the beginnings of a plan."

"I sure hope it's better than your cigarette plan."

"I need this card flown to Langley. The circus is probably watching Jack Cross so that's a risk. Overnight UPS is always a risk. Got any ideas?"

"Hand deliver. No other choice."

"Shit. I don't have the time. Anybody fly private jets out of Huntsville?"

"Sure."

"It's a risk but get me a right now, quick turnaround flight to someplace close to Cabin John."

Cabin John is a rural area in Montgomery County, Maryland, and is a bedroom community for elites, including some high-ranking government officials. Cole had covertly visited Cabin John years earlier to deliver a personal message to the Deputy Director of the CIA. This time it would be in full daylight and that came with uncertainties and risks.

Cole was just reaching the private terminal at Huntsville International when the phone buzzed. It was Reed. Reed had sent the text and was waiting for a response. Cole recognized the nervousness in Reed's voice. The call was probably more for reassurance than anything, concluded Cole. But Reed now knew his lifeline really would answer the phone and be there for him. Cole expected Kuoto to give it some time for consideration before responding, hopefully, a couple of hours. He desperately needed sleep and the airplane was probably as good as any hotel bed.

Chapter 38

Job Offer Accepted

Jeff Monson just finished mowing his lawn. It was one of the simple tasks he enjoyed doing the most. He prided himself on his gas mower and the precision engine tuning he had been able to accomplish with little more than a screwdriver. Some of his neighbors had mentioned the noise and environmental concerns, but an electric mower was out of the question. He was just too set in his ways.

His wife brought him a glass of iced tea and his cell phone. She said somebody had tried to call. Jeff sat on the back porch, took a long drink of tea, and admired his two-pass lawn-mowing job; he had first worked back and forth directly across the lawn and then went diagonally for the second cut.

Jeff nonchalantly glanced at his cell phone and then set it back down to further admire his lawn-mowing job. He reached for his glass of tea when it occurred to him. He grabbed his cell phone and studied the incoming number; it was his own! Jeff quickly went to voice messages: "Once upon a time you offered Kevin and I a job. We're going to take you up on the offer. Want to learn something about top-secret satellite communications? Check your email within the hour."

Jeff bolted from his chair and charged inside to his study and computer. The email was there. It was addressed to him and from him. He clicked to open without hesitation: "The attached photo is of a data card that was destined for the NSA, but it is a substitute. Consider what a substitute might result in. The data card will be arriving soon. Original cards are secure at the supplier's facility. Do not contact the supplier. Do you like Chinese, Korean, or artificial celestial dishes? Not sure what's on the menu. Maybe all of the above."

IN THE BASEMENT OF BUILDING L AT THE CIA's Langley Complex, Space Technology Analysis supervisor, Frank Wallace, just finished a performance evaluation meeting with one of his analysts, Sally McBride. It was the part of his job he disliked the most, but all part of being a section supervisor. He was new to the job, having been transferred from the FBI at the request of the higher-ups. Politics was the other part of his job that was a frustration, both with his superiors and some of those who worked for him. Some people believed perception was most important for career advancement but it just wasn't his cup of tea. He believed in accomplishment-based performance. And Sally was too much show and not enough output. She was near tears when she left his office. Sometimes he thought he would rather go back to just being a FBI field agent.

It was near quitting time. His computer beeped, indicating another incoming message. He probably had fifty yet unanswered. It was going to be another after-hours evening. He typed the passcode to open his computer and scanned down through the emails. His breathing stopped when he saw the last message. He hadn't spoken to Jeff Monson in months. Jeff had actually been responsible for his transfer from the FBI to the CIA and his promotion to a supervisory position. Frank opened the email. It simply had a forwarded email attached. The attached email was sent to Jeff Monson from Jeff Monson and had no subject.

IT rules said "DON'T EVER" and Frank knew he was opening the door to being hacked, but it came from a source he absolutely trusted. He briefly weighed the consequence of violating CIA computer security versus the value of potential information in the email.

He clicked on the email: "The attached photo...Do you like Chinese, Korean, or artificial celestial dishes? Not sure what's on the menu. Maybe all of the above."

The last few sentences made no sense but they would in the end. Frank yelled from his office, "Nobody goes home." He hit the print button on the attached photo. Frank hit 'print screen' to capture the email content and then emailed just the print screen version to everyone in his group, which might limit the spread of what he suspected was a virus of some kind. From his office door, he yelled, "Meeting. Five minutes." He told his secretary to pull up the photo on the big screen in the conference room and then dialed his boss, Bart McDonald. Before his boss could speak, Frank blurted out, "Do you remember the cryptic email on the Quaraysh Unity? I just got another similar email from Monson. I cut and pasted the content and will email it to you. I'll get IT to scrub my computer tonight—because we'll be here working. If I need anything, I'll call you at home tonight." Frank hung up just as his boss was beginning to speak.

In the conference room, Frank magnified the image for those who had arrived as directed. "Nobody goes home until I know what this is and how its modification could affect its intended use. Jeffery and Sally, I want you to get on the phone with the NSA and find out what this part number is. Don't quit calling until you find someone that can tell you. Jim and Dale, I want you to start a records search for anything similar to this card. Parker, Debbie, John, and Cecil I want you to evaluate the microchips on this card and brainstorm their possible design function."

Cecil interrupted as he studied the enlarged projection, "I can tell you one thing; its radiation hardened."

Hanky added, "That means it's space-based; either ballistic missile or military satellite."

"Excellent," said Frank and then remembered the confounding reference to 'artificial celestial.' "It's satellite. Narrow your focus to military-grade satellites."

Frank then continued to give out assignments and set nine that evening as the time for an open discussion and out-brief by each member of his team.

Chapter 39

CHRISSY

COLE GOT A COUPLE OF HOURS OF SLEEP BEFORE THE private jet touched down at the Leesburg Executive Airport. As the plane taxied towards the terminal, Cole's satellite phone buzzed. It was Kevin.

"You aren't going to believe this," blasted an excited Kevin. "From the codes they're running and outputs they're getting, it's definitely satellite. They ran a few cases linked to Beijing. But there are hundreds of orbital mechanics outputs they link to U.S. cities. I downloaded one of their complete files and I'm studying it. Running it now; some kind of orbital mechanics code, not sure what the output means. Oh, I'm currently recording a call between Reed Delahe and some guy who calls himself Yao. Reed's doing a pretty good job negotiating but he's nervous as shit. Yao says Kuoto will want to know Reed's plan for swapping out the cards and also where Reed plans on hiding. Yao says he better have it all figured out before he meets with Kuoto."

"Nervous is good. It'll make him believable."

Kevin didn't wait for more; he rolled on with his update, "Julie did everything she was supposed to. Native Americans paid in full. Warehouse waiting receipt of container. Trucking and driver taken care of. No records anywhere. Money all washed. Transfer account is set up for twenty-five mil receipt and washing. Container will be in New York by nine in the morning. But you have a problem with Julie. She's wrong. This is a stupid idea. This whole cigarette thing is going to go bad. Liu can talk to you about Julie."

"I know. But we're staying with it."

"Oh, their code just completed running. First and eighth path coverage is dead nuts over 38.8977° N 77.0365° W."

"Where the hell is that?"

"I'll figure it out. Here, talk to Liu about Julie. Bye."

A very pleasant feminine voice came on the phone. He recognized it, but it was somehow now more assertive: "Hello, this Liu. We need to talk about your friend."

"Okay. Nice to talk to you again," replied Cole. "Tell me about Julie."

"Sorry to say, but she isn't who she says she is. Her name is actually Chrissy Filer from Edmond Oklahoma. Julia Addison checks out from birth certificate to present. She has all the right pieces of data: grade school history and pictures, yearbook photos, diplomas, all of it. But it's all a creation. And somebody went to a lot of work to do it; it had to be the U.S. Marshall's Office, FBI, or some other government agency with a lot of capability."

Cole blew through his fist and recalled events, words, and actions. It was the "show." It was actually about Kevin. Cole inquired, "How did you find out?"

"Her parents check out on the surface, but have no genealogical history; they just appear. Then with facial recognition searches, I found a match with a Chrissy Filer high school yearbook photo. After high school, somebody erased the entire existence of Chrissy Filer. She just disappeared. I ran facial recognition several times and reviewed the actual biometric data itself; it's her. Then it gets worse. The cell phone at the Squire Inn captured some pretty incriminating video and voice data. Three men in plain clothes came in and set up hidden video cameras and substituted one of the paired cell phones with one of their own. I think Julie is working with them. I'm so sorry. "

Cole blew through his fist as thoughts formed. "Anyway this whole Julie thing could be related to Kevin?" Cole inquired.

There was no response. Cole waited. Liu eventually responded, "I don't know." She paused and then continued, "Not unless he's a Cool Fool."

"A what?"

"Well, when I was searching records on Chrissy Filer's parents, I came across a strange reference to some undefined government program called 'Cool Fool.'"

Cole blew through his fist and then responded, "Okay. Let Kevin know we are going ahead with the cigarette plan. We'll let it play out and see where it goes. Thank you, Liu."

As soon as Cole disconnected, one of his burner phones buzzed. Kevin was right about this cigarette thing all along. But it could not be a distraction to the Kuoto game. The big picture was still missing. How widespread was Kuoto's reach? How many other Reed Delahes were under his control?

Cole answered the burner, "Helmut."

"This is Reed Delahe. I just finished a call with somebody named Yao. He works for Kuoto. It was kind of a cryptic discussion because he said somebody might be listening."

"They were."

"Huh?"

"Go on."

"I didn't do that good. No agreement on money and he said Kuoto would have other demands."

"Yeah, I got the summarized version."

"What?"

"Don't worry about it. Next discussion will be a little more focused. But for now, just get some rest. We'll talk in the morning."

Inside the terminal building, a well-dressed man was holding a sign reading 'Helmut Hoelzer.' The greeting was short and Cole followed him to a waiting black Suburban executive taxi. It was a thirty-minute ride across the Maryland state line to Cabin John. Cole blew through his fist as new pieces of information melded with the frantic events of the past week. It was still incomplete. His real focus had to be on Kuoto. The rest of it would just take its course once he delivered the circuit card to Monson.

He had the driver deliver him four houses down from Jeff Monson's residence. He'd been there before, but not in such an open fashion. The driver was instructed to "go get a cup of coffee" and be back in an hour. Cole's senses went on high alert as the Suburban pulled away. It was an upscale neighborhood and he felt out of place. He was probably drawing attention to himself just by walking down the street. He accelerated his pace and quickly found himself at the front door he had clandestinely entered years earlier.

The doorbell camera was staring right at him. There was no hiding. "Shit," he said to himself. Cole pressed the doorbell. The door was almost immediately opened.

"I've been expecting you," said Jeff Monson. "Won't you come in Hamilton?"

Monson extended his hand and Cole took it. The handshake was long overdue. He really did like this man. "I go by Cole."

Cole followed Jeff to the living room. "Please have a seat," said Jeff. "Would you like something to drink: water, iced tea, coke?"

"No, I'm fine."

"I like my late evening news and hate to miss it," Jeff said and turned on the wall-mounted TV. He then set a small electronic box on the coffee table in front of Cole. A small LED on the electronic box illuminated and Jeff took a seat on the couch next to Cole.

"I'm sorry," said Jeff as he took the remote and increased the volume on the TV. "My hearing isn't what it used to be."

Jeff checked the LED on the electronic box and then said, "I suspect the menu is both celestial and Chinese."

"That's for you to figure out."

"I'm retired."

"I know, but you did offer me a job one time. And I now accept," said Cole as he handed Jeff the package he'd been carrying.

Jeff pulled open the corner of the wrapping and peeked at the computer card. "By the looks of your face, I assume you didn't come by this easily."

"I'll pass on the details. I'll just say that I now know who is orchestrating events and we'll have more information in a day or so. But we have no idea what the end game is. That's why this computer card part of the puzzle is now in your hands."

"Is this a domestic issue or international?" Jeff paused and then continued, "Since I left the CIA, I have less influence with CIA leadership than I do with the FBI or Marshall's Office. If this is domestic in nature, I might be able to get better engagement from them."

"It started domestic, but, as you said, it's probably Chinese. We have a plan to take care of the domestic and that leaves you to take care of the international."

"I assume the 'we' includes Kevin McKuel."

"It does. That is, unless the U.S. government gets to him first."

"I don't understand."

"I believe some agency of the United States government has targeted us. Maybe something called "Cool Fool.""

"I kept my part of the bargain after the Quraysh Unity. Kevin and your data were purged: DNA, fingerprints, FACE, all of it."

"Well, someone resurrected it."

"All right. I'll see what I can find out. But first, I need to drive this computer card to Langley. Can I drop you somewhere?"

"Nope. I have a ride."

The two departed as friends. Jeff drove past Cole on the street just as the Suburban taxi pulled up. Cole looked forward to another couple of hours of sleep on the flight back to Huntsville.

Chapter 40

MAHEM

Frank's next out-briefing with his group was only a few minutes away when he got the call.

"This is General Lance from the Air Force's Space Force. What the hell is going on? You are way out of line," lambasted the caller. "You are sniffing around in areas that are way above your pay grade. I want it stopped immediately. Do you hear me!"

"I hear you," Frank calmly replied.

"And!"

"I hear you, I said, and nothing."

"You don't even know what you're messing around with. You stay the hell away from it."

"Messing around with what?

"God Dammit," shouted General Lance. "You know exactly what I'm talking about! Mayhem, that's what the hell we're talking about!"

"Okay, so we're looking into Mayhem. You may have a security breach."

"Yes, we do and it's you. I direct you to cease and desist all activities associated with Mayhem. If you don't, I'm personally going to make sure your getting fired is the least of your problems. Do you understand what I'm saying?"

"Yes Sir. I absolutely understand what you're saying: cease and desist."

"Good! And good f-ing night," General Lance shouted and hung up.

Frank started his 3:00 A.M. session with his group by announcing the name of the program, "The program is called Mayhem and it's the U.S. Space Force. Let's shift our focus to look at them."

Cecil interrupted, "The Space Force is really just the new Air Force and it doesn't like the CIA. They wouldn't give us the time of day."

"Go after financial allocations. Look for anything unusual or excessive. Find something big, something buried. I have an uneasy gut feeling about the NSA. The NSA supposedly works for the CIA but sometimes I think they have their own agenda. Look for something that's got an inter-agency agreement or transfer of funds between the Space Force and the NSA. Next, go after NSA procurement expenditures. See if we can paste together a picture of what they've been buying. Do a records search for Mayhem acronyms. Find anything that's out there. Jeffery and Sally, I want that to be your focus." He looked at them individually and then finished, "You're excused. Let's go to work."

Sally raised her hand and said, "I'm tired and want to go home."

"When the sun comes up, you'll feel better. Now get on it."

The next group meeting would be at six A.M. And he intended to have a summary report out for his boss by eight.

Six A.M. came quickly but pieces were coming together. Robert had met Jeff Monson in the visitor parking lot and accepted the package. Hanky had run a number of satellite orbit scenarios. And the teams had other results as well, including finding data on a reference to a program called MAHEM. Each individual summarized what he or she had as Frank typed on his laptop.

The data card was similar to that used in the USA-224 series reconnaissance satellite offering optical and sensor resolution of ground sites. Two cards were used, one primary and one backup. The function of the USA-224 card was to receive and process input data from ground or a higher altitude H-9 relay satellite. Imagery data capture and download were triggered through the card. The USA-224 flew at a relatively low altitude of 92 miles in a circular orbit with a 39-degree azimuth for cycle coverage over a number of potentially hostile areas of the world, including Tehran and Beijing. It had eight-pass coverage, meaning that it flew over the same region below a latitude of 39 degrees every eighth orbit. The data card had no control function for satellite re-positioning; its only control function was to trigger data capture over a commanded location and relay the imagery data.

Hanky had verified the orbital coverage of a satellite using the USA-224 as the basis for orbital trajectory. In addition to Tehran, Beijing, and a number of other possible imagery targets, it would also be possible to trigger the data card over much of the U.S., including Langley and Washington D.C. In essence, details down to the 2.25 centimeters level could be captured with the latest digitally-enhanced combination of optic and sensor data. If the data card was triggered over Langley, you could find a quarter lying in the parking lot and tell if it was heads or tails.

The substitute data card provided no clear evidence of why it was so important. Without detailed side-by-side comparison testing to an original card, its compromise was only speculative. Speculatively, it could potentially compromise the latest Space Force spy satellite, leaving it just another piece of space junk.

A couple of references to MAHEM were discovered. At one time MAHEM, which stood for Mass-critical Accelerated Hypervelocity Explosive Munition, was a proposed DARPA program. The defunct program was to develop a hypervelocity cannon able to accelerate a tungsten projectile to a speed of nearly 36,000 mph using a massive sixty-foot barrel capable of withstanding pressures of 80,000 psi. Analysis at the time showed that the projectile would have such kinetic energy that it would completely destroy hard targets, such as a tank, and disintegrate soft targets, such as a person. The program was proposed in 2006 but never funded and never re-visited because of the impracticality of the massive barrel requirements. Strangely, two obscure references to MAHEM were found in classified documentation leading up to the assassination of Qusem Soleimani by the United States Air Force.

Frank captured and edited the information on his laptop for the summary report as the eight o'clock hour approached. He included everything relevant, including the reference to MAHEM. Frank hit the send button on the email to his boss, just as his secretary stuck her head in the conference room. She spoke, but a thought in the back of his mind came to the forefront. He knew opening the email last night was an avenue to getting hacked. Even though IT had cleaned his computer, he still wondered if he had just sent his report to more than just his boss.

"Bart McDonald is on your office phone and sent me to fetch you," his secretary said. "He says he needs to talk to you right now."

Frank gathered his thoughts as he walked to his office. Bart had been on hold for more than ten minutes when Frank answered: "Hello."

"Frank, I don't know what you did last night but you certainly got the attention of the higher-ups. I've had six conversations this morning with the Space Farce, NSA, DARPA, and even one with Director Higgins himself, all complaining about your inquiries. I'm just now scanning down through your report and don't see anything of real substance. It's more of a data dump. What do you think you really have?"

"I'm not sure. That's why I left out speculations."

"Okay, well give them to me now."

"I think we have a space-based weapon of some kind that is off the books and it's going for a ride on an upgrade to the USA-224 satellite. I think it somehow uses the onboard optic and sensor capability of the satellite to target more than imagery. It doesn't make sense as of yet, but somehow the defunct MAHEM program comes into play. And that's all speculation because I have no data."

"First, space-based weapons, lasers, nuclear or other, are banned by treaty. If the Space Farce is really dabbling in that arena, I doubt even the President would know about it. But it would explain the nervousness you've stirred up. Second, this suspect data card you got a picture of is far from justification for any kind of an investigation."

"I know. But I also know that the email I got last night is rock solid. The data card I now have in my possession has been discretely altered in some way for some devious purpose."

"All right. I'll hold them at bay for as long as I can. I'll hold your report—promise them a copy by COB today. But I won't tell them you have the substitute USA-224 card. We don't have any top cover on this one. We are on our own. Since Jeff Monson left the agency, all we have is a bunch of self-serving bureaucrats for leadership. They're only interested in their own image and creating a kinder-nicer-gentler agency that doesn't offend anyone, no matter how stupid. Damn, I miss the days of Monson. Be diligent and be fast because they are going to shut us down hard."

Top cover, Frank thought to himself as he hung up the phone. Monson was indeed top cover when he headed the CIA. Kinder-nicer-gentler was direct-specific-and-punishing, but things got done and there was no bullshit. He dialed the number of a home in Cabin John.

"Hello," answered Jeff Monson.

"This is Frank. How are you doing?"

"Fishing and traveling. Retirement is great. I should have done it years earlier. How about you?"

"I have another issue. I got your Christmas presents. Thank you very much. But Bart McDonald and I are about to get shut down. And it's serious. The problem is we don't have any top cover, as Bart calls it. I'm looking for help."

"Frank, I'd like to help but I don't have any pull with the agency anymore. I'm not sure Higgins would even return my call. It'll have to go over the top. I still talk to Evert Hooster on a regular basis. He might be an avenue to go over the top. I might be able to help if I had really good intel. So keep me up-to-date on the Christmas presents."

"Can't do that directly. Security rules and such. But there are always buts."

"Evert could provide the top cover you're looking for, but the information would have to be rock solid."

"I'll get on it. Thanks, Jeff."

"No. Thank you, Frank," said Monson before he touched the end button.

Frank stared at his computer. Hacked? Yes. Every keystroke? Maybe, he contemplated. He composed an email to himself, from himself, detailing all his findings and suppositions and concluding with a request, "If you get this, please get the info to Jeff Monson, now retired. This includes anything developed within my section." Frank hit send. It went to his Sent box and then almost immediately to his Inbox. Frank stared at his Inbox wondering?

Sally stepped through his office door, "I think I found something."

Frank's thoughts instantly transitioned, "Good. What've you got?"

She sat down opposite him and began, "A variation of something very similar to MAHEM was on the drafting boards in the Ronald Reagan years. It was part of the Star Wars thing that was terminated. The technology really didn't exist for it at the time but it might now. It's a tiny little projectile with a pin-sized aerospike that can be fired from orbit. The projectile is less than a centimeter in diameter and is accelerated with a complex converging-tubulated nozzle using superheated hydrogen from a tiny nuclear deflagration. The projectile rides on a compressed gas sabot to continue increasing acceleration. The projectile is accelerated to nearly 15 miles per second, which is as fast as even the most minute dust particle in space. But this projectile is thoriated tungsten and has its little aerospike to trip the hypersonic shock when it enters the atmosphere, which keeps the projectile body in its own little sheltered environment. This, in turn, keeps it from melting or disintegrating. The aerospike also keeps the projectile on target slipping right through clouds, rain, and just about anything else. I'm guessing, but with today's accuracy and state of art technical development, it could be an assassination weapon. From an altitude of 100 miles, the projectile would take only seven seconds to reach its target. And with the kinetic energy associated with 40,000 miles per hour, a soft target would explode, leaving nothing but heated mist."

"That's good Sally, really good. When this is over, I'm going to take another look at your performance review. Summarize it, if you will, in an email to me. Include all the details and references and make sure you include the little tidbit about the Qusem Soleimani assassination. And thanks. This is a huge piece of the puzzle."

Chapter 41

The Mogwai Angel's Nightmare Begins

Liu was working side by side with Kevin. She needed access to Kuoto's computer, but the IP address was indeterminate. They had bank routing and account numbers from Jamal's phone, but needed more. Kuoto's phone number from Jamal's phone led to a secure Chinese satellite line that Kevin had failed to access. The best he could do was capture numbers dialed, but even those were encrypted; eavesdropping was out. Then there was the information Kevin was extracting from the CIA. Frank Wallace was very smart. He knew Kevin had access to his computer and was now sending them clandestine messages. In the end, Jeff Monson would play a key role in their plan. But so much to make happen and so little time. The cigarette scam was just an irritation. And Julie's motives added confusion and more frustration. Kevin and Liu were doing all they could. But taken in total, it was overwhelming.

In an early morning conversation with Reed Delahe, Cole had told Reed to call this Yao back and demand a meeting with Kuoto, otherwise, the deal was off and he would destroy the data cards.

After the call with Yao, Reed frantically called Cole: "He knows. He knows you've been listening in on our phone calls. He told me Kuoto was testing me and I failed."

"Slow down," said Cole. "Take a breath."

"I can't. You got me into this and now—and now—I don't know what to do."

"Did you get to him agree to a meeting?"

"No. It never got that far. What am I going to do?"

"I'm coming to you. I'm already en route. Just give me ten minutes," said Cole as he mashed the accelerator pedal.

Cole was at Reed's home in seven minutes and dashed to the front door. Reed was waiting and opened it immediately. He was still in a state of disarray and Cole needed him to focus, focus as he'd never focused before.

"This is what you're going to do!" shouted Cole. "Call Yao back on his phone. Tell him your new bodyguard was eavesdropping. Tell him you need to send a file you prepared directly to Kuoto. Get his email address. Tell him the subject of the email will be Mayhem. You have to be strong here, Reed. Tommy's life depends on it."

"I can't remember all that."

"You're going to put this earbud in your ear and I will tell you everything to say."

"I hope you know what you're doing."

"I do, Reed. Now put this in your ear and dial."

Reed did as instructed but Kuoto, instead of Yao, answered after only two rings. "Yes Reed," Kuoto said in a devilish tone.

"I didn't finish my conversation with Yao. At least I didn't get to say all I had to say."

"Go on."

"First thing you should know is that I want a private meeting with you to discuss, ah, let's just say—space. Second thing, I've hired a bodyguard. He is the one eavesdropping on Yao and me. You're not going to beat on me again. And you won't get mayhem unless we meet. I…"

Kuoto interrupted, "Could you repeat that?"

"You heard me. It's spelled M-A-H-E-M. Do I have your attention?

"Indeed."

"Give me an email address and I'll send you something to peruse before our meeting, which will be two hours from now."

"Okay, Mister Delahe," Kuoto paused as if in thought and then resumed. "We'll let it be for now. But I warn you; be careful of the amateurish escapade you wish to conduct. You know the extent of my determination, but we shall see. Send your tripe to mogwaijyulping@baofu.com."

"Look for it shortly. It's just a summary, but I'm sure you'll find it interesting. I haven't shared the contents of the email with my bodyguard. But he will be attending the meeting."

"Well, you have yours," Kuoto paused and then said very slow and threateningly, "And-I-have-mine."

"I want one hundred million and my bodyguard will have routing numbers. You will pay. Be at the stock car dirt track just off 72 at 11:00 A.M sharp. There's no racing today so we will be alone."

"Very well then."

"Oh, just one other thing. You put me through the wringer to get me to agree to trade out the data cards, which I will do. But you need to understand that I know of two other individuals who went through a similar wringer and I do know what you're doing. So if I don't get what I want, it'll be more than just the cards that don't get to space. It'll be a very limited mayhem for you. Don't be late," finished Reed and Cole disconnected the phone for him.

"You did very good and were absolutely convincing," complimented Cole.

"What the hell was all that about? I didn't understand half of it?" questioned Reed.

"You may not, but Kuoto understood every word. Now sit down at your computer."

The email was there: To Reed Delahe from Reed Delahe with no subject. Cole pointed to it and Reed opened it. It included satellite trajectory data for Washington D.C. and Beijing, the description of MAHEM, and another demand for one hundred million dollars. Wire transfer account numbers were to be provided at the meeting.

"Add 'MAHEM' to the subject line and forward it to Kuoto's email address," said Cole.

They departed in Cole's rental car and drove straight towards his hotel room. Cole didn't waste time worrying about where the circus was. He assumed they were in Miami still trying to find Bob Goddard. If anyone was watching, it would be different; it would be Kuoto's surveillance teams. Cole called Kevin on his satellite phone as he drove.

"He bit," came a cheery Kevin. "Kuoto's making calls. Each one lasts about three minutes. It's Chinese encryption and I can't listen in. But I am capturing the encrypted phone numbers and will start crunching those. I should have names to go with them in a few hours."

"Rock and roll. How's Julie's game going?"

"She's winning. Cigarettes are stupid. And if they're just as stupid and buy our container, we'll have another twenty-five million," said Kevin, pleased with himself and added. "You know Julie's a phony and a liar, but she likes me."

"I doubt it."

"She wants to meet me. Do you think Liu will be jealous?"

"Don't get your hopes up," said Cole and shook his head.

Reed just looked at Cole and didn't ask. They reached the hotel and went straight to Cole's room. Cole pulled out a burner phone, dialed it, and handed it to Reed. "They're waiting for your call," he said.

It was Liz who answered the phone. Reed was elated. The Manti sheriff, both his deputies, and three other armed men were in hiding with Tommy and

Elizabeth. Cole had set it up with the Sheriff, giving him just enough information about foreigners leveraging Reed by using Tommy to make it believable. It was all simple terms that the country sheriff understood. Cole knew the resolve of small western town righteousness and knew Tommy and Elizabeth would be safe from the foreigners. Cole saw the delight in Reed's face when Tommy came on the line.

Cole interrupted Reed momentarily and told him to stay put in the hotel room until he got back. Cole departed without a goodbye, going straight to the parking lot and his rental car.

Cole raced down 72 headed for the off-the-beat dirt racetrack. He slid his hand down his leg and touched the butt of his boot knife. How many would there be? Going into battle without any reconnaissance, mistake—mine. He had only one real advantage: underestimation, mistake—theirs.

He passed the strip clubs on the fringes of the Huntsville city limits and pressed on. Gas stations, restaurants, and stores hugging the edges of the highway soon faded to heavily wooded areas. He was going to be late and pressed even harder on the accelerator pedal. He almost passed the sign for the racetrack but slammed on the brakes just in time to slide the turn onto the dirt road leading to the track. It was a mile or so before he got to the track. The track was probably a third-mile oval skirted with little more than field fencing. There were no bleachers for fans, just ringside parking all around the track. The flagman and announcer tower at the edge of the track was over what appeared to be a locked concession booth. Directly in front of the concession stand was a full-length black limousine with two men standing at its rear. A second car, probably a Toyota, was parked next to the limousine. Windows on the limousine were tinted and the Toyota was empty, leaving only two visible targets. But maybe as many as four others were posted somewhere on the perimeter and an unknown number inside the limousine. Eight total, worst case. Cole winced.

Cole pulled up behind the limousine staring directly at the two behind it. He put the car in park, turned off the ignition, and blew into his fist. He stepped out of the car as one of the bodyguards approached and said, "My name is Yao. Now if you don't mind, this way sir. Mister Kuoto doesn't like to be kept waiting and you're late." Yao had Cole raise his arms and did a pat down. Yao found Cole's boot knife. "Mister Kuoto expected something more lethal," said Yao. Yao opened the rear door of the limousine and gestured for Cole to get in. The limousine was idling and the cooled temperature inside was just right. Cole stepped in and was gently nudged with the point of his knife to the far side to sit directly across from a thing resembling a demon. The Oriental thing had bushy eyebrows, deep wrinkles of age, small mouth, and piercing eyes. Yao slid in next to Cole with Cole's knife in his hand.

"Oh that's a big one," said the thing looking at the knife. "Where is Mister Delahe?"

"He thought it was better that just I come," coolly replied Cole.

"That will not do!" lambasted the thing.

"Oh yes, it will."

The thing's hand flashed forward and grabbed Cole by the throat. Its face came forward to glare into Cole's eyes and said, "I am Kuoto and I will tell you what we will do."

Cole tensed his neck muscles against the grip and coldly replied, "You look like a Mogwai angel from Hell. But make no mistake about it, the Mogwai moved me to the head of the line and I will tell you what we will do!"

Cole accelerated his right hand in a sweeping arc to strike the Adams apple of the unsuspecting Yao, crushing larynx, trachea, and collapsing the subglottis. Yao grabbed his throat, gasped for air, and would be dead in minutes.

"Now release me," demanded Cole.

Kuoto's grip retreated as he jerked back into his seat. His eyes widened, his mouth opened slightly, and he just stared. Yao's body next to Cole was uncontrollably flopping and flailing as the man desperately searched for air. Cole's boot knife had fallen onto the seat next to him. The privacy window between the driver and the compartment started down. In a single motion, Cole snatched his boot knife from the seat and, just as the window reached bottom, dove his knife deep into the back of the driver's neck, separating vertebra and severing nerves. The driver's eyes momentarily focused on the rearview mirror—and then closed. Cole didn't retract the knife, he just left it in place and reached across to retrieve a Rugger 1911 pistol from the flailing man's waistband. Cole's thumb flipped the safety off as he stepped out of the limousine. The goon standing at the back of the limousine turned just as Cole fired. Cole didn't wait to verify the damage; instead, he whirled to face the concession stand. Two men were just emerging. Front-sight-bang at the first target and then front-sight-bang at the second. The second man started to crumble, but the first was a miss and was now bringing a pistol horizontal. Cole focused; aimed and fired at the same instant the man fired his weapon. Cole's shot was aimed and the other man's was not. Cole hit center of mass and the other man's bullet whistled past, off into the trees. Cole did a quick recon of the tree line and surrounding area. All was quiet, except for the groaning of a downed man. Cole fired three additional shots; one for each and just for insurance that they were, or would be, dead. Five down and it had all taken less than twenty seconds.

Cole slipped back through the open car door and sat down to face Kuoto. He briefly glanced at the knife sticking out the driver's neck and then stared at Kuoto. Cole pulled the door closed and calmly said, "Now where were we? Oh, I remember. I was about to tell you what you are going to do. But this flopping around is a real distraction. Excuse me for just another moment would you." Cole reached across the flailing Yao, still gripping his throat, and opened the opposing door. With a powerful thrust of Cole's leg, he shoved the man from the car and then closed the door. "Much better, don't you think?" Cole asked.

The glare from Kuoto's eyes was gone and it was now replaced by fear. "I'll take that as a yes. But from here on out, you will answer me," said Cole after getting no answer from Kuoto. "Yes, say it. Yes!" demanded Cole.

"Yes."

"Good. Now, I'm going to get paid a lot of money for this. If you don't pay Reed Delahe, then I won't get paid. And that's personal. And when it's personal, I sometimes get pissed. You wouldn't want me pissed, would you?"

"No."

"Good. So all you have to do is follow the instructions in an email sent to you by Mister Delahe and I won't get pissed. Does that seem fair?"

Fear was apparent in Kuoto's eyes and he failed to come up with a response. Cole reached over and grabbed the butt of his knife. He jerked several times to remove it. When it came free, the blade screeched as it slid from between the compressed vertebra. Cole toyed with the knife and examined the blood on its blade. "Do you think it will come clean? Maybe not. I guess I'll have to just leave it here with you. But maybe I'll do some carving first. Maybe like I did on your friend Jamal and his friends."

Kuoto's eyes widened and he pressed farther back into his seat. "Okay, okay."

"I have an electronic transfer number for you. All you have to do is make the transfer today and then I'll get paid. And I emphasize today. Then you'll never see me again," said Cole as he handed Kuoto a piece of paper.

Kuoto looked at the numbers and put the note in his shirt pocket.

Cole opened the car door and said, "Well I guess that concludes our business here today. I do hope I've made an impression on you. Tootle do." Cole slipped out of the limousine and looked back at the three gunshot goons. They were motionless. Yao was still flailing around on the ground.

As Cole drove away, he called Kevin to see if his discrete phone-pairing attempt had worked. It hadn't, but Kevin was still pleased with himself. Communication functions to and from Kuoto's satellite phone didn't pair. But security features for location were lacking and Kevin had been able to pair with its GPS system. They had him.

Chapter 42

REVELATIONS

COLE KNEW KUOTO WAS ALONE, AFRAID, AND HAD A mess to clean up. The last thing he would want is to explain five dead men to the police. Cole studied the cars going west as he drove east toward Huntsville. One, two, three, or more, he didn't know. But by now, Kuoto had summoned all his resources to come to him, at least that was the plan. And the result would be no surveillance on Reed Delahe. On-coming cars whistled by and Cole continued to look at faces trying to decide if they were part of Kuoto's goon squad: woman—no, senior citizen—no, young kid—no, two middle-aged men—maybe, pickup truck—no. It was a gamble but so were many other things. Cole called Reed Delahe when he was five minutes from the hotel and told him to meet him out front. Tommy was safe and now he needed to make sure Reed was safe as well.

Reed was waiting when Cole arrived at the hotel entrance. He climbed into the passenger seat and they quickly sped away. Cole worked his way circuitously toward Atlanta. He told Reed that he would check in to the Best Western under the name of Bob Goddard. He was to wear a mask and when asked for ID, use the one Cole provided. Reed's hair and facial features weren't too far different from his own. It would not be a problem with a Covid mask and a little confidence. When Reed checked in under the name of Bob Goddard, he would become the focus of a circus: FBI, ATF, or other. It didn't matter; Reed would have protection from the presumed surveillance of Bob Goddard. Reed shouldn't expect to ever see them because they were very good. Kuoto and his goons wouldn't see them either until it was too late for them, should Kuoto's goons somehow trace his location.

Reed slipped on the mask and studied the Bob Goddard driver's license and credit cards. Cole assured him it would work. It just required confidence. Cole pulled to the curb a half block from the Best Western. He told Reed that he would wait curbside for ten minutes. If Reed didn't reappear, he would assume the check-in went as planned. Reed stepped from the car and headed towards the hotel. Cole watched intently, not so much looking out for Reed, but looking for the FBI, or whoever they were. They were no doubt already watching Julie, but from where and how?

Cole called Kevin and the call was answered immediately. "Shit's happening," boasted Kevin. "Kuoto started making phone calls as soon as you left. I'm working on un-encrypting all the numbers. We won't know what's said, but we'll know who he's talking to. Even better, I'm into his computer. I've uploaded a Trojan bank sequencer code to maximize his transfer. Chinese banks update their sequencer every hundredth of a second on electronic transfers, and when Kuoto initiates the transfer, the code will hit it as many times as it can within the hundredth of a second. How's that for brilliant?"

"I count on it, Kevin. How's the GPS tag on his phone?"

"Oh, yeah. Kuoto's staying at an AirB&B on the outskirts of Huntsville. I studied it on a terrain map and it looks like a private compound of some type, security fence and all."

"So we got him. I hope timing of the transfers works out. I just delivered Reed to the Best Western. Seen the circus on hotel or traffic cams?"

"No. Are you sure they're there?"

"I'm counting on them being here for Reed's safety. They've got to be watching Julie. Her trail was easy to follow. And I doubt they all went to Miami. They were just too good. I'm going to go see Julie at three o'clock. Can you do your thing with the hotel cams?"

"What do you want to see her for? Maybe a little foreplay before you slit her throat?"

"Knock that shit off, Kevin! Can you kill the hotel cams or not?

"Sure."

"Good! I'll text you around three. Bye."

Cole pulled the car away from the curb and drove to the Denny's directly across from the Best Western. He donned his mask and put his glasses on. Once inside the Denny's, he asked for a booth against the window. It gave him a vantage point of the hotel's front entrance. He waited and watched while eating a burger and drinking coffee. A car pulled up to the front, and a man got out and went inside. The car sat there for several minutes. Eventually, a man came out of the hotel and got in the car, but it was a different man. It was them, Cole concluded. It was some kind of a shift change or something, but it was definitely them. Cole wondered why Kevin hadn't picked up on it. He seldom missed anything.

Three o'clock was approaching. Cole paid his tab and left the restaurant. He walked to the corner, crossed the street, and then strolled back towards the Best Western. At precisely three o'clock, he texted "now" to Kevin. He arrived at the side door and inserted an administrator key card to enter the building. Stairs were adjacent to the side door entrance and Cole went up. Julie's room was the fourth room down the hall. He inserted the key card and entered. She was sitting at a desk studying something on her phone. She was wearing just panties and a bra. Julie jumped in surprise at his entry but a warm smile instantly came to her face.

She met him halfway to the door, hugged him, threw his mask and glasses on the bed, and then began a long slow kiss that transitioned to the mingling of tongues. She pulled back and just stared at him for a moment. And then said, "I've had time to do a lot of thinking."

Cole started to speak but she put her finger to his lips. "I can't do this," she said.

The thought of sex with this beautiful woman was something that had been at the forefront of his mind ever since he'd first met her. But it was not going to happen. She was just part of the circus. Cole dismissed his desires, "We are not going to have sex. So don't worry about it."

Julie looked at him strangely and then, as tears formed in her eyes, she spoke softly, "That's not what I was referring to. I mean I just can't do this to Kevin— and you. You were supposed to be just a pawn to lead me to Kevin. And there's more. You won't even like me when you hear what I have to say." She paused and then continued, "You were profiled to identify every characteristic, every action, every reaction, to every situation imaginable. I spent six months interacting with an AI-generated hologram of you. The problem is that I fell in love with the hologram and now with the real man. I'm so confused. I'm so sorry."

Cole's phone beeped and he briefly glanced at it. It was a text from Kevin: "11 x money—Chinese government. Money—US government."

"Go on Julie," Cole said softly.

"I was recruited by the highest levels of the NSA to help track down Kevin McKuel. You were the path. And I should have known back then what I know now. Your AI profile tells a story of a very intense man, but also a true man, a man like few others—a man I could fall in love with. But the AI missed so much; the real man is so much more than I ever imagined. It's all been a charade and I have been such a fake."

"I know Julie," said Cole. "Or should I say, Chrissy?"

"What? You knew? How could you?"

"Chrissy Filer from Edmond Oklahoma."

"That name was purged from existence. I haven't heard it in so long that it sounds strange."

"You are very, very good. But it's the 'tells.' Wince of your cheek, slipped words, search of the condo, surveillance of the Squire Inn, and more. And then there's the simplicity of the cigarette scam. Kevin knew it from the start. And by the way, the stupidity and transparency of it was just confirmed; the U.S. government just paid twenty-five million for a cargo container full of newspaper. Where do we go from here Chrissy?"

"I don't know. I feel so," Chrissy paused and searched for the right words, "embarrassed and ashamed."

"Well, maybe it will make you feel better to know that your AI missed the boat. I'm not at all what you think. What would you say if I told you I killed five men this morning? Would it bother you that I did it without a hint of remorse?"

Chrissy looked at him strangely. "Why would you do that? You didn't. You couldn't have. I don't know." She paused and struggled with the thought before continuing, "You didn't really. I mean there is no way. The AI hologram has all your tendencies, core values, and innate character traits. It couldn't be; and the killing in the parking lot really wasn't your fault."

"Then you don't know me."

Chrissy hesitated again. "The parking lot thing, maybe, but only because you thought you were protecting me, which was predicted by the AI. But your predicted response was to just prevent the kidnap and then take me directly to Kevin. Killing is not in your character and was never contemplated."

"I wish it wasn't in my character. But it is. Listen, Chrissy," Cole said softly. "I like you. I know you were just doing your job. But you need to think about what I told you about myself. Then, if you want, we can spend some honest time sorting out where we go next."

"It can't work. The NSA is still going to want Kevin, with or without my involvement."

"Those three men in your parking lot, were they FBI?" questioned Cole.

"Yes."

"I was afraid of that. Who's been tracking us and watching you? FBI?"

"Yes, temporarily assigned to the NSA."

"What's the level of surveillance here in this hotel?"

"Two down the hall in 211. Two mobile. And then they're tied into hotel and traffic cameras. If I get close to Kevin, there are four additional standby agents that can be called upon at a moment's notice."

"Kevin wouldn't let his own mother get close to him. Myself and only one other person in the world know where he's at. What does your profile say about me diverging a secret like that?"

"Impenetrable wall, even with sodium pentothal."

"Right now Kevin and I are engaged in other business that needs to run its full course. I need you to keep up your charade for a little longer. There's a man checked into this hotel under the name of Bob Goddard. I need the FBI surveillance to inadvertently provide an umbrella of safety for him. Can you give me at least forty-eight hours?"

"I don't understand."

"You will when the time comes. Forty-eight hours, please," requested Cole.

"All right. But it's odd. I don't know which side of the line I'm on."

"Who initiated the investigation into Kevin and I?"

"NSA director Blaine Higgins. He, I, and only seven others know the full details."

"You mean Operation Cool Fool."

Chrissy looked away. When she turned back to him, she asked, "How could you possibly know? My God. I'm so stupid."

Cole stared deep into her eyes and asked, "Where does a woman named Liu fit in?"

"Who?" replied Julie without any indication of falsehood.

"Liu? No last name," Cole again inquired.

"I don't recognize the name," Chrissy said and shook her head.

"How much do you know about Higgins?"

"He's my boss in this whole thing."

"Higgins is a self-serving ass."

"You know him?"

"Know of him. Kevin knows more about him than I do. Call Kevin and ask about Higgins. He'll tell you what a conniving, lying, SOB you've been working for. Keep talking to Kevin; he likes you. Tell him what you told me about Cool Fool. He and his special person need to know. Its better they hear it from you than me." Cole paused. "Just help buy Kevin and I some time. Keep up the charade."

"I will, Cole," said Chrissy as she touched his face.

Cole backed away from Chrissy and turned to the door. He pushed the send button on his phone for the simple text "now." Kevin again put traffic cameras and hotel security cameras into replay streaming mode. Cole exited and made his way back to the exit. He was soon headed for Hartsfield-Jackson Atlanta International and a waiting private jet.

KEN KUOTO SAT AT HIS COMPUTER STARING AT HIS transaction history. He clicked back to his account balance. The transfer wasn't there. In fact, there was nothing there at all. He went back to his transaction history page. It made no sense. He was expecting a hundred million transferred in from the Peoples Bank of China, instead the transaction history showed eleven one-hundred million transfers in, and eleven one-hundred million transfers out. Then there was a twenty-five million transfer in, from the Wellington Reserve Bank of New York, but it also had been transferred out along with his two million in working capital. All of the transfers out went to the Central Bank of Russia.

Kuoto's intense study was interrupted when a computer window opened indicating he had a new email confirming his airline travel plans for Moscow. "What?" he said out loud.

Kuoto's satellite phone buzzed. He looked at the incoming number and thought, good. I can get some answers to all this. He answered the phone, "Yes, General Kenoug. I am glad you…"

"Kuoto. What are you doing?" asked the head of the Ministry of State Security.

"I am waiting for the hundred million transfer so I can ensure our success. I have not received…"

"Don't. Just don't lie to me. I know what you did. We are reconstructing it now. You get one chance, just one. You arrange for its transfer back right now, or you will face the consequences of Qincheng. And I will personally oversee your torture."

"There is nothing to transfer back. I do not understand."

"So be it, Kuoto. Do not expect the Russians to help you. My reach is far and you cannot hide," said the General and disconnected.

COLE CLIMBED ABOARD THE WAITING PRIVATE JET AND was soon airborne. Cole's thoughts were of Chrissy. He really did like her. And from her point of view, he was probably just as much a fake and a liar. She had said, "a man like you I could love." How could it be? She really didn't know me or the things I've done in this life, thought Cole. How could any woman love that? The hostility that lay just beneath the surface was always going to be there. I'm not even sane, he postulated. Did her profile identify that little fact? Cole closed his eyes and fanaticized about the two of them on a beach or skiing in the Alps, him just enjoying her company. He yearned for normalcy. Could she help provide it?

The plane touched down at Leesburg and jolted Cole's thoughts back to reality. Cole called Kevin as the plane taxied towards the executive terminal. "Does eleven X mean eleven transfers," he asked Kevin.

"Pretty McKuel, don't you think? One-point-one billion."

"Well, that will certainly piss them off."

"Yep. I'm still hiding it: moved, removed, bought, sold, divided, combined, acquired. I liquidated and acquired through dozens of banks, financial markets, and asset holding companies. Gone from existence, at least as far as anyone will ever know."

"Did Chrissy call you?"

"She did. And here I was all-righteous about her being wrong for you. But she likes you more than you know. Now you don't have to slit her throat. You can do the nasty hooty-tooty or maybe the kinky-winko. Who's going to be on top, anyway?"

"Kevin, someday I'm going to kick your ass."

"I doubt it."

"Goodbye, asshole."

Cole exited the plane and Helmut Hoelzer's rental car was waiting. An envelope was lying in the driver's seat and he briefly glanced at the contents. It was a single USB stick. He headed towards Cabin John. This time, he would just pull into the driveway.

And that's exactly what he did. Jeff Monson answered the door and extended his hand. "I didn't expect you back so soon."

Cole shook his hand and replied, "Things came together faster than I expected."

"Okay, Cole. Come on in. Can I get you a coke or something?"

"No, but thank you."

"I noticed you were admiring my grass. The secret is the lawn mower itself. Let's go out back."

Cole followed Jeff through the house to the backyard and a yellow storage building. The backyard was well-groomed and surrounded by a six-foot privacy fence. Jeff opened the storage building door and wheeled out a lawn mower.

Monson continued, "Most people have gone to electric mowers. They cut but don't have the RPM you can get out of an old-fashioned gas mower." He pushed the electric start and then increased the throttle. The lawn mower whirled at high rpm. Jeff said, "Now we can talk."

Cole handed the USB stick to Jeff. "This contains information on a NSA and Space Force program to put something called MAHEM in space. It's an upgraded version of a USA-224 satellite. Last I knew, weaponizing space was not part of the U.S.'s defense strategy. Maybe it is today. I don't know. The NSA has been helping them. And that's just part one.

"Part two, which is also on the stick, is that the Chinese government has compromised the design and is substituting critical components with those of their own, presumably so they can control the satellite's weaponry. It looks like targeting could have included Washington D.C. Their operation was headed by a Ken Kuoto and he was assisted by seven highly placed individuals within the secret community. Their names are on the stick. Don't judge them too quickly. Kuoto's measures of persuasion were extreme: beatings, financial ruin, threatened torture of family members, murder, and more. One of the names on the list is Reed Delahe, who was instrumental in bringing this information to you. His ex-wife was one of the casualties associated with Kuoto's persuasion.

"Delahe is in Atlanta, currently in hiding under FBI surveillance. He's using the name Bob Goddard. The FBI thinks I'm Bob Goddard, but I have Reed Delahe as a duped stand-in. He needs to remain under FBI surveillance to protect him from Kuoto.

"Which brings me to part three. None of which is on the USB stick. NSA director Blaine Higgins is conducting an operation called 'Cool Fool.' It is a dirty tricks ploy to lead them to Kevin McKuel. I don't know how, but Higgins somehow got the FBI involved.

"At one point, operation 'Cool Fool' went bad and two FBI agents died. I am really sorry. It was a charade with a damsel in distress ploy and I came to the damn rescue. Sounds all very stupid, I know. But at the time I had no idea they were FBI."

"Holy shit, Cole," said a stunned Monson. "That's a lot to digest."

"There's more. But you'll figure it out. Also, Kuoto just got the attention of the 'Cool Fool' operation by accepting twenty-five million dollars from the U.S. government. Kuoto is in Huntsville, Alabama. The government won't get any of its twenty-five million back. At this point, it's gone. Between you and me, it and more will make it to the widows and families of the FBI agents I killed. Kuoto's current location is on the USB stick. The FBI should get him under surveillance as soon as possible."

"He's a flight risk?"

"Yes, but Kevin and I have arranged for the Chinese government to want him more than the U.S. government. And they should have him. I suggest you assist the Chinese government in their recovery of Mr. Kuoto. It won't go well for him. But you're going to have to move fast."

"I can't do this by myself. Would you be willing to repeat what you just told me to Evert Hooster of the FBI?"

Cole thought about it for a moment. "No," he said. "Kevin and I do not exist. This information is for you to act on."

"If Higgins has tracked you, then you do exist."

"Yes. And the FBI is helping him. I'm not about to turn myself in and confess to killing two FBI agents."

"I'm retired and no longer in a position to get the intel high enough, fast enough. I need you to talk directly to Everett. You need to trust me on this one."

Cole brought his fist to his mouth and blew. "That's a lot of trust."

"You took my job offer. You're my asset. Sometimes you have to step into the fire pit. That's the way it is."

Cole slowly shook his head and then conceded, "I'll talk but only under the condition that Kevin and my records are purged, or somehow sealed forever. Then I'm done. I'm tired of hiding."

Cole drove as they headed for Evert Hooster's residence. Jeff called Evert Hooster's home phone and his wife confirmed he was home. As it turned out, the drive was less than six miles.

The sun was setting and Cole felt a great uneasiness as he pulled into the driveway. This was, in no way, part of the plan. Evert Hooster met them at the front door. Cole's internal alerts went high order when he was introduced to Hooster.

The man held Cole's hand too long after the initial handshake and said, "I recall the mention of a Hamilton Cole Davis somewhere in the past," and then smiled.

Cole began contemplating an escape plan and refused to enter when invited to enter the house. If this was a trap, at least he could see them coming. Cole firmly stated, "What I have to say can be said out here."

Evert looked at him strangely as Jeff interrupted, "This is not a social visit, Ev. Cole is my asset and I've invited him over here to share intel with you. Some of it you're not going to like. But you need to hear it all first hand. Just listen."

Cole repeated all he had told Jeff. Evert listened intently. When Cole got to the part about Operation Cool Fool, Hooster mumbled, "Damn Higgins." As Cole finished, he could see Hooster going through some kind of mental debate.

Hooster finally spoke, "That's a hell of a story. And I will take action. But I can't get past the death of my two agents."

Jeff interrupted, "First, he's working for me. If he's guilty, I'm guilty. Second, anybody who observed a woman about to be stuffed in the trunk of a car and took action is hailed as a hero. Your agents made all appearances of doing harm to the woman, play-acting or not. How would it play out in court? Or even worse, in the media? Do you want to tell that story?"

Evert reluctantly conceded. Cole stood by while Evert and Jeff strategized options. In the end, the simplest answer was the best. Evert would schedule a Code 3 meeting with the President. Jeff would get a specialty invite.

Going forward, the FBI would rally forces in Huntsville as requested for containment of Kuoto, cease and desist on Operation Cool Fool, and protect Reed Delahe. All satellite design, manufacture, and assembly would be halted until the impact of Kuoto's activities could be assessed. When it came to Cole and Kevin, they were Monson's retired assets and all agencies were to close their books on them.

Chapter 43

ARROGANT BASTARD

EVERT HOOSTER REQUESTED AND GOT AN URGENT audience with President Cluttle. It was scheduled for 6:00 A.M. the following morning. Evert and his staff, along with Jeff, worked feverishly with Frank Wallace's CIA section to assemble a report on MAHEM.

After all the basics were captured, Jeff continued to work on a report of his own. He sat at his computer late into the night generating a summary of Operation Cool Fool based on what Cole and Evert had told him. He included a summary of MAHEM and added what he knew about program authorizations; this speculated detail was also included in the report.

He knew Blaine Higgins was an expert ass-kissing brown-noser. Surely he would have gone looking for his little pat on the head from the President. Surely the President already knew about Cool Fool and MAHEM, concluded Jeff. But it would have been presented in such a way that the President could always claim deniability. That's just the way things worked.

As Jeff reviewed what he'd just created, he tapped a pencil on the desk. Jeff had survived the politics and bureaucracy of government for forty-one years, clear up to his forced retirement. He knew more about how the clandestine world worked than probably anyone else in the world. Washington D.C. was a sanity-free zone where almost anything could happen. Politics and perception always outweighed the most basic elements of right and wrong. The clandestine world was expected to support the politics and perception of those at the top. Sometimes Jeff had been forced to do things he wasn't particularly proud of during his long career. This meeting with the President could result in unintended, and potentially terminal, consequences.

Jeff copied his files to a USB stick and password-protected it. The CIA, NSA, or some other agency was no doubt monitoring his personal computer and would have the contents of the USB stick along with its password. He also hoped someone else had access to his computer. Kevin McKuel had cyber capabilities as good as most intelligence agencies.

Jeff made six copies of the USB stick and hand-wrote six individualized notes. He then addressed and stamped four envelopes, packaged the USB sticks and notes, and sealed them for mailing. Jeff checked the time. It was going to be tight. Before leaving the house, Jeff turned off his cell phone and wrapped it in multiple layers of tin foil. It would be unwrapped only once he reached the D.C. area.

En route to Washington D.C., Jeff stopped at four post offices, first Cabin John and then others along the way. Two of the envelopes went into UPS overnight drop boxes. Jeff arrived at the White House security gate shortly after five. He went through the normal sign-in, body scan, and physical search before being assigned an escort. They kept his cell phone and promised its return upon his departure. He assumed they would start its interrogation as soon as he stepped away. But there was nothing on it worth their while. He also submitted his USB stick. They were to scan it for viruses and authorize its use in the President's computer terminal.

He met Evert Hooster in the hall outside the Oval Office. Evert asked, "You ready for this?" Jeff could sense his nervousness. Evert knew the politics of the insanity zone almost as well as he did. They were granted entrance and guarded by two aides and a Secret Service agent until the President stepped through the side door. The greeting was brief and all took seats.

Evert advised the President that the discussion was extremely classified. Secret Service and aides were dismissed. Evert opened his briefcase and slid a top-secret report across the desk to the president. The report was entitled "Quaraysh Unity Summary."

The President glanced at it and said, "I've been briefed."

"Then you know the intel assets were Jeff's," stated Evert.

The President raised his eyebrows, stared at Jeff, and then said, "I guess I do now."

"Blaine Higgins has been running an operation called Cool Fool to hunt down and incarcerate or kill one of those assets," stated Evert. "Those very same assets have identified Chinese compromise of MAHEM."

The President's eyebrows again raised. Jeff could read both recognition and surprise. An aide opened the door and interrupted, "Excuse me, sir. This has been cleared by IT for use." The aid entered and handed the USB stick to Evert before quickly departing.

"MAHEM is unknown to me," said the President. There it was: deniability. Jeff knew better.

"It's being developed by the Space Force with help from Higgin's directorate," stated Evert. "It's an unauthorized program involving space-based weaponry, which has implications for international agreements. What's worse is that Chinese components and software substitutions have been incorporated to potentially turn its lethality against us. It's all on the USB Jeff brought with him."

Evert slid Jeff's USB across the desk towards the President. A few moments lapsed as the President inserted the USB and waited for a response from his terminal. "Password," commanded the President.

"Arrogant Bastard," Jeff said boldly.

Both Evert and the President were stunned and stared at Jeff. The President's stare transitioned to an angry glare. Jeff read the thoughts, nobody talks to me that way. Jeff glared back.

After a few moments of silence, Jeff continued, "Password is 'arrogant bastard;' type it all caps, no space.

Now, there are six copies of that USB stick and at least one free-floating e-file out in the world. It would be absolutely devastating if the information on that stick got out. It's imperative that you, Mr. President, ensure the contents of the USB are always kept secure. And just for general information, I intend to live a happy life until the age of ninety-five. I also assume that my assets, Hamilton Cole Davis and Kevin McKuel, will also live a happy life to the age of ninety-five. Now, we're all pretty self-sufficient and very capable so I don't anticipate needing any help or any further action from the intelligence community, or anybody else for that matter. Which, by the way, is actually also in your best interests. Now please Mr. President, open the file named 'CoolFool' and read the first sentence."

The President quickly typed in the password and opened the file. The first sentence read: "President Cluttle authorized misappropriation of funds, space-based weaponry, targeted assassination of U.S. citizens, and risked the sanctity of the United States of America."

"Oh, I have an additional request," continued Jeff. "The CIA needs to have trustworthy, top-notch leadership with impeccable character and commitment. Director might be a stretch. So I'll just suggest that Frank Wallace be moved into my old office as Deputy Director of the CIA."

The President was more than livid. He glared at Monson. Clinched his fists, and said, "You son-of-a-bitch! Get the fuck out of here!"

Jeff knew he'd made his point. As he and Evert exited the Oval Office, all Evert could say was, "Holy shit."

"Say that now. What are you going to say when the house cleaning begins? Hold on to your hat." Jeff laughed.

Chapter 44

Aftermath

NSA director Higgins was early for his scheduled 8:00 A.M. meeting with the President. He was confident he had assembled an impressive file on 'Operation Cool Fool' that would further advance him in the eyes of the President.

It didn't; the meeting lasted five minutes during which time the President did all the talking—and yelling. Higgins was fired on the spot. His firing was quickly followed by the firing of the head of the Space Force, CIA director, Homeland Security director, and the President's own Secretary of Defense.

Purging the Nation's top-level security leaders was leaked to the press before 9:00 A.M. and the breaking news flurries ensued with false and misguided information. Members of both the House and Senate voiced their ire at the President for his irresponsible actions and used their media interviews to bolster their own political agendas.

Ken Kuoto was alerted by the sound of a helicopter flying over the estate. His bodyguards informed him that the estate was surrounded by men in suits, obviously a law enforcement agency of some type: ATF, FBI, or something similar. They were in plain sight, which was quite unusual. His plans for escape and flight to Mongolia would, at a minimum, be delayed.

Then, just as if a light switch turned off, the helicopter and all the agents disappeared. It was quite disconcerting. Kuoto joined one of his bodyguards sitting in front of the surveillance camera screens. Four SUVs burst through the estate's main gate and sped towards the front door. Occupants of the SUVs sprang from the vehicles and charged the house in military style. When the first of the occupants breached the front door, Kuoto heard the familiar rattle of 7.62 mm automatic gunfire. He stood and backed against the wall as the surveillance camera screens showed the systematic search of the house. Eventually, they found him. Kuoto's concerns turned to terror when they began yelling commands at him in Chinese.

He was whisked off to a waiting Chinese National airplane at the Huntsville private terminal. Kuoto was strapped into something resembling a dentist's chair with six white-gowned attendants in waiting. The floor of the plane was covered in plastic. Surgical and electronic instruments were laid out on towels on the table between two sets of opposing seats. Two of the white-gowned attendants were inspecting and organizing the instruments. Three other white-gowned attendants sat farther to the rear of the plane and were fastening their seat belts. Kuoto stared in fear at the surgical tools. The lead attendant faced Kuoto and said in Chinese, "General Kenoug said we were to wait until after takeoff. He wanted you to know that it will be an especially long flight. General Kenoug, himself, will be joining us via video conference to participate in the extraordinary agonization that has been arranged for you."

CAROL SWANSON WAS STILL IN MOURNING FOR HER husband killed in the line of duty for the FBI. She sat in the kitchen staring at the wall contemplating the reality of her and the children's future. She missed him terribly, but the future was frightening. The FBI's death benefit and pension would help, but the uncertainty of it all was overwhelming. She was near tears when she received a call from the Gentlemen's Outreach Charitable Organization. A representative would be arriving today at her door to explain the assistance program, which included a basic ten million dollar award and another ten million set aside for her children and their education. She and the widow of another FBI agent were to be this year's recipients.

ARMANDO ALZEBRI PULLED HIS CAB INTO THE YEL- lowOne shop for maintenance. As soon as he stepped out of his cab, he was greeted by the service manager, who referred to him as Mister Alzebri. The normally lackadaisical shop hopped with a flurry of activity and everyone was discreetly watching Armando. It felt weird. Soon a corporate representative announcing himself as the Chief Operating Officer appeared and asked Mister Alzebri if there was anything he could do for him. Armando had never seen the man before. The man told him that his office was being reconditioned on an expedited basis and would be complete by noon; he hoped the accommodations would be acceptable to the new CEO and majority shareholder of the YellowOne cab company.

MARCY OGALSBY STOOD MID-BLOCK ON 5TH Avenue hoping her next John would tip her more than the twenty she got from her last customer. She had given full service for only three hundred bucks and with the smile she left on his face; the tip should have been at least a hundred. But it was all right. In total, it was enough to get her the coke she so desperately needed. A limousine pulled up and the rear door swung open. A man smiled at her and she climbed in. She studied her next trick, only this was different.

He was well-dressed and offered her an unbelievable deal. She would be flown to an exclusive rehab facility in southern California where she would meet celebrities and undergo the best drug rehab treatments available. He was to be her financial manager and she would receive five hundred thousand dollars a year for life as long as long as she stayed straight. It was all funded by the Gentlemen's Outreach Charitable Organization.

REED DELAHE WAS ESCORTED FROM THE ATLANTA Best Western to the airport and was soon on a direct flight to Salt Lake City, Utah. He was accompanied by two FBI agents who would remain his companions for the next several weeks. A black SUV with two additional agents was waiting for them in Salt Lake City. They were soon headed for Manti—and Tommy.

FRANK WALLACE ARRIVED EARLY FOR WORK AND turned on his computer. The CIA logo appeared and he waited for the log-on prompt to appear. Probably at least twenty-five unanswered emails were first on the to-do list. His manager, Bart McDonald, stepped into his office.

"What's up?" asked Frank.

"You. That's what's up!" McDonald replied.

"Who'd I piss off this time?"

"What I am about to tell you is unprecedented and I absolutely don't understand it. It violates a dozen HR policies, a dozen security requirements, and a hundred standard protocols. You've been promoted."

"That means I really pissed somebody off. What am I now? Head pencil sharpener?"

"No. You're now our new Deputy Director. And with the firing of our Director, it means you are now in charge of the world's largest intelligence agency."

"Yeah right. And last night Hell froze over and we're all going ice-skating. What do you really want?"

"I want you to accompany me to the main head-quarters building and your new office where your staff and direct reports are assembling. You are now by far the youngest Deputy Director in the history of the CIA."

Frank was without words and absolutely confused, "You're not serious. That's not possible."

"Oh, but it is. I checked and re-checked. The order came directly from the President. It's you—by name, rank, and employee number."

EVERT HOOSTER SAT AT HIS DESK AND REVIEWED the list of twenty-two names added to the FBI's most wanted list. It included human traffickers, drug dealers, money launderers, prostitution kingpins, murderers, and more. But more importantly, it included every surviving individual who had once used Isaac Laughlin to launder their ill-gotten funds. The full weight of the FBI was now relentlessly pursuing criminal charges against each. Hundreds of agents were tearing apart their lives to find every shred of evidence and build multiple cases against each. Even if they had some inclination that Kevin and Cole had once relieved them of funds, it would be the least of their worries.

Chapter 45

EDMOND OKLAHOMA

IN HER ATLANTA BEST WESTERN HOTEL ROOM, Chrissy Filer sat staring at the TV trying to sort it out. Head of the NSA, head of the CIA, Undersecretary, and many others were terminated without any reason given. Had the President lost his mind? The media was afire with speculation.

She received a call from someone asserting he was from the NSA. She was told to forget anything she ever knew about Operation Cool Fool and, if she ever divulged a single word about it, she would face prosecution, imprisonment, and maybe worse. She was also advised that her services were no longer required by the NSA. She too had been fired.

Mass firings, her firing, termination of the operation—none of it made sense. And what happened to Cole? She had received no calls from him, or Kevin. And her calls to them just went to "number-out-of-service" recordings. It was as if her world had abandoned her and all she had was the whirl of confusing media information.

Four days had passed and nothing from Cole. Cole had asked for forty-eight hours and she had given him twice that. The last time they talked, he had been curt and all business. Maybe he wasn't coming back. Maybe it was over and she was on her own.

The media and the four walls of the hotel room were about to drive her nuts. The Cool Fool operation had kept her from contacting her mom and dad for more than a year; it was time for a trip home. Except, she didn't have any real identification. Chrissy Filer had been erased. She would have to travel as Julia Addison or use the stupid Ellie Mae documentation. But Cool Fool was gone, which meant so was Julia. "Shit," she mumbled to herself.

Chrissy used her cell phone and bought a one-way ticket to Edmond Oklahoma as Ellie Mae Clampet. She packed the few personal items she had, called for a taxi, and waited. The thought dawned on her; the CIA owed her at least a year's back pay. Who were they going to pay it to because on record Chrissy Filer no longer existed? She didn't even have a social security number. She had cash that had come with the ID package, but it wouldn't last long. Then it would all be Ellie Mae. Would she have to go through life as Ellie Mae? And at some point, without the Ellie Mae credit card, she wouldn't even be able to buy a cup of coffee. The more she thought about it, the more she wondered why she'd ever accepted the assignment to begin with.

The taxi arrived. It was a long ride to the Hartsfield–Jackson Atlanta airport and the thoughts continued to churn. What had happened to Cole? The taxi left her at the departure gate and she retrieved her ticket at the kiosk. She inched forward in the TSA security line. When the TSA agent checked her ID and ticket, he just smiled. Damn Kevin, she thought to herself. She easily passed through security and headed for the "plane train."

As she entered the train, her senses went on high alert. A man was at the front of the car with his back to her. She had seen him before in the security line. He was wearing a hoodie and had his hands in his pockets. She got a partial look at the side of his face, but it was obscured by the hoodie. Probably nothing—but—what if? The train pulled into her concourse, the C-concourse, and the doors opened. The man started to move towards the door but then changed his mind. As he retreated back into the train, she was moments from jumping off but the doors closed and the train accelerated towards the D-concourse. She quickly exited the train at the D-concourse and started the hike in the underground tunnel back towards the C-concourse. Lighting in the tunnel was dim, but he was definitely following.

She took the escalator up to the C-concourse and headed for her gate. She glanced to her rear and he was there. He was intermingled with the horde of people about a hundred feet back.

The NSA man that had called and fired her was very threatening. Given all the events that had transpired, maybe she was going to get more than just fired. She joined the mass of people preparing to board at her gate and discretely searched the advancing crowd behind her. She captured every face and evaluated every movement. He had to be there.

Then, a pair of strong hands rested on her shoulders. This is it; she thought and closed her eyes. The hands slowly turned her around. She slowly opened her eyes; it was Cole!

"Oh my God," she cried and wrapped her arms around him. "Somebody's been following me."

"Nobody's been following you," consoled Cole. "I've been watching the Best Western for days and followed you ever since you left."

Chrissy studied the hoodie Cole was wearing. "Oh shit. I thought you were NSA, FBI, or someone worse. I thought maybe I was about to be a casualty."

"That's why I followed you. But there's no NSA, ATF, FBI, or circus of any kind. You're in the clear. Go anywhere you want. Do anything you want."

Just then, a man stepped forward, handed Cole an envelope, and said, "ID stuff." Cole simply said, "Thanks."

Julie hardly noticed, hugged him tight, and then pressed her lips against his. The plane for Edmond was boarding and people were moving all around them. When the kiss broke, Julie stared at him with admiration and more—much more.

Cole looked at the dwindling boarding process and asked, "Going to Edmond?"

"I was. I was going to see my parents. But I'm not going now."

Cole smiled, "That's too bad. I guess I'll just have to go to Edmond all by myself because I have a ticket. I hope your father likes me."

Julie smiled, gently slapped his shoulder, embraced him and the kissing started again.

Chapter 46

OF THE HEART

KEVIN HAD CONTRACTED FOR A HOUSE TO BE BUILT on a small rise above the Tobago beach. It was just barely within shouting distance of Joe and Sylvia Atkin's beachfront villa where Kevin had spent countless hours pounding on computer keys and nurturing his Fugaku Clone. Joe and Sylvia were the most special couple he had ever known. Joe was a big burly black man well into his seventies, yet more capable than most men in their fifties. Sylvia was a very special Hispanic flower that had beaten cancer and blossomed with strength; she cared for Kevin like a son and he reciprocated.

Liu and Kevin walked down the beach, hand in hand. They stopped and studied the flurry of construction activity up on the hillside. Completion was expected by year's end.

Kevin kissed Liu on the cheek. When she responded with a whisper, he bolted down the beach like a wild man, all the while screaming unintelligible sounds. He stopped fifty yards out, turned, and ran back toward Liu screaming, "I love you. I love you. I love you." He grabbed her in his arms and they kissed and kissed and kissed.

FOUR-THOUSAND-ONE-HUNDRED-NINETY-SIX MILES northwest, three men in tuxedos and top hats stood at attention in the lobby of Advanced Micro Corporation in San Jose California. The center man's tuxedo was purple; the other two men wore traditional black tuxedos. The man in the purple tuxedo demanded the immediate presence of Rolf and Lana Chen. The receptionist advised them that Rolf and Lana Chen were unavailable for the foreseeable future, not even an appointment was possible. But with continued insistence from the man in the center, the receptionist called six floors up to Rolf Chen's admin.

Rolf Chen's admin interrupted a meeting and advised him of the demand. Rolf Chen's cell phone buzzed for the fourth time but he ignored it. He directed his admin to call 911. The admin did as directed but was immediately forwarded to the San Jose Police Chief's office. The admin was advised that the San Jose Police Chief was waiting for Rolf to answer repeated cell phone call attempts.

Rolf Chen pulled his phone from his pocket and answered the incoming call. The Police Chief was brief and to the point, "This is an international matter coordinated by the President of Trinidad and our Ambassador. I have been advised to make sure you receive the invitation and then provide any escort or any other service needed to ensure you attend the event." Rolf was confused but excused himself from the meeting. He instructed his admin to get ahold of his wife and have her join him in the lobby.

Lana Chen was summoned from her workstation deep within the confines of Advanced Micro Corporation. She met Rolf in the foyer leading to the front entrance. Although they worked in the same place and lived in the same house, they seldom spoke. Work always out-prioritized everything else. She stared at Rolf and asked, "What's going on?" He just shrugged his shoulders.

They both stared in wonderment at the three men in tuxedos. Rolf Chen again shrugged his shoulders and said, "I guess we go see what they want."

The man in the purple tuxedo marched forward with the other two following alongside. They all converged in the center of the lobby. With the voice of an opera tenor, the man in the center began, "Hear ye, hear ye. From kings and queens to paupers and serfs, no union has ever been so righteous. From the far reaches of all the world, no union has ever been so founded. So hear ye and hear ye well."

Lana grabbed Rolf's arm and briefly stared at him in wonderment as the man continued, "Let it be known to Rolf and Lana Chen—and all the world—that Kevin McKuel and Liu Chen will forever be united in a magnificent ceremony of matrimony on the sixteenth of November in this year of the Lord. It is my pleasure to insist on the presence of Rolf and Lana Chen on the isle of Robinson Caruso for this glorious event.

Transportation will be provided by a private carrier. Lodging will be provided by the local concierge. Your journey begins on the tenth day of November in this year of the Lord. Refusal of this unforgettable journey is not an option. So hear ye, hear ye now, and make plans accordingly. Let it be known and forever written."

A formal invite in a cloth envelope with embroidered gold lettering was handed to Rolf and Lana Chen.

LIU WAS LEARNING NEW THINGS. SYLVIA HAD HER cooking everything from exotic island recipes to meatloaf. She helped Sylvia in the kitchen while Kevin and Joe debated some silly world event in the living room. Tonight's dinner was freshly caught snapper and a bodi, morai, and carailie vegetable mix. Liu prepared the vegetable mix while Sylvia basted the snapper with a blended lemon sauce that included finely chopped cilantro, chilies, bacon bits, and a cadre of island spices.

Sylvia asked Liu, "Have you told him yet?"

"Told him what?" replied Liu.

"I'm old and wise. I see things. You can't fool me, child," admonished Sylvia.

Liu smiled and blushed before replying, "I'm not sure I know what you're talking about."

Sylvia wiped her hands on a towel and frowned. The frown turned into a smile as she turned to Liu. The smile turned into a broad smile as she delicately placed her hand on Liu's stomach and said, "This."

Brian David Simmons

Made in the USA
Columbia, SC
17 August 2024

40175937R10248